More Love
of the
Great Composers

Basil Howitt

Sound And Vision

Contents

Dedication

To Clare
who trims my prose
rather than my waistline

Overture

"There's nowt so queer as folk." Thus averred my grandmother, Lancashire born-and-bred, when she was having a good gossip with my two maiden aunts round her kitchen range, soot-encrusted kettle steaming on the gleaming hob. The adage certainly holds true where reactions to my books on composers' love lives are concerned.

"I enjoyed your book. I skipped through it for all the naughty bits." Thus one fine amateur pianist, whom I was coaching in a chamber music session, on my first book of composers' love lives for Sound And Vision. At the other extreme was the TV wine pundit Jancis Robinson discussing another of my books on the same theme (*Grand Passions and Broken Hearts*) on BBC Radio 3. She didn't want to spoil beautiful music by reading about the often-sordid private lives of the men who wrote it. In which case, I ask, why did she bother, since the contents are so clearly signalled in the blurbs and fliers? (Fortunately Robinson's view was a minority of one on the programme.)

Most fascinating of all, however, have been the responses of the prurient prudes who are clearly obsessed by what they claim to disapprove of. A prominent librarian in Manchester UK, though ever helpful, has always been rather sniffy about my books, declining to make a copy of them available on his library shelves. At the same time, he has taken a furtive interest in them. On one occasion he vaguely remembered to happen on a feature on my first volume on a sheet of the *News of the World* (Britain's premier smutty tabloid) that was "lining the bottom of my budgerigar cage"; as though he had no conception of how it got there! More recently, after turning up his nose at my research on Gounod's love life, he sneaked up later and asked me if I knew about the composer's ménage à trois!

Although this book includes many fascinating naughty bits for the healthily salacious adult, they are not its raison d'être. For me. the primary interest, after now having explored in detail the lives of some forty male composers, continues to be the connections between their relationships and their music. (And yes, one of these days I will get round to including a female composer, though during the periods under consideration there haven't been any in the category of "great". There is a fascinating book to be written on why there were so many great female novelists in the eighteenth and nineteenth centuries, but not composers or dramatists.)

At one extreme there have been the composers who were utterly dependent on their lovers and muses for inspiration and emotional support. Elgar "needed muses always, that is inescapable," writes Michael Kennedy in his foreword to Kevin Allen's *Elgar in Love*. Wagner, we saw, was virtually incapable of putting pen to paper without a comforting cleavage under his nose. Although the consequences became dire for his much younger wife Alma – and for his marriage – Mahler needed her unquestioning total sacrifice and devotion to him and his art in order to compose and conduct. Johann Strauss the younger was unable to function at all without a mother-muse-mistress-wife figure, replacing each of his first two wives almost immediately when he was left alone.

In complete contrast, a man like Bellini would not allow his women – whom he cultivated for "sentiment" and "sex" – to interfere with his work. In his last year (he died age thirty-three), he finally met his ideal woman – one who "gives me no trouble at all; every now and again I see her, I make love, and then I think about my opera." Of the other composers in this volume, neither Satie nor Sibelius drew significant inspiration from women. Although Sibelius's wife Aino was long-suffering of her husband's "blind egocentricity" to a fault, his main prop was alcohol, as, in his later years, was Satie's.

Other composers fall between the two extremes. Verdi benefited from the close interest of his long-time mistress and eventual wife Giuseppina Strepponi in his works in progress – "This is beautiful, Wizard. – This is not. Stop. Play that again. This is original." – but he wrote many of his operas without any muse at all. And although two of Debussy's finest piano works, *Masques* and *L'Île Joyeuse* embody his "uncontrollable feeling" for Emma Bardac in the first flush of their affair, Debussy was far more often inspired in his finest works by paintings, symbolist poetry and other art forms than by any woman. His women were complementary rather than integral to his works.

One constant remains in all three volumes. More great music has flowed from the pains of unrequited love than from love fulfilled: to wit, in previous volumes, the music of Beethoven, Brahms, Berlioz, Chopin, Tchaikovsky and so many others. The supreme case in this volume is Janácek, whose flood of late masterpieces in his sixties and early seventies derived, on his own explicit insistence, from his obsession over eleven years with a young married woman who never allowed any contact more intimate than a kiss!

Finally – here is a question especially for women readers. Can great art produced by bastards justify their behaviour? The supreme example in this volume is Debussy, who two-timed and jettisoned his women as his personal needs dictated. Christopher Palmer has this to say of not only Debussy, but also Wagner, Delius, and Arnold Bax, all composers of glorious sea music:

> ... a shared characteristic of these four great sea-poets in music was the strength of their sexuality. None could be fettered in the usual way to conjugal and family fidelity or responsibility, and It is surely true that any denial of this constant and restless need for gratification of the senses would have impaired the force of their creativity. ...
>
> [Taken from *Bax* by Lewis Foreman]

This is a man writing about men, of course. What do women think? I would be interested to hear from them (Basil_Howitt@ compuserve.com, or via the publisher).

A book like this relies heavily on the researches of specialist biographers, and on the *Grove* and *New Grove Dictionaries of Music and Musicians*. However, my largest single debt is to *Greene's Biographical Encyclopedia of Composers* (Collins 1985). It is an extraordinary feat of personal stamina containing one man's highly readable profiles of no less than 2,433 composers in 1,348 pages from Limenius (born Greece second century BC) to William Hugh Albright (born 1944). No wonder Mr Mason Greene described his tome to me as "seven years of slavery". I am particularly grateful that he gave me leave to rifle his tome in any way that is legal. If, when transferring notes to text, I have occasionally borrowed rather than quoted a few phrases from Mason Greene, and from other sources as well, it has not been deliberate and I hereby apologise for any transgressions.

***

Chapter 1

George Frideric Handel
"Same sex desire"
Born: Halle, 23 February 1685
Died age 74: London, 13-14 April 1759

> In light of the composer's extensive and intimate
> association with demonstrably homosexual men and/
> or milieux, the question becomes this: on what basis
> can or ought one to argue that Handel was everywhere
> he went an exception?
> [Gary C. Thomas in *Queering the Pitch*, 1994]

As long ago as 1994 Gary C. Thomas proposed very convincingly, albeit with due academic caveats, that Handel was gay. Thomas's case appeared in his chapter on the composer – "Was George Frideric Handel Gay?" from *Queering the Pitch: The New Gay and Lesbian Musicology,* published by Routledge.

For whatever reason, Thomas's work escaped the attention of the majority of media pundits in the UK. I only became aware of *Queering the Pitch–* thanks to a kindly Canadian reviewer – after the publication in 1995 of my *Love Lives of the Great Composers*. There I presented Handel's love life as essentially unfathomable.

Not until October 2001 did the UK media circus get in on the Handel Is Gay act. Journalists and broadcasters were obviously bombarded with either advance copies or (more probably) fliers from Harvard University Press for their January 2002 title, *Handel as Orpheus*, by Ellen Harris. Ms Harris, we learned from the flier, suggests that Handel's cantatas, written between 1706 and 1723, "exhibit a clear homosexual subtext." Handel wrote them for his patrons and hosts who, in both Italy and England, "moved in circles in which same-sex desire was commonplace."

The UK media orgy even inspired a suitably sardonic sendup of BBC Radio 3 in *Private Eye*'s Anniversary Issue (Forty Glorious Years) on 2 November 2001:

Was Handel gay? *You* decide.

Ten Tell-tale Signs That Could Help You Make Up Your Mind.

1. He was unmarried.
2. Wore a wig.
3. Lived near Soho.
4. Liked playing with his organ.
5. Looked like Elton John.
6. Was "Musical".
7. Wore stockings and high heels.
8. Wrote music admired by many members of the gay community.
9. ... er ...
10. ... he must have been.

What's more, just look at these top Handel "homo" hits.

- *The Hellosailor Chorus*
- *The Entrance of the Old Queen of Sheba*
- *Gaydock the Priest*
- Plus millions more

British residents may wish to phone the Radio 3 "Was Handel Gay Line" and say why you're switching to *Classic FM*.

*

Inevitably, most of Thomas's evidence for Handel having been being gay is circumstantial and the interpretation of the evidence speculative. But how can the situation ever be otherwise in the elusive area of a private life considered without the benefit of documentation? In Handel's case, there were no flies-on-the-wall, no private confessions to confidants, no kiss-and-tell stories from jilted hangers-on, no cameras with telephoto lenses – nothing to give the game away. The whole world knows Tchaikovsky was gay because he wrote repeatedly to his brother Modest about what he called his "damned pederasty" and "pernicious passions." Lully was happy to flaunt his pederastic passions quite openly in the court of Louis XIV. But in Handel's case there is no proof of his gayness. Nor for that matter of anything very much else in his private life apart from his renowned gluttony.

Basically Thomas's case is that you can reasonably judge a man by the company he keeps. During his sojourn in Italy between

1706 and 1710, and during his permanent residence in England from the time of his second visit to London in 1712, Handel moved extensively among circles whose members are known to have been, in various mixes, "homosocial," "homoerotic" or homosexual.

*

Handel in Hamburg (1703-1706) and Hanover (1710).

According to one scholar mentioned by Thomas, Marion Ziegler, two of Handel's associates whom he met after leaving home for good in 1703 belonged to a cluster of men she "suspected" or "identified" as being gay. One of these was Johann Mattheson, the composer, singer, and prolific scribe with whom Handel had his famous duel at the Goosemarket Opera in Hamburg on 5 December 1704. The other was Agostino Steffani, by turns priest, Kapellmeister and diplomat. Handel reported to his biographer Sir John Hawkins that Steffani treated him "with great kindness" after he arrived in Hanover from Italy in 1710. Some thirty years older than Handel, Steffani moved in indisputably gay circles when visiting Rome between 1708 and 1709, and the two men may have already met there.

Interestingly, Ms Ziegler also claims that Thomas Arne, Telemann, and Handel's librettist for *Messiah*, Charles Jennens, were gay. All this in her essay *The Great Gay Composers*, in a volume entitled *Gay Source: A Catalogue for Men* (1977). Some of Ziegler's claims may be pushing speculation to its limits (I haven't read her book). Mattheson married an Englishwoman, Catharina Jennings, in 1709; Telemann was twice married and sired up to ten children; whilst Thomas Arne also had a wife, Cecilia, whom he treated abominably, and reportedly had a son by another woman.

Far less conjectural, however, were the proclivities of the two men Handel met in Hamburg who probably most influenced his decision to go to Italy: Prince Giovanni Gastone de' Medici ("Gian", the last of the Medici line) and his brother Ferdinand. Gian, something of "a ne'er-do-well Italian drifter" was, according to Ziegler, "one of the most open homosexuals in Europe in his day." Her claim is substantiated by the Enlightenment cultural historian George S. Rousseau, who quotes accounts of Gastone as having been a "rampant" sodomite, and an instigator of "bacchanalian orgies," at least in his later years.

Gays' Paradise
Handel in Italy (1706-1710)

Why for so long did Italy have the reputation of being a breeding ground and safe haven for gays, not to say also a sodomite's paradise? Anecdotal evidence abounds from at least the time of Boccaccio's *Decameron* in the mid fourteenth century. In Neifile's *Third Story* (First Day), Boccaccio has the Jew visiting Rome discover, tongue in cheek, that practically all the priests there "from the highest to the lowest were flagrantly given to the sin of lust, not only of the natural variety but also of the sodomitic."

In the time of the composer Lully (1632-87), himself an Italian-born rampant sodomite who achieved untold status and stardom in the court of Louis XIV, the term "Italian morals" was synonymous with sodomy. "Horrible, execrable, odious," was how the poet and satirist Boileau described them. Two centuries later, in January 1880, we find Tchaikovsky having a whale of a time in Rome (while working on his *Capriccio Italien)* because, in the words of his biographer Alexander Poznansky, Italy was "widely considered an erotic paradise by European homosexuals."

Is it because Italian men are such notoriously oedipal mummy's boys? In 1997, according to a piece originating in *Süddeuttsche Zeitung* (The South German Times), forty per cent of men in the 25-34 age group still lived at home with mamma mia, as opposed to only 25.9 per cent of women. The skier Alberto Tomba dreamed "of finding a wife like my mother," while the prominent "mammista" politician Sig. Francesco d'Onofrio lived with his 85-year-old mother who waited up for him every night. His marriage had collapsed because his wife could no longer tolerate his mother dropping in so frequently "with newspapers or cheese." North Americans know about these goings-on from a recent segment on CBS-TV's *60 Minutes*.

To return to Handel. During his three years in Italy the budding composer moved about between Florence, Rome, Venice, and Naples. In Florence he stayed with the above-mentioned Gian Gastone de Medici and his brother at the ducal court of Tuscany – Gian Gastone having been catapulted onto the throne as the last of the Medici dukes. By January 1707 Handel was in Rome (reputedly "the city of sodom") as guest in turn of Marchese Francesco Ruspoli, and the cardinals Colonna, Pamphili and Ottoboni.

"Here's yet another queer cardinal."

In Rome especially, music is known to have flourished within the "homosexual subcultures" fostered by the clergy. And there can be no doubt about the proclivities of one clergyman, Cardinal Pietro Ottoboni who owned a lavish villa, the Palazzo della Cancelleria, and nurtured a thriving and extraordinarily rich musical culture there. He was notorious for attracting men like Paolucci (a famous young singer) and Corelli into his service. And the aforementioned Steffani was ever a welcome guest of Ottoboni during his visits to Rome.

Of Corelli's gayness, incidentally, there can be little doubt, not least because of his known inseparable attachment to his former pupil Matteo Fornari who, after joining his master on the first desk of violins, was "rarely to be absent from his side." Fornari was also the legatee of all Corelli's instruments and manuscripts.

The widely quoted French diplomat and historian Charles de Brosses, who travelled in Italy in 1739 and 1740, pulled no punches about Ottoboni. In effect de Brosses was saying in coded language "Here's yet another queer cardinal" when he described Ottoboni as

> without morals, without repute, debauched, decadent,
> lover of the arts, and a fine musician.

Ottoboni presided over what was called an "Arcadian Academy" – Arcadian academies in general, in Italy, having had "a long and rich history of homosexual appropriation". Because he was not yet twenty-four, Handel could not officially join Ottoboni's Academy but its members nevertheless received him "with open arms."

Masquerades

According to Handel's first biographer, the widely quoted and reliable Rev. John Mainwaring (actually the first biographer ever of any composer), Domenico Scarlatti first met Handel playing the harpsichord and wearing a visor at a masquerade in Venice in 1709. As by now you may well imagine, masquerades in Italy were known venues for "unauthorised" sexual activity and also provided many opportunities for transvestism. Whether Handel also later attended, on the quiet, the "infamous" masquerades in London is not recorded.

*

Handel in London's gay aristocratic circles.
We are to walk, ride, ramble. dine, drink, and lie
together.
[Alexander Pope to Mrs Martha Blount (1716) on a
prospective visit to the Earl of Burlington's retreat at
Chiswick.]

On his first return visit to London for its opera season in the
autumn of 1712, Handel first stayed with a gentleman by the
name of "Mr Andrews" of Barn Elms (now Barnes). Nothing is
known of Andrews beyond his probable membership of the Kit
Kat Club, an all-male Whig coterie. Later this same year Handel
went to live for three years in the decidedly "homoerotic milieu"
of Burlington House in Piccadilly, the palatial residence of Richard Boyle, Earl of Burlington. The earl, then "a youth of barely
nineteen," still living (in Hogwood's words) "under the watchful
eye of his mother" was the first of Handel's generous English
patrons. Boyle also possessed an idyllic country residence, built
in the Palladian style, at Chiswick. In effect it was another Ital-
ian-inspired Arcadian retreat "where evidence of circumstantial homosexuality," (writes Thomas) "is difficult to suppress."
Here Handel mingled with such homosocial if not homoerotic
bachelors as Alexander Pope (England's leading 18th-century
poet) and John Gay (Handel's exact contemporary, best known
for *The Beggar's Opera* of 1728). Another intimate of the Chiswick
circle was William Kent ("Kentino"), an architect, landscape designer and painter and, according to Thomas, indisputably a homosexual.

Alexander Pope penned a revealing vignette of life at
Chiswick (including Handel's music) to a Mrs Teresa Blount in
1716:

I am to pass three or four days there in high luxury,
with some company, at my Lord Burlington's. We are
to walk, ride, ramble. dine, drink, and lie together. His
gardens are delightful, his music rewarding.

Not a woman in sight among these young men in their
twenties or early thirties. Except, of course, for the maids
changing the sheets, the washerwomen and the pastry cooks!

*

After returning from a visit to Germany in 1716, Handel found similar refuge and employment for some two years with another patron, this time at Cannons, an idyllic retreat nine miles out of town near Edgeware in Middlesex. Again in Palladian style, Cannons was owned by James Brydges, the first Duke of Chandos. The Duke, of course, was immortalised in Handel's eleven *Chandos Anthems* and also a *Chandos Te Deum*.

Molly houses

Did Handel, one wonders, so impenetrable in his private life, ever visit one or more of London's molly houses that sprung up in the eighteenth century – one of the most notorious of them being run by a certain Mrs Margaret Clap? Gay aristocrats gathered in these haunts to drink, dress up – and have sex in the back rooms, just like in heterosexual brothels. About the back rooms the mind boggles, especially after reading Edwina Curry's cameo of a gay bordello in Amsterdam in *A Parliamentary Affair*: couples, or even threesomes or moresomes, having whimpering, grunting, heaving, writhing, sweating, slithering sex in the same darkened room on sometimes inevitably stinking mattresses ...

Gary Thomas – to whom this chapter is obviously deeply indebted – must have the last word about his fascinating and painstaking investigations:

> If Handel belongs on the long and impressive list of queer men and women (in vast disproportion to their numbers), who have created, performed, cultivated, and adored music, I want to know about it and talk about the ways in which that might be meaningful. And if this knowledge gives one hate-mongering bigot pause, or makes one young lesbian or gay man proud, then so be it: for that the effort will have been worth it.
>
> ***

Chapter 2

Vincenzo Bellini
" a sigh in dancing pumps."
Born: Catania (Sicily), 3 November 1801
Died age 33: Puteaux (near Paris), 23 September 1835

I look for sentiment as well as sex.
[Bellini on his love life, to Florimo, 27 September 1828]

Carve in your head in adamantine letters: *Opera must
make people weep, feel horrified, die through singing.*
[Bellini to Carlo Pepoli, librettist for *I Puritani*,
May 1834]

How much is that fucking hat, please?
[Bellini in a Parisian hat shop]

Bellini cared far more about his music and himself than about
his lovers. But whereas other self-centred composers drew
indispensable creative inspiration from their women, Bellini
could compose without them.

The women in his life were important to him while they
lasted – for what he called "sentiment" and "sex" – but he dumped
them sooner or later in a determination to remain unencumbered
for the sake of his work. Only in the last year of his short life did
he set about searching in earnest for a wife, after the parents of
his long-favoured choice turned him down.

The young lady in question was Clelia Pasta, on whom the
composer had been keeping an interested eye since 1831 when
she was only 13 years old. Clelia was the daughter of the colo-
ratura diva Giuditta Pasta (1797-1865), one of the very finest in
the history of opera – and once pointedly described as Bellini's
"Minerva."

Well she might be! Minerva was the goddess of the arts in
Roman mythology and if any woman inspired Bellini to compose
it was Pasta – though there was no question of any kind of
amorous relationship. Unusually for divas of those times, Pasta
remained respectably married, with a husband, Giuseppe, who
gave up his singing career to be her manager. She was neither
promiscuous nor even open to persuasion on the casting couch.

Adoring her voice, acting abilities and personality, Bellini created star roles for her, including those in his two masterpieces, *La sonnambula* (The Sleepwalking Girl, 1831), and *Norma* (1831). *Norma* is one of the finest of all bel canto operas and took Pasta to the peak of her career. Readers unfamiliar with Bellini may have heard the two endlessly relayed lollipop arias from these operas: *Casta Diva* (Chaste Goddess) from *Norma* and Elvino's *Prendi: l'anel di tono* (Take this ring of fidelity) from *La sonnambula*.

Pasta became Bellini's "angel" who elicited from him a "grateful adoration that will end only with my life." One painting shows her hair wound tightly round her head from a central parting and braided on top into a large bun; a rosebud mouth, long slender nose, an elaborate ruff high round her neck, a tight dress with puffed-out upper sleeves ...

Bellini's other singing "angel" was the renowned French soprano Maria Malibran (1808-36) whom he got to know in 1833 in London. Here again the relationship was platonic and Bellini dismissed as "utter fabrication" all the gossip about a duel with a jealous rival.

Had she been alive 170 years ago, Joan "La Stupenda" Sutherland would also unquestionably have secured Bellini's adoration. Her singing in the four of his operas she recorded between 1962-66, with her husband Richard Bonynge conducting, is surely unsurpassed on record.

La sonnambula and *Norma* are both awash with Bellini's unforgettable and unmistakable kind of "long, long, long spun-out melodies" (Verdi's words). They are wide arched, meandering almost – like butterflies that move off time and again when you think they are going to settle on a flower – and (in Bellini's own words) "full of true passion and tears." The meandering aspect may have come from the folk music Bellini heard as a boy when peasant musicians came each year with their bagpipes from the north east tip of Sicily to his home city of Catania.

No wonder Bellini was so highly esteemed by Wagner, Berlioz and Donizetti. But perhaps his greatest admirer was Chopin, who adored his bel canto melodies and was powerfully influenced by them in his own *Nocturnes* and slow movements. The two men may well have met when they were based in Paris

(1831-35), and both being fastidious dandies, they no doubt talked about clothes as well as music. (Bellini once ordered two dozen pairs of gloves, remarking that "one can never have too many").

Bellini's paranoid tendencies seem to have made him less inclined to reciprocate the professional admiration he enjoyed. "Friendship within the profession is quite impossible," he wrote on 5 April 1828, while on another occasion he declared that "Donizetti's friends" were "my enemies." With some justification he was ever on the lookout for intrigues imagined or actual against him. In this he was nothing less than a through and through working musician of the theatre who realised that it was a tough and not very friendly world out there. All the surface luvviness failed to paper over the cracks of back-biting, of in-fighting, job pinching, partner pinching, and all the rest. To stay at the top meant being able always to deliver top quality products.

*

Francesco Florimo (1800-1881)
"Bellini's widower" and "spiritual heir"

Outside of his closely-knit family, the only person who mattered crucially to Bellini was his friend and peer Francesco Florimo. They first met while they were studying at the Real Collegio di Musica in Naples, where Bellini had arrived in 1819 with a grant from the City Council of Catania. Florimo was a native of Calabria, the southernmost region of the Italian mainland. In true Mediterranean fashion there were to be many territorially-inspired flare-ups over the years between the two young men, with Florimo denouncing Bellini's Sicilian origins and Bellini cursing Florimo as a *stupidino Calabresino*. The reconciliations were, of course, as passionate as the rows had been.

Bellini would remain in Naples for eight years before being catapulted to fame in Milan and Paris. Florimo stayed there for the rest of his life as librarian at the Real Collegio and became Bellini's most intimate male correspondent. After Bellini's death in 1831 Florimo assumed the mantle of biographer and memoirist to his friend. Much, however, that Florimo wrote about or attributed to Bellini needs to be taken with pinches or even shovelfuls of salt. Florimo was apt to touch up, obliterate, and otherwise edit parts of Bellini's life into a soulful melodrama in which the composer could do no wrong. Thus it was, for instance, that many of Bellini's letters revealing his callous conduct towards Giuditta Turina (see below) were thrown on the fire.

Some have suggested that the fervent correspondence between the two men indicates an actively homosexual rather than a more generalised homoerotic friendship. However, such epistolary effusiveness should perhaps be seen as no more than part of the gushing *schwärmerisch* style then so prevalent between young male friends throughout continental Europe and even England: to wit Paganini's passionate outpourings to his closest friend Luigi Germi, or Chopin's to his friend and mentor Tytus Woyciechowski during and after their years at the Lyceum in Warsaw. Even the correspondence between Tennyson and Arthur Hallam in bottled-up old Blighty is in the same vein!

Here is Bellini in fervent mode to Florimo (taken from Rosselli):

> [ours are] hearts made only to be friends to the last breath ...
> [12 January 1828]
> your existence is necessary to mine ...
> [23 January 1828]
> my excellent, my honest, my angelic friend! ... The more we know of the world the more we shall see how rare is our friendship.
> [11 February 1835]

When Bellini became involved with Giuditta Turina he had to assure Florimo that their love was intact:

> Do you understand or not? That in me love for you has become an element necessary to my peace, to my life? And that I don't want to hear about doubts, even though they are only an impulse of your love? Enough.

Enough indeed! Apart from informing the reader that since so little is known about Bellini's relationship with his mother Agata née Ferlito – other than that he inherited his blond looks from her – this piece will give a miss to all Freudian speculations about mother fixations and male bondings! We can say precious little either about Bellini's father, Rosario, of whose career as a musician virtually nothing is known. Rosario Bellini worked in the shadow of his more talented father Vincenzo Tobia Bellini, who was the maestro di capella of a distinguished Sicilian nobleman. Vincenzo Tobia was undoubtedly the most important influence on the early musical education of his grandson, "our"

Vincenzo Bellini. Inevitably so, because in 1813, due to severe overcrowding in his family's apartment, our Bellini left his parents and seven younger siblings to live with his grandfather.

Bellini would always keep in touch with his family, showering them, on one occasion, with "lots of kisses to Papa, Mama, my sisters, brothers, boy cousins, girl cousins, in particular Pudda and Zudda, Zia Saruzza, Zia Mara, Zia Jusdda, etc etc etc." He regularly sent them substantial sums of money, though only managed to return home twice in his lifetime (the second time triumphantly in 1832) after first leaving Catania in 1819.

*

"A sigh in dancing pumps"

Bellini undoubtedly projected an aura to some of what John Rosselli has called a "wavering" or "uncertain" sexual identity. One of the composer's exotic and influential hostesses in Paris, Princess Cristina Belgioso, described him as

> rounded, effeminate, though most elegant. His whole person was in harmony with his tender and dreamy compositions.

A more bitchy cameo of Bellini in Paris (where he settled in 1831) comes from the pen of the prominent German romantic poet Heinrich Heine, who noted that Bellini

> was a tall slender figure that moved in a graceful, I might say coquettish way; always finically dressed; face regular, long, rosy; hair light blond, almost golden, lightly curled; forehead noble, high, very high; nose straight; eyes pale blue; mouth well cut; chin round. His features had about them something vague and characterless, rather like milk, and this milky face sometimes curdled into a sweet-sour look of sadness. This sad look on Bellini's face made up for its want of spirit but it was a sadness without depth. It glimmered without poetry in his eyes, it quivered without passion about his lips. The young maestro seemed to wish to make this shallow, languid sadness visible in his whole appearance. His hair was dressed in such a romantically wistful fashion; his clothes fitted his frail body so languorously, and he carried his little malacca cane in such an idyllic manner, that he always reminded me of the young shepherds in our pastoral plays mincing about with beribboned crooks, in pastel jackets and breeches. And his gait was so maidenly, so

elegiac, so ethereal. The creature altogether looked like a sigh in dancing pumps.

Heine was clearly something of a stirrer. At one Paris salon he reminded Bellini that geniuses died young. Bellini responded with the Italian sign against the evil eye.

Bellini and his women

Bellini was neither highly sexed nor remotely macho. He was disinclined to make the first moves in sexual encounters, telling Princess Belgioso it was like "attacking a brand-new heart" or "breaking in a horse or a pair of new boots." "I don't like playing Don Juan or Don Quixote" was how he put it to Florimo.

He was, however, undoubtedly attractive to women and it can safely be assumed that when he felt in need of sex, any number of adoring, married, and maternally inclined admirers at whom he tweaked an eyebrow would be only too willing to drag him into their boudoirs, loosen their stays, peel off his shirt, and tumble onto the four-poster. As he wrote from Paris to Florimo, "I see a few women but the husbands are against duels on principle."

Besides his music and his looks Bellini had other attractions for well-to-do-women. Unlike Mozart, Schubert and so many others, he became a legend in his own lifetime, earning a fortune and being showered with honours. The most prestigious of these was perhaps the French Légion d'Honneur conferred on him in 1835.

And he was certainly a good catch financially! A slow worker, producing only one opera a year on average, as opposed to, say, Donizetti who produced up to five, Bellini insisted on and secured very high fees. His earnings shot up from 100 ducats for *Il Pirata* in 1827 to 1,800 ducats for *I Capuleti* (1830), 2,000 ducats plus half of author's rights for *La Sonnambula* and 3,000 ducats plus rights for *Norma* (both 1831). Verdi could not top such a figure until his tenth opera, *Macbeth,* in 1847. Had Bellini's works not so often been pirated in Italy, where there were no copyright laws until 1840, he would have been richer still.

*

Maddalena Fumaroli: Naples 1822

"The daughter of a Fumaroli can never be the wife of a poor suonatore di cembalo" [harpsichord player].
[Signor Fumaroli, father of Maddalena]

Whatever youthful flings Bellini enjoyed during his first two years as a student in Naples remain his (and Florimo's) secret. Unlike both Rossini and Donizetti, who were both severely plagued by venereal diseases contracted from prostitutes in their mid teens, Bellini remained free of any form of the pox. It seems in any case that he had only limited time or energy for women, since his working day at the Collegio under its Director Zingarelli stretched from 5.30 am until 10.00 pm. He had much to catch up on, apparently, since although his precocity had been clear to all in Catania, he lacked proficiency in the basic disciplines of *solfegio* (sol-fa exercises). However, he was a fast learner: as well as completing his first successful opera in 1825 he also composed many sacred and secular pieces, the best known of the latter now being his tuneful *Oboe Concerto*.

Outside of music, Bellini briefly involved himself with the Carbonari revolutionaries, getting off lightly with a reprimand from Zingarelli. He also fell seriously under the spell of a magistrate's daughter called Maddalena Fumaroli. It was love at first sight – and through a telescope at that. After Bellini spotted her Florimo arranged an introduction.

Maddalena, who naturally had all the accomplishments of a magistrate's daughter (sketching, singing and versifying), came to reciprocate Bellini's admiration during her singing and keyboard lessons with him in 1823 and 1824.

Bellini must have been keen to judge by an incident later recalled by both Florimo and Bellini:

> One evening the eager young lover followed the Fumaroli carriage from Piazzetta Marina, through Via Chiara and Piazza San Ferdinando, along Via Toledo and finally up Montecalvario to the Teatro Nuovo and right into the theatre, where Mercadante's *Elisa e Claudio* was being performed. Signor Fumaroli took exception to his daughter being subjected to what seemed to him unwelcome attentions, and lodged a complaint with the rector of the college.
>
> [Taken from *Bellini* by Leslie Orrey]

It was only after Bellini's composing career took off that Signor Fumaroli would eventually change his tune. Bellini's first success with *Adelson e Salvini*, premiered at the Collegio in 1825, encouraged him to ask – in vain – for Maddalena's hand through a go-between, his painter friend Giuseppe Marsigli.

Then came Bellini's first sensational success in Naples, sealing his career as a professional composer: *Bianca e Gernando,* premiered at the sumptuous San Carlo Theatre on 30 May 1836. But still Signor Fumaroli refused to budge. When Bellini again sought Maddalena's hand through Marsigli the reply came back, "The daughter of a Fumaroli can never be the wife of a poor suonatore di cembalo."

It was only Bellini's next overwhelming success that would finally impress Fumaroli. But by then – as you've already guessed – Bellini had lost interest.

The irrepressible, larger-than-life impresario at the San Carlo in Naples, former café waiter Domenico Barbaja, was also Director of La Scala in Milan. A sharp-eyed spotter of talent, Barbaja now invited Bellini to present his next opera there in collaboration with Italy's foremost librettist Felice Romani. Romani, who during his career would write over 100 texts for 40 different composers, wrote the libretti for all Bellini's operas except the last, *I Puritani.* A furious row between the two men in 1833 was fortunately patched up.

Thus it was that after a final secret rendezvous with Maddalena, full of tears "unrestrained and heart-rending," Bellini left Naples in April 1827 to make his home in Milan.

The first Bellini-Romani collaboration, *Il Pirata,* was a smash hit from the first night (24 October 1827 at La Scala) causing Bellini to "burst into convulsive sobs." The "povere suonatore di cembalo" had arrived, and Signor Fumaroli sent word through the usual go-between that Bellini's approaches for his daughter's hand would now be acceptable. However, Bellini had already decided (in a letter to Florimo from Milan) that "For my part I could never have made her happy, because that's what the needs of my career and my finances dictate." But instead of doing the decent thing and writing to Maddalena telling her it was all off, he ducked his duty – as so many of us do, men perhaps especially.

He now asked Florimo to reply on his behalf to Fumaroli's offer as he was too pressed for time. Maddalena then wrote him two letters which unfortunately arrived in Milan while he was in Genoa for two months supervising a substantially redrafted version of *Bianca e Gernando.* More than that, while in Genoa he first became smitten by the greatest and longest love of his life, Giuditta Turina.

Inevitably, on returning to Milan, Bellini was in a pickle after reading Maddalena's two letters, and once again commissioned Florimo to reply on his behalf. Poor Maddalena must have been desperate, for she wrote yet again to her former swain. And yes, Bellini yet again passed the buck to Florimo. All this, remember, in an era in which it took eight days for letters to be carried to and fro between Milan and Naples.

The devastated Maddalena left it at that and Bellini never heard from her again. But after her death only six years later at age thirty-two, he seems to have felt some remorse. A letter to Florimo (authenticated by Rosselli) agonises thus:

> The news of poor Maddalena's death afflicted me excessively; ... when I got this sad news, when I read the poems you set to music, I wept bitterly, and I saw that my heart was still capable of feeling sorrow: enough, let's not talk about it. Get the author of the poem *Due Speranze* to write another for me, in keeping with Maddalena's virtues and tender affection, and I'll set it to music ... it'll certainly be tender, and [will] arrange for me to speak to her beautiful spirit!!

Bellini may have been sincere in his intention to set a poem to music in Maddalena's memory – but his own death less than four months later thwarted his plans.

*

Giudetta Turina (1803-1871)
This passion will protect me from marriage.
[Bellini to Florimo, 27 September 1828]

The final rupture was no more to Bellini's credit than the conclusion of the earlier affair with Maddalena.
[Leslie Orrey: *Bellini*]

Giuditta Turina was everything Bellini could wish for: adoring, beautiful, rich – and above all married to someone else! Turina's husband tolerated his wife's affair as long as discretion was assured. Since marriages in high society were primarily about breeding and booty and rarely about love, adulterous affairs were commonplace. And the tradition lives on, of course, as the triangular sagas within the present British royal family have testified.

No wonder Bellini fell for Giuditta when they first met in Genoa in 1828. In one pastel by Luigi Bianchi she is extremely pretty, with her hair falling everywhere in ringlets, a slender, slightly crooked nose, thin lips, wide mouth ...

Born in Milan, the eldest child of a wealthy silk merchant from Pavia, she was slightly younger than Bellini and had married Ferdinando Turina in 1819. Before he returned from Genoa to Milan in the summer of 1828, Bellini had arranged to present Giuditta with a copy of a *Rondo* from his redrafted opera with the dedication "to Signora Giuditta Turina".

Bellini reported his conquest of Giuditta at great length, and in his typically clumsy, not to say boorish fashion, in a letter to Florimo. The Pollinis he mentions in the extract below were an elderly couple who took him under their wing after he arrived in Milan, regarding him as their "dearest son" and later nursing him back to health during a first serious illness (1830). The illness of Giuditta to which Bellini refers may have been one of her recurring bouts of severe menstrual pains that could lay her up for weeks at a time.

[27 September 1828]

On arriving in Milan last year, after having got to know as many people as possible, I began to be well received and had a few affairs; but they did not last long, for as you know I look for sentiment as well as sex; I soon discovered that with most of them only the latter prevailed, and that was sufficient for me to give them up, though remaining friends. So I went on, dropping one and picking up another, until I went to Genoa, where I got to know my present lover, of whom the Pollinis had often spoken to me, knowing her sister–in-law and her children's governess ... [Giuditta Turina] is about 28, affectionate, with a sweetness of manner that quite bowled me over; ... I first got really interested in her about a couple of days after I had been introduced, when I went to see her for the first time at her apartment, where she was with her brother, her only travelling companion, her husband being tied up with his business affairs. When I was shown in and she saw me she blushed scarlet, and this unexpected phenomenon rather surprised and enchanted me, and made me think of making love to her. The visits were kept up the next few days, and then when she had to

take to her bed in great pain I took advantage of her
indisposition to show my loving concern by keeping her
company the whole day; so I was several hours alone
with her, and you know how the thoughts uppermost
in one's mind can slip unintentionally into the
conversation, so we got to calling ourselves lovers, but
she expressed grave doubts as to my constancy, because
I had to travel about so much, and because she could
not always be in Milan; we kept arguing these points,
and all the time we were in Genoa the pleasures were
confined to conversation, and hour-long embraces, and
amorous kisses, and whisperings to each other of love,
but she continued to have doubts of my love, and for
my part I privately wondered if in fact it would be any
different from my other Milanese affairs. ... after a few
evenings of amorous discourse and embraces and kisses,
I gathered the flowers of love almost by stealth, since
her father [Signor Cantù] was in the house and we had
to keep all the doors open: fainting with love she asked
me: 'Bellini, will you love me always. will you love me
more and more ... I answered that I would love her if
she deserved it; in fact being a woman very rich,
beautiful and with all the qualities that make her
desirable company she had previously been invited
everywhere, but now this is all put behind her, she
goes to no more noisy parties, her only pleasure is to
be with me, and when she does find herself in a crowd
of people she is afflicted with melancholy; and so now
all the signs are that she truly loves me, my mind is
tranquil, the affair seems to be serious so now I confide
to you our secret. ... We are in perfect harmony, and I
am quite the happy lover, and go no more wandering
from one beauty to the next.

The course of the affair was never smooth for long. Even
during its first year Giuditta's illnesses meant that she missed
several of Bellini's premières or revivals: first *La Straniera,*
another knockout success, on 14 February 1829 at La Scala, with
Bellini taking five curtain calls and the audience yelling "like
mad." Then *Zaira* on 16 May in Parma (initially a failure in which
a 2.00 am final curtain didn't help). Then in the following year
Giuditta missed her lover's two brilliant successes during the
Venice Carnival: the revived *Il Pirata* (16 January 1830) and his
new *I Capuleti e i Montecchi* (11 March).

Giuditta's illnesses meant also that during her visit with Bellini to Naples (with her brother as chaperon) in the winter of 1832 she spent "more than twenty days in bed." And ill or not, she was inevitably excluded from the triumphant two-month return home to Catania that Bellini made (with Florimo) in February 1832.

Fortunately their passion was undoubtedly mutual for a while and they enjoyed idyllic sojourns together. In the summer of 1830 they lived discreetly in her family home on Lake Como while he did some preliminary work on an abortive opera *Hernani* – consulting his other Giuditta (Pasta) who lived nearby – before later settling on *La sonnambula*.

The lovers also spent the following summer similarly, between the premières of *La sonnambula* (6 March, Teatro Carcano, Milan) and *Norma* (26 December La Scala). By this second summer, however, Bellini, then aged twenty-nine, was already contemplating marriage with thirteen year old Clelia Pasta. There were even indications that the Pastas looked favourably on the idea.

The first signs of serious lovers' troubles came while they were together, at Bellini's insistence and against Giuditta's better judgement, during the Venice Carnival season of 1833 for the premiere of the grimmest of his operas, *Beatrice di Tenda*. Back home in Cassalbutano, Ferdinando Turina received an anonymous letter about the affair, but Giuditta nevertheless managed to prevent a terminal showdown. It was only in May of that same year, when Ferdinando was somehow presented with un unmistakably compromising letters written by Bellini (from London) to his wife, that he cried "Enough!" Ferdinando immediately threw her out, and filed for divorce.

Even then, however, by Giuditta's own account, she may have been able to save her marriage had she known that Bellini's interest in her was waning. Only her side of the story from now on has survived, though it seems plausible enough given Bellini's selfishness and commitment-phobia.

*

He says [he must set] his career avant tout, is this the way to speak to a woman who has sacrificed everything for him?
[Giuditta, 17 February 1834]

The essence of Bellini's excuse for an escape lay in rumours that had reached his ears of Giuditta's flirting with "an old man" in Naples (during Bellini's return to Catania), and of her displays of "coquetry." Hardly convincing, when she had all along risked so much in the way of security and status for the man she loved. Nevertheless, Bellini had also been told by some gossipmonger that a man had been courting Giuditta in Milan, staying with her "till 2.00 am," while he was in Venice preparing for *Beatrice di Tende*. Hence Bellini's insistence that Giuditta should join him there.

From Paris in September 1833 came further pretexts from Bellini for cooling off. These centred round not only "the Venice jealousy" but also "other gossip people fed him in Paris."

"There seems little doubt that he behaved ill," writes Rosselli. Indeed! When Giuditta Turina needed him most, he shied off. When he learned in March 1834 that she might come to Paris he made plans to escape quickly.

Return to Sender

In the early part of 1834 Giuditta refused to receive letters with Bellini's name on them. Business matters between them – Bellini having, for example, placed some of his capital with her at five percent interest – were discussed through a third party.

By July 1834, however, Bellini had received a "most affectionate" letter from Giuditta saying that although she still loved him she would content herself with his "cool friendship." Although tempted, Bellini resisted, writing to Florimo on 24 July:

> ...if it weren't that I have to pursue my career I would have decided to take up our relationship once more, but with so many commitments in various countries, such a relationship would be fatal to me, because it would take away my time and my peace as well; so I'll send her an evasive note, if possible without hurting her.

Thereafter Bellini seems to have escaped further tempting offers from Giuditta, or for appeals to his non-existent sense of duty. He was soon involved with another woman in a free and easy arrangement that suited him perfectly: above all, she was "docile and undemanding."

Giuditta Turina survived Bellini by more than thirty years, many of them troublesome. She had to nurse her sick mother and was also short of money. However, it seems that she eventually acquired the comforting companionship of a doctor.

After Bellini's death she mourned him and

> forgot everything, in order to think only of the tender affection that once bound us.

She died in 1871. Her tombstone in Milan cemetery pays tribute to the "essential goodness of a cultivated and gracious lady."

*

Paris

> You find here the greatest splendour, the greatest filthiness, the greatest virtue and the greatest vice.
> [Chopin]

By mid August of 1833 Bellini had been performed widely in Italy, also in Vienna and London. But like his compatriots Rossini before him and Donizetti after him, he realised that the route to real fame and big money in the opera world was to play the theatres of Paris, then the "centre and vortex" of cultural activity and fashion in Europe: first at the Théâtre-Italien, and then, hopefully, the Opéra, which specialised in the grandest of grand five-act historical operas (including a ballet) always presented in French. (Enough work "to fell a bull" was how Verdi put it later).

Within Paris, the salons of aristocratic ladies were the hubs of social and cultural interaction. Prominent among these hostesses was Princess Cristina Belgioso in whose salon Bellini may have met Chopin, the pianist Ferdinand Hiller, Heine, and various Italians including Rossini. Known as "The Romantic Muse", Princess Belgioso was the kind of woman who must have overwhelmed Bellini. A slim Italian beauty, she was known for her "black protruding eyes ... as big as saucers", her very slender hands, and her "grand and gracious manners." She wore large turbans and diaphanous, "excessively low necked dresses."

Not surprisingly, such men as Heine, Liszt, and the famous General Lafayette saw and enjoyed far more than her low neckline. However, we may safely assume that Bellini did not, even though he confided in her, as we have seen, his reluctance

31

to make the first moves in love. In any case it seems that Bellini didn't feel at home in these aristocratic circles, necessary though they were in his finely calculated "system" of self-advancement. A particular difficulty for him was the language barrier – sometimes embarrassingly so as when he once ordered a "fucking hat" (chapeau de foutre) instead of a "felt hat" (chapeau de feutre).

Bellini took two rooms at a pleasant private hotel, Les Bains Chinois, on the Boulevard des Italiens, conveniently near the Théâtre-Italien where four of his operas were to be presented. *Il pirata* and *I Capuleti* were successful in the autumn of 1833, and *La sonnambula* likewise in November 1834. *I Puritani*, Bellini's last opera, was (with a helpful push from Rossini) commissioned specially by the Théâtre-Italien and premiered there on 24 January 1835. Had he lived longer, it is near certain that he would have achieved his ambition of being commissioned by the Opéra itself. Before his death he had entered into negotiations for libretti with the extremely popular French dramatist Eugène Scribe, author of over 300 plays, as well as libretti for Meyerbeer and Verdi.

In May 1834 Bellini abandoned Les Bains Chinois for about six months of peace and quiet in the leafy suburb of Puteaux, half-an-hour's coach ride out of town. He moved out there again in May 1835.

It was the perfect hole-up for his final uninvolved and perhaps rather seedy affair during which he also set out in earnest search of a suitable wife.

1834

"No trouble at all": Mlle Olivier
I know a beautiful woman here [in Paris] who loves me extremely: for my part I can't say as much; but I find her beautiful, and kind and very docile, so much so that she gives me no trouble at all; every now and again I see her, I make love, and then I think about my opera.
[4 August 1834]

Until he found a suitable wife – well-off, compliant and faithful – this "beautiful woman" would do nicely for Bellini. She provided sex when he wanted it and then let him get on with his work without any nonsense about love and commitment.

John Rosselli – to whom the rest of this chapter is deeply indebted – suggests that, according to rumours put about after Bellini's death, the lady in question might have been a certain Mlle Olivier. She was the mistress of Bellini's intimate English friend ("mio stretto amico inglese") Solomon Levy with whom he stayed in Puteaux. Levy sounds to have been a rather dodgy character – "a foreign Jew with a dubious source of income and theatrical connections" is how Rosselli describes him, whilst Giuditta Turina would later describe Mlle Olivier as a "kept woman." For all that, Bellini found the couple to be "kind and good-natured."

To complicate the issue, there are two possible candidates for the identity of this Mlle Olivier who shared her favours between Levy and Bellini. She may have been either the soubrette by the name of Jenny Olivier, who became one of the many mistresses of Heine, or a former ballet dancer at the Opéra, Mlle Honorine Olivier. Either was about twenty-five or twenty-six in 1834-35 and therefore up to ten years younger than Bellini.

Since the question is entirely open, let's go for a biopic story. Bellini's Mlle Olivier was the less respectable woman, the soubrette Jenny who later transferred her favours to Heine. She seems to fit Bellini's bill slightly better than Honorine the ballet dancer, who may have been in any case less overawed than Jenny by Bellini the composer of bel canto. Jenny the soubrette realised that climbing into bed with the maestro would do her career, however modest, no harm, and her cynical partner Levy was ready to hand her over, rent-free, for similar reasons. On the other hand, the ballet world is rather androgynous and Bellini's "uncertain sexual identity" may have attracted Honorine.

No! Let's settle for Jenny and a nice cosy triangular arrangement.

Bellini's search for a wife

To have for my own a young girl, pretty and well brought up, will lead me no longer to have any relationships with women who are not mine, which bring continual ill-feeling. As for my wife (supposing her too to be inclined to flirt), I am the master: I will receive whom I please, I will take her travelling if the fancy takes me, etc. etc.: yet I don't think I shall be compelled to such measures; I know myself: if l marry

a woman who is agreeable and good-looking, and kind
as well, I believe I shall keep her company as
affectionately as can be: now women, all of them
without exception, behave ill to their husbands only
when they are neglected; so for the moment I am
imagining a happy state. ...
[30 November 1834]

Bellini made two proposals of marriage before his death, and
also specifically considered two other women.

Charlotte Hunloke
"150,000 francs without love isn't much."

The sister of a baronet from Roman Catholic stock in Lancashire,
Charlotte Hunloke, was one of the first women Bellini met in
Paris. They had been introduced by Giuditta Pasta, who had
earlier entrusted Charlotte with the care of Clelia.

Bellini proposed to Charlotte in vain – and it was just as
well. She made it clear that she felt "only esteem and friendship"
for her suitor, and Bellini's own feelings were no stronger. He
even disliked her teeth! This being the case a dowry of only
150,000 francs – "without love" – wasn't enough. It seems there
may also have been a problem of sexual identity – this time on
Charlotte's part since she had a fixation on Signora Pasta that
was no less than "idolatry." Whether after Bellini's death she
treasured the lock of hair he gave her is doubtful – all she could
recollect about him was his worship of Giuditta Pasta.

Clelia Pasta

In October 1834 Bellini formally approached the Pastas about
marrying their daughter Clelia. This time the response was "most
polite but icy." Hardly surprising in view of how they had seen
Bellini treat their good friend Giuditta Turina, now struggling
after Bellini's abandonment of her.

Determined to keep her away from theatrical influences,
the Pastas lost no time in marrying Clelia off to one of her cousins.

Mlle Vernet
200,000 francs but "too lively"

Another possible Signora Bellini came into the frame following
a suggestion from the wife of Bellini's financier friend Baron

Sellieyre. This young lady was the daughter of the renowned military painter Horace Vernet, Director of the French School in Rome.

Bellini began to imagine "a happy state" with Mlle Vernet, who was a pliable eighteen years of age, probably spoke some Italian, and would be worth 200,000 francs. Alas, when he met her his hopes were dashed: she was "too lively" and too self-willed. Within a few months she married someone else.

Baron Sellieyre's niece

Finally there was the niece of Baron Sellieyre – "rather pretty, sweet-tempered, of good family ... full of religion and good principles and very well bred." Bellini even wrote back to his folks in Catania about her – a sign indeed of seriousness.

But alas! It was not to be. Her family could not come up with the necessary minimum dowry Bellini demanded of 200,000 francs. Only such a sum would make him "independent of every-body and everything."

And that was it. The very last letter Bellini wrote to Florimo about marriage – concerning Baron Sellieyre's niece was on 18 July 1835. Two months later he was dead, after having in August written a canon for the composer Cherubini and another in four voices for Zimmerman.

*

Death

Although Bellini had suffered a brief bout of what was probably gastric fever in June 1834, he recovered fully and reported to Florimo on 24 July of the following year that he was in excellent health. Still, he was worried that a wave of cholera around Provence and the Riviera might spread.

On 2 September (in his penultimate known letter to Florimo) he reported that he had been "slightly troubled" by diarrhoea and on 11 September he mentioned "a slight dysentery" to a caller. He died twelve days later on 23 September at 5.00pm.

The actual causes of his death were the consequences of amoebic dysentery: "loss of blood from multiple ulceration of the large intestine, and loss of water from dysentery." His condition had been seriously aggravated by the development of a liver abscess "the size of a fist."

The Levys may have panicked and fled, fearing that Bellini was Paris's first cholera victim. When Bellini's friend Auguste Aymé arrived at the Puteaux residence on 23 September (having on several previous occasions been turned away) he found Bellini's corpse, the gardener having disappeared to buy candles and summon help.

Rossini, who was one of the pallbearers at Bellini's funeral, reported that it was carried out "with true royal splendour." He was buried in the famous Père Lachaise Cemetery but in 1876 his remains were transferred to the cathedral of Catania where there were days of processions, public meetings, concerts and masses.

Too short a short life, certainly. But long enough to create a cornucopia of uniquely enchanting, intoxicating melodies.

***

Chapter 3

All Those Strausses
Johann Baptist Strauss (the Elder or Father)
Born: Vienna, 14 March, 1804
Died age 45: Vienna, 25 September, 1849

Johann Baptist Strauss (Junior or Son)
Born: Vienna, 25 October, 1825
Died age 73: Vienna, 3 June 1899

Josef Strauss
Born: Vienna, 20 August, 1827
Died age 42: Vienna 22 July 1870

Eduard Strauss
Born: Vienna, 15 March, 1835
Died age 81: Vienna, 28 December, 1916

Which Strauss is which?

Who's who among all those Strausses? And which of them wrote what? After maybe a heavy New Year's Eve, you can be forgiven if you are confused on New Year's Day. If, that is, you are up in time to tune in to the ever-enchanting New Year's Day concert given by the Vienna Philharmonic Orchestra in the Musikverein. Or if you and yours have manfully made it to one of the scores of New Year's Day's concerts presented in many parts of the world.

Recharge your glass with champagne (a sparkling wine will do fine) and relax. It's easy.

In a nutshell, the man who started the Strauss ball rolling was known as "Johann Strauss the elder," or "Johann Strauss father" (hereafter called Strauss I). He is now best known for his immortal *Radetzky March*. In 1827 he broke away from his boss and elder colleague Joseph Lanner – who has sometimes been dubbed The Father of the Modern Waltz – and formed his own orchestra. Strauss I's first important booking was a six year contract (1829-36) to perform at the elegant and fashionable establishment Zum Sperlbauer, its several halls bedecked with palms and "more than a thousand lamps burning in the high and mighty chandeliers." In 1833 Strauss I began the first of many European tours in which his waltzes would win him untold fame.

Strauss I's legitimate family included three musical sons, the eldest and most famous of whom was also Johann, born less than four months after his father's marriage to Anna Streim, a lady he met in the line of business.

This first son of Strauss I was distinguished from his father on concert billboards of the time as "Johann Strauss son" or "Johann Strauss junior." Strauss II, a prolific composer with around 500 published works, is best known for his waltzes *The Blue Danube, Tales from the Vienna Woods*, and *The Emperor;* for his *Thunder and Lightning* and *Tritsch-Tratsch Polkas*; and for his operettas *Die Fledermaus* and *The Gypsy Baron*. Strauss II formed his own orchestra in 1844, and after his father's death merged his father's band with his own.

The other two musically distinguished sons of Strauss I were Josef and Eduard. Josef composed over 300 original compositions – distinguishing himself especially in his polkas (*Harlequin, Without a Care* ...) – and produced 500 arrangements of other composers' music. Eduard produced more than 350 original compositions, showing a special flair for the schnell-polka. However, Eduard's greatest claim to fame – or rather infamy – was his insane fit of pyromania in 1906 when he burned "several hundred kilos of waste paper" that turned out to be precious and irreplaceable manuscripts of his family's music.

None of these Strausses was in any way related to the famous opera composer Richard Strauss, who, along with many other "serious" composers (especially Brahms), was an ardent admirer of Johann II's music. Nor did they have any connection with Oscar, a Straus but not a Strauss. Oscar wrote *The Chocolate Soldier* and often features in New Year's Day programmes.

*

Johann II, Josef, and Eduard were all part of Strauss I's legitimate family of six children, one of whom died as a baby at ten months. Strauss I, however, was undoubtedly what the tabloids now call a love-rat, able to resist everything except temptation. Given his endless and prolonged touring schedules and inordinate popularity (apart from the time around the 1848 revolution), it is hardly surprising that he had umpteen mistresses. Women especially were intoxicated by the waltz craze that he and Lanner so astutely exploited. As one aristocratic

chronicler had put it at the time of the Congress of Vienna in
1814-15:

> One can scarcely conceive of the power which the waltz
> exercises. As soon as the first bars are heard, counte-
> nances brighten, eyes come alive, a tremor of delight
> runs through everyone. The graceful spinning-tops take
> shape, start to move, interweave, overtake. One has to
> have seen the ravishingly beautiful women, aglow with
> flowers and diamonds, drawn like bright meteors by
> this irresistible music ...".

According to Richard Wagner, writing in 1832, Strauss I
"very often made the audience frantic with delight", his music,
rather than the drink they gargled, raising their worship for the
bewitching violinist to "almost bewildering heights of frenzy."

In about 1833 things became very serious between Strauss
I and one of his mistresses. Between then and 1844 he fathered
no less than seven "love children" by one, Emilie Trambusch. An
attractive nineteen year old milliner when Strauss I first met
her (he was then 29), Emilie was the daughter of a military
surgeon.

Anna Strauss suffered acute humiliation when just two
months after the birth of her aforementioned Eduard in March
1835, her husband openly admitted paternity of a daughter by
his Emilie. Further shame came when the next illegitimate child
was christened Johann! – though this Johann thoughtfully didn't
make life more complicated for us by also becoming a dance
musician.

Anna Strauss had no choice but to tolerate this situation
until 1863 when she finally managed to obtain a divorce. In the
meantime Strauss I lived in a separate apartment in the home
of his legitimate family, the Hirschenhaus.

Johann II was deeply affected by the parental split, since
he adored both his mother and his father, to whom he wrote in
1844:

> Neither you, dear father, nor the world, if they consider
> it carefully, will disapprove of this, my immutable
> resolve, to remain at the side of my mother.

One wonders whether Anna felt it was rough justice when
her ex-husband caught scarlet fever from one of his illegitimate
brood and died from meningitis during the night of 24-25
September, 1849.

*

The Waltz King – Johann Strauss II –
"The Pampered Darling of our City of Song."

no bigger than Charlie Chaplin

Appropriately there's a McDonald's on the ground floor
of his apartment at 54 Praterstrasse. You feel Strauss,
always with an eye on making a *schilling* or three, as
composer, violinist and conductor, would have cashed
in with the *Mickey D Polka* if he was still around.

...Strauss is cheerfully lowbrow: scrumptious as
marrons glacés for some; sickly as *sachertorte* for
others.
[John Cunningham, *Guardian Travel* 27 March 1999]

[Strauss II] turned a bawdy dance form into a vehicle
for symphonic poetry.
[Mason Greene]

"Cheerfully lowbrow" or not, I would not exchange one bar of
Johann Strauss II for a million bars of Mahler, nor two million
bars of Hindemith, nor three million bars of ... Enough! In my
score of years as a jobbing cellist, the date I most loved on the
calendar was the New Year's Day Viennese show in the Free
Trade Hall Manchester UK, inaugurated by John Whibley and
his Manchester Camerata (in which I played) in the early 1990s.
Enchantment!

In spite of his father's implacable opposition to his taking up a
career in music, Strauss II, his ambition to learn the violin having
been fulfilled in secret by his mother, finally wore down paternal
resistance. In 1844 he took out a music license and, as noted,
hired his own orchestra. It performed for the first time, very
successfully, at a "Soirée Dansante" at Dommayer's Casino on
14 October. From then until Strauss I's death five years later,
the two men were in competition, though the father was never
ousted by his son. Johann II included his father's works in his
own less prestigious concerts at smaller venues, patronised by a
large proportion of youthful Bohemian, Serb and Slav minorities.

By the time that debut at Dommayer's was celebrated fifty years later in a series of Golden Jubilee festivities, Strauss II's astronomical successes as the Waltz King had made him (according to a poll of 1890) the third most popular figure in Europe, beaten only by Queen Victoria and Prince Otto von Bismarck. Tokens of esteem included a magnificent laurel wreath wrought in silver and solid gold from two hundred American admirers, and two huge giraffes from a former viceroy and khedive of Egypt. But perhaps his greatest honour was the conferment of honorary membership of the Gesellschaft der Musikfreunde (The Society of the Friends of Music), a distinction putting him on the same pedestal as such illustrious fellow friends as Brahms, Bruckner, Liszt, Verdi and Wagner. Strauss was so honoured that, with certain provisions, he willed his entire estate – worth more than £1M in today's money – to the Society.

During the intervening fifty years, Strauss II had reached one sensational landmark during the Viennese Carnival of 1861 when, on 5 February, he fielded three bands under the Strauss name in one evening, with Josef and Eduard as the other conductors. That evening three hundred musicians bowed, blew or banged their way through fifty dances including fourteen waltzes, ten quadrilles, nine French polkas, eight polka mazurkas eight quick polkas and a schottische. By then Strauss II had, not surprisingly, convinced the authorities that he had abandoned the revolutionary fervour of his youth and, in 1863, had been granted the ultimate royal accolade in his line of business: the Directorship of Music for the Imperial-Royal Court Balls.

Another landmark in Strauss II's career was his appointment by a consortium of railway barons to direct very lucrative five-month summer seasons of music at the Russian resort of Pavlovsk, recently connected by a nineteen mile stretch of railway to St Petersburg. Strauss appeared there each summer from 1856 to 1865 and again in 1869 and 1886. Many of his best loved pieces originate from this period, and often received their first performance at Pavlovsk – including the *Egyptian March* (celebrating the opening of the Suez Canal in 1869), the *Champagne Polka*, the *Tritsch-Tratsch Polka* (named after a contemporary Viennese satirical weekly which took its name from a contemporary play) and the *Pizzicato Polka,* composed jointly with Josef because Johann II failed to persuade his brother to write the piece on his own.

41

"Besieged by Russian women" [Peter Kemp]
Olga Smirnitskaya ("The mischievous one")

Inevitably during those long summer seasons in Pavlovsk Strauss II was bombarded by adoring groupies. So many, in fact, that he immortalised them in his waltz *Les dames de St Petersbourgh,* later tactfully renamed *Wiener Frauen* (Viennese Ladies). In 1858 he became acutely smitten by one of these admirers, Olga Smirnitzky, the musically talented daughter of a Russian aristocratic family. The passionate letters Strauss wrote to his "mischievous one" – sadly not available to us in English – show that he was keen to marry her. But however large his bank balance by now, as a strolling player he was not considered at all suitable as husband material by Olga's parents. It all ended abruptly when she wrote to her "dearest Jean" in the spring of 1860:

> Do not condemn me when you read these lines. I will be brief and omit explanation I have been engaged for two weeks ... Forget your unfaithful imp ...

*

Henriette Carolina Josepha Chalupetzky otherwise known as Jetty Treffz "the happiest of wives"

Two years later Strauss found happiness when he married a woman seven years his senior, Jetty Treffz, in St Stephen's Cathedral on 27 August 1862. One of his wedding presents was a Polka française, *Bluette,* that he dedicated to her.

Described as "pudgy" when Strauss met her, Jetty's lifestyle had been colourful, even by female singers' standards of the time. A fine warbler whose greatest triumphs had been in England performing with Strauss I in 1849, she returned to Vienna and retired with a bulging purse. Over the years 1841 to 1852 she had seven illegitimate children, most of them by her lover Moritz Todesco, a wealthy banker with whom she lived for eighteen years. It was at one of Todesco's many soirees with music that Jetty met Strauss II, rekindling a friendship that had been simmering for eighteen years. After her marriage to Strauss, Jetty kept contact with her children but concentrated all her energies on supporting Strauss in his meteoric career.

Perhaps her single most important contribution to that career – certainly from posterity's point of view – was to persuade her husband in the late 1860s to cut down radically on his concert appearances in favour of composing, particularly operettas. And thank goodness for that, since the third of them, *Die Fledermaus*, composed in six weeks in 1874, is arguably the most popular light opera ever written, and certainly the only one to be firmly in the repertory of every major opera house around the world today. In Vienna especially, *Die Fledermaus* is still "as compulsory as apple strudel" on New Year's Eve, with guest stars each taking the limelight in Act II to do their party pieces. *The Gypsy Baron* (1885) has proved almost as lasting.

Many of Strauss's greatest waltzes for the ballroom were also written in the later 1860s after his marriage to Jetty: *Artist's Life* (1867), *The Blue Danube* (1867), *Tales from Vienna Woods* (1868), and *Wine, Woman and Song* (1868).

Upstaging Robbie Williams

Strauss didn't stop touring and conducting altogether in the 1870s. Perhaps his most complicated conducting date ever came in 1872 when he directed *The Blue Danube* at the Boston Jubilee. A chorus of 20,000 and a 'regular' band of 809 players performed it to an audience of reportedly 100,000 in the largest building then ever constructed in America, the Coliseum. (That's five times as many as Robbie Williams performed in front of at the Wembley arena.) Strauss himself described the occasion to a friend:

> A hundred assistant conductors had been placed at my disposal to control these gigantic masses, but I was only able to see those nearest to me ... Suddenly a cannon fired, a gentle hint for us twenty thousand to begin the concert ... I gave the signal, my hundred sub-conductors followed me as quickly and as well as they could, and then there broke out a fearful racket that I shall never forget as long as I live! As we had begun more or less simultaneously, my whole attention was now directed towards seeing that we should also finish together. Thank Heaven, I also managed that. The hundred thousand-strong audience roared their approval, and I breathed a sigh of relief when I found myself in the fresh air again and felt the firm ground beneath my feet. The next day I had to flee an army of impresarios, who promised me the whole of California for a tour of America. I had already had quite enough of the music 'festival', and returned to Europe with the very greatest possible speed.

Returning to Jetty, she also had a crucially stabilising influence on her Johann as he became ever more prone to bouts of depression and increasingly dogged by ill-health. In Peter Kemp's words, she was (until her death in 1878) her husband's "wife, lover, artistic adviser, private secretary, organiser, music copyist, and even nurse."

A German journalist Albert Wolff penned a vivid impression of the husband Jetty had to handle when he was possessed by the creative demon:

> Strauss works "feverishly": he composes with the same nervous energy with which he conducts the orchestra. His workroom is everywhere. In a velvet suit and top boots, his hair in a mess, he rushes through his apartments ... Madame Strauss sees to it that in every room there is a table with writing implements ... Whether Strauss is composing an operetta or a polka, he gets into an indescribable state of nervous excitement. After two or three hours of work, he is as exhausted as a native bearer ... He belongs to that breed of artists who spend their lives doubting themselves ...

Nevertheless Jetty seems to have been blissfully happy in her role. When she had accompanied Strauss for his annual stint in Pavlovsk in 1863 she wrote that she was "the happiest of wives", her life "idyllic" with her "Jeany boy" who had "made life seem desirable to me again after it had become loathsome and a torment to me."

After years of being "a poor old cripple" – her own words for the persistent and painful illnesses she increasingly suffered – Jetty died at the age of fifty-nine on 8 April 1878; reportedly from a heart attack triggered off by an upsetting letter from one of her illegitimate sons. (According to Mason Greene, this son had "injected himself into the menage unannounced and had proved so demanding that Strauss threw him out").

Unable to cope with either arranging or attending Jetty's funeral, Strauss fled his villa in the suburb of Hietzing for good, and left Eduard to make all the arrangements. Strauss had been similarly absent on the deaths of his mother, his brother Josef, and his Aunt Pepi.

Ever afraid of being alone, Strauss plunged into a disastrous marriage only seven weeks later – with a woman with whom he had reportedly been having an affair; this being the most recent affair of the thirteen that Jetty had noted (according to Mason Greene) during their marriage.

*

Lili

Ernestine Henriette Angelika Dittrich, known as Lili, was twenty five years younger than Strauss when they were formally introduced to each other by Lili's singing teacher (having already met clandestinely of course). Besides adoring Strauss's music, Lili saw marriage with Strauss as a certain entree into her chosen career of theatre management.

The attraction of Lili for Strauss, in the flower of her youth, is obvious. She looks winsome and bewitching in one portrait, seated in a sideways pose featuring her extremely long hair parted in the middle, and an apron dress with an elaborate dog-tooth frill at the hem – the whole enhanced by draped foliage in the style of the times.

In spite of the elegant Stadt Palais the couple moved into at No 4 Igelgasse – the design and construction of the whole having been closely supervised by Jetty – the marriage soon foundered. She was less than thrilled to be left so much alone while her elderly, workaholic husband spent hours composing fretfully at his desk. Even a lovely *Kuss-Walzer* (Kiss Waltz) that Strauss dedicated "to his beloved wife Angelica" failed to pull in her lead as she pursued twenty nine year old Franz Steiner. Whatever his personal charms, Steiner's most important asset for Lili was surely his directorship of the Theater an der Wien.

In September 1882 Strauss's sister Anna confirmed what he had already suspected three months earlier, when he had written in lapdog fashion to Lili in Fraznensbad:

> Let yourself be well and truly kissed dear Lili, but don't run away from me.

Alas, she did just that on 27 September and the couple obtained a divorce in the civil courts by mutual consent as early as 9 December.

Although Lili moved in with Steiner and became his assistant at the Theater an der Wien, they were together only for about two years, and she seems to have come to regret parting from Strauss. Having moved from theatre management into a career in photography, during the First World War Lili took on the responsibility of fostering two children whose father had been drafted to the Front. After her death her grateful foster-children inscribed her gravestone thus:

> Here lies Lili Strauss (1849-1919)
> Your goodness is not forgotten.

*

Adèle Strauss née Deutsch

Once again Strauss and his bed, like Nature, abhorred a vacuum. After Lili moved out in September 1882, another woman he had known socially for several years would soon clamber up beside him in the four-poster – by November at the latest. In that month Adèle Strauss (no relation) accompanied him to Pest where he was to conduct his opera *Der lustige Kreig* (The Merry War).

Even more attractive than Lili, wasp-waisted Adèle was a twenty six year old Jewish widow (just half Strauss's age) with a two year old daughter Alice. Her husband Anton Strauss had died less than three years after they married. The long-time link between the unrelated Strauss families had been Anton's father Albert, a high-flying financier who had advised Johann II on his investment portfolio.

Adèle moved in with Strauss at the Stadt Palais and provided him with the kind of emotional and practical support he always so intensely needed. In the words of the normally satirical journal *Der Floh* on 25 March 1883:

> Frau Adèle Strauss ... will have a beneficial effect upon his nervous artistic temperament, and will be happy if she can give again to the honoured and beloved composer the peace of mind and happiness necessary for his creativity.

So confident was Strauss that he had found a woman to replace Jetty in his life, that as early as 19 April 1882 he conferred on Adèle an irrevocable life annuity of 4000 gulden – worth at the millennium perhaps £10,000.

Marriage between Strauss and Adèle was obviously going to be a problem, Strauss's civil divorce from Lili not being recognised by the Catholic church to which he at least nominally subscribed. Nevertheless, due to his contacts with admirers in very high places, together with an adroit transfer from Austrian to German citizenship and a change of denomination to Lutheran, a divorce and marriage became possible. Strauss received his divorce from his Teutonic fan Duke Ernst II of Saxe-Coburg-Gotha in July 1887. A month later the final scene in this real-life playlet was the wedding of the couple on 15 August in the ducal Chapel. Strauss had already prepared Adèle a wedding present in the shape of his lovely *Adelen-Walzer*.

And yes, they lived happily ever after. They really did. As happily as they had been during their previous years of cohabitation. How often do you read a story like that in these pages?

So much was Adèle a treasured part of Strauss's life that he kept a bell by his desk to summon her to hear his latest tunes. These days he composed while standing at a specially constructed high desk, rather than sitting at a piano, and also worked out his more complex orchestrations on a bespoke harmonium.

For all the uplift and ecstasy in his music, the Waltz King became in his last years ever more subject to psychiatric illnesses. "Morose, unspeaking, hardly looking up" wrote his librettist Ignatz Schnitzer,

> he would skulk for days or weeks on end unsociably around the house, or kept himself cocooned in his workroom. His own wife scarcely dared to speak to him, since to be disturbed in this ill-humoured silence could bring him to furious agitation.

Nevertheless Strauss retained a close circle of kindred spirits with whom (besides Adèle of course) he found moments of peace and happiness: among them Brahms, the composer Karl Goldmark, and the conductor Hans Richter (Musical Director of the Vienna State Opera from 1893 to 1900). According to legend he also spent the occasional afternoon in the company of the Emperor – for whose jubilee in 1889 he dedicated his *Kaiser-Jubiläum Jubelwalzer* – at the home of the Emperor's mistress Kathi Schratt.

Strauss had always harboured an obsessive fear of death (as well as of dying in poverty!) and must have dreaded his own. After catching pneumonia in late May 1899, his end came relatively quickly. He died in the arms of his devoted Adèle shortly after 4.00 pm on Saturday 3 June. Adèle survived her husband by more than thirty years and ensured that his posthumous interests were honoured and protected. The finely wrought art-nouveau statue of the composer in the park on the Ring was erected in 1921.

*

Josef Strauss

Unlike his elder brother, Josef Strauss became a musician almost by default. Although a keen amateur poet and painter, by 1850 he was working under the municipal architect and later became a factory chief engineer. He also made "the design for a water-works, published a book of useful mathematical formulae and tables, and invented a mechanical street sweeper that was bought by the city."

The musician by default emerged only in 1853, when Johann II collapsed from overwork and cajoled his brother into taking over his band at the already mentioned Sperl establishment. The deputising brother was an immediate success and, in a gesture of family loyalty, took a crash revision course in music and introduced his "First and Last Waltzes". From then on he was constantly overworked as a substitute for his brother both at home and abroad, with "little sleep and too many cigars."

"Pearls of Love"

Josef married his childhood sweetheart Caroline Josefa Pruck-mayer on 8 June 1857, presenting her with a lovely present of a specially composed concert waltz, *Perlen der Liebe* (Pearls of Love). Their only child Karoline Anna was born on 27 March 1858. Josef's dream of freeing Caroline from the jaws of his family's voracious music monster could never be fulfilled.

His mother's death in 1870 exacerbated his increasingly fragile condition, and in spite of the attentions of his beloved Caroline he became "enervated, depressed and subject to black-outs." Whilst in Warsaw in May 1870, he suffered an attack of "cerebral apoplexy" and a fall on the rostrum which, eventually, led to his death on 22 July 1870.

**

Eduard Strauss

Eduard took sole charge of the family Orchestra from 1870 (the year Josef died) until his retirement in 1901. According to legend, for which there is no supporting evidence, his notorious bouts of pyromania were triggered off by fits of jealousy against his eldest and more famous brother. As mentioned above, in 1907 Eduard destroyed "several hundred kilos of waste paper" in two large pottery-firing kilns of a Viennese furnace manufacturer. He also burned a further two cart-loads elsewhere. The "waste paper" turned out to be the extensive music archives of the Strauss orchestra. Fortunately, the existence of Strauss archives in other countries is making possible a gradual compilation of copies of some of the destroyed material.

Notwithstanding such devastation, we must credit Eduard for his enormous success in sustaining the Strauss family's renown. He became not only Imperial Court Ball Director but also Hofkapellmeister to the Emperor of Brazil and, writes Mason Greene, "held (and wore) decorations from Austria, Spain, France, Russia, and Persia, to name only some sources. (His chest, in full regalia, would have put Idi Amin's to shame").

"... completely alone ... I *no longer* have a family "
Eduard's marriage at the age of twenty seven to twenty-two-year-old Maria Magdalena Klenkhart (daughter of a friend of Johann I) took place on 8 January 1863. They had two sons, Johann Maria Eduard (born in 1866) and Josef Eduard Anna (born 1868). I'm loth to tell you that said Johann is known as Johann III – but don't let it spoil your (by now I hope) umpteenth glass of bubbly. Johann III would "carry the family musical tradition well into the [20th] century."

As to Eduard's marriage and family life, it seems to have fallen apart in spectacular fashion by 1897. Peter Kemp explains that in a period of three-and-a-quarter years from 1894, Eduard's two sons, with their mother's connivance, dissipated a total of 737,600 kronen (perhaps not far short of £1M) of their father's earnings.

Of this Eduard wrote to a friend Jacques Kowy on 21 July 1897:

> I do not know if you have heard of the limitless distress which I suffer due to the prodigality of members of my family, and the position and the circumstances force me to stand completely alone. I *no longer have* a family! Let *men* not dwell on this unspeakably sad situation any longer ...

It is hardly surprising to learn that Johann III and his father were thereafter "almost totally estranged."

※※

Chapter 4

Giuseppe Fortunino Francesco Verdi
"as unafraid as any man who ever lived."
Born: Le Roncole, 8.00 pm, 10 October, 1813
Died age 87: Milan, 2.50 pm, 27 January, 1901

Passion! Passion! Never mind which, but passion! ...
Poetry with great big balls...
FEW WORDS ... FEW WORDS ... FEW, BUT
SIGNIFICANT.
[Verdi to his librettist Piave, 1840s]

I met an old man who had been a loose friend of Verdi's
From him I learned that Verdi loved women to an
exaggerated degree and not only that, but this rich,
filthy-mouthed farmer said that he learned from Verdi
to like a certain kind of kiss that until then he had
never given any woman.
[Toscanini to his mistress Ada Mainardi, 7 November
1936]

Strepponi declared 'Either this woman leaves this house
or I leave it,' and Verdi replied 'This woman stays or I
blow my brains out.'
[Frank Walker: *The Man Verdi*]

... in his music he expressed through the personalities
of other human beings the wildest extremities of
passion, desire, and despair.
[Willard Mellers: *Man and His Music*]

*

Verdi was a colossus of Italian opera, unrivalled in popularity
from the waning of Donizetti until the arrival of Puccini. He is
still an enduring favourite, of course. Many are familiar with
the Verdi pop tunes that flood the airwaves today, just as they
pounded out of barrel-organs all over Italy in his day: *La donna
e mobile* and *Caro nome* from *Rigoletto*; the *Anvil chorus, Stride
la vampa, Il balen,* and *Miserere* from *Il Trovatore*; the *Grand
March* from *Aida; Va, Pensiero* from *Nabucco; Brindisi* from *La
Traviata* ... They thrill us today as much as they did millions
across the world within his own lifetime.

"Mr Cunt"

Fiercely guarding his privacy as he did, much of Verdi's love life outside of his main relationships is a closed book. If he did ever go astray, even after beginning to live with Giuseppina Strepponi in 1847, it was probably in the company of the man he nicknamed "Mr Cunt", Francesco Piave, who was the composer's tame librettist for ten of the operas. Piave was known for what Strepponi called his "erotic zeal" or nights of lechery on the town, and his readiness to act as procurer for his friends.

Of course, given his stature, genius, and strings of honours within his lifetime – not to mention also his inscrutable, increasingly handsome, even noble appearance – beautiful women, married and single, were there for the taking if he wanted them. He had a "straight blunt nose," a "steady gaze," a beard, long hair, and typically wore "baggy suits," an "artist's flowing bow tie," and a broad-brimmed hat.

When it came to high honours, no Italian musician could possibly ever match Verdi – even though he much preferred the admiration for his work of labourers, landladies and tram drivers. He received honorary citizenships galore and at least a score of decorations, including two in the French Legion of Honour, many similar awards in Italy, one in Russia, one in Turkey ...

In the political arena he represented Busseto in the assembly of Parma provinces, later became a member of the Italian Parliament (1861-65) and after that was sworn in as a Senator in Rome (1875) – though he soon quit. Considered by the Italians as a hero of the Risorgimento, the movement that led to the unification of Italy, Verdi shared passionately the republican visions of Giuseppe Mazzini and Luciano Manara.

Verdi's love life and his music

There are few direct links between Verdi's love life and his operas. As Rosselli has noted, love is often not even central to many of them. And even where it is, the love is "as often that of parent and child, of friends, or of country as it is the mutual love of young men and women."

One link, however, between Verdi's love life and his music is enshrined in a manuscript score of his little-known opera *Jérusalem* (1847), a reworking of *I Lombardi*. The words of the love duet in this opera between Gaston and Hélène are "filled in alternately in Verdi's and Strepponi's handwriting, indicating a secret and early declaration of their love."

Another link is the soprano Teresa Stolz with *Aida* and the *Requiem*. Verdi was besotted with Stolz while composing *Aida* – coaching her personally in the title role – and also the *Requiem,* the manuscript score of which he gave her after Strepponi's death. The leading soprano parts in both these works were inevitably shaped to Stolz's vocal talents as closely as the many finely-cut dresses in her wardrobe flattered her person.

Verdi's love life may also have suffused the tender music of *La Traviata*. The heroine Violetta's early death from consumption may have been linked unconsciously in Verdi's mind with his first wife Margherita, who died at the age of only twenty after a mere four years of marriage. There are some resemblances also (as we shall see) between Violetta's life as a demimondaine and that of Strepponi before she met Verdi. In the eyes of many she was "the real *Traviata*" in his life.

*

A "scoundrel" with "boorish manners"

Verdi began his musical education at his birthplace, Le Roncole (a hamlet in the North Italian plains in the Duchy of Parma), with the village organist Pietro Baistrocchi. From age seven, when his father bought him an old spinet, Verdi began to deputise for Baistrocchi, taking over his post at age nine for a stipend of about £4 a year.

After transferring at age ten to the ginnasio (grammar school) in Busseto, a small town about three miles from Le Roncole, Verdi continued his musical education with Ferdinando Provesi, then the town's most prominent professional musician. He was municipal music master, director of the Philharmonic Society, and also of the music for the collegiate church, San Bartolomeo. Provesi provided Verdi with many of his earliest opportunities for composition and serious music making, his first concert being an organ recital when he was thirteen in the chapel of the ginnasio.

Ailing in health, Provesi had Verdi deputise for him at San Bartolomeo. When he was sixteen Verdi was given the task of writing music for a service, a procession and a concert for the Holy Week of 1830.

Early musical openings came Verdi's way not only through Provesi, but also through Provesi's friend Antonio Barezzi, the man who very soon became a second father to his "beloved son" Verdi. After Barezzi's death in 1867 Verdi would write to his close friend Countess Maffei, "You know that I owe him everything, everything, everything ... I've known many people in my life but never a man better than he."

A prosperous Bussetan grocer and wine merchant who supplied goods to Verdi's father (who was an innkeeper), Barezzi was a "maniaco dilettante." Proficient on the flute and other instruments, and founder of the local Philharmonic Society, Barezzi did everything he could to develop his protégé's talent. Verdi not only composed all kinds of music to be performed at the Philharmonic Society's concerts, the small Busseto theatre and the church; he also directed rehearsals, taught young pupils, and played the piano, especially at soirees in the Barezzi household.

In May 1831 Verdi, then seventeen, moved in with Barezzi and his large family at their house at the end of the arcaded street in the piazza – a move welcomed by Verdi's father whose circumstances, however, were never nearly as humble as Verdi later claimed. Having left home, Verdi would remain close to both his parents, especially to his mother. His sister Giuseppina, mentally retarded as a result of meningitis, died aged seventeen in 1833.

It soon became apparent that a romance was blooming between Barezzi's eldest daughter Margherita and her newly-resident piano and singing master, a mere seven months older than she. But marriage was out of the question until Verdi could earn a decent living. Spotting that Verdi's future may well be in opera, Barezzi steered him towards the Milan Conservatoire.

The problem was money. Although Verdi would later receive a small grant from a charitable foundation, here and now – in 1832 – Barezzi would have to stump up all the costs of his protégé's musical education. (In the long term he paid about three-quarters of the total, and also provided him with a spinet.) The Milan Conservatoire, however, refused Verdi a place, not without with good reason (including his failure of the entrance exam) but to his everlasting pique. Barezzi therefore arranged for Verdi to be educated privately in Milan by one Vincenzo Lavigna, whose teaching was uninspiring and limited.

Holidays apart, Verdi remained in Milan until July 1835. Little is known of his stay there, though he took advantage of a regular cheap bench seat in the gods at La Scala, probably also went to other theatres, and made good use of the city's many book shops. A city seething with activity, Milan had a good deal to offer also in the way of more debauched pursuits. Visiting the city in 1836 Antonio Ghislanzoni (librettist of *Aida*) was struck more by Milan's squalor than its glories:

> pavements crossed by open sewers, crowded back-street
> dwellings, and dingy streets frequented by drunkards,
> thieves and whores. The signs of poverty and squalor
> were everywhere. Houses of ill repute from which
> prostitutes solicited from doors and windows were to
> be found even in the city centre near the cathedral.

The signs are that Verdi sowed a few wild oats during these student days. His landlord (Signor Giuseppe Seletti, a Bussetan) threw him out after fifteen months on account of his "boorish manners" and unacceptable behaviour. In declaring that Verdi was "something of a scoundrel", Seletti may have been hinting that his lodger had been trying to seduce his daughter!

Verdi returned to Busseto in 1835 with a big professional feather in his cap. In April 1834 he had been called in an emergency by Milan's Philharmonic Society to direct a rehearsal of Haydn's *Creation* He was so impressive conducting with his right hand and "playing with my left hand alone" that he ended up directing the actual performance at the Casino de 'Nobili, in which he enjoyed "a great success – all the better for being unexpected."

*

Marriage to Margherita Barezzi ("Ghita") "In the flower of her years"

In the year following his return to Busseto, Verdi became Town Music Master and Director of the Philharmonic Society – though only after endless, labyrinthine argy-bargy known as the Busseto War. In essence, Verdi's supporters wanted him to have the former combined directorship of both town and church music (held by Provesi who had died in 1833), whilst others had vehemently supported a man named Ferrara. In the end the authorities in

Parma decreed that the post would be split. On 20 April 1836 Verdi signed a nine-year contract as town music master, renewable every three years.

He could now marry his beloved Ghita.

Sodomite blackbirds and all – a wedding with a difference "... the bed will be fine for the newly weds."

The couple were betrothed on 16 April 1836 and married two and half weeks later in San Bartolomeo on 4 May, Margherita's birthday. The officiating priest, one Don Pettorelli from Ferrara, had written a ribald poem centred round the Philharmonic Society. He cast himself as an Owl, "Barezzi as The Great Blackbird, Verdi as a Parrot, Margherita as a Dove, and the lesser Philharmonic members as Sodomite-Blackbirds." After the wedding, the entire Philharmonic Society went to Casa Barezzi for the shindig, after which the couple left for their honeymoon in Milan – Verdi's father accompanying them! Amusingly, they stayed at the lodgings of Signor Seletti from which Verdi had been evicted as a student. But all was well enough and Seletti avowed that "the bed will be fine for the newly weds."

An oil painting of Margherita by August Mussini shows her as demure and pretty, holding a closed fan, with a long chiffon scarf round her neck and a very elaborate hairdo: thick coils wound round her ears like huge headphones and up into a tightly plaited diadem almost as long as her face.

Back in Busseto, Verdi soon involved Margherita in his arduous teaching duties, which were on top of his obligations to compose music for the Philharmonic Society and direct rehearsals and concerts.

The couple's children were given politically significant names of Roman Republican martyrs who had surrendered their lives under a tyrant. Virginia was born 26 March 1837 and Icilio Romano 11 July 1838.

Sadly, each child died early in its second year and both before the premiere of Verdi's first completed opera, commissioned by La Scala's "Napoleon of impresarios" BartolomeoMerelli. *Oberto, conte di San Bonifacio* opened at La Scala, Milan, on 17 November 1839. After Virginia's death in August 1838 Verdi had resigned his job in Busseto and in

February 1839 moved with Margherita and Icilio to a small apartment in Milan. Until his breakthrough with *Oberto* they were sometimes so hard up that Margherita is said to have pawned her jewels to help pay the rent.

*

So soon a widower

In Milan at midday on the feast of Corpus Cristi my beloved daughter Margherita died in my arms of some terrible disease perhaps unknown to medical science. She was in the flower of her years and at the height of her good fortune, for she had become the lifelong companion of that excellent young man Giuseppe Verdi, maestro di Musica. I beg for peace for her pure soul, ever as I weep over this tragic loss.

[From Barezzi's diary, June 1840]

Verdi had been able, just, to cope with the deaths of his children. But then the boost of *Oberto*'s reasonable success with both critics and audience (fourteen performances, and a contract from Merelli for three more operas at La Scala) was soon obliterated. Only eight months after the death of Icilio, Verdi's beloved Ghita died on 18 June 1840 from what the civil records called "rheumatic fever," what Verdi called a "brain fever," and what in truth was probably meningitis or encephalitis.

A relative, Giuseppe Demaldé, recorded that Verdi's "profound sorrow"

led him to give up everything completely and forever. He thought of nothing but hiding himself in some dark place and living out his miserable existence.

So violently did he rage against his fate that those close to him thought he was on the verge of insanity.

*

"Life is sorrow."

No wonder so many of Verdi's operas end with corpses on the stage, especially *Il Trovatore*. After its premiere in 1853 Verdi would write to the dearest of his confidantes, Countess Maffei:

People say the opera is too sad, and that there are too many deaths in it. But after all, death is all there is in life. What else is there?

Later still he would write at various times in similar vein:

Life is sorrow.
Misfortune rules the world.

What have we achieved? What shall we achieve? ...
Nothing.
I think that life is such a stupid thing, and what is worse,
a pointless thing. What shall we do? What shall we do?
Taking it all together, there is only one answer,
humiliating and extremely sad: NOTHING!

"Gloom and horror, violence and hatred, despair and death"
pervade not only *Il Trovatore* but also Verdi's two other operas
from his so-called middle period: *Rigoletto* (1851), which climaxes
with the eponymous hunchback hero ripping open a sack to
discover the corpse of his only daughter, and *La Traviata* (1853).

*

Margherita died just as Verdi was working on his second opera
for La Scala – a comedy *Un Giorno di Regno* (A One-Day Reign).
He returned to Busseto and tried to pull out of his contract. But
Merelli (wisely) insisted on its fulfilment and Verdi therefore
returned to Milan and the small and now desolate apartment on
the Carrobbio – with its "prim walnut sofa and side-chairs, the
empty beds, [and] all the furnishings of the home he had shared
with his wife and son." Yet he somehow managed to finish the
opera in time for its premiere on 5 September 1840. That it failed
dismally is hardly surprising in view of Verdi's traumatic
experiences. Nevertheless Demaldé's view that there were "at
least four strong pieces" in *Un Giorno* has been vindicated by
occasional twentieth century revivals of the work.

Verdi would not write another comedy until his very last
work, *Falstaff,* fifty years on.

*

Oh that *Nabucco*! Beautiful! Beautiful! Beautiful!
[Donizetti]

Verdi is supposed to have vowed to give up composing after his
triple bereavements, though in fact he worked on revisions for
the revival of *Oberto* in Genoa in 1841. Nevertheless, Merelli
can take the credit for easing the composer out of depression
and back into work. Gently but firmly, Merelli pushed his maestro
in the direction of a libretto by the flamboyant dramatist
Temistocle Solera: *Nabucodonsor* (Nebuchadnezzar, now known
as *Nabucco)*, a tale to Verdi's taste of "religion, armies, politics,
kings and priests, death and betrayal."

The rest of the *Nabucco* story is history. Although never specifically intended as such, the chorus of enslaved and homesick Jews craving deliverance from Nebuchadnezzar, leader of the Babylonians – *Va, pensiero sull' ali dorate* (Fly, my thoughts on golden wings) – became an unofficial national anthem after the unification of Italy in 1861. In that year the proclamation of King Victor Emanuel II as King of Italy ended forty six years of Austrian hegemony.

The first night of *Nabucco* at La Scala was a spectacular success and followed by seventy-five performances before the end of 1842. Offers of contracts flooded in to Verdi from other theatres. Also flooding in were messages from aristocratic ladies inviting Verdi to visit their Milanese salons. In the words of his devoted amanuensis and only pupil Emmanuele Muzio, Verdi, when not at work, was from now on "always out and surrounded by noble satellites who seem unable to do without him." We can mention these admiring ladies only fleetingly.

Countesses and Confidantes

Verdi clearly became extremely fond of, perhaps even fell in love with, Donna Emilia Zeltner Morosini, a "distinguished matron" nine years older than himself. Her attraction for him may have been partly maternal in the wake of his bereavements. Conversely, for Donna Emilia, Verdi in his handsome late twenties may have been a welcome distraction from her husband, who was old enough to be her father – and who at some point appears to have separated from her.

Verdi's letters to Donna Emilia (and her daughters) are full of such endearments as *tenero, tenerissimo,* and *tenerezza*, while in one letter written in 1842 he made an explicit declaration of love:

> I am always loving, passionate, on fire, half-dead over you. ...How many things I would like to say to you!

Of more enduring importance in Verdi's personal life was Countess Clarina Maffei whom he also first met after the success of *Nabucco*. Then twenty-eight, she had married at age sixteen the poet Cavaliere Andrei Maffei, later to be one of Verdi's librettists. By the time the Maffeis befriended Verdi their marriage seems to have been in name only, Maffei reportedly indulging in "a quick mass in the morning, a little flutter of cards in the afternoon, a bit of dalliance in the evening."

The couple separated in 1846, by which time Clarina had begun an open and lasting affair with Carlo Tenca, editor of the literary magazine *Rivista Europea*. Wisely not taking sides, Verdi had witnessed the separation agreement and remained on friendly terms with all three members of the triangle until their deaths.

Another fervent supporter of the Risorgimento, Countess Maffei presided over Milan's premier salon for fifty years. She was close enough to Verdi to receive from him all kinds of personal news concerning his work and health, both during and after his "sixteen years in the galleys!" – his own words to her for the period 1842-58 covering his score or so, of premiered operas and revisions from *Nabucco* to *Un ballo in maschera*.

After thirty years of friendship Clarina wrote to Verdi that time had "done nothing but add to your great mind experience, knowledge, depth of feeling." She herself had undoubtedly fostered these very qualities in him by introducing him at her salons to all manner of intellectuals, artists, journalists, poets, and such passionately political activists as Luciano Manara. To his everlasting delight, in 1868 she also introduced Verdi to the frail, eighty-two year old poet and novelist Alessandro Manzoni. Verdi considered Manzoni's novel *I Promessi Sposia* (The Betrothed), to be "one of the greatest books ever to have come out of the human mind ... a consolation for humanity."

After Clarina's death Verdi wrote that she was "so kind, so considerate, and so sensible. Oh, I shall certainly never forget her! We had been friends for forty-four years!! Poor Clarina!"

Another especially fervent admirer of Verdi was Countess Giuseppina Appiani – "kind-hearted, hospitable and generous" – whom he probably first met in December 1843. Sixteen years his senior, she was particularly fond of musicians. Bellini had composed his *La sonnambula*, and Donizetti his *Linda di Chamonix*, in her house in Milan. Donizetti's rapturous response to *Nabucco* meant that Signora Appiani would not offend him by also welcoming the rising star Verdi into her salon.

Fanciful biographers have had a field day suggesting that Signora Appiani was a "flirtatious Merry Widow" ensnaring her protégés. While she obviously doted on Bellini and Donizetti – to the extent of retaining the walking sticks and a cushion of the former, and bestowing a pair of slippers on the latter – this is hardly the stuff of grand passions or even discrete affairs. Nor is the Christmas present of a pair of braces that she sent to Verdi that seem to have been lost in the post in December 1845!

The friendship came to a sudden end in 1854 after Appiani had sent a letter to Sant' Agata (where Verdi and Strepponi lived from 1851) addressed to "Giuseppina Strepponi". Oddly, and not very understandably, both Verdi and Strepponi were seriously piqued by what they regarded as a breach of etiquette – even though they had been living together for five years and would not marry for another five!

Jane Phillips-Matz seems to be the only writer in English to have thoroughly investigated the possible identity of an "angel" with whom Verdi seems to have become loosely involved for seven years. He first mentioned her in a letter to Piave from Venice in March 1844. Then in various letters up to March 1851, Verdi referred to "that Angel whom you know" and "the woman I like." Had Piave, one wonders, made the introduction? Whether or not, Verdi had clearly not quite exorcised his angel by the time he made a serious commitment to Strepponi in 1846!

To Verdi's eternal glee from the grave, Phillips-Matz's possible candidates for the angel are legion and highly speculative. Apparently the angel had "expectations of her own" about the relationship and even a mind to do the impossible and visit Verdi at Sant' Agata.

*

Giuseppina Strepponi (1815-1897)
> one of the most remarkable [women] ever to figure in
> a composer's biography.
> [Julian Budden]

It was through their work that Verdi and Giuseppina Strepponi first met. She herself had been unable to sing in the premier of *Oberto* (1839) but had recommended it to Merelli.

That Verdi was making a marked impression on Strepponi is clear from the portrait of herself in operatic costume that she sent him from Venice as early as November 1841. The mysterious dedication in Italian reads: 'In your narrow street, you guided my steps, life-giving Venice.' She signs herself as Giuseppina Strepponj – a letter j often seeming to be used in Italian names in place of an i.

It was Strepponi also who persuaded Merelli to mount *Nabucco* by undertaking to sing the role of Abigaille in 1842. Soon afterwards Donizetti was talking of Strepponi (for whom he had created the title role in his opera *Adelia*) and "her Verdi." The couple met next in Parma in 1843 where she again sang Abigaille, and where *I Lombardi* was premiered on 11 February. At Verdi's request, Strepponi had advised him on a suitable fee for *I Lombardi*: the same, she suggested, as Bellini had received for *Norma*: 10,000 Austrian lire. He closed the deal, but the sum was later raised to 12,000.

The couple's next meeting was in 1844 in Bergamo, when she again nurtured Verdi's professional interests in a letter concerning the publication by Giovaninna Lucca of his *Six Romances*. Later in the year, she sang in performances Verdi directed of *Ernani*.

Verdi and Strepponi may have become lovers in Parma in 1843 – his at least according to Strepponi herself who in a letter to him dated 3 January 1853 defined that new year as the "the eleventh year of our relationship." Perhaps mistrusting Strepponi's memory, Frank Walker has suggested that the couple became lovers in Paris in 1846.

Women, however, surely have a habit or remembering such things as "the first time:" "I remember the red silk curtains in the hotel room, the mouse in the wainscot, and the limping chambermaid." In any case, Strepponi was not the kind of woman, as we shall see, to wait blushingly for Verdi to make a move.

Strepponi's previous career makes good tabloid copy even today. She seems to have been hell-bent on auto-destruct in her professional and personal lives, both being sensational and gripping enough to rival plots by Balzac and Zola.

Born in Lodi, Lombardi, in 1815 and the eldest daughter of a minor composer, Strepponi went to the Milan Conservatoire at age fifteen. Soon recognised in her career as a "prima donna assoluta" with a rare gift for being able to take on both comic and serious roles, her career was brilliant but brief. Not only through serious over-work – she would sometimes sing extremely demanding roles five or even six nights in a week – but also because of a succession of debilitating pregnancies. She had three illegitimate children within three years.

Camillo was born in 1838 and adopted by Strepponi's former maid. Later he studied sculpture and medicine before dying in 1863. Sinforosa was born in 1839 and after some three weeks was placed in the turnstile of an Ospedale for abandoned infants, but lived to the ripe old age of 80. Adela was born in 1841, adopted by a working class couple in Trieste and then never seen again by her mother before dying from dysentery in 1842. There may also have been a fourth child, possibly still-born.

According to Frank Walker, the father of Camillo and Sinforosa was probably Napoleone Moriani, a star tenor with a wife and two children. The complication is that Strepponi's theatrical agent Camillo Cirelli admitted paternity of these first two children, possibly to save Moriani's reputation. However, Moriani was definitely the father of Adelina.

Plans to marry Strepponi off to one admirer – referred to by Moriani as "that nasty lame devil who gives her such bad advice"– came to nothing, as did attempts to link her permanently with another lover, Count Filippo Camerata dei Passionei. This nobleman was understandably put off not only by the child Adela who had arrived in late 1841 but by Strepponi's simultaneous affair with a man named Calvi, about whom he irately tackled her in her dressing room in Trieste.

Under a doctor's warning of consumption and with a voice in ruins, Strepponi retired at the age of thirty to Paris, where she set about establishing a private teaching practice and giving small-scaled concerts. Verdi asked his friends the Escudiers (his publishers in France) to give every possible assistance to "the woman I entrust to your care" – and they did.

When Verdi went to Paris for the premier of *Jérusalem* in November 1847, he and Strepponi began their life of fifty years together, he staying either just round the corner from her or in the same apartment block. Their entries (mentioned above) into the autograph score of *Jérusalem* are touching evidence of their love for each other – a love that unfortunately would all but crack up twenty or so years later.

Verdi had, in fact, already made an unequivocal commitment to Strepponi in a letter to her of October 1846. But no-one other than her has ever read it, nor are they ever likely to. On its sealed envelope at S.Agata, Strepponi wrote:

They shall lay this letter on my heart
when they bury me!
[5 or 6 October 1846]

It was her most treasured possession. When she died at Sant' Agata fifty-one years later Verdi, remembering her wishes, had the house searched for the letter but it could not be unearthed at the time. Since then, by agreement with Verdi's adoptive heirs, the letter has remained unopened.

*

"Pasticcio" and her "Wizard"

Planning to return to his roots since at least 1845, Verdi had bought in that year the Palazzo Dordoni in Busseto. In August 1849 he moved in on his return from Paris, and Strepponi joined him a month later.

The tongue-wagging and worse that this cohabitation caused in small-time Busseto needs no elaboration. Verdi's house, the Barezzis', the collegiate church and the town hall were all within 200 yards of each other in the town's piazza. Verdi, in spite of the disapproval of both his father (a strict Catholic) and his former father-in-law, could tough out all the scuttlebutt, especially as he was often away and approaching the most intensive working years of his life. (The years 1849-53 saw two revivals of *Macbeth* and premieres of *La battaglia di Legnano, Luisa Miller, Stiffelio, Rigoletto, Il Trovatore* and *La Traviata*). But poor Strepponi was stuck on her own in Busseto much of the time and had to bear the brunt of scorn, hatred and ostracisation – even to the extent of being ignored in church. Undoubtedly she had guts and must have loved her man intensely.

Sant' Agata

By 1851 the situation in Busseto had become intolerable and the couple moved to Sant' Agata, the Verdi family's ancestral estate with three tenant farms (later to be repeatedly expanded) that the composer had bought in 1848. The pull of his roots had become irresistible, the Lombard plain being hardly otherwise beckoning with its extremes of weather and expanses of monotonous flatness relieved only by poplars, church spires and vine-carrying pollarded mulberries. After eighteen months, Verdi was the proud owner of four oxen, seventeen cows, ten bullocks, eleven calves and six rams. He would forever keep scrupulously detailed accounts of all transactions in wine, corn, hay, manure, flour, salt and livestock. Though with an abundance of cheap labour on hand that he ruled with a rod of iron – eighteen staff worked on the garden alone – he was more a gentleman farmer than a working one.

Rosselli, who has obviously been there, offers a businesslike cameo of Sant' Agata:

> The house, though they added to it, claims no aristocratic status; the rooms are of middling size and height, easily kept warm in winter, the furniture solid and elaborate in the Italian variant of mid-Victorian style, the pictures for the most part anecdotal or of personal interest. The garden, again of middling size for a villa, adds more trees and a pond to the few oaks already there in 1848; magnolia grandiflora, willows, cedars, further oaks made a shaded oasis in the plain, though the Verdis were old before they could enjoy their new trees at full height. It is a gentleman farmer's house, with far more books and music than such a person might normally collect.

No sooner had Verdi and Strepponi moved into Sant' Agata than his mother Luigia died on 28 June 1851. Sorrow, intensified perhaps by guilt and remorse, induced fits of sobbing and raving. "I cannot describe his grief," wrote Muzio to Verdi's publisher Giulio Ricordi, "for it is too great."

> Peppina is suffering, watching him weep, and I have the sad task of making arrangements for the funeral, priests, etc. I had persuaded him to leave and come [to Milan], but he has changed his mind and does not want to leave his house.

*

Placating Barezzi

That Verdi's beloved second father Barezzi was put out by the presence on home ground of his former son-in-law's mistress can hardly be doubted. Verdi obviously felt it necessary to tackle the issue head-on in a long, defiant though respectful letter of 21 January 1852 responding to Barezzi's "stinging phrases." Here is a small part of it, taken from Phillips-Matz:

> Carissimo Suocero [Dearest Father-in-Law],
> ... I have nothing to hide. In my house there lives a free, independent lady, a lover – like me – of the solitary life, with means that cover her every need. Neither I nor she owes any explanation for our actions

to anyone at all; but on the other hand, who knows what relationship exists between us? What business connections? What ties? What rights I have over her, and she over me? Who knows whether she is or is not my wife? And if she were, who knows what particular motives, what reasons we have for not making that public? Who knows whether it is good or bad? Why could it not also be good? And if it were bad, who has the right to hurl curses at us? But I will say that in my house people owe to her the same respect owed to me, or even greater [respect], and that no one is allowed to fall short in that, for any reason whatever; ...

... if, by chance, something should offend you because it has not been said, then I swear to you on my honour that I have no intention of giving you any kind of unhappiness. I have always considered you and I consider you my benefactor, and I am honoured by that and I boast of it. Addio, addio! With the usual friendship. ...

This same letter also indicates that Barezzi was more hurt by Verdi no longer needing his help, for what he called "errands," than by the presence of Strepponi, whom he liked.

*

"So often alone" ... "a body without a soul" ... "these days when you have condemned me to a cell."

After the couple's arrival in Sant' Agata in 1851, Verdi was often away – for revivals of *Macbeth* and *Luisa Miller* in Bologna, and for about three months in Paris. In 1852-53, his work trips included two to Venice, two to Rome, and a further one to Paris.

Verdi didn't allow Strepponi to accompany him on any of his Italian travels until an eventful visit to Naples in 1858. She was therefore often alone with the servants at Sant' Agata, or perhaps in hotels where he had left her, or seeing relations.

Strepponi consoled herself by sending her beloved long love letters that are a joy to read, especially perhaps when she writes as his indispensable day-to-day muse – persuading him to put the right notes in the right place.

In her letters of 2 and 3 January 1853 she is worldly-wise, well read, full of the little domesticities of Sant' Agata (omitted here) – and above all desperately missing her man and wondering repeatedly why she is not allowed to join him in Rome. The first letter from a hotel in Leghorn is addressed to 'Signor Giuseppe

Verdi, Compositore di Musica a Roma' where he is preparing for the premiere of *Il Trovatore* ("our Trovatore" she called it) at the Teatro Apollo:

> [2 January]
> ... You can't imagine how impatiently I am awaiting your return! I have started reading, and I read, read, read until my eyes are red; but I am afraid that sadness and boredom will attack me violently during these days when you have condemned me to a cell. You will say 'Spend money and have a good time.' First of all, I do not like you to tell me 'Have a good time,' when I don't know where to look for amusement! If I could see you for a quarter of an hour out of every twenty-four, I would be in high spirits, would work, would read, would write, and the time would pass if anything too quickly. As it is. ..but let's drop this argument because I am about to cry! ...
> Addio for this
> evening.
>
> [3 January]
> My dear Pasticcio,
> I have just this moment received your [letter] and I cannot describe my joy! I read the newspaper articles that you sent me. ...
> I am very, very pleased that you are lost without me, and I hope you will be so bothered that you will give up your barbarous idea of leaving me alone like a saint from the *Thebaid* [a Roman epic by Statius]! My dear Wizard, your heart is *an angel's heart*, but your head – as far as language and certain Ideas are concerned – has a skull *so thick* that if Gall were alive, he could add certain curious observations to his treatise on *Craniology*. ...
> Addio, write me a nice letter and hurry and give *our Trovatore*. A kiss on your heart.
> Peppina.

On this same day (3 January 1853) she received another letter from Verdi, replying immediately with passion and caring tenderness to 'Sig. Maestro Giuseppe Verdi, Roma'. Fractions of the letter read:

> Dearest
> I received your second letter and I thank you for thinking of me on the first day of the new year, the

eleventh [year] of our relationship! If I didn't send you [holiday greetings] it was because I know such things do not matter to you ... but you can imagine how much I desire you and will desire you on the first and on every day of every year of the rest of your life! ... Without you, I am a body without a soul. I am (and I think you are the same) different from so many others who need frequent separations to keep their love alive. I would stay with you for years and years without being bored, or weary.

... We will not have children (since God perhaps is punishing me for my sins in not granting me any legitimate joy before I die!) Well, then, not having any children by me, I hope you will not make me sad by having any by another woman. ...

... And you haven't yet composed anything [of *La Traviata*]? You see, you do not have your poor Pest in a corner of your room, tucked away in an armchair, saying to you *'This is beautiful, Wizard.– This is not. Stop. Play that again. This is original.'* Now without this poor Pest, God is punishing you, making you wait and rack your brain, before opening up the little boxes and letting your magnificent musical ideas out of them.

... Good evening, Wizard. Tomorrow before leaving, I will finish this letter.

Verdi seems to have been miffed by a few days' gap in Strepponi's letter writing. Her response on 12 January 1853 includes a further uninhibited declaration of love and commitment, and the assurance that:

excepting for you, I have nothing on earth that consoles me. I (and perhaps this is bad) love you above everything else and above all others. No matter how great, how many, and how unrelenting my sorrows are, your love is for me such a good thing that it is enough to give me the courage to bear all the bitter things that torment me. ...

Love me as I love you.

Your Peppina.

Verdi must have again mentioned that he was having difficulties with composing *La Traviata*. Again also, in her reply of 12 January she raised the vexed issue of their separations. And yet again she asserted before everything else her undiminished love for the man "who alone in the world has never made me unhappy." This same letter also contained Strepponi's detailed professional advice (obviously solicited) on his projected commitments in Naples and Paris.

"As for the rest of your body..."

"Her devotion runs like a refrain," writes Budden. Yet for all their mutual devotion, Strepponi was enough of a realist and woman of the world to realise that when in Venice preparing for *La Traviata's* premiere on 6 March, Verdi may well have had a night or two of womanising with Piave:

[26 February 1853]

...

Addio, I kiss you on your angel heart, which I hope will be mine forever; as for the rest of your body, I would not swear to that, not even at this moment when I am writing to you, particularly as you have Piave nearby. Addio addio.'

*

After what Verdi called the "utter fiasco" of the premiere of *La Traviata* in Venice, he returned to Sant' Agata. Then in October the couple went back to Paris – still then El Dorado for a successful Italian opera composer. The couple were based there for some fifteen months, though with Verdi making two work trips to London. The French premiere of *Trovatore* took place at the Théâtre des Italiens on 26 December 1854, while the world premiere of *Les vêpres siciliennes* at the Opéra (in June 1855, after endless delays and problems) more than satisfied the insatiable demands of the French for grand operas in five acts.

Altogether Verdi made about twenty visits to the French capital during his lifetime.

*

The couple returned to Sant' Agata in December 1855 and during the following two years Verdi again often left Strepponi to her own devices whilst his travels took him to Parma, Venice, Paris, Reggio Emilia, Rimini ... The couple did, however, take a short holiday for sea bathing in Venice in the early summer of 1856.

As noted, the first business trip he made with Strepponi in Italy was to Naples in 1858 where she cut a matronly figure, "voluminous in black crinoline," helping Verdi to track down their "errant Maltese spaniel Loulou." ("Ah there you are, you son of a bitch!") Strepponi also no doubt gave Verdi sound advice on how to deal with the unacceptable censorship imposed by the authorities on his opera *Un ballo in maschera*. After endless haggling, he withdrew *Un ballo* and agreed to replace it with a revised *Simon Boccanegra* staged in November.

After working in Rome for the premiere of *Un ballo* on 17 February 1859 Verdi finally made an honest woman of Strepponi by marrying her in Collonges-sous-Salèves (in the Savoy region of France) in a very private ceremony on 29 August. The only others in attendance were the two witnesses, the bell-ringer and the coachman. Verdi may possibly have waited so long before marrying Strepponi to avoid any risk of paternal responsibility for her two illegitimate sons, Camillo by now having reached the age of majority and Sinforosa about to do so.

Later, in 1867, Verdi would further enhance his family by adopting Maria Filomena Carrara-Verdi – "Fifao." The orphaned daughter of one of his cousins, Filomena would in due course marry the lawyer Alberto Carrara and Verdi's heirs today descend from this union.

The honeymoon was probably neither madly passionate nor deliriously romantic. Just intensely affectionate. Verdi was forty-five, Giuseppina was forty-four, and they had been living together for ten or eleven years. The marriage simply sealed a union of deeply committed and faithful friends. A year later, Strepponi implied as much when she wrote to Verdi that she held him close "as in the active period of our life." In any case, her appetite for sex may have been severely hampered by the acute "stomach cramps" that afflicted her from the early 1860s, followed by many other "internal troubles."

Whatever their life in the bedroom, Giuseppina got Verdi composing again after a prolonged period in which he concentrated on his farming interests. The year 1860 was spent managing his estates, spending the late winter in Genoa, high summer at Tabbiano Spa and buying rifles for the Busseto militia. There is no doubt that it was her influence that set his creative juices flowing again after he was approached for an opera in St Petersburg. She told Mauro Corticelli (whose idea it had been) that she would agree to

> using the methods which are said to be successful with the most illustrious St Peter ... that is, to worry and make a nuisance of oneself until you get what you want.

> It is true that Verdi is less patient than St Peter; but after all if he packs me off to bed it won't be the first time ...

The result of Giuseppina's prodding – and also of Verdi's own quickly excited interest in the project and of the prospect of a record fee to date of 60,000 francs – was *La forza del destino*, eventually premiered at the Italian Imperial Theatre in St Petersburg on 10 November 1862. For good measure the Russians added to Verdi's pile of honours by awarding him the Cross of the Imperial and Royal Order of S. Stanislas.

Strepponi nursed not only Verdi's creativity but also the ever-important inner man. For the Russian trip she ordered in advance:

> 100 bottles of light Bordeaux dinner wines, 20 bottles of fine Bordeaux, 20 bottles of Champagne, as well as rice [arborio of course], maccheroni, and cheese fine enough to keep her temperamental husband in good spirits.

*

Strife: "The Bear of Busseto"

The year 1867 saw documented strife and stress in the Verdi household. It was a bad year for Verdi anyway – in spite of the successful premiere *of Don Carlos* in Paris in March – with his father's death on 14 January, and that of his beloved Barezzi on 21 July. But these bereavements and other irritations cannot alone account for his increasing fits of depression and vile tempers over trivial matters at Sant' Agata. Strepponi described in her entry for 2 July how Verdi, after searching for his copy of Plato and being helpfully reminded by his wife that it was in the "cupboard in the dining room," accused her of "premeditated" aggravation amounting "almost to an abuse of power."

Strepponi's diary notes for January 1868 provide further glimpses of domestic trouble, with her references to the "thousand things that set him off", his brusqueness, and his dissatisfaction even with her "tone of voice in casual conversation."

*

The Other Woman

The real plunge in the Verdis' marriage came after the entrance into Verdi's operatic orbit of thirty-three year old Teresa Stolz when she sang Elisabetta in the premiere of *Don Carlos* on 11 March 1867.

Born near Prague in 1834 into a family of musicians, she trained there and began her career in Tbilisi in 1857, soon afterwards appearing in several European theatres, Rio de Janeiro, and London. "Plump and equable," she had "an impeccable vocal technique," and "an instinctive feeling for Verdi's music," bringing to his operas "a powerful, luminous and ... imposing dramatic presence." Her career on the Italian circuit was given a huge boost by the admiration of the conductor Angelo Mariani, a close friend of Verdi since 1857. Over the following twelve years, until a quarrel in 1869 which notably discredited Verdi in the eyes of many, Mariani conducted three of Verdi's operas, perhaps most notably the premiere of *Don Carlos*.

Mariani was in raptures with Stolz's singing: "the range and beauty of her voice, the artistry with which she inflects it, sentiment, mastery of line – all perfect, all sublime," he wrote of her Amelia in *Un ballo in maschera* early in 1868. But more than that, he was also in raptures with her person, and later that same year they became engaged.

"Repudiated"

It appears that Verdi himself may have first become interested in more than just Stolz's singing early in 1869. Budden suggests, convincingly, that Verdi's refusal to invite Giuseppina in February 1869 to the rehearsals in Milan for his revised *La forza del destino* (with Stolz singing Leonora) may be "significant." Certainly this letter from Giuseppina to her husband two weeks or so before the premiere (on 27 February) speaks volumes:

> ... when last Spring my heart counselled me boldly to introduce myself to Clarina Maffei and to Manzoni [in Milan] so as to come home bearing all sorts of things you would like – and when we took that trip together to Milan and visited Manzoni and sailed along the lake and the consequence of it was to bring you back to the land of your first triumphs. little did I forsee the strange and cruel outcome, that I should be disowned thus ... May God forgive you the sharp and humiliating wound you have dealt me.

In this same letter she also accused him of wanting to slip her into Milan "like a bundle of contraband goods" and described herself as having been "repudiated." It does seem likely that Verdi, perhaps on the cusp of male menopause at the age of fifty five, didn't want his ageing wife in the way while he paid excessive court to this much younger woman who would soon enslave him.

Nevertheless, when it suited his purpose to have Strepponi sit in a box during the dress rehearsal and on the opening night, he went to collect her in Genoa (where he had rented winter quarters at the Palazzo Sauli since 1866) and brought her back to Milan. (In 1874 the couple would move from Palazzo Sauli to Palazzo Doria.)

And so Giuseppina's suffering continued and intensified exponentially. Stolz made the first of her regular visits to Sant' Agata in the late summer of 1871, soon afterwards breaking off her engagement to Mariani. Giuseppina's tactics in handling this ménage à trois were (as Budden puts it) those "recommended by the average woman's magazine." After Stolz's visit Giuseppina wrote to her rival:

> ... what I want above all is to embrace you again and stay as long as possible in your company, because I love you, admire you and am attracted by your frank, sincere and elevated character in no way tainted by the air of the *coulisses* [meaning behaviour "behind the scenes"] ...

During this year Verdi was coaching Stolz intensively in her title role in *Aida,* which had its Egyptian premiere on 24 December1871 (in the absence of both Verdi and Stolz) and its Italian premiere (Stolz singing) at La Scala on 8 February1872. Next would come the preparations for her soprano solos in the *Requiem,* premiered at the Church of San Marco, Milan, on 22 May 1874.

By now Stolz was fully aware of her power to bewitch her maestro and was coming over all "kittenish" with him:

> Couldn't you spare a moment of your precious sleep to come and say hello to us in the theatre ... Maestro, you are *naughty*! very naughty!

By the spring of 1872 Strepponi was desperate. She even suggested to Verdi that Stolz should buy a villa in Castione dei Marchesi, conveniently close to Sant' Agata. When the ménage à trois were in hotels together during the tours of the *Requiem* and *Aida,* Strepponi noticed how blatantly her husband contrived ways to be with Stolz even at mealtimes. After performances of

Aida in Milan and Parma in 1872, she wrote on a packet of Stolz's letters (described by Walker as "garrulous, sometimes malicious and not very intelligent"):

> Sixteen letters!! In a short time!! What *activity*!

A hack's hatchet job

From August through November 1875 Verdi's behaviour reached its nadir and Strepponi's humiliation its zenith. He was now nearly sixty two, Stolz forty-one. An article on 22 August in the Florence newspaper *La rivista indipendente* promised to publish

> the story of the career of Signora Teresa Stolz, Singer; the late Maestro M[ariani] of Bologna; Maestro Verdi of Busseto; and the Signori Ricordi and Tomaghi of Milan', including '[her] intimacy with Maestro M. – cruelty to the same Maestro M. Favours and intimacy with Maestro Verdi – a wallet lost and found in Signora Stolz's room, etc., etc.'

The articles began on 4 September and ran through four further issues into November. Here are short extracts, adapted from Phillips-Matz, from three of the articles:

> [Second instalment]
> ... And so there they are, Philemon and Baucis [a jibe at Verdi's advanced age] right in the middle of their honeymoon! Here is Verdi and here is Stolz, who pretends to adore green [verde], a green that is no longer green [young]; and here is Verdi, who becomes small in spite of his reputation, becomes like a baby, and – poor little love-struck heart – lets himself be led around by the nose by Teresina. Indeed he acts like a boy who asks his teacher for permission to go to the lavatory. His alter ego schemes, has her own way, and gives orders. And Verdi obeys. Poor reputation, and poor name, how tiny have you become! ...
> [Third instalment]
> And here we are with our soprano's comical adventures. The first act begins in the classical, beautiful city of Milan. ... See how proper these little people were! They were not living in the same hotel; but that did not stop Maestro Verdi from hurrying to honour the plump, appealing soprano with a visit, which we believe was platonic. Verdi was received with all the honours and dignity required on such a visit; and soon the amorous couple lay down, or rather, did not lie down – they

> made themselves comfortable, they relaxed, they stretched out on a soft sofa. We really do not know what odd things they did on that sofa, what struggles went on, or what discussions, as they thrashed around, because they were in the room, and the door was closed. The adventure lies in the fact that in the heat of the encounter neither Stolz nor Verdi was aware of anything; Verdi's wallet, containing 50,000 lire, fell out of his pocket. ... Unnoticed by the two wrestlers, the wallet slid on to the sofa. When the two wrestlers calmed down, Verdi went back home ...

Verdi later recovered his wallet, though the episode "gave rise to odd remarks and made people laugh like mad." Part of the Fourth instalment reads:

> ... once Stolz knew Verdi, she wanted to be introduced to his dear Other Half, Signora Strepponi, who kindly welcomed Stolz and was gracious to her ... but when this good lady became aware that Stolz, in addition to interpreting Verdi's works, was also showing him her intimate charms, she thought it wise to leave her in the dirt on the stage floor; and then *Anger* came. ... But Signora Stolz, profiting from Maestro Verdi's good-heartedness, took too much advantage of him and began to boss him around, (if I can be permitted a vulgar expression) taking off his trousers. And if you want a proof of that, look at her on the stage in Ancona where she is running the season, accepting and refusing singers and orchestra players, and with the blessing of Verdi, who is letting himself be led around by the nose and wants everyone to bow before the Goddess soprano. ..

Although further revelations were promised, nothing else was published. Another newspaper, *Il presente*, later pontificated that although Verdi's private life was his own affair it was "a scandal" that any man could afford to have 50,000 lire in his wallet

> when hunger was rife in Italy and unarmed, starving farm-hands were defying armed government troops in a desperate bid to get their pay raised by a few centesimi a day.

Strepponi's fear, after at least eight years of marital misery, that Verdi might leave her altogether is harrowing in this contempory letter draft. After suggesting that they move their winter quarters from the invasive "coal smoke" of Genoa to Milan, she continued:

> As you know, I do not need society, and it is enough for me to have some good person to whom I can speak from time to time. I love to stay in the house; I ask you only for an apartment with light and air, and that you not abandon me completely in these last years of our lives; by that I mean to say do not desert our house completely. In that flat city I can take an occasional walk, visit [someone] occasionally, and have the chance to spend a bit of money myself, something I have never had the chance or the desire to do in Genoa.

All this while Strepponi continued to struggle to maintain some sort of sanity in her relationship with La Stolz who, by now, was clearly worried about her effect on the Verdis' marriage:

> So, my dear Teresa, your fear of being unwelcome because you detected a hint of unhappiness in me is a fear to be put aside ... You will never be unwelcome in our house so long as you and we remain those honest, straightforward souls that we now are. With this and a kiss, I end my sentence.

After a reply from Stolz, Strepponi declared:

> Now that I have received your dear letter, where you tell me that I was mistaken in what I believed, I am happy, and I thank you for all the affectionate words that you sent me to lift any doubt from my mind. Oh! I hope that the moment of disillusionment will never come in our friendship; and to make sure that does not happen, let us always stay just this honest and sincere, and let's enjoy pleasure and suffer sorrow together; it is so unusual to find hearts that are good and unselfish!!!

*

"If she is. ... Let's end this once and for all."

The boil had to burst, Strepponi mounted a direct offensive on her husband in this letter of 21 April 1876, the day before he conducted both *Aida* and the *Requiem* at the Théâtre des Italiens in Paris. They were all three staying at the Hotel de Bade.

> ... since she is not ill and there is no performance, it seems to me that you could go twenty-four hours without seeing this signora;

> ... I do not know whether she is or is not ... I know that
> since 1872 there have been [added and erased: febrile]
> periods of assiduity and solicitude on your part that
> no woman could possibly interpret more favourably. I
> know that I am always ready to love her frankly and
> honestly.
> You know how you have thanked me! with hard,
> violent, heart-rending words! You cannot control
> yourself.
> If she is ... Let's end this once and for all.

In the early the Autumn of 1876 there was, according to
Walker, "a tense and dangerous situation" at Sant' Agata so
tense, in fact, that sometime in the first weeks of October
Strepponi went to see her sister "for a few days" in Cremona.
There had been a "final traumatic confrontation" after Verdi had
brought Strepponi, Stolz, and his adopted daughter Filomena to
Sant' Agata. Strepponi reportedly ordered Verdi to send Stolz
away, and Verdi threatened to "blow his brains out" if Stolz left.
Strepponi therefore left the Sant' Agata until Stolz had returned
to Milan.

Return to ménage à deux

To her credit, Stolz, having announced her retirement from the
stage, decided by October of this disastrous year to resume her
career after receiving an offer from St Petersburg. Her motive
seems to have been as much to opt out of the impossible love
triangle as to seize the chance of earning "140,000 gold francs".
She broke off all communication with the Verdis from the time
of her departure from Sant' Agata in October until December.
When correspondence was resumed Strepponi, as Walker says,
was "almost superhuman" in her readiness not only to forgive
"offences" but also to love "the offender."

After the crisis of October 1876 the Verdi household returned
to relative normality. According to Phillips-Matz, in 1878 Stolz
addressed only two letters to Verdi alone, in 1879 three, in 1880
one. Propriety was restored. But far more than that,

> The two women developed a sisterly relationship as
> they sent lace, hats, furniture, and advice back and
> forth, traded coats and furs, paid each other's small
> bills, and settled their petty cash accounts.

In 1880 there was a pleasant and unthreatening ménage à trois at the Hotel de Bade in Paris when Verdi conducted *Aida* at the Opéra, sung in French and this time with a ballet incorporated in deference to rigid French traditions. Stolz was also at Sant' Agata for the Christmas and New Year gatherings of 1881-82.

The indisputable evidence of a full reconciliation between the two women in Verdi's triangle comes from Strepponi's will in which she left Stolz:

> a watch framed with small diamonds, a gold chatelaine with green enamel, and a bracelet of Roman work with the word 'Souvenir' in small diamonds.

*

"... believe in my love, great, very, very great, and very true."

After Strepponi's death in November 1897 Verdi and Stolz remained in love with each other to the very end of their lives. He was now free to give her the autograph score of the *Requiem:*

> To Teresa Stolz the first interpreter of this composition.
> G. Verdi. Sant' Agata, December 1897.

The letters between the eighty-seven-year-old composer and his sixty-six-year-old former diva speak for themselves. After Stolz left Sant' Agata for Tabiano in the early summer of 1900 he wrote:

> Dearest,
> Delightful hours but [they were] too short! And who knows when even ones as short as those will come again! Oh an old man's life is truly unhappy! Even without real illness, life is a burden ... Love me well always, and believe in my [love], great, very, very great, and very true.

And later, after arranging her next visit to Sant' Agata:

> So everything is set for Saturday morning at nine; ... If you approve, just send me a word: 'All right!' Oh! Joy! Joy! I am truly happy, even though my health is a bit off.

Stolz confirmed the arrangements from Tabiano on 22 June:

> Your letter received yesterday evening. Thanks. It is settled. I will be in Borgo [San Donnino] tomorrow Saturday at nine in the morning. What joy!! What happiness!! Your very affectionate [Teresa].

They then stayed for a month together in Montecatini, and she was present when he celebrated his eighty seventh birthday with friends on 13 October.

During Verdi's final week of unconsciousness, induced by a stroke on 21 January 1901, she fainted. She herself died a year later at the age of sixty eight.

*

Death of Strepponi

To pick up the threads of Verdi and Strepponi: after years of torment they settled in to a mellow and peaceful old age together. Since they were often with each other either at Sant' Agata or elsewhere there are few letters between them. One Verdi sent to Giuseppina in the Autumn of 1880 ends:

> I have nothing else to tell you and have nothing else to do, other than give you a kiss and say I am your !!!
> Addio, addio

> ... Stay well and keep going. I am not bad. Moving around is positively good for me. You understand, [I mean] travelling.
> Again, addio.

Giuseppina was determined to make sure her husband did not overwork. In 1893 when Arrigo Boito (Verdi's last librettist who provided the scripts for *Otello* and *Falstaff*) suggested that he and Verdi should set to work on *King Lear*, Giuseppina remonstrated "For heaven's sake Boito! Verdi is too old and tired."

Verdi was with Giuseppina at the last when she died of pneumonia at 4.30 pm on Sunday 14 November 1897 at age 82. The funeral, attended by large numbers from every rung of the local community ladder, took place at dawn in the Sant' Agata parish church, with no flowers and no eulogies. "I came into the world poor and without pomp," she had insisted, "and without pomp I want to go down into the grave." She was buried (for the first time) in the Cimitero Monumentale in Milan in a ceremony attended by all and sundry, including several senators, members of the Ricordi family (Giulio Ricordi had mounted all Verdi's Italian premieres since 1869), Toscanini ...

Stolz was not there. She had already gone with Giuditta Ricordi to Sant' Agata to be with Verdi. In her will, Giuseppina named Verdi her universal heir. Besides the gifts to Stolz she also left substantial annual sums to the poor and deserving, 24,000 lire to her sister Barberina Strepponi, and a total of 18,400 lire to other members of her extended family.

This last item must have created a huge lump in Verdi's throat:

> With tears in my eyes, I beg him to keep one single thing with him until his death and then leave it to my sister Barberina, if she is alive, or to Maria Verdi Carrara, that they will keep it as a sacred memory! It is my gold bracelet, given to me in Naples, which bears the inscription "To my dear Peppina 1872".

Her last words in the will to her husband were:

> And now, addio, my Verdi. As we were united in life, may God rejoin our spirits in Heaven.

*

After Strepponi died, Verdi was rarely left alone, enjoying especially the practical and emotional support of his adopted daughter (now married for some twenty years), Stolz, and Giuditta Ricordi. Early in December Verdi wrote to Boito that "his hands trembled so that he could barely write, that he was half-deaf, half-blind, and unable to focus on anything." But he soon recovered sufficiently to go on writing clearly enough.

He had written his last two operas, *Otello* (regarded as one of the greatest of all music dramas), and *Falstaff* ("one of the miracles of operatic music", not least because of Boito's unsurpassed libretto) in 1886 and 1892 respectively. His most important work in his last five years was undoubtedly the founding in December 1899, at his own expense, of a rest home in Milan (Casa di Riposa) for retired and impoverished musicians. He had begun planning its construction in 1895.

Verdi was finally beaten by a stroke on 21 January 1901 in the Grand Hotel, Milan. After being unconscious for a week in which the streets were covered with straw to deaden the traffic sounds, he died at 2.50 pm on 27 January 1901.

Although a grand public funeral had been planned, this was changed when it became known that his will requested a "very modest" ceremony, "either at dawn or at the time of the *Ave Maria* in the evening, and without music and singing." He was buried alongside his "Peppina" in the Cimitero Monumentale. Well before dawn on that damp, foggy morning a crowd of 28,000 lining the streets sang softly the *'Va, pensiero'* chorus from *Nabucco.*

Following the request in his will, both his body and Giuseppina's were transferred to the oratory in the Casa di Riposa on 28 February. At this ceremony, attended by a crowd of some 300,000 Toscanini conducted a choir of 820 singers in the *Nabucco* chorus.

We can do no better than finish with this tribute of Peter Southwell Sander:

> Verdi's life had spanned a world of almost incredible change. His music, though part of his country's history, is also part of human experience for it reflects the deepest and yet the simplest human emotions. During his lifetime, and since his death, countless thousands have discovered in that music something of themselves; but the man who composed it continues partially to elude those who seek to find him.

***

Chapter 5

Charles François Gounod
"The Philandering Monk"
Born: Paris, 17 June, 1818
Died age 75: Paris, 18 October, 1893

She [Isabel Archer] had had everything a girl could
have ... the music of Gounod, the poetry of Browning,
the prose of George Eliot.
[Henry James: *The Portrait of a Lady*, 1881]

...there are persistent rumours of a wandering extra-
marital eye.
[*New Grove Dictionary of Music and Musicians*, 2000]

a base soul who went about pouring a kind of bath
water melody down the back of every woman he met.
[Irish novelist George Moore]

Emotionally fragile and prone to nervous breakdowns as he was,
Gounod was putty in the hands of determined women. Being
managed by one at a time was often wonderful – unless that
woman was his wife. But when she and someone else scratched
each other's eyes out over him, life became very trying and he
"whirled helplessly about like a leaf caught up in raging cross-
winds." Someone aptly called Gounod a man of sand.

Also forever very trying for Gounod were the competing
pulls of the spirit and the flesh. Throughout his life he retained
yearnings to take the cloth. From around 1870 he would sport a
velvet skull cap and quilted smoking jacket, endlessly study the
writings of church doctors with scholarly care, and discuss them
with all comers. On the other hand, in James Harding's words,

The promptings of sensuality were a constant trial,
and respect for the chastity of his saintly idols failed
to overcome his taste for young and pretty girls – the
younger the better.

His appetite for these ladies never waned. Although chapter
and verse of his adventures are hard to establish, his love life
was said, according to Harding, "to be full of incident by turns
amusing and outrageous." Bizet mentioned that while in Rome,
Gounod repaid the kindness of a friend by having an affair with

his wife; and the Irish novelist George Moore, himself a practised seducer, claimed Gounod to be

> a base soul who went about pouring a kind of bath water melody down the back of every woman he met.

Contradiction also permeates his work. At his best – as in the delightful love music of *Faust* – his music is almost Mozartian in its "purity, clarity, subtle colouring and refined craftsmanship." But too often he allegedly succumbed to the temptations of vulgarity and bombast in order to put bums on seats in Parisian theatres. In this he succeeded spectacularly, affording to live, in his last fourteen years, in the Place Malesherbes in the Avenue de Villiers – an opulent Parisian neighbourhood favoured by bankers, senators, and millionaire industrialists. Gounod's three-storey mansion, shared with relations, had (according to La Mure) a wrought-iron gate, a stately carriage entrance, silk curtains, and "that air of elegant aloofness that comes with money." Here it was that he gave generously of his time to such promising musicians of the next generation as Debussy. Earlier he had made positive contributions to the careers of Saint-Saëns (a very close friend less than half his age), Bizet, Lalo and Massenet.

Whatever his musical shortcomings, Gounod was one of the most respected and prolific composers in France in the second half of the nineteenth century. Nowadays he is rather out of fashion. Apart, that is, from the enduring appeal of his five-act opera *Faust* and his sentimental descant tune, *Ave Maria*, first improvised in 1853 (and later jotted down by his father-in-law) to fit over the first of the forty eight preludes from Bach's *Well-Tempered Clavier*. Wind players both amateur and professional also very much enjoy playing his *Petite Symphonie*. And a few octogenarians and nonagenarians still cling lovingly to their crackly recordings on shellac of Heddle Nash singing *Nazareth*.

*

His father François, a painter whose considerable talent Charles fully inherited, died when the lad was five, prompting an intensified reverence of child for mother. Gounod later claimed that he imbibed his precocious musical talent from his mother's milk, since she sang as she breast-fed him. According to his great grandson Jean-Pierre (on an attractive internet site, www.charles-gounod.com) Gounod's call to music came after hearing Maria Malibran singing Desdemona in Rossini's *Otello*, and a performance of Mozart's *Don Juan*. Mme Gounod was for some time reluctant to allow her precious charge to become a musician, but eventually gave in and arranged for Charles to have one day off school each week for music lessons with Anton Reicha. This paid off and led to his entering the Paris Conservatoire in 1836 and to his gaining the coveted Prix de Rome on his third attempt, in 1839, with his cantata *Fernand*. The sacrifices his mother was making for him – getting up at 5.00 am in readiness for her twelve-hour days of piano teaching – were being rewarded.

In Rome Gounod was particularly drawn to the music of Palestrina he heard sung in the Sistine Chapel, and also to the company of a circle led by a liberal and fiery Dominican orator, one Father Lacordaire. At the same time Gounod steeped himself in the Romantic poetry of Lamartine (setting two of his poems to music) and in Goethe's *Faust*, which even then he dreamed of turning into an opera.

Mendelssohn's sister Fanny made Gounod's acquaintance in Rome and found him to be "passionate and romantic in the extreme," even hysterical in his enthusiasm for her playing. She also remarked on his rapid mood swings from "excitable, effusive and eminently charming to contemplative, aloof and mystical." The more passive aspects of his character are caught in an exquisite pencil portrait drawn in 1841 by Jean-Auguste Dominique Ingres. The artist was himself a former Prix de Rome winner and was now Principal of the Villa Medici where the French prize-winners lived and studied. Ingres thought very highly of Gounod's drawing ability and even offered to secure him a chance to stay on in Rome as an art student.

En route back to Paris in 1843, Gounod spent time in Vienna, where his *Requiem* and his *Mass* went down well, and in Leipzig, where he established a cordial friendship with Mendelssohn. Back in Paris he took a post as Music Director at the Seminary of Foreign Missions, writing several works for the choir during his tenure (1843-48). He also made it plain to friends that he intended (to his mother's deep dismay) to become a priest, and in the autumn of 1847 formally enrolled as a student of the St Suplice seminary. He lived at the Carmelite monastery, was authorised by the Archbishop of Paris to wear a cassock, and to sign himself Abbé Gounod. However, he abandoned his studies at St Suplice in 1850: perhaps the lure of the theatre, and the sins of the flesh it encouraged, were too strong to resist.

Pauline Viardot (1821-1910)

Gounod's big break came in 1850 with the patronage and support of the legendary Spanish-born mezzo soprano Pauline Viardot-Garcia, then twenty nine. Wife of the impresario Louis Viardot, she would later be the dedicatee of Saint-Saëns's *Samson et Dalila*. Intelligent and cultivated (by no means always the case with opera divas), Pauline Viardot was also a brilliant linguist, a composer, and a pianist who had taken lessons from Liszt. She could more than hold her own in the company of the leading artists and intellectuals floating between the Parisian salons so often mentioned in these pages. She herself held her own salons at her house in the rue de Douai on Thursday evenings.

She it was who, believing his talent was on a par with Mozart's, secured for Gounod his first commission, *Sapho*, from the Paris Opéra. Viardot also found Gounod a librettist (Émile Augier) and agreed to sing the title role. With such backing, Gounod's career was assured, though lacking all the spectacular effects of French Grand Opera à la Meyerbeer, *Sapho* was a box-office flop: not only at its premiere on 16 April 1851, but also at Covent Garden later that same year. Nevertheless, several prominent writers gave the opera the thumbs-up, including Berlioz, who experienced "one of the keenest emotions" he had felt for a long time at the premiere, and also the English critic Henry Chorley, who had already become one of Gounod's champions.

Equally important is Viardot's more personal relationship with her sensitive and ultra-polite protégé. In April 1850, after the sudden death of his elder brother Louis Urbain, Gounod and his mother went for a five-month stay with the Viardots at their country residence at Courtavenel so that Gounod could compose *Sapho* in peace. Also staying as a long-term "house guest" was the Russian novelist Ivan Sergeyavich Turgenev who had fallen in love with Viardot in 1843. Over the years he would provide Viardot not only with "intimate companionship" but also with librettos for three of her operettas: *Too Many Women, The Last Sorcerer,* and *Ogre*.

"Too Many Men" may have been a more apt title! There was talk of a ménage à quatre at Courtavenel, with Viardot keeping up to three men happy. But possibly her husband was not overly welcome in her boudoir, since she later confided to the conductor Julius Rietz that Louis meant nothing to her physically. However, M. Viardot sometimes demanded his marital rights, since a baby – assuming it was sired by himself – was well on the way at the time of Gounod's marriage in April 1852.

Viardot was apparently far from beautiful but clearly had a sirenian personality as well as the stupendous talent inherited from her father, the great tenor Manuel Garcia. (Her elder sister was the equally famous singer Maria Malibran, whose career was cut short at the age of twenty-eight after a fatal riding accident.) Correspondence suggests, according to *Grove*, that both Turgenev and Gounod "were enthralled and possibly romantically involved with the singer." While it seems clear that Turgenev was Viardot's lover – why else would such a genius pen operetta librettos, other than to please his mistress? – it is much less certain that the name "Charles" appeared on Pauline's bedroom rota. ("Which one of them left this night cap?" I hear her murmuring to her maid who has retrieved one from under the bed.)

*

"Le fiancé malgré lui"
("The Fiancé in spite of himself")
Marriage to "a Japanese crockery dog":
Anna Zimmerman Rift with the Viardots
"I do not accept gifts from my husband's mistress."
[Anna Zimmerman after her marriage to Gounod, quoted by Georgina Weldon]

It was after renewing acquaintance with his elderly and much-respected Conservatoire piano teacher Pierre Zimmerman that Gounod came to be married. Zimmerman's wife, in spite of substantial dowries on offer, had trouble in finding husbands for her four daughters because they had inherited her own unappealing traits, not least her pettiness. When Gounod – now thirty two, handsome, gushing, affable and ever pliable – stepped into the family circle, Mme Zimmerman snapped him up for her daughter Anna. True, Gounod still had no money but his prospects were good.

Gounod's feeble protestations to Mme Zimmerman that he was at present unable to afford matrimony were swept aside. Accustomed as he was to doing what he was told by women, Gounod by default became, in his own words, a suitable subject for a comic opera: "le fiancé malgré lui."

But although romance was singularly absent from his feelings for Anna, Gounod realised the sound value of her father's connections, his money, and his superb property in the country at St Cloud. Accordingly he married her on 20 April 1852 in the church at Auteuil (a fashionable suburb of Paris).

Family-wise, there were three deaths over the next few years – a baby daughter, Gounod's father-in-law Zimmerman (1853), and his own mother (1855). A son Jean was born in 1856 and a daughter Jeanne 1864. Because Zimmerman had no sons, Gounod inherited the property at St Cloud.

It does seem that in spite of Mme Zimmerman's failings, Gounod came to develop an affection or tolerance for her, referring to her as "mother" in his correspondence. He also showed "much affection" to his plethora of in-laws.

The marriage was too much for Pauline Viardot, then heavily pregnant. Not only had she heard Gounod repeatedly mock the Zimmerman daughters: her distress was compounded when on his mother-in-law's insistence Gounod returned the bracelet Viardot had sent Anna as a wedding present. (Someone had informed the Zimmermans about Gounod's former friendship with the diva.) At the bottom of it all was Anna's venomous jealousy, only too evident when she spat out the words "I do not accept gifts from my husband's mistress."

Deeply wounded, Pauline Viardot never recovered from the insult. But though she told George Sand that Gounod was a Tartuffe (the ultimate in religious hypocrisy), she continued to admire and support his music.

Career-wise, Gounod's marriage paid off very quickly, because M. Zimmerman secured for him a well-paid and interesting permanent post as director of the Orphéon de la Ville de Paris. This was a network of local choral societies for which Gounod composed several short works including a hugely popular *Vive l'Empereur* (March 1854) in honour of Napoleon III. Gounod also became director of vocal instruction in the capital's schools.

The Zimmermans further supported Gounod's career by financing the publication of his incidental music for François Ponsard's play *Ulysse*, and of his next opera, *La nonne sanglante* (The Bleeding Nun). Although *La nonne* was a dismal failure in spite of (or because of) a lurid libretto written by the all-powerful Eugène Scribe, Gounod was undaunted and proceeded quickly to compose two symphonies and his popular and sumptuous *St Cecilia Mass* (dedicated to his late father-in-law).

Delirium

He advanced on every possible front, writing music for "state, church, salon, concert hall and theatre," and his work was recognised by the award of Chevalier in the Légion d'Honneur in January 1856. (He was later promoted to Officer in 1866 and Commander in 1877.) Success came at a personal price, however. The demands being made on him as a public figure, combined with his failure on the first attempt to become a member of the exalted Académie des Beaux Arts (he succeeded ten years later) resulted in the first of many breakdowns. In October 1856, after a riding session at St Cloud, he returned for dinner:

> ... his face deathly white [writes James Harding]. He burst into tears and rushed up to his room. There he was found lying on the floor in a dead faint. On reviving he clamoured to go back to Paris. He was convinced that his mother, who was ill at the time, had taken a turn for the worse. Once in Paris he went straight to bed and fell into a delirium.
> For two days he moaned and shrieked. 'Peace! peace!' he was heard to shout over and over again, his eyes starting from their sockets. ...

The family sent him for a fortnight to Dr Antoine Emile Blanche's famous clinic at Passy.

Earlier that year (1856) he had begun composing *Faust* to a libretto by Jules Barbier in collaboration with Michel Carré – they provided Gounod with five libretti altogether – but set it to one side because of a rival production. He then turned to what he considered to be his first real success, *Le médécin malgré lui*. Based on the comedy by Molière, it was premiered at the Théâtre-Lyrique, owned by the flamboyant Mauritian impresario Léon Carvalho, on 15 January 1858.

On the following day Gounod's mother died at age seventy-seven. He had lost the most valued, understanding and supportive woman in his life.

The high point of his career

Although *Faust,* premiered at the Théâtre-Lyrique on 19 March 1859, was not an initial smash hit, it soon picked up in opera houses in provincial France, Germany (much to the chagrin of Wagner), Belgium and elsewhere. And when Carvalho chose it to open the newly built hall of the Théâtre-Lyrique in 1862, it took Paris by storm as well. (There were 314 shows in the opera's first ten years.) When the Théâtre-Lyrique went bankrupt in 1869, the Opéra immediately snapped up the rights to a revamped version with the obligatory ballet, staging 166 shows by 1875.

In the eight years following the *Faust* premiere Gounod capitalised on his success by writing a further five operas, the most important being *Roméo et Juliette.* It was premiered at the Théâtre-Lyrique during the International Exposition of 1867 and soon afterwards performed in London with Adelina Patti in the star role. Still quite often performed, and containing some of his most ravishing music, *Roméo et Juliette* proved in Gounod's lifetime to be his most rapid and sure-fire international success.

He had now reached the high point of his career – a time when, wrote Saint-Saëns,

> all women sang his songs, all young composers [in France] imitated his style.

Gounod was even considered, along with Verdi and Wagner, for an opera to inaugurate the Cairo Opera House in 1871. Verdi, however, got that job with *Aida.*

The Sculptor Marcello

Shortly before the *Roméo* premiere, Gounod began another friendship with a woman – this time with the Duchesse Castiglione Colonna, known to the world as the sculptor Marcello. They enjoyed, according to *Grove,* "a close and warm relationship" based on "a lively exchange of ideas." In an e-mail to the author, the composer's great grandson writes that he has found "no trace of carnal [or] erotic innuendo" in Gounod's letters to the Duchess.

In 1868, Gounod complained of "mental fatigue" to Emile Perrin (the Paris Opéra director) and was reluctant to get on with the *Faust* ballet music. Buckling under career and business pressures, he retreated for the third time to Dr Blanche's clinic up in the pure air on the heights of Passy. (He had paid his second visit there in 1863 after being shattered, understandably, by the vast sums that went to his publisher Choudens rather than to himself from successful performances of *Faust* in London.)

Therapy continued after Gounod's third retreat, in the form of another trip he made to Rome at the end of the year (1868). There he not only met Liszt, by now a womanising priest in minor orders, but also found inspiration for two religious works, the opera *Polyeucte* about the early Christian martyrs (based on a play by Corneille), and an oratorio *La rédemption*.

*

"the Pauline of my dreams"
England and Mrs Georgina Weldon

"… a woman of the town who slept around for a fiver a time."
[Anna Gounod on Mrs Weldon]

Under pressure of political events unfolding from the summer of 1870 (France's reckless declaration of war on Prussia, the fall of the Second Empire, the declaration of the republic and the siege of Paris) Gounod moved his family in September to London, where his standing was already high. Needing funds, he successfully set about finding publishers and promoting himself as a singer of his own songs at high society functions. He also received a commission for a choral piece *Gallia* (published by *Novello*), to celebrate the opening of the Royal Albert Hall on 1 May 1871. This led to his directorship of a large new choral society – "Gounod's Choir" – based at the Hall.

Earlier this same year Gounod first met Mrs Georgina Weldon, a singer and teacher who was a prime mover in the formation of the choral society. Harding describes the coup-de-foudre:

> On the 26 February 1871, Gounod was at the home of Sir Julius Benedict, the conductor and composer recently knighted for his versatile services to English music. Among the guests were Mrs Georgina Weldon and her husband. As usual when a new and attractive

face arrived, Gounod offered it his full attention and sang his song *A une jeune fille* with many a significant glance at Mrs Weldon. 'He seemed to be specially addressing himself to me,' she wrote. '1 did not know which way to look. My tears, which had begun to flow at the first line, had become a rivulet, the rivulet had become a stream, the stream a torrent, the torrent sobs, the sobs almost a fit!'

... She calmed herself by retreating to a window and drinking a glass of water behind the curtain. ...

Mrs Weldon – daughter of a rich barrister who had cut her off when she insisted on marrying Weldon, an army officer of insufficient means – was then thirty-three. Gounod had now passed the dangerous age of fifty-two. It is easy to see from an earlier portrait of Georgina why she turned his head: dark-haired and full-lipped, she looks bewitchingly attractive, and knows it. In choosing Georgina as the soloist in the Conservatoire premiere of *Gallia,* and in promising her the role of Pauline (the "Pauline of my dreams") in *Polyeucte,* Gounod may well have been influenced by her non-vocal attractions, impressive as her singing reportedly was.

One thing is certain, at least according to Mrs Weldon in her highly colourful memoir, *My Orphanage & Gounod in England.* Anna Gounod – described by Georgina as "this little old brown woman," "the most ill-natured, cross-grained woman I ever met" and as looking like "a Japanese crockery dog" – returned to France on 21 May 1871 "in a jealous rage" without her husband. (She would soon reportedly give as good as she got by declaring Georgina to be "a woman of the town who slept around for a fiver a time" – prompting Gounod to slap her and rip her dressing gown.)

"Chère Mimi"

After pleading to Georgina to help him escape from a wife who had caused him "twenty years of hell on earth," Gounod became a long stay house guest in a ménage à trois for the second time in his life. Only this time, it was for nearly three years, at the Weldons' eighteen-roomed mansion in Tavistock Square where she had opened a singing school for orphaned young ladies with vocal talent. Harry Weldon was content with the threesome arrangement, having already found more receptive female arms outside home. He even enjoyed his role as Gounod's male nurse.

To Georgina, her guest was "an angel from heaven," whom she looked on as a "saint" and as a "father" to nurse and to manage obsessively. Gounod's interest in Georgina was altogether more earth-bound, though he soon realised that he would never succeed in climbing into her four-poster. Nor, even, catch a glimpse of her garters or petticoat. The most he enjoyed in the way of intimacy, it seems, was when she soaped his back and brushed his hair "until it gleamed."

In Harding's words, Georgina learned to evade Gounod's advances with "a mixture of deft footwork and tact." After all, he was only a simple male who early made the mistake of thinking that her extravagant declarations were the sign of a passionate nature. He could not have been more mistaken ... Georgina would never have allowed the slightest liberty.

Georgina in any case claimed to find Gounod unattractive with his "muddy complexion ... clothes scrubby and too short ... short neck, [and] round stomach." She wanted Gounod in bed only "to nurse rather than to love" and immediately prescribed a regime of "india rubber baths and cold ablutions." It was all just as well because after conducting her in three successful *Gallia* performances in Paris during October and November 1871 – and after horrendous scenes with Mme Gounod – he returned with Georgina to London and suffered yet another breakdown. (If you haven't been counting them, this is the fourth mentioned.) This time it was complicated by "eczema, dysentery, influenza, haemorrhoids, swollen glands and rheumatism." In Georgina's picturesque words,

> He fluttered into our nest like a wounded bird; he crouched down in bed like a poor hunted animal, and there lay for several days without moving.

Gounod's recovery was not helped by recurring visitors from the Mme Gounod camp, not least his librettist Barbier whose belligerence on her behalf earned him the monicker "Mme Gounod's parrot".

Threat of the slammer

Mrs Weldon more or less took over as Gounod's business manager. With a penchant for litigation she encouraged him to take action against what he called his "vampires" – his publishers in France

(Choudens) and England (Novello) who were forever sucking him dry. (He had, for instance, sold *Faust* outright to Choudens and so lost out on its later manic success.) Skipping all the myriad details, we can note only, with the kind help of *Grove*, that

> In 1873 he ended up in court with a suit against Littleton [of *Novello*], who initiated a counter-suit. During the proceedings it emerged that Weldon had sent a libellous letter to the press in Gounod's name. This did not prevent the composer from being fined, and when he refused to pay [a £2 fine and £100 costs], it looked for a while that he might be briefly imprisoned. Despite the comical side of this and other misadventures with Mrs Weldon, flattering to neither party, they should not obscure the many valid points that they expressed about artistic property nor Gounod's contribution to improving the financial lot of composers in France ...

Inevitably the French press had a field day of gossip and innuendo, and there was speculation among critics as to whether Gounod would ever come home. When the Conservatoire directorship had become vacant after the death of Auber in May 1871, Gounod, under Mrs Weldon's influence, had declined the honour of being considered as Auber's successor. This was surely wise, because under the continual care of his "chère Mimi" Gounod continued to compose intensively, while he may have buckled under the strain of such responsibility.

Back to the missus; Mrs Weldon's fury
Gounod suffered another severe relapse in May 1874, This, together with his loathing of Mrs Weldon's dogs (one was called Whiddles), continuing jibes in the French press about "the Englishman Gounod" and his "passionate love affair" finally pushed him into returning to Paris. On 8 June, with the help of his good friend and physician Gaston de Beaucourt who made the trip across the channel especially to help, it seems he did a hasty daytime flit from Tavistock Square while the Weldons were out.

Within a few months Gounod was reconciled with his wife, but also became embroiled in extended legal and diplomatic negotiations to recover various personal belongings and manuscripts fromTavistock Square – including, most importantly, the draft score of *Polyeucte*. Mrs Weldon had flatly refused to co-operate, having become ever more angered by the slanderous rumours that she accused Gounod and his wife of spreading about her. More than that, she initiated an absurd and protracted suit against her former idol, demanding money he had promised her for the orphanage, and retaining his score of *Polyeucte* as hostage. If Gounod had set foot in Britain after 10 May 1885, when a judgement was made against him in favour of Mrs Weldon, he would have been arrested and liable to pay her the huge sum of £11,640 on pain of summary imprisonment. He was thus unable to accept either a royal invitation to conduct his latest religious work *Mors et Vita* on 26 August 1885 in Birmingham, or the offer in 1892 of a Cambridge doctorate. By way of compensation in the former case, Queen Victoria requested a performance in February 1886 and sent Gounod her personal congratulations. Gounod was also pleased that the Cambridge honour was transferred to Saint-Saëns.

Mrs Weldon's retention of the *Polyeucte* draft proved to be no real problem for Gounod. He simply wrote it out again from memory. But when, in September 1875, he had nearly finished the rewrite, Mrs Weldon sent the original music back to him. Her parting shot had been to scrawl her name across every single page of the score to make sure she was not easily forgotten. (*Polyeucte* did finally reach the stage – at the Théâtre-Lyrique on 7 October 1878. In the words of Gounod's great-grandson, it was "un échec" or failure.)

Thereafter Mrs Weldon, who for all her madnesses evokes considerable love and admiration, separated from her husband and continued to pursue a plethora of good causes. These included conjugal rights, Land Reform, The Salvation Army – and also reform of the lunacy laws!! Childless herself, she ended her days as a respected "Grannie Weldon" to all the children of her friends.

When she heard of Gounod's death she was an ardent spiritualist living in a hospice surrounded by her dogs, a pet monkey and various birds. "Poor old man," she noted in her diary, "how I did love him and how hard all hope died."

*

"... the last modulation resolving to the tonic of the eternal concert"

Gounod's last two decades saw, amongst many things, the emergence of several failed operas, an outcrop of religious music, his wonderful *Petite Symphonie for Winds* (1885), and articles "on such things as faith, beauty, and breast feeding" (writes Mason Greene). On 19 May 1888 his mother-in-law died, and on 4 November of this same year he conducted the 500th performance of *Faust*. In his palatial rebuilt country home at St Cloud (it had been destroyed in the siege of Paris) he welcomed pilgrims, played the local church organ for Sunday services, argued points of theology with willing disputants and attempted the conversion of Sarah Bernhardt ("Divine Sarah", the leading romantic and tragic actress of her day). Not even the offer of 1,000,000 francs would entice Gounod away for an American tour. After producing his *Requiem* for his grandson, and discussing its arrangement for organ with his protégé and amanuensis Henri Büsser, he died while thumbing through the manuscript — on what he himself had anticipated as "the last modulation resolving to the tonic of the eternal concert". He had been suffering from sciatica, chronic bronchitis and the failure of his vascular system.

He was given a state funeral on 27 October at the Madeleine Church, with Saint-Saëns playing the great organ and Fauré leading the cortège. He was interred in the cemetery at Auteuil.

***

Chapter 6

Camille Saint-Saëns
"Orgies with Arab boys and fellaheen"
Born: Paris, 9 October 1835
Died age 86: Algiers, 16 December 1921

... the greatest organist in the world.
[Liszt]

On one occasion he is even said to have worn a "pink dress" when visited by the Archbishop of Carthage. Given that flashy frocks come with the job for cardinals and archbishops, Saint-Saëns's pink dress will surely have met with clerical approval.
[Author]

Dear Reader, I already hear you groaning. "Not *another* mother-fixated musician with gay or bi tendencies?"

Well, it does look like it! A complex and private man who once declared that "one cannot make over one's personality," the gossip about Saint-Saëns perhaps suggests more of the gay than the heterosexual in him. Though the more one writes about gender in human beings, the more uncertain everything becomes.

Of the mother fixation there is no doubt, and for good measure we can throw in a great-aunt fixation as well. Camille Saint-Saëns knew nothing about his father, Jacques-Joseph-Victor, who died when Camille was a babe in swaddling clothes. For the rest of his life, until their deaths, Camille lived with and was mollycoddled by his mother Clémence, and her aunt Mme Charlotte Masson, who perhaps more than anyone lovingly nurtured the extraordinary talent of her great-nephew. In his formal debut at ten he played concertos by both Beethoven and Mozart. Saint-Saëns adored both women, and when at the age of thirty nine he decided to pluck out nineteen year old Marie Laure Emilie Truffot from the boondocks and marry her, he never dreamed of quitting the domestic hearth. Poor Marie had to endure the stares of four ever-disapproving eyes until the marriage collapsed after six years in the wake of a double domestic tragedy.

*

Pink dresses and broad beams
Gender stories (taken mainly from Studd)

The most colourful story about Saint-Saëns and women is undoubtedly one relayed by the English soprano Maggie Teyte who met him in Chicago during his second working visit to the United States in 1915. The composer caused a stir in his hotel by suddenly demanding a woman from the Director of the Chicago Opera. A lady of the evening, duly escorted to his room found him

> lying in a post-orgasmic languor, only to discover that the seventy-nine-year-old lamenting that she had arrived "too late".

"The March King" John Philip Sousa (of *Stars and Stripes Forever* fame) met Saint-Saëns in California on the same tour and noted that

> the Frenchman "seemed always to have an eye" for the ladies, especially those of ample proportions. During their walks together "he would nudge me, calling my attention to 'yonder beaming beauty!' The broader the 'beam' the greater his delight!"

Perhaps one telling clue to the gender issue is the vein of misogyny in many of Saint-Saëns's operas and symphonic poems. Their themes are often of men "ruined by the seductive charms of a woman:" *Ascanio, Samson et Dalila, Déjanire ...*

That Saint-Saëns believed the male body to be more aesthetically pleasing than a woman's because of its classical proportions in itself tells us little. But if there is any truth in the scandalous rumours surrounding his many visits to Algeria (the first in 1873) then his gay proclivities cannot be doubted. "Gide-like orgies with Arab boys and fellaheen" were (according to James Harding in his respected biography of the composer) a reported but unconfirmed feature of the composer's Algerian sojourns. On one occasion he is even said to have worn a "pink dress" when visited by the Archbishop of Carthage. Given that flashy frocks come with the job for cardinals and archbishops, Saint-Saëns's pink dress will surely have met with clerical approval – though it does seem that the composer's garb was probably a djellaba that he often liked to wear with a fez on these visits to warmer winter climes. Sexual shenanigans notwithstanding, not much else is known about Saint-Saëns's many visits to Algeria. More than anything, as a Parisian rather frail in health, he craved its winter sunshine and "clear, transparent sky of a blueness unknown to us." Algeria was a country where "everything breathes life, abundance and fertility." He also loved its "multi-coloured mountains", and treasured the opportunities for "perfect, absolute silence." Certainly a blissful environment for composing when the spirit moved him.

Saint-Saëns's penchant for cross-dressing at society charades and parties was legendary. But perhaps his most famous turn was at the Moscow Conservatoire in 1875. As light relief during a concert tour, he and Tchaikovsky danced impromptu, in an otherwise empty hall, to the piano accompaniment of Nikolai Rubinstein; Tchaikovsky as Pygmalion, Saint-Saëns as his usual Galatea.

Saint-Saëns was certainly fond of the company of talented and charming young men, two of his closest friendships being with homosexuals. One of them was his one-time pupil, the now-neglected composer Reynaldo Hahn, whose death drove his lover (the tenor Guy Ferrand) to commit suicide. The other was Marcel Proust, who once described Saint-Saëns's brilliant piano-playing as "regal" in its lack of "writhings, shakings of the head and tossing of the hair."

Like Schubert, Paganini, Chopin, Bellini and other men in these stories, Saint-Saëns used effusively affectionate language (in "schwärmerisch" vein) in his letters to male correspondents, this recipient being unidentified in a letter dated 17 August 1907:

> "You are adorable, and I do not deserve to have friends
> such as you."

*

Some of Saint-Saëns compositions are no less flamboyant than his personal eccentricities. Though very much what Debussy called "the musician of tradition" in his musical constructions – characterised as they are by "moderation, logic, clarity, balance and precision" he nevertheless loved to present works of bravura and panache on an epic scale. Perhaps the most spectacular event with which he was associated was the staging in 1898 of Louis Gallet's drama *Déjanire* in Béziers (in the south of France), for which Saint-Saëns wrote the incidental music. (A wealthy wine merchant, Castelbon de Beauxhostes, had restored the vast arena there for the staging of epic theatrical performances.) Saint-Saëns's orchestra included the Garde Municipale of Barcelona, a Lyre Biterroise (an instrument of the zither family originating in Béziers), 110 orchestral strings, a "curtain" of 18 harps, 25 trumpets and choruses of more than 200. The audience of 10,000 came from all over France and endured scorching temperatures as Déjanire (the jealous wife of Hercules) made her grand entrance in a horse-drawn chariot onto the vast set depicting an ancient Greek city.

Hardly less impressive in terms of impact was Saint-Saëns's *Le feu céleste* (The Celestial Fire), a cantata or hymn he wrote celebrating the arrival of electricity for the opening in 1900 of *The Exposition Universelle* (The Universal Exhibition). The work climaxes in a blaze of trumpets and organ "proclaiming a world lit brilliantly by the new electrical wonder."

The Exposition reminds us just how much of a polymath Saint-Saëns was. Besides being a world-class concert pianist of dazzling virtuosity, he also produced scholarly editions of other composers' works; wrote poems and plays, and impeccably informed pieces for a wide variety of newspapers and journals. The topics ranged through literature, philosophy, mathematics, archaeology – and most especially astronomy, on which he became hooked as a child.

Saint-Saëns was also very widely travelled, concert tours taking him not only to Russia and North America, but also to southern Europe, South America (including Uruguay, where he wrote a hymn for the national holiday), the Canary Islands, Scandinavia and East Asia.

No wonder he was awarded the highest honours in the Légion d'Honneur, was feted by royalty, and had the rare distinction, for a musician, of being alive to see the unveiling of a statue of himself in Dieppe, where he created the Musée Saint-Saëns in 1890.

*

Saint-Saëns's music is at last making a serious come-back, at least on disc. For decades since his death he has been known only for *Carnival of the Animals* and particularly for *The Swan* which was so often danced by Anna Pavlova in the early 1900s – the *Danse Macabre* (used as the signature tune for a classy detective series from the late 1990s), the *Wedding Cake* waltz, the little cello show-piece *Allegro Appassionato*, the *Third Violin Concerto*, the stupendous *Third* or *Organ Symphony* – and his opera *Samson et Dalilah* (most especially Dalilah's ravishing aria *Softly awakes my heart*). The *Organ Symphony* (1866) is nowadays a real crowd-puller in concerts of classical pops – as well it might be, for the composer wrote of it that

> I have given all that I had to give. What I have done I shall never do again.

Works of Saint-Saëns now making a comeback include his five piano concertos - the first described as "a little-known peach, cool as crystal at its centre" – and such showpieces as *Rapsodie d'Auvergne,* and that "feast of catchy syncopations," *Africa*.
And now back to the business of love!

*

1868 Augusta Holmes
"veritable orgies of youth, art, music and poetry"

> We were all of us in love with her. Literary men, painters, musicians, any of us would have been honoured to have had her for a wife.
> [*Saint-Saëns*, taken from Studd, from whom much of this section derives.]

*

Whatever the gender complications, Saint-Saëns must have appealed to women more for his dynamic personality and talents than his looks. According to Mina Curtiss, in his twenties

> He was short and always strangely resembled a parrot; the same sharply curved profile, a beak-like hooked nose, lively, restless, piercing eyes. ... He strutted like a bird and talked rapidly, precipitately, with a curiously affected lisp. But his external lack of charm was soon dispelled by the quickness of his wit and the extraordinary breadth of his interests and culture.

By his thirties, however, according to Studd, he

> cut a rather more dashing figure than the rather bookish young man of ten years before: almost handsome, the head slightly too large for the body but with a fine mane of dark hair and neatly trimmed beard, impressively earnest, knowledgeable eyes and an intense expression of burning inquiry.

This was the Saint-Saëns who at around age thirty three proposed to the dazzling Augusta Holmes (or Holmès). Apparently "a successful composer of symphonies and symphonic odes," she was twelve years Saint-Saëns's junior and was born in Paris. Officially her parents were Irish, though she did nothing to dispel persistent rumours that her real father was the poet Alfred de Vigny.

Everybody was after her, especially Saint-Saëns's poet and painter friends. She joined them all for summer picnic parties to Versailles and Fontainebleau, after which they would return to her flat in Paris for musical evenings.

According to the painter Georges Clairin, Augusta was

> tall and well-built, majestic and serene, with fine golden hair that fell in a sheet down her back, and green eyes that made us imagine the sea of Ireland. She was not so much a woman as a goddess.

Clairin recounted how one night when Saint-Saëns was playing Gluck on the piano, and the moonlight was spreading "a pallid and mysterious light" through the stained glass windows

> Augusta comes forward like a goddess and, with her arms raised to the sky, unloosens her hair with a sudden movement and begins to sing, exciting us to ecstasy and to arms. ...

Those were the days, in the last years of the Second Empire under Napoleon III! In Saint-Saëns's case, they were the happiest of his life. Maman and great aunt Charlotte were there to look after his every need at home, and he already enjoyed a formidable reputation as a composer and virtuoso pianist.

Although increasingly bewitched by Augusta's beauty and musicianship as he gave her (it seems) informal composition lessons, Saint-Saëns's proposal to her may have also been with an eye to his own career, her parents being rich and well-connected. Alas, she turned him down, determined to put her own career first. Though according to one source she did find time along the way to bear three children to the poet Catulles Mendès!

Saint-Saëns bore up under Augusta's refusal and later dedicated some of his works to her. But he was rather bitchy about her compositions, declaring they were

> full of grotesque exaggerations, effects overstated to the point of absurdity and orchestral sounds subjected to "a system of forced growth."

*

Marriage to Marie Laure Emilie Truffot
Proposal by proxy in the swimming baths

While working on his *Danse Macabre* Saint-Saëns made another proposal of marriage, this time successfully. The lady in question was Marie Laure Emilie Truffot, the nineteen-year-old younger sister of one of Saint-Saëns's favourite pupils Jean. Apparently Saint-Saëns broached the question of marriage to Jean in the swimming baths, asking him playfully if he would like to become his brother-in-law. Later Saint-Saëns formally asked Marie's father for her hand, as they used to say. Saint-Saëns having already many solid achievements behind him, the deal was made.

The fact that Marie had no serious artistic ambitions or interests was probably now a bonus for the composer. Half his age, she was pliable and in no way a threat to his career, as Augusta may have been. The couple married in Marie's home town of Le Cateau (south east of Lille in Northern France) on 3rd February 1875.

Marie stood little chance of happiness living with a workaholic obsessed with his art, under the roof of a possessive and strongly-disapproving mother-in-law and a great aunt.

Double Tragedy

> Life is full of sadness, but I shall never grow accustomed to it.
>
> [Saint-Saëns to his publisher Durand, 25 July 1881]

The permanent presence of the in-laws was bad enough for any marriage, but two terminal blows were dealt to the union in 1878. In that year both their sons died within six weeks of each other. André fell out of the fourth-floor window of their apartment when he was two and a half, and then Jean François died of a childhood illness at six months.

Saint-Saëns held his wife responsible for the deaths and never forgave her. On 28 May he returned to his apartment in the evening to be told by a cousin that André was dead. That afternoon Marie had been busy in the next room, mother-in-law had nodded off, and the servant had been doing the washing in the kitchen. Hearing through an open window the shouts of his playmates on the floor below, André climbed out onto the window-ledge, slipped, and fell four storeys to his death.

According to one report, Saint-Saëns is said to have refused to speak to Marie, writing "Farewell" on a note. But in any case she was so distressed by André's death that she was unable to feed baby Jean François, who was taken to be nursed by her mother in Reims. The infant died on 7 July.

As usual, Saint-Saëns buried his feelings rather than give vent to them in torrents of Italianate grief. His only known written reference to the deaths is in a postscript of a letter to a friend:

> I have just lost two children in the space of a month and can assure you that my gaiety is notably restrained.

Three years later, while on holiday with Marie in the spa town of La Bourboule in the Auvergne, Saint-Saëns suddenly vanished. In desperate straits, Marie finally discovered that he had gone back to mother. When Marie returned, she was horrified to discover not only the full extent of mother-in-law's hatred of her, but also the venomous hostility of her husband's favourite cousin, who had spared no effort to poison Camille's mind against her.

After receiving a formal note from Saint-Saëns announcing his decision not to return to her, Marie went back to her own family. There was no divorce, but the couple never set eyes on each other again.

It has often been said that Saint-Saëns longed to be "a father without being a husband." He achieved partial compensation for his grievous losses through his deep friendship with his pupil Gabriel Fauré, whose career he did much to support. As the years went by Saint-Saëns tended to regard Fauré's growing family as his own, becoming an adopted and benevolent uncle.

In the circumstances, Marie's verdict on her husband was generous:

> I suffered many injustices through the capricious nature of my husband, but he had good qualities too.

Marie attended Saint-Saëns's funeral but was spurned by his relatives, who still blamed her for the tragedy. Only after acrimonious legal battles did she win rights to the proceeds from all his works written after their marriage. She lived to a ripe but lonely old age, dying at age 95 near Bordeaux.

*

It remains only to report two other deaths in Saint-Saëns' life followed by a funny story. (At least I think it's funny.) When great-aunt Charlotte (whom he often described as his "second mother") died in January 1872, he was so devastated that he cancelled all his engagements for a month. Inevitably, from now on Saint-Saëns relied even more heavily on his other emotional lifeline. Now sixty-three, Clémence Saint-Saëns accompanied her son more frequently to his concerts, and acted as hostess at the Monday soirees he continued to give.

After a healthy old age, Clémence Saint-Saëns caught a chill late in 1888 that soon developed into pneumonia, from which she died at age seventy nine on 18 December. Within ten years Saint-Saëns had lost his two sons, his great aunt, and now his mother.

Clearly his mother's death was the most shattering blow of all. A brief note he sent to Fauré, whose mother had died a year earlier, reads:

> My Dear Gabriel, I too lost my mother this morning at nine o'clock. Not much point in saying more, is there? Not much point either in coming to see me, I am receiving only my relations because I cannot do otherwise – unless you would like to see her for the last time.

After Clémence's funeral and burial in the family vault at Montparnasse, Saint-Saëns was unable to face returning to the family apartment, and on doctor's advice travelled south to the resort of Tamaris, near Toulon.

A letter he sent to his publisher Durand dated 28 January expresses his quiet desolation:

> I began to work again today. Will better times come? I can doubt it. *Tristis est anima mea usque ad mortem* (my spirit is sad unto death)."

In February he still had "a horrible dread of returning home". Instead, he went to his beloved Algiers in March, returned to Paris in April, and abandoned the family apartment for accommodation in the suburb of St Germain-en-Laye. He sent most of his own possessions and the family heirlooms bequeathed to him – including his telescope, his mother's paintings, and the little piano on which he had received his first lessons from great aunt Charlotte – to his favourite cousin who lived in Dieppe.

They later formed the basis of the Saint-Saëns museum established there.

*

On 9 October 1889, his fifty-fourth birthday, Saint-Saëns again set off south, this time the Canaries becoming his ultimate destination. Not only did he crave the winter sun he so much needed, his constitution suffering markedly in the Parisian winters; he also needed to be alone – to come to terms with his bereavement, and, hopefully, to start composing again. Money was never a problem for him, especially since in 1877 an admiring benefactor, Albert Libon, had bequeathed him 100,000 francs to devote himself to composition.

The trip encompassed the most hilarious episode of his career. "M. Charles Sannois, businessman"

The stories of Saint-Saëns's four-month retreat in the Canaries come mostly from newspaper reports, and are inevitably embellished. In his search for privacy Saint-Saëns assumed the alias of M. Charles Sannois, businessman. Doubts about this disguise soon surfaced, however, when the locals and holiday-makers on Las Palmas observed his keen and informed interest in astronomy, his landscape sketches, his attendance at chamber concerts, cafe concerts, brass band concerts ... Even less "businessman" – like was his ability at one soirée to transpose Mephistopheles's serenade from *Faust* a semitone down at sight!

At first it was thought that he was "un anglais" holidaying on the island who happened to speak French. Now let Stephen Studd, to whom this chapter is indebted, finish the story:

> ... a chambermaid, seeing the manuscript sketches of the Africa fantasy on his desk, drew sinister conclusions from them and reported it to the already suspicious hotel manager, causing the supposed spy and his coded messages to leave Las Palmas for less conspicuous lodgings outside the town. Reports of him thereafter under constant police surveillance are, however, almost certainly an exaggeration. For the next month he explored the other islands, visiting Tenerife and Lanzarote, before returning to Las Palmas. There he checked into a different hotel, but almost immediately began to excite curiosity again, chiefly by his renewed attendance at concerts. According to *Le Figaro*, when

an Italian opera company arrived with a production of *Rigoletto* he offered to sing the part of Monterone when the company's baritone fell ill. Not surprisingly the manager turned down this approach from a total stranger, who then asked the conductor if he could play percussion. This offer too was declined. In the *Musical Times* version of the story, however, Saint-Saëns's offer to sing was accepted; he rehearsed, but the performance never took place because the company went bankrupt at the last moment. "It is quite refreshing in these mercenary days to know that there are eminent composers who will sing for nothing", the journal commented.

Saint-Saëns died on 16 December 1921 under the winter sun and blue skies of the country he loved most to visit – Algeria. His funeral took place at the cathedral, and his body was then taken to the Madeleine Church in Paris, where he had officiated for some twenty years as its renowned organist. He was given the honour of a state funeral.

***

Chapter 7

Georges [Alexandre-César-Leopold] Bizet
"Mr Prude"
Born: Paris, 25 October 1838
Died age 36: Bougival (near Paris), 3 June 1875

a whole society hurling itself at the c ***
[Bizet's Parisian contemporary Émile Zola]

... From Palo to Civita Vecchia. In the train we met
two sweeties. I would almost have **** one, but was
still thinking of her.
[Bizet: *Notes de Voyages*, 1860]

His susceptibility to [his mother-in-law's] charm seems
to have been quite as real and strong as his love for
his wife.
[Mina Curtiss: *Bizet and His World*]

*

With the seeming exception of a mysterious young woman called
Zeph, Bizet's very active sex life was mainly confined to prostitutes and "women of the theatre" until his late twenties. (Zeph
was a woman to whom he said goodbye in a last "tender, agonising
night" of lovemaking in Rome on 26 July 1860.) Without even
realising it, Bizet upheld the same old hoary double standard.
Women were either whores or Madonnas – to be rutted and got
rid of, or worshipped and wedded.

In Bizet's case, the latter would prove to be a disaster. After
an initial period of marital bliss, his wife Geneviève's chronic
mental instability, inherited from both sides of her family, would
increasingly make his life hell and severely jeopardise his creative
activity. As also would the endlessly draining antics of his classic-
case mother-in-law, Léonie Halévy.

Bizet might possibly have been happier in the long term if
he had married the woman who, seven years before his marriage,
bore him an illegitimate child. Bizet was twenty-three and she
was the family's maid Marie Reiter, who nursed the composer
through his harrowing last illness when he was thirty-six. Their
son Jean Reiter, who was brought up with the Bizet family "as a
sort of cousin," lived a seemingly normal life before he died at

the age of seventy seven. By contrast, Bizet's legitimate son, Jacques, committed suicide at age fifty-one after founding the first auto-rental agency in France.

*

Bizet's sexual double standards are writ large in his letters and his actions. He deplored loose women yet pounced on them. Shortly after his arrival in Rome in 1858 as the prize-winning Grand Prix music scholar at the French Academy (following in the footsteps of Berlioz and Gounod) he wrote to his mother:

> The women here have about one franc's worth of virtue. The same applies to the upper classes, only it's more expensive. ... A virtuous Italian woman has all my admiration. I esteem and admire her more than Jeanne d'Arc or Lucretia. ...

On his way home two and a half years later, after that last night with his beloved Zeph, he would record in his *Notes de Voyages*:

> From Palo to Civita Vecchia. In the train we met two sweeties. I would almost have **** [?fucked] one, but was still thinking of her.

And this:

> search for women, in vain, alas!

And this, after a night in a bordello:

> [She was] a little on the skinny side!!! Oh, Berlioz, where wert thou?

(Scholars have burned midnight oil trying to fathom the reference to Berlioz, who was then in his late fifties. Perhaps Bizet somehow knew that Berlioz, no angel himself, had enjoyed using skinny prostitutes?)

Later on his journey, Bizet wrote to his adored mother assuring her that although he was anxious to live in separate accommodation when he returned home, the reason was not so that he could entertain ladies of easy virtue:

> There is no problem there. I don't like women of questionable morals; ... It is merely a question of my individual liberty.

Even at the age of 34, three years after his marriage, he would write to his mother-in-law:

> ... I am unwilling to have a woman whom I know to be of doubtful reputation set foot in my house. As for women of the theatre, under no circumstances will one of them cross my threshold. You see that I am inflexible-so much so that Geneviève [Bizet's wife] calls me M. Prud'homme [Mr Prude].

The world can only be glad that Bizet broke his own rule before he married. Without the visits of one infamous and loveable "woman of the theatre" to his home, there may well have been no *Carmen*, arguably the most popular opera ever written.. The woman in question was Madame la Comtesse de Moreton de Chabrillan, also known as Céleste Mogador, who was fourteen years older than Bizet. Although he never claimed La Mogador as his model for *Carmen*, Mina Curtiss has suggested persuasively that the parallels between her personality and that of the *Carmen* whom Bizet created are too close to be accidental. La Mogador may also have influenced Bizet's creation of the exotic heroine in his failed opera *Djamileh*.

"... the wife of your best friend"

Aside from Zeph and La Mogador, only one other woman, unidentified, is specifically referred to in Bizet's love-life before his disastrous marriage. She was "the wife of [his] best friend," mentioned as one among many of his women by La Mogador in this amusing exchange she recorded. After an evening at Bizet's cottage in which he had enchanted his guests with his music,

> our evening ended late. The gentlemen accompanied me home. It was a superb night. I gave Georges my arm, congratulating him on his inimitable talent. Without realising it I pressed against him. So, leaning toward me he said, 'I would like to call your attention to the fact that I have always been very guarded with you. Now, tonight you are making advances to me!'
> 'My dear,' I replied laughing, 'my dear, you mustn't misunderstand me. I adore your talent. I am proud of your friendship, of walking arm-in-arm with you by moonlight, but my admiration is absolutely platonic. As for my emotions, I have never dreamed of finding a place in a heart that is like a rooming-house for transient lodgers.'
> He laughed and said, 'I could give notice to my other lodgers.'
> 'No. One of them has a lease, the wife of your best friend.'
> 'I think that is finished. I no longer love her.'
> 'You may love her less, but you are still fond of her. Let it run its course, and we shall see later what to do with our fine, free friendship. But for now let's stay

the way we are, good companions. Otherwise it's a
hundred to one we'll quarrel later.'
So the matter was understood and settled
at least for the time …

*

It is not difficult to see why Bizet's heart never lacked "lodgers,"
however brief the tenancies. His friend and fellow student in
Rome, Felix Henri Giacomotti, described him thus after painting
him in July 1860:

> The very embodiment of adolescent genius, his proud,
> virile brow was haloed in ash-blond hair. He had rosy
> cheeks …. a delicate nose with quivering nostrils and
> an eye full of mischief when it wasn't alight with
> inspiration.

Later, one of his pupils, an American lady, was clearly
bewitched by him in his mid thirties:

> He was very plump and vigorous – a very showy,
> attractive man without ever thinking that he was or
> seeming to care what his effect was on the other people.
> He had light-brown hair and a full beard, almost russet
> or reddish-brown. His eyes were dark grey or blue. He
> dressed with extreme care and for his own personal
> satisfaction. He wore the finest linen I ever saw. His
> gloves were gants de Suède – ladies' gloves – very
> long, soft, light-brown, with no buttons. And then he
> would come in and strip off his gloves, throw them on
> the piano and reveal those beautiful hands! …
> [Mina Curtiss: *Bizet and His World*]

*

An only son, Bizet was always deeply devoted to his mother Aimée
(née Delsarte), a talented pianist who taught him his notes along
with his letters when he was four. His father Adolphe, a singing
teacher and minor composer, taught him elementary music theory
from age eight, when he was showing an exceptional capacity
for aural memory. He entered the Conservatoire at ten and by
the time he left at nineteen to take up his prize-winning place in
Rome, he had won several other prizes. He had also, when barely
seventeen, composed his enduringly fresh and popular *Symphony
in C*. Still a regular concert item around the world, its sparkle
and vitality capture the essence of his personality.

In Italy, Bizet revelled in the scenery and cultural sights
during his travels to such places as the Alban Hills, Cape Circe,

Terracina, Naples (where he had the first of his many severe attacks of throat trouble) and Pompeii. It may well be that he also visited bordellos as often as basilicas.

On his way home from Italy with his friend Ernest Guiraud (during which they visited all those bordellos), he wrote a long letter to his mother after receiving news of her illness. These extracts reveal not only the deeply devoted son, but also a fiery and volatile temperament:

> It was terribly rash of you to date your letter from a hospital. ... That letter was the first one the post office employee gave me. I opened it and saw those two lines. The blood rushed to my head and to my heart. I could no longer read the rest of the letter or throw off this terrible state of mind. Then, after a quarter of an hour of rage, I managed to find sufficient provocation to quarrel with the gondolier; I hurled myself at him with the firm intention of strangling him. My kind Guiraud snatched him out of my hands. Two minutes later I arrived at St. Mark's. The sight of this enchanted splendour brought me to my senses, and I decided to leave at once for Paris. Again Guiraud was helpful. 'Read the letter preceding that one,' he said. And in the earlier letter I found some small comfort. ...
> ... Adieu, dear, beloved Mama; I am overcome with sleep, with fatigue. For two nights I haven't slept, thanks to the insects that ornament the hotels of Padua. All this, combined with the blow of your letter and the sharp regret that a certain letter from Rome caused me, has exhausted me physically .

He also included a letter to his father in the same envelope:

> Force the doctor to give a sincere opinion of what there is to fear. Tell me whether your financial condition is sound enough to permit of the necessary care. Why is she in a six-bed room? Your reply will determine my decision. But write to me by every post. ...

Arriving home to find that his mother's condition was not yet life-threatening, he was able in the following months to impress Liszt greatly with his piano playing, and to complete two works for orchestra. However, about a year after his return his mother died after a prolonged illness on 8 September 1861. Freudians, Jungians and others will doubtless be able to interpret the dream that Bizet frequently had in the aftermath of her death:

[To Giacomotti]:
At night I would feel a terrible agony. I would be forced to throw myself down in an armchair, and then I would think I saw my mother coming into the room. She would cross and stand beside me and put her hand on my heart. Then the agony would increase. I would suffocate, and it seemed to me that her hand, weighing on me so heavily, was the true cause of my suffering.

Perhaps it was the traumatic loss of his mother that drove the twenty-two year old composer into the comforting arms of the family maid, Marie Reiter. Their child Jean was born in June 1862, nine months after Mme Bizet's death.

Between Marie and La Mogador: 1862-1865

Opera was the only viable medium by which composers could make their name in France at this time, and Bizet slaved away at his scores when he could free himself from giving much-loathed but bread-winning piano lessons.

The returns on his composing labours were hardly ever fruitful within his lifetime, his career being a depressing catalogue of completed works unperformed to this day, and others that either he or theatre managements soon abandoned. (The spectacular success of *Carmen* came only after he was dead and buried.)

His symphonic ode *Vasco de Gama* (written as one of his assignments in Rome) had a hearing at the Société Nationale des Beaux Arts on 8 February 1863 and was panned by the critics. Of more interest is the fate of his opera *Les Pêcheurs de Perle* (The Pearl Fishers), composed at white heat, and now his most performed opera after *Carmen*. The *Friendship Duet* from *The Pearl Fishers* is now one of the most popular and frequently broadcast arias ever written. In 1863, however, the opera met with only a mixed reception at its premiere at the Théâtre-Lyrique on 30 September and was dropped after eighteen shows. It was not revived in Bizet's lifetime.

He spent much of 1864 undermining his fragile health by doing hack work for publishers and theatre directors. One of these latter, Léon Carvalho (director of the Théâtre-Lyrique), at least had faith in Bizet but was ever compelled to worship at the altar of the Box Office. Thus it was that an opera he commissioned from Bizet in 1864, a second version of *Ivan IV*, was repeatedly postponed throughout 1865 – so often, in fact, that Bizet offered it to the Opéra, which refused it. On the brighter side, however, Bizet made his first acquaintance with a pupil who became a life-long friend and disciple – Edmond Galabert – and also met La Mogador.

*

Madame La Comtesse de Moreton de Chabrillan (Céleste Mogador)

… wasp-waisted, supple as a willow, lively as a linnet.
… just pock-marked enough to suggest a slight resemblance to the Venus de Milo, except that she had two beautiful arms, generously displayed. … Proud Mogador voluptuously flaunts curves Minerva might envy.
[contemporary newspaper]

My life has been one long excess.
[La Mogador: *Mémoires*]

Bizet first met this exceptional lady in the autumn of 1865 on the twelve-mile train journey between Paris and Le Vésinet, where he occupied a one-room cottage on estate land his father had bought for a summer residence. In September 1865 La Mogador had also bought land on the same estate and met Bizet when she was travelling to supervise the construction of her house, Le Chalet Lionel, adjoining Bizet's cottage.

Here are some landmarks in La Mogador's staggering career to date.
• Prostitute
The illegitimate daughter of a laundress and an unidentified soldier living in the poor Parisian district of Belleville, she fled home at age thirteen to escape the attentions of one of her mother's many lovers. Her career began as a "fille inscrite," a prostitute registered on the police lists. Her ambition was to move upwards in her profession to become a high-society courtesan. There were openings galore, because according to Bizet's contemporary, Zola, sex-obsessed Paris was a "whole society hurling itself at the c***." (His *Nana*, published 1880, tells all.)
At age sixteen she was installed in a bordello patronised by dukes, musicians and writers. Among her clients was the renowned Romantic poet Alfred de Musset, the former lover of

112

George Sand who had abandoned him (she said) to a life of "drunkenness, wine, whores again and always." La Mogador accepted his "fistful of gold pieces" while offering as little in return as she could get away with. Her stint at this bordello ended when on one occasion she was in a restaurant with de Musset:

> Our waiter brought a bottle of seltzer water. ... He took the siphon as though he were going to pour a drink and, pointing the nozzle at me, drenched me from head to foot. ... I burst into tears of rage. The more I cried, the more he laughed. If I had stayed another minute in that room I would have thrown a carafe at his head in spite of the consequences. ...

• Dancing

She then became a dancer at the Bal Mabille (ballroom), and was chosen by the proprietor, one Brididi, to be his partner in the launching of that brand new dance, the polka. Men clamoured to dance with her and resistance, Brididi warned, was futile. "It would be easier to defend Mogador," he said, Mogador being the Moroccan city recently attacked by a French squadron. Thus did Céleste acquire her nickname. She was now in the news.

• Circus rider at the Hippodrome

La Mogador's acrobatic feats on the back of a horse brought her many more admirers, including a duke who placed a horse and carriage at her disposal.

• The theatre and music

While circus riding, La Mogador eased her way into the social circle of Alphonse Royer, a Director of the Opéra. Predictably, she caused many admirers heartache, especially the young German Jewish pianist Hermann Cohen, "Puzzi," who was a favourite protégé of Liszt. Cohen fell madly in love with La Mogador, who loved his playing but not, alas, his body. (Being anti-Semitic didn't help.) Broken-hearted, Puzzi converted to Roman Catholicism and became a priest, Père Augustin Marie du Très Saint Sacrement. He surely deserved such a long title as recompense for his sufferings.

• Attachment and marriage to Lionel, Comte de Moreton de Chabrillan. Best selling author.

Son of a former gentleman-in-waiting at the court of Charles X, Lionel was the black sheep of his aristocratic family from Berry, and found himself relying on funds from La Mogador after they got together. Having abandoned circus riding because of a serious accident, La Mogador now turned to acting at the Théâtre des Variétés, where the younger Alexander Dumas (author of *La dame aux camélias*) wrote a part for her into one of his plays. To supplement her income further she turned to memoir writing "with the aid of a former lover who was also her lawyer." In spite of its phonetic spelling and poor literacy, this volume was the first of her many best sellers.

Meanwhile, relations with Count Lionel went through a stormy patch, doubtless because his reckless gambling had bankrupted the couple once again. To give each other space, he went to Melbourne, Australia for a year, and on his return had La Mogador's name removed from the police lists before marrying her.

They then went back to Melbourne where the count had somehow fixed himself up with the post of French consul. Two years later La Mogador returned alone with "two little dogs and a green parakeet," and also a completed novel featuring life down under – *The French Consul's Wife* (still advertised for sale on the Internet) – that was published by Michel Levy. (Levy's prestigious list included George Sand, Flaubert, and Balzac.)

The novel was extremely well received by La Mogador's many friends including Dumas the elder (of *Three Musketeers and Count of Monte Cristo* fame) and the influential critic Jules Janin. Half a century later Marcel Proust also became a fan.

Altogether La Mogador would produce a hundred or more volumes including – her Mémoires, sixteen novels, twenty-six plays, seven operetta librettos, and twenty nine songs and poems.

• Theatre Director

With the death of her husband in 1858 La Mogador abandoned her title of Countess and, as plain "Mme Lionel" became Director of the Bouffes Parisiens (Paris Comic Opera), which had until recently been the venue for Offenbach's operettas. For four years she produced a string of operettas, also supplying librettos for many of them. Eventually hounded out by malicious critics, La Mogador next took over the management of a large theatre in the poor district of Belleville (her birthplace), and presented a stage version of her novel *The Gold Robbers*, transcribed (anonymously and as a favour) by the elder Dumas, no less. A smash hit, it played to full houses of working men in Belleville before touring many provincial theatres.

The Gold Robbers made La Mogador enough money to buy her treasured acre and a half of wooded land at Le Vésinet, and to build her house next door to Bizet's little cottage. She was then forty-one, he twenty-seven.

Although La Mogador never admitted in her memoirs to having an affair with Bizet, the hint was there in the banter about his fickleness (quoted above). It is hard to imagine that she never succumbed to the advances of a man whose music and passionate personality so clearly enthralled her. She even bought a piano so that Bizet could use it in her home. Sitting quietly, she would watch his "beautiful hands" in action, holding her breath so as not to disturb "the master's adorable playing." In 1866 she would for sure have observed him working on his grandiose and the now seldom performed, second symphony *Roma*, as well as his opera *La Jolie Fille de Perth* (The Fair Maid of Perth), now known mainly for its orchestral suite.

La Mogador noted that Bizet was too often morose, in such comments as "I never saw him laugh freely," and "he was not very cheerful at this time." Hardly surprising, in view of all the setbacks he had been experiencing (with *The Pearl Fishers* and *Ivan IV*), and the depressing amount of hackwork he had to undertake for publishers. Even his venture into journalism in 1866 was cut short when he withdrew a second article for *The National and Foreign Revue* rather than allow the editor to tamper with it.

Nevertheless La Mogador provided him with consolations:
At your house [he told her] I can at least hear myself work. My own hole-in-the-wall is so tiny that the sound doesn't rise. ... It seems as though your presence inspires me. ... If I see you on the days I go to Paris, I am sure to come back in the evening with good news.

The chamber pot story
La Mogador's rough-trade mother, Mme Vénard, particularly disliked Bizet's casual manners. One evening she decided to cure him of his habit, after returning on the midnight train from Paris, of "rapping violently" on the shutters of Le Chalet Lionel with his cane or his umbrella before continuing on his way laughing. "The dog would bark" wrote Céleste, and

we would all wake up with a start, my mother, my adopted daughter, my servant and myself. ... Everybody would scream from one end of the house to the other, particularly my mother, who was nervous and excessively afraid of being in the country. Once awakened she could not go to sleep again. She had said to me, 'If he plays these practical jokes again he will have me to deal with.' ...The window of her room was just above mine. One evening when I was writing, Georges saw a ray of light between the cracks of the Venetian blinds. ..and he kept rapping to tell me he had good news. I was more or less undressed, and answered, 'Wait a minute.' At that moment I heard something fall from the window above and Georges crying, 'How stupid! I've been drenched in an unexpected shower .' He yelled, he swore, he stormed out on the avenue while my mother, the little girl, and my maid, all practically undressed, came into my room, where they laughed like idiots escaped from a lunatic asylum. The dog, Blanchette, her hair bristling, her eyes popping out of her head, kept barking in a voice hoarse from yapping.

And Bizet called from outdoors, 'It is shameful to empty chamber-pots on the heads of poor late passers-by. 'My mother replied, 'You should have kept on going, you devil.'

If the very essence of *Carmen* in Bizet's opera is a handsome, shameless, bewitching gypsy, born to make men mad, that is surely also a good part of the profile of La Mogador. It also seems certain that Bizet drew directly or indirectly on her cabaret repertoire at the Concert Du XIX'me Siècle for the opera.

If further evidence of a direct link here between life and art is needed, might not La Mogador (suggests Curtiss) have written these words of Carmen in her act one Habañera?

"Si tu ne m'aimes pas, je t'aime" ["If you don't love me, I love you."]

Indeed yes! La Mogador wrote in her memoirs:

I have always been capricious and proud. No one, among women whose tendency it is to say yes, derives more pleasure than I do from saying no. So the men to whom I have given the most are those who asked least of me.

*

Geneviève Halévy: "an emotional mess"

The mother has been mad for several months, and Bébé [Geneviève's pet name], who is now a woman, is more and more unbalanced.
[The composer Paladhile to his father, 1864]

The La Mogador-Bizet friendship must have cooled down by the summer of 1867. In October he became engaged to Geneviève Halévy, only to find that her mother rescinded the betrothal later that same month. Aside from Bizet's lack of prospects as a husband, Mme Halévy and her relations seem also to have had wind of Bizet's association with La Mogador.

Love was indeed blind for Bizet as far as Geneviève and the Halévys were concerned. Tremors of mental instability rumbled through both sides of the family, and in Mme Halévy's and Geneviève's case frequently erupted into quakes. True, Geneviève's father Fromental Halévy, who had died when she was only thirteen, had earned deep respect for his achievements as a composer of thirty seven operas, and as a teacher of such geniuses as Gounod, Saint-Saëns and Bizet himself. He suffered severely, however, from neurasthenia, a neurotic disorder characterised by chronic fatigue and weakness ("torpeur habituelle") and loss of memory. (Was this the nineteenth century version of ME?)

For all her talents as a sculptress, Geneviève's mother Léonie née Rodrigues-Henriques was far more problematic. Daughter of a Sephardic banker, she had married Halévy at age twenty-one, less than half his age. Their first daughter Esther died at age twenty before she could marry her cousin Ludovic Halévy. Léonie later became fixated on blaming Geneviève for the death and banished her to relatives. Léonie's other dysfunctional symptoms included wildly irresponsible spending sprees and regular committals to an asylum.

Delacroix, who painted some scenes from Halévy's operas, had this to say about the Halévys:

> His poor wife fills the house with old pots and pans and old furniture; ... How can he do any serious work in the midst of this hubbub? ...
> How do these Halévys ... these people, hounded by debts and the demands of family or of vanity, manage a calm and smiling manner through all their troubles? They can be happy only by blinding themselves and

ignoring the reefs through which they steer their course, often desperate and sometimes ship- wrecked.

Marriage

No more evening parties! No more fits and starts! No more mistresses! All that is finished! Absolutely finished!

[Bizet to Galabert, October 1867]

Bizet was besotted with Geneviève, with her "black eyes, feverish, deep-set," her complexion "pale as a camellia under her helmet of brown hair" and a mouth with "thick, quivering lips, drooping at the corners." He was jubilant about both his life and career prospects with Geneviève at his side, though it was not until spring 1869 that Mme Halévy consented to the marriage. Meanwhile his opera *The Fair Maid of Perth* was premiered at the Théâtre Lyrique, only to be scrapped after eighteen performances. In the following year he began work on *The King of Thule's Cup,* never completed but considered by scholars to contain some of his finest work. While working on it, he suffered a severe attack of quinsy ("forty tiny abscesses in the gullet, etc., etc.") as well as a spiritual crisis concerning his beliefs and the world's value systems. He was then almost thirty.

No doubt to curry favour with Mme Halévy, Bizet also began work on completing her late husband's opera *Noé.* Mme Halévy seems finally to have been persuaded that Bizet was an acceptable son-in-law by her elder brother Hippolyte Rodrigues, who remained an eternally loyal friend to Bizet. Bizet and Geneviève were married on 3 June 1869.

Since neither Bizet nor his bride were believers, the marriage was a civil one, attended by Bizet's father but not by Mme Halévy who was once more laid up in a sanatorium. The dowry ("between 150,000 and 200,000 francs, with 500,000 to come later") and further bequests to Geneviève were not sufficient to enable Bizet to give up those hated piano lessons.

Bizet described his new-found bliss to Rodrigues, at whose home the couple had spent their honeymoon:

I am tremendously happy. Geneviève is marvellously well. – We love each other and we love you, for it is you who have made our life possible.– Come, come soon. We call you, we long for you. – Here there is happiness for all three of us.

The couple took an apartment at 22 rue de Douai in Montmartre, its façade covered (Bizet wrote) with "columns, scrolls, and angels so that it looked like the work of a delirious mason who had passed through Rome." Montmartre was then a residential district with grass and trees in squares and gardens rather than the plethora of cheap hotels and seedy dives it is now.

Inevitably Bizet was heavily burdened with the practicalities of marriage during September and October, leaving him with precious little time to compose. "I have spent the last six weeks at the upholsterer's, the locksmith's, the carpenter's, etc," he wrote to his correspondence pupil and confident Paul Lacombe in early November. And to the mezzo-soprano Marie Trélat he wrote:

> What a job! It's frightful. We are dead tired at the moment. We spend the day buying casseroles; at night I work on *Noé* ... for which I have a short-term contract with Pasdeloup which fills me with terror. As soon as there is a pillow under my head, as soon as I have our furniture, I shall come to see you."

National Guard

In 1870 Bizet began working on two more operatic projects that came to nothing: *Clarissa Harlowe* and *Grisélidis*. The couple's holiday that summer in Barbizon was cut short by the outbreak of the Franco-Prussian War on 19 July. Bizet, the upright patriot, joined the Sixteenth Battalion of the National Guard at the end of August and remained in Paris throughout the siege. "Our gun weighs 14 pounds," he wrote to Geneviève

> – that's heavy for a musician. These weapons kick back, spit, and do everything possible to be more disagreeable to those who fire them than to the enemy. In short, they are, *par excellence*, Prussian arms.

The strain of continual separation from her husband soon began to tell on Geneviève. By mid-October she was mostly staying in bed and not eating. Bizet did his best to comfort her with letters, and solicitous notes left on the kitchen table:

> My dearest love, I can't see you this morning. I am on sentry-duty at 11 o'clock-and I haven't even time to grab a bite to eat on the run. But I shall come back for dinner. I don't know just what time. In any case, have dinner ready at six o'clock. I love you, my love, with all my soul.

119

By December 1870 the couple were living on horsemeat, and Geneviève dreamed every night of "chickens and lobsters." Nevertheless, he fervently welcomed the fall of the Second Empire under Napoleon III and the removal of "the thick coat of shame and ordure" with which it had "bespattered the country."

"acute hysteria" in Bordeaux: "nervous tics"

On both their pleadings, but much against his better judgement, Bizet took Geneviève to see her long-estranged mother in Bordeaux in February 1871. Inevitably, there was a crisis. After forty eight hours Geneviève was reduced to a state of such "acute hysteria" that she begged Bizet to take her away at once.

The strains inflicted on Bizet by an unstable wife and mother are all too clear in this part of his letter to Rodrigues written on the return journey to Paris:

> ... [Geneviève] was terribly shaken. This morning she heard someone talking in the corridor of the hotel, If you could have seen how pale she turned, if you could have seen the way she threw herself into my arms screaming: 'She's here! Save me, I'll die if I see her again,' you would have been frightened of the way she looked. ... [Mme Halévy's] vanity is overwhelming! 'I am Mme Halévy. Everybody must obey me.' ...
>
> ... Their illness (for it is morbid of both of them) excuses everything, but it does not enliven the situation.

Back in Paris the situation hardly improved for some time:

> ... the external manifestations of her nervous shock are frightening. I can't give you any idea of the extent of the nervous tics. ... In five or six days I think she will be able to hold a pen (which today is absolutely impossible; her nervous tics preclude any occupation, even if it takes only a few minutes).

After the insurrection of the Commune on 18 March 1871, the Bizets moved out to Le Vésinet, where he resumed work on *Clarissa Harlowe* and *Grisélidis*, the latter being rejected by the Opéra-Comique. He therefore offered the management another opera instead, *Djamileh,* which he completed in the late summer. Also in 1871, Bizet completed his very popular twelve pieces for piano duet, *Jeux d'enfants* (Children's Games, later transcribed as a *Little Suite for Orchestra*). In October he resigned on a matter of principle from the post of chorus master at the Opéra that he had been offered only in July. (In securing the post he had res-olutely rejected his mother-in-law's interfering moves to lobby on his behalf, insisting that "For many reasons I need absolute moral independence.")

Suppressed love triangle

Still in this same year (1871), Bizet became involved in a sort of love triangle, not overtly sexual, between Geneviève and her mother. Many letters from Bizet to Mme Halévy end in warmest declarations:

> [March, after returning from Bordeaux]
> I love you more than you choose to think and send you
> the most tender expressions of my filial affection. ...
> I love you with all my heart.

It never occurred to Bizet that his need for his mother-in-law's approval, and the intensity of his affection for her, perhaps not entirely platonic (she was then fifty-one to his thirty-three), would exacerbate Geneviève's emotional and psychiatric prob-lems. His often-expressed "horror" of losing Madame Halévy's love induced a "strange terror" of him in Geneviève, who probably felt threatened by the attachment.

To deflect Bizet yet again from composition, in September Mme Halévy required him to co-operate with a lawyer in handling her business affairs, and arrange for the transport to Bordeaux of furniture from her house at Bas-Prunay (near Reims). Sheaves of correspondence show that Bizet took endless pains with the commission, only to be repaid by accusations that he had been careless over the furniture and had withheld or lost some of Madame's belongings. Deeply wounded, Bizet replied with pages of facts and figures, ending poignantly:

> Let us hope that this letter is the last I shall write to
> you about your household goods. We will discuss art, a
> subject which is perhaps less alien to me.

All the while he had been trying to compose *Djamileh*, and had also suffered his eleventh attack of quinsy (defined as an "acute inflammation of the tonsils and the surrounding tissue, often leading to the formation of an abscess").

Bizet generally showed remarkable resilience in the face of in-sults, crises and setbacks. Louis Gallet (his librettist for *Djamileh)* left a delightful cameo of him at Le Vésinet while working on the opera:

He walked about in a straw hat and loose jacket with the easy assurance of a country gentleman, smoking his pipe, chatting happily with his friends, receiving them at table, with a conviviality that always had a touch of banter in it, between his charming young wife and his father, who was his host and spent all day gardening as a change from the fatigue of giving lessons.

The year 1872 saw the failure of *Djamileh* in May – in spite of its charming music, it was dropped after ten shows – and the birth of the couple's son Jacques on 10 July. No doubt spurred on by the need for cash, Bizet very rapidly wrote his ever-popular and fresh-minted incidental music for Alphonse Daudet's *L'Arlésienne*, a play about peasant life in Provence. The play failed, but the music was performed as a suite with great success under the baton of Jules Pasdeloup on 10 November. Perhaps everybody's favourite number is the *Adagietto*, which in the play celebrates the touching love of an ageing couple who meet after fifty years' separation.

Composition-wise, 1873 was unproductive. Bizet began working on *Carmen* in the spring, but had to lay it aside because of difficulties with the Opéra-Comique. Yet another work was abandoned (*Don Rodrigue*) when the Opéra was burned down on 28 October.

Separation (1874)

There are several witnesses to his settled melancholy at this period; Henri Maréchal said he "often sensed tears in his voice, but an immediate effort at self-control quickly suppressed them".

[Curtiss]

Marital problems became so difficult early in 1874 that the couple separated for two or three months, Bizet remaining in Paris and Geneviève staying with her cousin Ludovic at Saint-Germain. Little is discoverable because, in Mina Curtiss's words

the faithful Galabert, who until his death in 1913 treasured every word and note his master had written, kept no letters from Bizet written after 1873 because, as he told his son, he felt that they revealed facts about the marriage which Bizet would have wished to remain secret.

Once again Mme Halévy added to Bizet's miseries:

Dear Baby [sic], Your mother. ... tells me that she wants

to have the child either constantly with her or not at all. We came to the latter arrangement. – Do give me the satisfaction of keeping Jacquot or sending him elsewhere. Your mother has informed Mme Brun of the decision. So the question is settled, and I have had enough of this subject, which is beginning to besmirch me singularly.

And how is your little head – in good order? I love you, I love you, I love you. Don't worry. Good-bye for the present.

Ton baby [sic].

According to Henry Malherbe (a later director of the Opéra who wrote books on both Bizet and *Carmen*), during the Bizets' separation the pianist Élie Delaborde made advances to Geneviève, who was reportedly in love with him. Although many of Malherbe's recollections are not substantiated, he had his ear close to the ground, and some of them may be true.

The Bizets somehow became reconciled and married life resumed at Le Vésinet. Fifty years later the painter Jacques-Émile Blanche recalled not only "the beautiful Geneviève" but also Bizet working at an extraordinary table with a piano built into it on one side, and also a piano hidden behind false drawers:

... At the piano-desk an invention of Fromental Halévy's, specially made for him by Erard — Bizet was working. An enormous head, a Diocletian with glasses, hunched up in his pea-jacket, a red scarf around his neck, his feet in Turkish slippers. At the request of Mlle Valentine, he opened the score of his overture, *Patrie* [1874], played for us the instrumental parts of the score, whistling the notes he couldn't play with his hands. I was in an ecstasy, wordless. He asked me whether I liked the music. I dissolved in tears.

The young American pupil (already quoted) recalled in detail how Bizet would talk, show pictures and "bring in his beautiful baby. He was very proud of it. Mme Bizet would almost always come in." The pupil also described how when working on *Carmen*, Bizet would temporarily abandon her during her lesson when tunes were running thick and fast through his head.

That summer (1874), after a renewed and severe attack of quinsy, the family went to Bougival (on the Seine) where Bizet completed *Carmen*. Rehearsals began in October and were fraught with problems: primarily the objections to the portrayal on stage of such a loose heroine. In January 1875 the publisher Choudens and Bizet signed a contract for the publication of the score for 25,000 francs.

Bizet's appointment as a Chevalier of the Legion of Honour was announced on March 3 1875. That same evening *Carmen* received its premiere in its original version with spoken text instead of accompanied recitatives, and caused ructions. The audience of glitterati became ever more disenchanted during the evening and sat on their hands at the end. Gounod complained he had been plagiarised wholesale, though never took any action. Critics panned the opera mercilessly, homing in on its obscenities. Bizet was mortified and depressed, quarrelling especially with one critic, Oscar Commetant. The crux of the objections seems to have been that in *Carmen* he had created an unrepentant heroine. In opera, fallen women were supposed to die wracked with guilt and remorse.

In late March Bizet was again taken seriously ill, his quinsy being aggravated by rheumatic pains and severe breathing difficulties:

[To Guiraud]
Colossal quinsy. Don't come on Sunday. Imagine a
double pedal a flat-e flat going through your head from
the left ear to the right. I'm quite done in.

Towards the end of May he moved out to Bougival. The next day, being addicted to icy water and cold showers, he went swimming in the river – setting off (writes Mason Greene) "an even more severe rheumatic attack and fever that climaxed in a coronary spasm on June 1. He recovered but suffered another attack the next day. He seemed to have weathered this one too, but during the night [3 June] the faithful Marie ... found him dead in bed." The cause of death was "a cardiac complication of articular rheumatism, aggravated by a chill."

After a moving funeral on 5 June, Gounod read out a statement supposedly, and implausibly, coming from Geneviève:

There was not an hour or a minute of her married life
that she would not gladly have again.

Gounod then broke down and had to stop. Geneviève was ill in bed at the time and had certainly not seen Gounod.

Bizet's body was buried in the Montmartre cemetery. That night the cast of *Carmen* could barely get through the opera, often weeping openly. In the Autumn it was a smash hit in Vienna. Though dropped by the Opéra-Comique, within three years it was on its way to becoming the most popular-ever opera.

After Bizet's death Geneviève devoted her life to her salons and her health, and took no interest in Bizet's autograph scores save those of *Carmen* and *L'Arlésienne* which she left to the Conservatoire. She gave many of the others away as souvenirs.

*

Postlude

Did Bizet have an affair with the soprano who premiered the title role in *Carmen*?

> She managed to combine with the display of unbridled
> passion an element of mystical fatalism.
> [Tchaikovsky on Galli-Marié's performance of *Carmen*]

It was widely reported that Bizet's chosen soprano for the premiere, Célestine Galli-Marié (then in her mid thirties), had played the opera on the night of Bizet's death in a state of angst she was unable to explain. In particular, at the point in Act 3 where Carmen reads her death in the cards – "me first, then him, for both death"– she experienced a horrifying sense of premonition and broke down at the end of the show.

Galli-Marié had always admired Bizet's music and, indeed, told him she knew his last two operas almost entirely by heart, "both voice and accompaniment". She soon became as keen to play *Carmen* as Bizet was for her to do it – his main worry being that her fee might not be affordable. A deal was made, her main musical request being that the role should exploit the same vocal range as that of Marguérite in Gounod's *Faust*.

The idea of an affair, albeit from Henry Malherbe, is entirely anecdotal. In his book *Carmen* (1921), Malherbe relays information from the tenor Paul Lhérie (the very first Don José), and Jacques Bouhy (the first Escamillo) that Bizet had a tempestuous affair with Galli-Marié, often broken off after quarrels.

All gossip, of course, but in view of all the tensions at home, Bizet may have been only too eager to fall into the arms of a woman whose artistry and personality he so adored. However, none of the surviving letters from Galli-Marié to Bizet confirm any kind of intimacy. Besides, Galli-Marié had for some years been living with the composer Émile Paladhile.

Once again, respected reader, it is for you to decide. Either way, these words of Mina Curtiss on Galli-Marié's role in Bizet's last year make a suitable conclusion:

> Throughout the embattled rehearsals of *Carmen*, it was not the composer's wife who sustained him either as a man or as an artist. It was Galli-Marié, the woman of the theatre, who became the embodiment of his creation by her own gifts, her faith in his talent, her fierce loyalty to his conception ... It was she who gave him wholehearted support.

***

Chapter 8

Leoš Janáček
'Good God, not again?'
Born: Hukvaldy (Moravia, now
Eastern Czech Republic), 3 July 1854
Died age 74: Moravaská, Ostrava, 12 August 1928

My father looked at me and suddenly asked:
'Why aren't you writing to your husband?'
'What's so strange when he's got another woman?' [Mrs
Gabriela Horvátová]
He wrung his hands: 'Good God, not again?'
I told him everything. He nodded: 'Well, that's what it's
like with such a person. You've got what you wanted.'
[Zdenka Janácková: *My Life with Janáček*]
*

Let me stick my neck out. No composer anywhere, at any time, wrote more great music fired explicitly by one obsessive and unconsummated grand passion than did Janácek. After he met twenty-six-year-old housewife Kamila Stösslová in the summer of 1917 when he was sixty three, Janácek identified her with a whole cluster of his late masterpieces. The first was the song cycle *The Diary of One Who Disappeared*. Then came four female-oriented operas: *Kát'a Kabanová, The Cunning Little Vixen, The Makropulos Affair,* and *From The House of The Dead*. After these, he shouted from the rooftops a more reciprocal phase in their relationship – though still unconsummated – with his *Love Letters*. This was the subtitle he originally used for his *Second String Quartet* that was completed in a frenzy of passion in February 1928. (Later he changed the subtitle to *Intimate Letters*.)

Even the other masterpieces of Janácek's last eleven years – including his largest orchestral work, the *Sinfonietta* of 1926 and his *Glagolitic Mass* of 1927 – were part of the fall-out from the explosion of his feelings for his dark-eyed, dark-haired "Negress," Kamila. We know so much about this relationship since although it was never consummated, Janácek wrote her a total of 722 letters over the last eleven years of his life. They have been compiled by John Tyrrell, who has also translated the memoirs of Janácek's long-suffering wife, Zdenka Janácková. "My life with Janácek" may not be a model of objectivity when Mrs Janácková is talking about her husband's mistresses, but the basic integrity of the document is undoubtedly accepted by Janácek scholars.

It is easy enough to think of other works by other composers – including Beethoven, Berlioz, Chopin, Mozart and Tchaikovsky – that were fuelled by unrequited love, but not on such a grand scale as this. Perhaps Brahms came closest, for although he had many muses, he himself acknowledged to Clara Schumann that "by rights, I should have to inscribe all my best melodies, 'Really by Clara Schumann.'

A late developer

Janácek only really became regarded as the third and last of the great Czech nationalist composers, carrying the torch after Smetana and Dvorák, as a result of his uniquely obsessive relationship with Kamila Stösslová. A truly late developer, his only work to have made the international headlines before 1917 was the opera *Jenufa*. Although premiered with enormous success in his native Brno in 1904, it was not until its staging at the National Theatre in Prague on 26 May 1916 that *Jenufa* took Europe by storm. After publication and promotion by *Universal Edition* it was soon being performed in Vienna, Berlin and other German cities.

Until 1916 Janácek's sphere of influence was essentially confined to Moravia and its capital Brno. Here he was highly respected as a composer, as a passionate folklorist, and as director of the Brno Organ School he had effectively founded in 1881. Outside of Moravia he was probably only known for thirty printed minor compositions. The first performance of any Janácek work outside Czech lands had been his chorus *Ah, the War*, by the Smetana Choral Society in Spa, Belgium in the summer of 1905.

A marriage doomed from the start

Kamila Stösslová was by no means the first of Janácek's extramarital interests. His marriage on 13 July 1881 to one of his piano pupils Zdenka Schulzová had never been a happy one. She was the daughter of the director of the Brno Teachers' Institute in which he had qualified as a music teacher in 1880.

When they married, Janácek was almost twenty-seven, Zdenka still only fifteen! Janácek was a fervently patriotic, highly impulsive, temperamental and libidinous Czech, Zdenka an innocent girl from a staid German middle class background – "carefully brought up so that one day she might become the respectable, painstaking and capable wife of a notable townsman."

About fifteen months after their marriage the couple separated for nearly two years. Their daughter Olga was born shortly before the split and died of typhoid at age twenty. Their son Vladíček was born in 1888 and died two years later of meningitis.

*

1890: affair with Františka Rakowitschová

Janáček was invariably and inevitably often given the glad-eye by women, not only because he was attractive and charismatic, but also because, by 1890, he was a local big shot in Brno and Moravia. Not only had he expanded his organ school into a thriving teaching establishment of conservatoire dimensions. He had also been appointed to the staff of the Brno Gymnasium (grammar school), had run a journal for two years, and had completed his first opera *Sarka*. He had also conducted the Beseda choral society for fourteen years, swiftly turning it from a male voice choir into a 250 strong mixed voice group that could tackle many of the great classics of the choral repertoire. In 1890 he published his first collection of Moravian folk songs – these being the life blood of his art.

In the spring of 1890 Janáček began carrying on with another woman right under Zdenka's nose when the family went with some friends to stay in the village of Hukvaldy, Janáček's birth place in the forested mountains of northern Moravia. Zdenka tells the story of how her husband humiliated her:

> I was happy, nothing worried me, I lacked for nothing. And here again of course the inevitable shadow had to fall. Once my husband and I were walking from the park. As we were approaching the brewery, a carriage in which a lady was sitting was just going into the gates. Leoš entirely brightened up, he took off his hat and waved it in greeting. The lady returned the greeting in a friendly fashion. 'You know, that's Mrs Rakowitschová', he said to me.
> I already knew that it was the sister of Mrs Jandovil, the daughter of the old lady from the Hukvaldy brewery,

and that she was married to a forestry official and that she was coming with her children for the holidays. I soon got to know her personally: a chestnut brunette with wide lips, slow-witted, she got bored in women's company, she enjoyed being with men, she smoked a cigar and had no interest in art. Otherwise I didn't notice anything remarkable about her. But my husband changed in a trice. We no longer meant anything to him, he was now in the service of this lady. On excursions, in the inn, at chance meetings, everywhere he saw only her. The next Sunday there was a firemen's expedition to the Matulov wood. The whole of Hukvaldy was there and all the local dignitaries. Mrs Rakowitschová came too. Here my eyes were opened when I saw how my husband hovered around her. And what I didn't see people filled in with hints and knowing smiles. I learnt that my husband had already had a good time with Mrs Rakowitschová the previous holidays. And now it got worse and worse. We all slept together with Vladícek in one room, my husband alone in the kitchen. When we were all already in bed I'd hear him sneaking out quietly and returning late. He began to make it clear to me that he didn't want me to go walking with him, later he even behaved as if I wasn't there at all. After a short moment of complete happiness I regretted his behaviour twice over. ...

Zdenka's grief after Vladícek's death later that same year was compounded by Janácek's refusal to give her another baby, such was his continuing obsession with Rakowitschová:

... I went to Leoš and begged him to give me a child. ! I'll never be able to forget what happened next. With a grimace, he looked at me and said harshly: 'Hm, that's what you would want, but I don't.' With a feeling of terrible shame and humiliation I endured this cruel blow. Only now, after many years, can I understand why he hurt me in this way. After Vladícek's death I mattered less to my husband than I'd suspected. Leoš thought of the other woman with all his violent passionate being, so that there remained no more room for me; with my request I appeared to him like an interloper. ... Those few words and that glance froze in me for ever not only any desire for a child, but also for my husband. I say 'desire for my

husband', not love for him. That seemed as if it welled up within me from a quite different source, having nothing to do with mutual' physical contact. ...
Only Olga was left to me and I transferred all my faith, hope and love on to her. ...

The affair continued until at least the summer of 1902, when Olga "let something slip about her Dad and Mrs Rakowitschová." Olga's death in 1903 inevitably further destabilised the marriage. There was now little more than "habit and convenience" to keep the couple together.

*

"An angel" and "an anonymous letter from Brno" Kamila Urválková

In 1903, while taking a separate holiday from Zdenka in his favourite spa resort of Luhacovice, Janácek met "an angel." She was Mrs Kamila Urválková, from Zaháj u Dolních Krávolic. Another forester's wife who had taken a shine to him, Mrs Urválková cheered the composer up by sending a bunch of red roses to his table because he looked so "sad and isolated." Their friendship then developed after rehearsals had started for *Jenufa* in Brno.

Mrs Urválková it was who provided Janácek with crucial inspiration for his semi-autobiographical opera then in progress *Osud* (Fate). Set in Luhacovice, the opera's heroine is Mila who, under pressure from her mother, has been obliged to stop meeting the composer Zivny. It all ends very badly, with the Mother throwing herself from a high staircase and dragging Mila with her to their deaths. The real life parallel for Janácek was that Mrs Urválková had told him of her love for the conductor Ludvíc Celanský.

At Janácek's request he and Zdenka had recently resumed conjugal relations. But these soon stopped when Zdenka found intimate letters from Mrs Urválková's to her husband.

He ran to me angrily:
'Where are my letters?'
'I've hidden them.'
'Give them back to me at once.'
'Certainly, when I've read them.'
'No, no, give them to me at once, or I'd have to kill myself.'
He begged, he threatened, eventually he promised me

that we'd read them together. I believed him and brought the letters. He tore them out of my hand and hid them. I got angry. I told him that he was unfaithful and asked why should he come to me when he then wanted to deceive me. He didn't defend himself, he didn't make excuses, he was clearly very frightened. Christmas 1903 we didn't even celebrate at home. He went to Hukvaldy, I to Vienna …

What must have been a short and fitful affair between Janácek and Urválková was abruptly terminated when her husband instructed Janácek to stop seeing or writing to his wife. According to Zdenka, Urválková's husband "had received an anonymous letter from Brno."

*

Gabriela Horvátová (1877-1967)

Janácek's most passionate extra-marital affair was with the singer Gabriela Horvátová. When he arrived in Prague for the last time before the premiere of *Jenufa* in May 1916 he was already completely besotted. She was then 38, he 61.

A Croat by birth, Horvátová had sung in Zagreb and German opera houses, and had joined the Prague company at the age of twenty-three. Although her voice was past its best when she and Janácek first met, Horvátová had been one of the company's most useful and versatile singers, taking in mezzo roles such as Carmen and Kundry (in *Parsifal*) and also such dramatic soprano parts as Tosca, Libuse (the title role in the opera by Smetana) and Brünnhilde (leader of the Valkyries in three of Wagner's music dramas).

Janácek began a passionate correspondence with Horvátová soon after her casting as Kostelnicka in *Jenufa* early in 1916. The composer and singer were soon flaunting their affair in public, even spending a summer holiday together in Luhacovice. All this resulted in an out-of-court legal separation between the Janáceks signed on 17 January 1917.

Janácek's interest in Horvátová would wane only after he met Kamila Stösslová in 1917. By 1918 his correspondence with Horvátová had died out, and references to her after that were derogatory ("that disgusting H.").

Zdenka Janácková poured out some 18,000 heartrending words on this affair in chapter seven of her *Memoirs*. Here is just a morsel or three, taking up Zdenka's story after Janácek said "So see you in Prague" before leaving Brno for the premiere of *Jenufa*:

> Suddenly I was gripped by terrible pain and anxiety. I remained standing in the vestibule. For a moment it was as if I could see into the future. I hid my head in the corner behind the clothes rack and I knew it: Leoš was lost to me.
>
> ... Leoš came to meet me [at the station in Prague] and took me to the hotel Imperial. He was pleased that I was there now, but I felt as if turned to stone. He took me to meet Mrs Horvátová right away. ... She caught hold of me, she embraced me and kissed me as if I were an old and beloved friend – she knew how to do things like that. I examined her discreetly but nevertheless thoroughly ... She was about forty-four [she was actually thirty-eight], taller than me, quite well-built, a brunette, with large black eyes, I'd call them 'Junoaugen' [i.e. prominent or bulging], a large, sensuous mouth, coarse features, the expression of the face at times almost predatory. Lots of gestures, an exceptionally lively manner; she knew how to speak without stopping. Her behaviour wasn't natural, everything was calculated for effect, but she did it so skilfully that she dazzled the unwary. And my husband, unfortunately, was one of those. ... Every moment he jumped up and kissed her hand. She told us many things which aimed to demonstrate her interest in *Jenufa*. ...

Zdenka's crushing humiliation over the next few days, often in front of her many friends from Brno, reached the point where she "had a mind to jump off the observation tower." Back in Brno, her suicidal state was later examined by the chief doctor of the Cernovice lunatic asylum, one Dr Papirnik. This singularly phlegmatic gentleman prescribed cold baths, lukewarm baths, Veronal (a barbiturate) and other medicines. He also offered these pearls of wisdom to Zdenka privately

> Madam, your nerves are in a very bad way and you must definitely not go to Luhacovice if Mrs Horvátová is going to be there.

– and this gem to man and wife together:

'There, there, make it up now and give each other a kiss.'

Janácek's infatuation with Horvátová drove him into the realms of deranged fantasy. Abetted by his mistress, he even tried (unsuccessfully) to convince Zdenka that his lover was pregnant with his child, and that she had then had a miscarriage.

The Janácek's legal separation enjoined them to keep the peace, to continue to keep house together but to sleep apart: Janácek in his office in the Organ School, Zdenka in the house that had been built for them in the grounds of the School.

*

Janácek's "Negress": Kamila Stösslová
"my guardian angel on all sides"

When Janácek first met Kamila Stösslová in early July 1917 in Luhacovice, he had been separated from his wife for nearly seven months. Kamila had been married for five years and had born her husband David Stössel, a dealer in antiques and pictures, two sons: Rudolf in 1913, and Otto in 1916.

At first Zdenka welcomed what looked like a wholly innocent friendship between her husband and Kamila, corresponding with her and having the couple to stay. Although there was some friction between the two women, the Janáceks and the Stössels publicly made up a respectable foursome for the first ten years of the friendship. And most crucially of all for Zdenka, it killed virtually overnight Janácek's obsession with Horvátová.

Janácek began to visit the Stössels at their home in Pisek in 1924, but it was only from Easter 1927 that his friendship with Kamila took a more intimate turn. During two walks she first agreed to the more intimate form of address between them – Ty instead of the more formal Vy. He used it for the first time in his letter to her of 21 April – actually the 432nd of those 722 that he sent her between 16 July 1917 and 25 July 1928! Kamila would sometimes thereafter reciprocate by signing off her letters with Tvá or Tvoje Kamila (Your Kamila).

From this point the flow of presents between them also increased. (During the entire course of the friendship Janácek gave her books, magazines, cakes, clothes, accessories, flowers, rings, royalties and scores. From Kamila, or more usually from

Kamila and her husband, came notepaper and envelopes, a ring, a silver writing set, sweets, and a tie and tie-pin.)

The first kiss

After the transition to "Ty" Janácek visited Pisek more frequently and began writing to Kamila daily. His full-blown obsession with her peaked after she permitted their first kiss on 19 August 1927, less than a year before his death. On this momentous day he was seventy-three, Kamila thirty-six. Although the intimacy never went beyond kisses, it inevitably led to a marked deterioration in his relationship with Zdenka. Thereafter he had to burn most of Kamila's letters.

Lovemaking or no, Kamila was now offering Janácek something he could hang on to:

> [14 March 1928]
> Dear Maestro
> ... I really don't know what I'd have done during this bad weather if it weren't for your letters. ... they're nice and even if I didn't want to I'd have to think of you all the time. ... Reading your letter today I thought so much of everything past of all I've lived through and I'm happy. You remind me of it when you write how your life was before and is now. And what about mine I've not known anything else I've not longed for anything else my life just went by without love and joy. But I always went along with the thought that, that's the way it had to be. Now I think that God was testing you and me and when he saw that we've been good and that we deserve it he has granted us this joy in life. If you told anyone he wouldn't believe that I've perhaps waited for you that all my life I'd found no-one who would offer me his love. I steered clear of everything I didn't look for anything and you were the only one in all the years you've known me and that really is the truth. ... you are much dearer to me than if you were young. I can assure you that my life is pleasant that I don't wish for any better. And for that only you are guilty ...I thank you for it also. [...]

Janácek's progress with Kamila was undoubtedly helped by – and contributed to – her deteriorating relationship with her husband. Whereas on 9 July 1924 she could write to Janácek that "I long for him just as you for me," by 18 June 1928 it was a very different story:

...My husband arrived from Vienna only on Saturday evening and went off early this morning.
I didn't even speak to him he's inconsiderate. ... Believe me, his presence irritates me I'm glad he's away. I'm happiest on my own now. And even if the worst was to happen I don't want you to come to see us. ... So don't be angry with me I know very well that you're suffering with me but to come to us is impossible now. ...

Kamila and Janácek's music
The Diary of One Who Disappeared

In any History of Love, the Janácek and Kamila story is amazing. But the musical fallout from the relationship is in every sense stupendous and unique. In his sleeve notes to EMI's thrilling recording of *The Diary of One Who Disappeared*, John Tyrrell explains how Janácek began to compose the work days after his first meeting with Kamila.

On 14 and 21 May of the previous year (1916), the Brno daily newspaper *Lidové noviny* had published a sequence of twenty three short poems written in a dialect of Czech from the remote region of Valassko. They were reportedly the work of a "self-taught man", a farmer's son who had mysteriously disappeared. The poems first tell the tale of his attraction to a Gypsy girl, Zefka, who seduces him and lures him away. They end with his farewell to his parents and his home. The verse being expertly crafted, no-one believed for a moment that the poems were written by a peasant. But the mystery of their authorship was finally solved only in 1997 when a local historian came across a letter written by a Moravian poet, Josef Kalda (1871-1921), to a friend. The letter reveals that Kalda disguised his authorship of the poems as a hoax.

A year later Janácek took cuttings of the poems to read on holiday in Luhacovice. After meeting Kamila and becoming instantly besotted by her, he very soon set to work on *The Diary of One Who Disappeared*, the first and most revealing of his Kamila-inspired compositions. The young man in the poems who abandons parents and home for the Gypsy woman is the mirror image of the impetuous Janácek, anxious to leave his dutiful but boring Zdenka and elope with the black-haired, dark-skinned Kamila.

Back home after his holiday, in his very first letters to Kamila, Janácek recorded the sketching of some of the songs. (The first dated song is marked 9 August.) *"Regularly In the Afternoon,"* Janácek wrote to Kamila

> a few motifs occur to me for those beautiful little poems about that Gypsy love. Perhaps a nice little musical romance will come out of it – and a tiny bit of the Luhacovice mood would be in it.

Janácek completed a final revision of *The Diary* in 1920 and it was premiered in Brno on 18 April 1921. The work soon became one of the composer's best-known compositions, with performances the following year in Berlin, London and Paris.

Janácek later revealed all to Kamila on 24 July 1924:

> And that black Gypsy girl in my *Diary* – that was especially you. That's why there's such emotional heat in these works. So much heat that if it caught both of us there'd be just ashes left of us. Luckily it's just I who burn – and you are saved.

To this letter Kamila replied provocatively that she dreamed she was Janácek's wife!

> Such silly things [she continued] where do we get them from? Mummy laughed when I told her about it. She said my head's full of nonsense, and I had to admit she was right. ... Please burn these things that I write to you. Someone would think I am sixteen, that I have no sense. ...

Janácek had even wanted an image of Kamila – with her "hair let down" – to be printed on the cover of the score

Kát'a Kabanová (1920-1921)

The first of his operas to be inspired by Kamila, *Kát'a Kabanová* tells the all-too-pointed story of a married woman having an affair during the absence of her husband on a business trip. Janácek dedicated the opera to Kamila and arranged for her to have the royalties from it.

The Cunning Little Vixen (1923)

Although Janácek nowhere specifically identifies Kamila with this work, its theme of the self-renewing power of nature is clearly resonant with the powerful rejuvenation Janácek so often celebrated after meeting his beloved.

The Makropulos Affair (1925)
From the House of the Dead (1928)

In just one letter to Kamila of 8 June 1927, from his holiday cottage in Hukvaldy, Janácek explains her part in both these operas – and also his utter dependence on her for his creative and personal sustenance:

> Dear Kamila
>
> ...
>
> Yesterday I wrote down for Zdenka what binds me to you. It was an open confession; I think she'll understand it. She imagined more than was remotely possible. For surely between us there's just a beautiful world, but what's beautiful in it, these desires, wishes, the ill and all, all just made up!
>
> I told her that this imaginary world is as necessary for me as air and water is for my life. ...
>
> I told her how in my compositions where pure feeling, sincerity, truth, and burning love exude warmth, you're the one through whom the touching melodies come, you're the Gypsy with the child in *The Diary of One Who Disappeared*.
>
> You're poor Elina Makropulos, and you're in my latest work as the loveable Aljeja [a breeches role in from *The House of the Dead*] I told her that if the thread that binds me to you were to be broken, the thread of my life would be broken. I think that she'll understand all this and especially this eleven-year riddle of ours!
>
> ...
>
> Yours for ever

At the end of this same year Janácek associated Kamila intimately also with the part of Akulka, the heroine in *From the House of the Dead:*

> [30 December 1927]
>
> But my Akulka – Kamila – and I are merry. There's much laughter and fooling around and meanwhile the light burns red in the stove and spreads its glow. ...
>
> So you see how you get mixed up with me! My little soul! Let's celebrate this year of ours! It's going out, but we'll remember it as long as we live!
>
> Thinking of you and /
>
> Yours for ever
>
> L.

Glagolitic Mass 1926

In just one letter of 28 March 1928 Janácek told Kamila of her importance to his *Glagolitic Mass,* and yet again waxed beautifully on the power of love. The mass is so called because its text was written in the Glagolitic or old church Slavonic alphabet formerly used in various Slavic languages, but nowadays only in the Catholic mass and other services of some communities along the Dalmatian coast.

> You can see what sadness and memories about you, of places where I used to see you in Luhacovice, you can see what sort of influence they had on this venerable work. Well, love is a wizard. Submit to it faithfully and it gives a person joy. It intoxicates, it envelops, it isolates. It creates fragrance from the air, ardour from coldness, it beautifies everything around it. Everywhere you see and want only black eyes, raven hair, the silk of the body, soft, smooth like velvet -in short, everywhere you want just your Kamilka. And I feel good on it, I'm content. [...]

Second String Quartet
"Love Letters"-"Intimate Letters"

'Written in fire' rather than his usual "hot ash", between 29 January and 19 February 1928, Janácek's glorious *Second String Quartet* celebrated his more erotic though still very much hands-off relationship with Kamila. He changed his original subtitle for the work, *Love Letters,* to *Intimate Letters.*

Just one letter – "1 February 1928 at night" – says it all.

Love Letters

> I think that it [the *Second Quartet*] will sound delightful. There have already been so many of those dear adventures of ours, haven't there? They'll be little fires in my soul and they'll set it ablaze with the most beautiful melodies. Just think. The first movement I did already in Hukvaldy. The impression when I saw you for the first time! I'm now working on the second movement. I think that it will flare up in the Luhacovice heat [one word inked out]. A special instrument will particularly hold the whole thing together. It's called the viola d'amore — the viola of love. Oh, how I'm looking forward to it! In that work I'll be always only with you! No third person beside us. Full of that yearning as

there at your place, in that heaven of ours! I'll love doing it! You know, don't you, that I know no world other
than you! You're everything to me, I don't want anything else but your love.

And how bitter it was for me when I read from your
letter how you wanted to forget everything nice that
had happened between us!

Kamila as Janácek's "wife"

In the last year of his life Janácek increasingly saw himself as
being married to Kamila, and also began to ponder how he might
end his marriage.

In a letter to Kamila dated 1 July 1927, he described her
as his "hoped-for wife." On 17 November of that same year he
abandoned "hoped-for" in favour of something more certain:

tomorrow's the day where I wait [to see] what my 'wife'
will write to me; if I'm a husband then you're my 'wife'.

On and after 16 February 1928 the quotation marks vanished.
During the time they spent together in Prague in April, they
lunched as a "married couple" and knocked back five drinks,
probably cognacs, after which their heads "didn't ache even a
little." Janácek's next move in the realms of fantasy was to
describe Kamila with his surname as "Mrs Dr Janácková" adding
with more realism that she was "Sort of chubby" (25 May). Later
he also expressed the wish to dedicate his *String Quartet* to "Mrs
Kamila Janácková."

Kamila's baby

Janácek's related fantasy was to pretend that Kamila was
pregnant by him. He made approving comments on her increasing
waistline, incorporated the "birth" in his programme for his *String
Quartet* ("Today I wrote that sweetest desire of mine in music"),
and mentioned that a lullaby he had set to words by Jan Amos
Komenský might be useful "for stock" (16 April 1928).

All the while, physical contact with Stösslová was a long
way from producing babies! The first kiss, as we saw, had taken
place in August 1927 and even a year later embraces were not
permitted:

Now I'd so like to hug you! Oh, if only you would once
let yourself be hugged. And you always just escape like
a slippery little fish!

Janácek's death

Janácek's death a few weeks after his seventy-fourth birthday was sudden and unexpected. In July 1928, after spending three weeks in Luhacovice, he went to the cottage in Hukvaldy where he was joined by Kamila, her son Otto (then eleven) and, for a short while, her husband. One night Otto wandered off alone and Janácek caught a chill while helping to search for him. This rapidly developed into pneumonia, and on 10 August he was taken to the nearest large town where he died at 10 a.m. on Sunday 12 August.

At his large public funeral in Brno on 15 August the final scene of *The Cunning Little Vixen* was performed. Shortly afterwards his *Second String Quartet* was premiered — though few if any of those attending the performance will have known just how much of his beloved Janácek had poured into the work.

Kamila died in 1935. After his wife's death David Stössel pawned the letters Janácek had written to her, along with other Janácek documents, and emigrated to Switzerland.

Zdenka Janácková died in 1938.

*

Could they have married if they had wanted to?

In an appendix to John Tyrrell's volume of the 722 letters, Richard Klos considers whether Janácek and Kamila could ever have married. He concludes that

> it would have been difficult for Janácek to have entered the marriage chamber with a carnation in his lapel sooner than towards the end of 1930. And it would not have happened after dramatic battles in the court house, revelations by brilliantly clad lawyers and sensational testimonies of witnesses but after a series of tussles and private deals. A miserable prospect for the old lion.

***

Chapter 9

(Sir) Edward William Elgar
"Renownedly susceptible"
Born: Broadheath, Worcestershire, 2 June, 1857
Died age 76: Worcester, 23 February, 1934

His attractiveness to women was never in doubt: his
aquiline features, his dark insecurities, and glinting
appeals for quick reassurance spoke louder than any
words. ... [Alice Elgar] knew that in the long run
Edward's music must be more important to him than
any woman; that every other woman would make more
demands than she; and that ultimately he would not
stand for it.
[Jerrold Northrop Moore: *Edward Elgar: A Creative
Life*]

... one moment so disillusioned and materialistic, the
next so mystic and visionary.
[Vera Hockman, Elgar's "mother" "child" "lover" and
"friend" in his last years. Taken from *Elgar in Love*
by Kevin Allen]

"a naughty old man"
[one of Elgar's servants after his wife's death]

A keen supporter of Wolverhampton Wanderers, he
composed a few bars of music for his favourite, player,
Malpass, in 1890.
[*The Guardian*, 19 January 2002]
*

Nowadays, Elgar is known by the great British public mainly
for two big tunes: first and foremost *Land of Hope and Glory,*
from the *Pomp and Circumstance March Number 1*; and also for
Nimrod, one of the *Enigma Variations* he wrote as portraits in
music of his wife and friends. These two tunes turn up repeatedly
in concerts of classical pops all over England, and also on the
radio. *Land of Hope and Glory* still sends almost any British
audience anywhere into nauseating spasms of maudlin, flag-
waving jingoism.

For me personally, even in the big *Nimrod* tune, Elgar's famed nobilmente style slides too easily into maudlin self-indulgence. Maybe it's all those sevenths: forever falling in *Nimrod,* and rising in, say, the slow movement of the *Cello Concerto.* And although I must have played in *The Dream of Gerontius* maybe twenty times, I have never taken to its cloying, incense-ridden score.

Yet, for what it's worth, I love Elgar's intimate serious works, especially the *Violin Sonata,* the *String Quartet,* and the *Piano Quintet,* all dating mainly from 1918. (Elgar's wife commented that they were "different from anything else of his.") And I'm not ashamed to say that I love the salon lollipops. As Elgar himself said, good Delibes is preferable to bad Brahms. He even loved the dance music of his times – especially *Monah* by Jay Wilbur and his band.

It's impossible not to love Elgar the man, in spite of his short fuse and his orgies of self-pity. Bafflingly complex, he himself was an enigma. Most of all, perhaps, because of the enormous chip he continued to carry about on his shoulder long after he had achieved world renown and had been accepted into the drawing rooms of dukes and duchesses, and even after he had been showered with honours, including a knighthood in 1904.

Elgar belongs especially to a book like this because, in Michael Kennedy's words, he "needed muses always, that is inescapable." I have (I hope) included something about most of Elgar's ladies below, apart from his influential American supporter Mrs Julia Worthington, and also Mrs Lalla Vandervelde, wife of the Belgian Socialist leader Emile Vandervelde. In neither case have I come across any soul-baring correspondence from the composer in the standard sources.

*

Nelly (Helen Weaver) and her "broken-hearted fiddler"
> my engagement is broken off & I am lonely. ...I have not the heart to speak to anyone.

> ... a miserable time for me.
> [Elgar to a friend, 1884, 1885]

The only woman with whom Elgar was deeply involved before his wife was his first fiancée, Helen Jessie Weaver. There were other brief romances, including one with an unidentified "E.E."

in Scotland in 1884, Elgar mentioning outings, adieux, flowers and "a little air" dedicated to her. He had also written a *Laura Valse* for a certain Laura Cox, whose parents discouraged any romance with a penniless piper.

Helen's father ran a thriving shoe shop on Worcester High Street almost opposite Elgar's father's music shop at number 10. A violin student at the Leipzig Conservatoire, Helen had a brother Frank who played first fiddle in the Worcester Amateur Instrumental Society that Elgar had conducted from 1882. This was one of the myriad odd jobs that Elgar's straitened family circumstances forced him to take on in his late teens and twenties in Worcester and district. (He never went to music college.) Elgar also earned his bread during those years as a solicitor's clerk, professional violinist, organist, conductor of the Worcester Glee Club, concertmaster of the Worcester Philharmonic, and conductor of the band of the Worcester City and County Lunatic Asylum. He also composed all sorts of music, the most important of which included pieces for wind quintet.

By the early 1880s Elgar had saved enough to afford to attend professional concerts in London, Paris and Leipzig. It was to Leipzig that he travelled in January 1883 to join Helen and another young lady, Edith Groveham who rather hero-worshipped him. Elgar put up at the pension where the girls had already been staying for six months – but of course in those days and in such respectable circles, hanky-panky was out of the question. (In any case the freezing bedrooms, lumpy mattresses and linoleum floors were passion killers.) Elgar heard "no end of stuff" in Leipzig, including lots of Schumann in concerts given by the famed Leipzig Gewandhaus Orchestra, and also "no end" of operas by Wagner.

Elgar and Helen became engaged in the summer of 1883, though he had been inscribing music to her – two polkas (one entitled *Nelly)* and two wind quintets – since 1878. How much she meant to him is clear in this letter he sent to his friend and mentor Dr Charles Buck:

> [1 July 1883]
> The vacation at Leipzig begins shortly; my "Braut"
> [bride] arrives here on Thursday next remaining till
> the first week in September; of course I shall remain

in Worcester till her departure. After that 'twould be a charity if you could find a brokenhearted fiddler much trio-playing for a day or two. Please do not let me intrude on you ... I can only say that I should dearly love to come.'

Helen had to abandon her studies in November and return to England to nurse her sick stepmother who was dying of TB. The engaged couple could therefore be "together a little now & then & consequently happy" (as Elgar wrote to Buck). For reasons not really clear, the engagement was broken off in April 1884. Possibly because Helen was a Unitarian and Elgar a Catholic. Possibly because there were misgivings about Elgar's prospects – he was still essentially penniless. But more likely because Helen had contracted TB in 1884 from her stepmother who had died the previous year. Helen may have wished to spare her fiancé the risk of catching what was still then very much a killer disease.

Elgar's misery is all too clear in another letter he wrote to Buck (himself now engaged) in the summer of 1884:

'my prospects are worse than ever & to crown my miseries my engagement is broken off & I am lonely. ...I have not the heart to speak to anyone. ... Once more accept my good wishes for your happiness, these I can give you the more sincerely since I know what it is to have lost my own for ever.'

A year later he wrote again to Buck:

Miss W. is going to New Zealand this month – her lungs are affected I hear & there has been a miserable time for me since I came home.

Helen's health improved in New Zealand and she married an Auckland banker in 1890. Outliving both her husband and their daughter, who also succumbed to TB, Helen died in 1927.

*

Caroline Alice Elgar, née Roberts.
"To say that she was the greatest influence on his life is no exaggeration, for no other interpretation is possible." (Kennedy)

Her features tended more to character than to conventional beauty: a high forehead, china-blue eyes under arched brows, a prominent nose, and trim lips were set off with abundant light-brown hair swept up and

plaited in the fashion of the day.
[Jerrold Northrop Moore on Alice Elgar at the time of
her marriage]

The care of a genius is enough of a life work for any
woman.
[Alice Elgar – diary entry 1914]

In my time of outer gloom
Thou did'st come, a tender lure
Thou, when life was but a tomb,
Beamedst pure.
[From the poem *Love*, written by Elgar for Alice on his
fiftieth birthday]

Undoubtedly Caroline Alice Elgar was her husband's most important muse. She was his bedrock for the entire twenty-one
years of their married life together. One of the most moving of
the many tributes Elgar paid to Alice after she died in his arms
in April 1920 appears in a letter written some two years later to
a friend and colleague. Looking back over his early years of
struggle, and in particular the problem of getting his cantata
Scenes from the *Saga of King Olaff* printed in 1894, he wrote:
  .. but thro' it all shines the radiant mind & soul of my
  dearest departed one: she travelled to London (I was
  grinding at the High School) & became bound for one
  hundred pounds so that my work might be printed –
  bless her! You, who like some of my work, must thank
  her for *all* of it – not me. *I* should have destroyed it all
  & joined Job's wife in the congenial task of cursing
  God.

"There's more in it than music lessons."
The daughter of a Major-general who died when she was twelve,
Caroline Alice Roberts – Alice – became a piano pupil of Elgar in
1886. She was thirty seven and he only twenty nine. One thing
led to another – as they often did between teacher and pupil.
One day the coachman who drove Alice to her lessons in Malvern
was overheard by his son to say that "there was more in it than
music lessons."

Alice was soon writing poetry inspired by what became
(almost certainly) the ever-popular *Serenade for Strings* (1888),

and also presented her Edward with a poem entitled *Love's Grace*. Elgar reciprocated with what became his *Salut d'Amour*, dedicated "à Carice" – this name being an amalgam of Caroline and Alice.

Braving family opposition – one aunt going so far as to cut Alice off from a substantial inheritance – the couple married on 8 May 1889. It was quite extraordinary bravery on her part, she being a lady of the Victorian landed gentry and he the son of a man who (as one woman was overheard to say) "kept a wretched little shop in Worcester and even tuned their pianos". Even worse, those Elgars were *Catholics* as well!

Such was Alice's belief in her husband's genius that he came before everything and everyone else in her life – not only before her own aspirations as a writer, but even also before their own daughter Carice, born on 14 August 1890. As Kennedy has pointed out, "if a rehearsal involving Elgar coincided with an event in Carice's life, such as a confirmation, the rehearsal won every time." As a result Carice – "a very beautiful little girl with flaxen hair and a roseleaf complexion" – grew up, in Kevin Allen's words, "a repressed, shy and dutifully obedient child." It seems almost as if there was an element of jealousy on Alice's part towards her daughter, making her board at The Mount nearby, and (according to Northrop Moore)

> dressing her up frumpishly in eternal brown stockings, surmounted with an outmoded lavishness certain to arouse the spite of other girls – a red plush cape, [and] a black velvet neckband with a gold cross to advertise her Catholicism to the Protestant community.

The fervour of Alice's belief in her husband – her "High Priest of Art" – burns incandescently in her letters and diary entries. "He has written his *Dream of G.* from his very *soul*," she wrote to a friend on the day Edward completed the full score (3 August 1900). Here is a snippet she wrote after the first performance of his *First Symphony*:

> Orch. & large part of audience simply rose, people *wept*.
> E. looked very *apart* and beautiful being recalled again
> & again

And another after he completed his *Second Symphony:*

> This is a day to be marked. E. finished his *Symphony*.
> It seems one of his very greatest works, vast in design
> & supremely beautiful. It really is sublime ....

And again another after he put the finishing touches to his "symphonic study" *Falstaff* at the crack of dawn on 5 August 1913:

> 'E. down at 4 a.m. – A. made him tea &c. &c. & he finished his great work *Falstaff*.

For some, including one of Elgar's closest friends August Johannes Jaeger *(Nimrod* in the *Variations* and Elgar's editor at *Novello & Co)*, Alice's worship was amusingly de trop. Writing to *"Dorabella"* (see below) after the first rehearsal in Düsseldorf of *The Dream of Gerontius* in 1901, Jaeger noted:

> As for dear Mrs E., you can imagine her state of seventh-heaven-beatitude, with eyebrow-lifting, neck twisting, forget-me-not glances towards the invisible Heavens! Don't think I am making fun of her! I am not; but you know her signs of deep emotion over the Dr's music, don't you?

For all that, Alice was far from being the submissive wife. She would crack the proverbial whip when necessary, showing a "quite ruthless determination" to keep Elgar at his desk. Once she made short shrift of his move to play with the children of their host rather than answer a sheaf of letters he had impulsively thrown on the floor:

> "Oh, Edward, that was naughty. These must be answered *at once*." With a shout of ribald laughter he took them from her and went straight back upstairs, without another word.

She "ordered his life" (writes Kennedy), "kept him at his desk, badgered his publishers and understood that she was the immovable rock in his life wherever else his fancy might roam for more poetic inspiration." Frank Schuster (a close friend of Elgar and a renowned patron of the arts) referred to her as an "indefatigable hostess and marvellous manager." Whenever Elgar was in the depths of composition, there was always a tray of food and a flask of tea outside his study. Likewise when he was in the depths of depression (most often before a new fit of creativity), Alice was always there to dig him out. However, she never took his threats of suicide too seriously.

Alice also made constructive suggestions about Elgar's compositions that he invariably adopted. Elgar recalled that in the case of the ending of the *Violin Concerto:*

I played some of the music I had written that day, and she nodded her head appreciatively, except over one passage, at which she sat up rather grimly, I thought. However, I went to bed leaving it as it was; but I got up as soon as it was light and went down to look over what I had written. I found it as I had left it, except that there was a little piece of paper, pinned over the offending bars, on which was written "All of it is beautiful and just right, except this ending. Don't you think, dear Edward, that this end is just a little. ..?" Well, Billy, I scrapped that end.
[from *Elgar As I Knew Him* by W.H. Reed]

If there was a downside for Elgar, it was probably nothing worse than her refusal to have dogs, even though he was passionately fond of them. He also accepted honours against his inclinations because they meant so much to her. (He laid his court sword beside Alice in her coffin.) And had it not been for Alice's explicit disapproval, he may well have continued with his "fun" sketches for a raunchy ballet project on Rabelais that she roundly declared was inappropriate for the composer of coronation odes and *The Apostles*. More's the pity, since for some of us Elgar is at his best when more genial and less serious!

Alice certainly pandered to Elgar's hypochondria! When they were staying with the Bantock family, Granville Bantock's daughter noted that

Elgar's wife ... surrounded her husband with a ring-fence of attention and care which was almost pathetic. The composer himself depended upon his wife to a surprising extent ... my newly-wed mother was, I am sure, awed by Mrs Elgar, with her array of rugs, shawls and cushions, extra body-belts and knitted bedsocks for Edward's comfort. One evening Helena [Bantock's wife] noted with astonishment no fewer than seven hot water bottles being filled for his bed on the occasion of Elgar's complaining of a slight chill!

Like many other couples (including those of the Victorian gentry), Elgar and Alice indulged in private baby talk. To a poem she had written before their marriage, she later scribbled:

'I spec this is to E's own souse Braut wopse' (meaning, Kennedy suggests, 'I expect this is to E's own self. Bride ?? ...').

After Alice had written Edward another poem in 1892 there was
this exchange:

> For my Beloved's booful music. Pease not beat. Will
> this do
> [Elgar]: Vessy nice

And Elgar wrote this in the margin of Alice's typescript:

> If zu smells sis, zu'll find it's not fesh! Grrh!
> Let us go hence, my songs; she will not hear.

When Alice died on 7 April 1920, Elgar was for a time paralysed
with grief, unable to face even the immediate practicalities of
the funeral. Rosa Burley, the first, most vigilant and long-
standing of his "extra-marital" muses, recalled that Elgar was

> So stunned ... by the blow, so withdrawn into himself,
> that no one at Severn House dared to approach him
> even when the undertaker had to be interviewed. I
> was in the house at the time and, realising that
> something had to be done, I went into the study and
> told him as gently as I could that he really must pull
> himself together.

*

Rosa Burley

> ... the be-all and end-all of his existence was to write
> great music.
> He would discuss with me at enormous length the
> works on which he was engaged and would sometimes
> explain with pride the ingenuity of his technical
> devices.
> [Rosa Burley in *Edward Elgar: The Record of a Friend-
> ship*]

In 1891 Rosa Burley, then aged twenty five, became headmistress
of The Mount school in Malvern where Elgar taught the violin,
and where Carice later became a boarder. Elgar clearly loathed
his duties there, later describing teaching the fiddle as "turning
a grindstone with a dislocated shoulder". The girls always had
their lesson with an elderly female "dragon" in attendance to
ensure "proprieties."

Discovering that Elgar's lessons were very unpopular with
the girls – he was often bad-tempered and spent the lessons
playing the piano to himself – Miss Burley, instead of putting
him on "special measures" or sacking him, hit on the idea of

learning the violin with him herself in an attempt to win him round and soften his approach. She also joined the Ladies' Orchestral Class that Elgar had created in Worcester.

Miss Burley soon plumbed the deeper levels of Elgar's character, recorded in her book *Edward Elgar: The Record of a Friendship*:

> His shyness masked the kind of intense pride with which an unhappy man attempts to console himself for feelings of frustration and disappointment ... He seemed to me to be a man whose emotional reactions were out of all proportion to the stimulating causes. It was thus very difficult to be at ease with him since he was so manifestly ill at ease with himself.'

More than that, he was

> one of the most repressed people possible to imagine ... enclosed, as it were, by a haunting fear of innumerable disapprovals.

Although he spoke with a noticeable Worcestershire brogue, Elgar was fanatically determined to project, by his mode of dress, the image of the military man, country gentleman or middle-class professional. (There is a marvellous photograph of him in plus fours and full country garb launching a huge kite on a heath.) Whenever possible he avoided being seen carrying his violin case!

Rosa Burley also spotted Elgar's resentment of his religion – or at least of the work opportunities that being a Catholic denied him. Combined with his sense of social inferiority as the son of a shopkeeper, "he felt himself branded as something very like a social pariah." Even marrying so far up the social ladder "was disastrous for Elgar's psyche." He was in a double-bind: although he longed to be accepted by the county set, he despised their barbaric indifference to the arts. All this insecurity betrayed itself in "rudeness, snobbery, and insensitivity to others."

Very much Elgar's muse during his composition of the *Enigma Variations,* Rosa mentioned that he seemed to enjoy composing them more than any of his previous commissioned works. She heard the theme and the first two variations when Elgar visited The Mount in October 1898. As he completed more variations he invited her to identify which of his friends they represented. It is possible that Rosa herself inspired the "extremely intimate and personal feelings" of the thirteenth *Romanza* variation, above which there are asterisks rather than initials. But against this must be set evidence that Elgar intended the variation to represent a certain Lady Mary Lygon, together with Rosa's own remark that "I'm not a variation; I'm the theme". In other words she was the woman who sparked off the entire composition. Well she might have been, for she had ever been eager to help Elgar with his creative plans. When he had been working on Longfellow's *King Olaff* in 1895, for instance, she had "spent a fortnight of my holidays in the British Museum" reading up on the "Longfellow movement". And she recalled that when Elgar was composing *Gerontius* in 1900,

> we talked of little else on our walks and Edward seemed to think of nothing else. Again and again manuscript fragments would be brought to The Mount on the lesson days, tried over and discussed.

Interestingly, however, Elgar never dedicated any piece of music to Rosa.

Trouble a' t' Mill

Their friendship dwindled when the Elgars moved in 1904 from their home in Malvern, Craeg Lea, to Plâs Gwyn (White House) in Hereford. But one letter Elgar later sent to Rosa, in July 1906, particularly reveals his continuing deep affection for her. By then Rosa was teaching in Portugal, having closed The Mount after crises which included an embarrassing series of epidemics, allegedly originating in the school kitchen supervised by her mother. Elgar is deeply missing their cycling expeditions to places like Upton, Tewkesbury, Hereford, the Vale of Evesham, Birtsomorton, and the pretty villages on the west side of the Malvern Hills:

> [17 July 1906]
> My work [*The Kingdom*] nears completion & will send it to you as soon as it is ready. I can get about again but have not cycled yet. *I have no one to cycle with.* The world seems very old to me now and all [so] changed ... I seem *tired* — oh! so tired. Everything is senseless. I was away when your trying time at Malvern came & it is a grief to me to know that I was unable to do anything ... You know I wish you everything good now & always. ...

Rosa returned from Portugal in 1911 and made her home in London. When in that same year Elgar took her to see his prospective new home in the capital, Severn House, he told her that

> he never conducted his music without finding that his mind had slipped to summer days on the Malvern Hills, to Birchwood, or to the drowsy peace of Longdon Marsh.

Was it something I said?

After Alice's death Elgar cut Rosa off, and pointedly ignored her at festivals. It seems that Rosa had given Elgar the impression, intended or not, that "she herself now stood as Carice's mother and would take over the running of the household".

Out of the blue Elgar sent Rosa a Christmas card "from Edward" in 1932, two years before his death. Rosa could never understand what had led Elgar to renew the contact unless it was a wish "to recapture some of the youthful urge to composition of past years."

> As he had resolutely cut me off for many years and as even our years of friendship had brought me a good deal of pain, I was careful in writing a letter of thanks to indicate as gently as possible that I did not wish to resume our past friendship.

*

Dora Penny, later Mrs Richard C. Powell: the Dorabella of the *Tenth Variation* "the grace of youth and a stammer in her speech".

> *The Variations* are finished and yours is the most cheerful ... I have orchestrated you well.'
> [Elgar to Dorabella, February 1899]

> My mind was in such a whirl of pleasure, pride, and almost shame that he should have written anything so lovely about *me*.
> [Dora Penny: *Edward Elgar: Memories of a Variation*]

Dorabella was Dora Penny, the attractive daughter of the Rector of Wolverhampton, Albert Penny. In her book *Edward Elgar: Memories of a Variation* (first published in 1937), she recalls how she first met Elgar at the rectory in 1895 when she was twenty-one:

> ... He came into the drawing-room before luncheon: 'Hullo, there's the black piano! Let's see how its inside has stood the move. Although I had not left school very long I had heard a number of good pianists, but I had never heard anything quite like this. He didn't play like a pianist, he almost seemed to play like a whole orchestra. ...
>
> After luncheon that first day we all went to the drawing-room for coffee and he took hold of a high-backed wooden chair to bring it forward-and its back came off.
>
> 'Here's another old friend and its back still comes off. Why don't you mend it?'
>
> I said it was a job which got put off to another day.
>
> 'Well, this is the day. Got any tools?' So, after coffee, bearing with us the chair, we departed to my sitting-room and started on it.
>
> 'Now clearly understand,' he said, 'if this is a success *I* mended it; if it's a failure *you* did it.'
>
> That, I think, sealed our friendship.

Dora's book contains a cornucopia of memories of Elgar through the course of their twenty year friendship before he so abruptly ended it. Among many other things she recalls:

- How he gripped people's arms so that they were black and blue with bruises the next day.

- How on impulse she improvised dancing steps for him as he was composing a number in *Lux Christi*.

- How he first referred to her as his "Sweet Dorabella" (in 1898).

- How they sat in a wood and watched the birds come closer and closer to "talk" to them.

- How he conducted at lunch with a carving knife.

- How she found him a bible passage which was just what he needed for his current oratorio *The Apostles*.

- How when she was once staying at Plâs Gwyn he was in "a composing fit", locking himself in his study until 1.30 am, when they all had a "grand meal". And how on this same night he complimented her on her "charming frock", instructing her never to wear one that was "dingy" or "smoky".

- How he would grunt rather than sing when he was reading through his work at the piano ...

And so much more!

Elgar took his playful nickname for Dora from Dorabella in Mozart's *Così fan Tutte*. Dora's stepmother was the sister of "W.M.B." (William Meath Baker) dedicatee of the fourth variation.

Dora recalled how she first heard sections of the *Enigma Variations* at Birchwood (then the Elgars' Malvern home). After hearing her own variation, "she was overcome by many emotions" and sat down:

'Well, how do you like *that* – hey?'

I murmured something about its being charming and rather like a butterfly, but I could think of nothing sensible to say. ... I had been as much the victim of E. E.'s impish humour as had R. B. T. ... My mind was in such a whirl of pleasure, pride, and almost shame that he should have written anything so lovely about me.

The ever readable journalist Martin Kettle presented his version (inspired by Dora's memoir) of how Elgar shared the creation of his best known tune with Dorabella one May morning in 1901:

... Edward Elgar, aged 44 and at the height of his creative powers, is seated at his piano in the study at his house in Malvern Wells. Hearing his friend Dora Penny arriving downstairs for a visit, the composer calls down to her, "Child, come up here. I've got a tune that will knock 'em — knock 'em flat." Penny goes upstairs as bidden, and Elgar plays her the tune that would become known throughout the country as *Land of Hope and Glory*

It's a lovely story, but what makes it special is less the music itself than Elgar's unrestrained excitement about his new tune ... he just knows, without needing anyone to reassure him, that this time he has hit the bull's-eye. ... Later, he was to call it "a tune that comes once in a lifetime".

[*The Guardian*, 20 September 2001]

Dora, like Rosa Burley, was suddenly and inexplicably all but wiped out of Elgar's life. When in 1912 she innocently suggested that *Auld Lang Syne* was "the hidden theme" in the *Enigma Variations* that was that! She had touched a ridiculously raw nerve.

*

Elgar's Goddess: Alice Stuart-Wortley (1862-1936)
"Windflower" "soul" and "stepmother"
of the *Violin Concerto*

I would write a sonnet to you but it would not rhyme &
if it did, it would not be good enough for you otherwise.
[Elgar to Alice Stuart-Wortley, 21 December 1909]

you will be conducting the concerto wherever you are.
[Elgar to Alice in 1910]
… you've had her a thousand times in your head.
[Jaeger to Elgar in David Pownall's play, *Rondo*]

On the available evidence Alice Stuart-Wortley was surely the muse Elgar most adored and revered during the time of his marriage to his own Alice. Alice Stuart-Wortley was the daughter of the British painter Sir John Everett Millais, a co-founder of the Pre-Raphaelite Brotherhood, President of the Royal Academy, and creator of such well-known masterpieces as *Christ in the Carpenter's Shop,* and *Order of Release.* In Millais's painting of his daughter, Alice looks the embodiment of Pre-Raphaelite womanhood, refined, ethereal and otherworldly. She was also a good pianist and lover of the countryside and it is easy to see why she so much appealed to the mystic and visionary in Elgar. If, as David Pownall suggests in his play *Rondo*, Elgar "had" Alice "a thousand times" in his head, there is no evidence whatsoever that he ever tried to turn fantasy into reality.

Alice was the second wife of Charles Stuart-Wortley (Lord Stuart of Wortley from 1916), Conservative M.P. for many years for the Hallam district of Sheffield. Elgar gave him some sketches of the *Violin Concerto,* whilst Alice Elgar wrote many affectionate letters to "my dearest namesake".

Elgar frequently mentions in his letters to Alice "our own concerto", and also refers to "your symphony" (the *Second*). Just how much he needed her emotional support while composing the *Concerto* is clear in these snippets from letters he wrote her in April 1910:

I am not sure about that Andante & shall put it away
for a long time before I decide its fate. I am glad you
liked it.

I am now ablaze with work & *writing hard*; you *should*
come & see (& hear it!)

I have been working hard at the windflower themes -
but all stands still until you come and approve!'

Before the first performance in November, referring to a
spare ticket, Elgar wrote to Alice:

I wish I could use it and you might conduct – but you
will be conducting the concerto wherever you are.

And soon after a rehearsal for the second performance that
same year he wrote:

'The concerto at 9 a.m. in the dark was divine – all
seats empty but a spirit hovering in Block A.'

The most conclusive evidence Kennedy provides, if any
more is needed, for Alice being the soul of the work was found on
a sheet of Alice's notepaper: the Spanish quotation, written in
Elgar's hand, which heads the score of the actual work. Dated
22 September 1910 the note reads:

Aquí está encerrada el alma de ..... (Here is enshrined
the soul of .....')

The five dots must stand either for Alice or for her initials A. S.
C. S.-W.

Elgar shared his bleakest moods with Alice – ever an
indication of deep friendship. When he had completed the
orchestration of his *Second Symphony* in August 1912 he wrote

... the end of my work is as dreary as that awful day
when I finished the composition & perished with cold
on the Heath. I cannot live much longer in this weather
& loneliness.

Elgar and his wife were frequent visitors to the Stuart-
Wortleys' home on Cheyne Walk, Chelsea, where Elgar loved his
other Alice to play through many of his works to him:

I love to hear you play [he wrote in 1911]. ... I do not
like piano solo players' playing but I love yours — you
will understand the difference. I am not going to praise
you now because you are quite vain enough! but you

must play when I ask & I would not think of asking
you to play to ordinary people who wd. not understand
what poetical playing really is.

At Christmas 1914 Elgar sent Alice something she must
have treasured immeasurably:

I cannot buy you pearls of untold worth ... so I send
you a little scrap of my old, old lonely life in which no
one shared; I had my dreams &, I suppose, ambitions
& I send you one of the little school-books which
lightened my entire loneliness.

Equally touching is a letter Elgar wrote to Alice on 27 April
1916, after she had been unable to attend an evening of private
music-making at Severn House (Elgar's London home from 1911)

'The things sounded lovely & the room is divine for a
small orchestra – only the goddess of the feast was not
there. ... they all thought it was nothing without you
& so did I.

(Reed was W. H or "Billy" Reed, Elgar's longtime friend,
leader of the London Symphony Orchestra and of
practically everything Elgar ever conducted.)

When Charles Stuart-Wortley was notified of his elevation
to a peerage in December 1916, and Alice became Lady Alice
designate, Elgar reminded her of the humble "coronet" he had
given her (the *Violin Concerto):*

My dear Windflower:
I am out of bed for the first time since Saturday & I
use the first minute to send you love & congratulation
on the event,– I gave you a coronet long ago – the best
I had but you may have forgotten it – now you will
have a real one, bless you!
I cannot tell you how glad I am – I expected it - wanted
it for you long ago & now it's come I feel afraid of you
& wonder in a vague sort of way what will be the
difference? But you are still the Windflower I think &
hope. ...
Bless you,
Your EE
[P.S.] I wonder what the new name will be – this may
be the last time I address you in the old familiar way.

Lady Alice encouraged Elgar to write a piano concerto, after
Elgar sent her a fragment of it and instructed her to practise it.
In February 1917 he wrote:

Where are you? I wanted to tell you that the theme
and every note must be approved by you (bless you!)
before anything can be done. Oh! why are you so far
away and so difficult to get at??

Two letters from 1918 show him overjoyed at the prospect
of a visit from her to his Sussex cottage, Brinkwells:

[12 May]
I rise about seven, work till 8.15 – then dress, breakfast
– pipe (I *smoke* again all day!) work till 12.30 lunch
(pipe) – rest an hour – work till tea (pipe) – then work
till 7-30 – change, dinner at 8.00. Bed at 10.00 –
everyday practically goes thus. ...We go lovely walks.
... I am looking forward to your coming with
acute joy: it really is lovely here – food good & plentiful
– *much beer!* – but do not mention it.

And a few days later:
I have been down the wood & told [the bluebells] you
are coming & asked them to remain for your loved
visit. ...You need bring very little of anything but if
quite convenient some dry biscuits *might* be a joy ...
but the thing is to bring yourself & rest: there will be
a full moon & all lovely & nightingales.

Perhaps his most loving and romantic-ever message to her
was not in words but music. When he heard by telegram that
Alice had broken her leg in August 1918, Elgar immediately sent
her an expansive melody of more than fifty bars – marked
dolcissimo or very sweetly. The theme became the central section
of the *Romance* in his *Violin Sonata*.

The intimacy between composer and muse did not long
survive Alice Elgar's death on April 1920. In July and August of
this same year he was inevitably felled by his bereavement,
writing to Alice

Music I loathe – I did get out some paper – but it's all
dead.
... the fields are as bare as my mind & soul.

Two years later, on 9 June 1922, he was still feeling deeply
sorry for himself:

I have *seen* no one, *no one* has written or taken the
slightest notice & I have read nothing & seen no papers:
truly I am a lonely person if I liked to think so; – but

my 'friends'! ! ! where, oh, where! are they? Silence
profound. …

Most of the remaining letters lack the closeness of former
years. Lord Stuart of Wortley died in November 1926. Elgar's
last letter to Alice (at least of those quoted in Northrop) is dated
14 December 1927 from Battenhall Manor – a residence he was
occupying on a short-term lease in Worcester:

> I wish I could have given you a Christmas here – it is a
> real Yule-loggy house & you wd have met, in spirit,
> Oliver Cromwell, Charles I & II & a lot of agreeable
> restoration ghosts.

Elgar had retreated into sullen bachelorhood, and would
remain there until he set eyes on his last and perhaps most
adoring muse, Vera Hockman, in 1931.

*

My darling Tenth Muse
Jelly d'Aranyi (c.1921)

Elgar's "renowned susceptibility" to young women and his reputation for being a "naughty old man" were nowhere more evident
than in the unwanted attentions he briefly inflicted in about
1921 on the very attractive Hungarian violinist Jelly d'Aranyi.
She had delighted him with a performance of his *Violin Sonata*
at the Wigmore Hall in May 1919, and then played it again in
1920 at Severn House in a private recital for Lady Elgar. Soon
afterwards Elgar – by then widowed – developed a "violent
affection" for d'Aranyi and addressed her as "My darling Tenth
Muse." After taking her out to lunch in Pall Mall, he invited her
back to Severn House. Not to see his etchings, but rather to give
her a book he wanted her to have. All we know is that within the
four walls of Severn House

> a little scene took place which ended in Jelly ensconced
> in a taxi 'cursing old men'.

All this according to Joseph Macleod in his biography *The Sisters
d'Aranyi*.

*

Age-gap romance
Vera Hockman (1897-1963)
"Hyperion" and "Sweetness"

.. earth mother as well as white goddess ..
[Kevin Allen]
.. my mother, my child, my lover and my friend.
[Elgar to Vera Hockman]

Where both deliberate, the love is slight:
Who ever loved, that loved not at first sight?
From *Hero and Leander* by Marlowe
[Lines underlined by Elgar in Vera's copy of *Pageant of English Poetry*.]

*

Exactly what led one of Elgar's servants at Marl Bank to call their widowed master "a naughty old man" is not known. (Marl Bank was Elgar's final and spacious home on Rainbow Hill in Worcester.) From late 1931 the composer's most frequent "lady friend" visitor was undoubtedly Vera Hockman, forty years his junior, and it may be that the good-humoured gossip referred to her. However innocent or otherwise the relationship, "naughty" is precisely the complexion that cooks, maids and gardeners would put on any man in his mid seventies entertaining regularly a young separated dark-eyed Jewish lady in her early thirties.

The research on this relationship carried out so meticulously and sympathetically by Kevin Allen in his recent book *Elgar in Love* leaves no doubt that it was in no way exploitative on either side. Many age-gap romances are, of course, often just that. Professional violinists in Vera Hockman's position might well exploit the infatuation of a great composer to further their careers, while the man in the case would exploit the young woman's need, and perhaps adulation, to revive his libido and boost his ego.

Age gap romance, of course, is as old as history, and not only in the music world where we have already explored many examples. Outside of classical music there is (at the time of writing) Lucien Freud at 79 living with 27 year old Emily Bearn. (She "gradually fell under his spell" while posing for him and they have now set up home together.) Then there's Rod Stewart and twenty-two year old Rachel Hunter, Chris Evans (35) and Billie Piper (18), Paul McCartney (60) and Heather Mills (31, and younger than one of his daughters), Michael Douglas (56) and Catherine Zeta Jones (31), Rupert Murdoch (70) and Wendy Deng (32), Eric Clapton (56) and Melia McEnery (25), the tenth Earl of Shaftesbury (63) and the lingerie model Nathalie Lions (27), Norman Mailer (79) and his sixth wife Norris (51) ...

"Shut up, you fool!"

Elgar had been desperately lonely since the death of Alice. With no muse throughout the 1920s to ignite his creative fires he wrote little of lasting interest: orchestrations of Bach and Handel, potboilers, incidental music, part songs, a *Civic Fanfare*, and a few other odds and ends. Looking as always like a retired general, white-haired, moustached and very erect, he settled into the life of a lonely, sad and all-too-often grumpy bachelor. Sometimes a downright rude one, too, as when in Harlech in 1924 he told a local worthy speechifying too long before a performance of *The Apostles* to "Shut up you fool."

He amused himself with reading voraciously (as always), writing letters to the *Times Literary Supplement*, having fun with his microscope, horseracing, walking the dogs, buying new cars, listening to records, talking to actors at his club, going to the cinema and theatre – and pursuing an unlikely but firm friendship with George Bernard Shaw.

Eventually some fine tunes began to surface again. In 1929 came *Pomp and Circumstance No. 5* (one of the best of the set). Then in 1930 came the much-loved *Nursery Suite*. But in 1931 came the conducting engagement that would lift the rest of his life as close as he perhaps ever came to paradise.

It was to conduct an all-Elgar concert at the Triennial Croydon Festival in November 1931. The Croydon Philharmonic Society then sported one of the finest choirs in the country, its orchestra led by Billy Reed.

The programme consisted of two Elgar oratorios, *The Light of Life* and *The Dream of Gerontius*. Vera Hockman was playing almost under Elgar's nose on the second desk of first violins. Although a competent semi-professional violinist, she had no need to earn a living at fiddling, her father (who died when she was twelve) having been one of London's leading diamond merchants. At age nineteen she had married a successful, much older man, Joseph Hockman, by turns a Rabbi, barrister, legal adviser to the King of Siam and barrister again. The Hockmans had two children, John and Dulcie, of whom Elgar would become very fond. However, the marriage soon began to founder, and the couple separated permanently in the late twenties – Joseph, nevertheless, never giving up hope of a reconciliation.

It seems reasonable to suppose that the loss of her father at age twelve drove Vera instinctively towards father figures: first her husband, then Elgar, and perhaps also (judging only by a photograph in Allen's book) the bassist Don Cheeseman, who became her "common-law husband." Vera also developed a close friendship with "Uncle Ralph" Vaughan Williams, some twenty-five years her senior.

"The Story of November 7, 1931"
"(Written on EE's Italian (Florentine) notepaper)"

Snippets from Vera Hockman's own account of her meeting with Elgar, together with Allen's commentary, reveal more about this intensely soulful, mutual adoration society than any amount of comment from me – other than to note the extraordinary frequency of Vera's deification of Elgar as Him with a capital H.

At the first rehearsal on Saturday 7 November, Vera noted that

> No sooner were we all assembled than He came. My heart stood still. ...

Elgar took up his baton announcing "in his quiet vibrant tones" that they would begin with the *Meditation* from *The Light of Life*:

> From that moment I hardly seemed to have looked at the music, my music and soul went out to him because his way was not to command the orchestra but to implore of them to give all the fire and energy and poetry that was in them. You could feel the love and veneration like great clouds of incense enveloping him.

"Trembling limbs"

After the rehearsal she approached Elgar "with trembling limbs," he having asked for an introduction to her because, he told her, "I could see by your face that you understand my music." "I hope I do," was all she could say, "hopelessly intoxicated (& blind to the world) for the rest of the evening."

They next saw each other at the soloists' rehearsal on the day of the concert when

> He knew that I understood the music and I understood that He knew.

After the concert, which lifted her onto a "celestial plain", they met at a party at Billy Reed's house, during which Elgar ordered her "not to leave me for one moment or I shall scream." The evening ended with Elgar mooting the prospect of further meetings, both in London and also at the Shirley Park Hotel where Vera and her children were staying. (She was having a house built, Robin Hill, in a nearby pine wood.)

From this moment onwards Elgar became her "Hyperion" (a Titan in Greek mythology) or sometimes "My Wondrous Being."

Elgar followed up the suggestion with letters, a signed photograph ("In remembrance Croydon Festival") and an autographed miniature score of his *String Quartet*. They finally met for lunch at the Langham Hotel on 26 November, when "their previous rapport flourished again." They lunched together again the following day. Ten days later, following a further phone call, she dropped everything she had planned for the day to lunch with Elgar a third time. "I was absolutely ill with apprehension for fear I should disappoint him," she wrote,

> ... I cannot remember the train journey or the taxi journey ... I wore a simple coat frock of reddish woolly material with gilt buttons (which he noticed immediately by asking whether they were bought with the frock or separately!!!)

The friendship was now firmly established. She expressed her "overwhelming joy" to be meeting him again and he confessed that never before had he asked for an introduction "to any lady in the orchestra."

They discussed literature, of which his knowledge was "stupendous." He would "gaze and gaze into my eyes and murmur portentously:

> Millions and millions of years. I can read it all there. Aren't you divine? What music would I write if I could have you near me always."

It would never be for always, but from now on they were very often together. Vera "knew henceforth and for ever more that we somehow miraculously understood one another."

"My Sonata-Our Sonata"

Vera made her first visit, with her violin, to Marl Bank in Worcester on 2 December "for an afternoon of conversation, dogs (Marco a spaniel and Mina a cair) and music." During the afternoon, in which he displayed "such a gorgeous medley of Michaelangelesque grand faults & virtues," he christened his violin sonata as they worked on it *My Sonata-Our Sonata*. He was "delirious with joy" over the *Romance* (the slow movement), exclaiming

> Oh this is such a *lonely* passage – I nearly always cry when I hear it, but I am not lonely today — we are together – I am so happy.

Elgar's niece Madge joined them with the dogs for tea, the dogs hogging the armchair and the couch, and getting most of the cake. They then played through the *Sonata* to Madge (the *Romance* twice), and it was time to catch the train back to London.

At their next meeting on 7 December – their "most romantic and intimate meeting so far," in Vera's aunt's house – Elgar gave Vera an intimate present: a copy of Longfellow's prose romance *Hyperion.*

At the first "mensiversary" of their meeting, again at Vera's aunt's house (December 7), the famous, often quoted exchange took place

> "With you that most perfect three fold relationship is possible – so rare on earth. Guardian – Child – Lover."
> "And friend as well," I added.

After this they sat "side by side on the couch in the half light gazing into the fire and sometimes into each other's eyes ..." It was also at this time that he spoke to her of his late "dear little wife" and of his daughter Carice. Having married a farmer Sam Blake in 1922 (none too happily, but stoically), Carice would soon welcome Vera's friendship with her father.

The lovers' friendship was sealed for life: in Allen's words "she would often be where Elgar was, not only his human spark to start a flame, but before everything a friend."

From now on also they introduced each other to their close family, friends and relations. In particular, Elgar was enchanted by Vera's young daughter Dulcie (taking infinite pains to write her a "joke score"), and Vera warmed to Carice. Vera also met the widow, Adela, of Elgar's former friend Frank Schuster.

Vera's own account of the romance ends shortly after the apocalyptic "mensiversary", with two letters to her from Elgar a few days later. Enclosed with the second on 11 December, was the original manuscript score of "their" sonata, Elgar penning against his signature a characteristically cryptic message. He also included all the preliminary sketches for the *Sonata,* dismissing them as "waste paper."

"V.H.'s own theme"

Near the end of her story Vera had summed up her role as that of "bringing divine happiness into the life of a giant." Her success in doing so was incalculable, as was her role in gently persuading her "giant" to take up three projects long shelved: the *Piano Concerto*, an opera *The Spanish Lady,* the third part of the projected *Apostles* trilogy, – and also the *Third Symphony.*

Nothing came of the opera, trilogy and concerto, but Bernard Shaw persuaded the BBC to commission a *Third Symphony.* That Vera was at the heart of this work is incontestable from Elgar's marking over the second subject of the first movement: "V.H.'s own theme." It is one of those "Windflowerish themes" (in Michael Kennedy's words) "cantabile, tender, yearning, passionate." At New Year 1933 Elgar sent Vera his first sketches of the opening bars of the first movement with the note

> First thought for Sym III and last thought for V.H.
> Jany. 1933 E.E. Or rather, 31st Decr 1932.

In a further undated letter he sent her a page of sketches including ten bars of the second subject of the First movement with the ominous note

> 1st sketch of VH's own theme above. Will never be finished.

Elgar died without sorting out the material into a coherent structure, but left enough to enable Anthony Payne to construct a version of the symphony as he imagined Elgar might have written it. Payne's realisation was premiered at the London Proms in 1998.

"A source of comment"

Part of Elgar's new lease of life included, in May 1933, a flight from Croydon airport to France to meet Delius, bedridden, in his home at Grez-sur-Loing. When he returned, Vera stayed away from the cameras at his airport reception because she had been "gently warned that her relationship with Elgar was beginning to be a source of comment." Little of her relationship with Elgar in the last months of his life is known because neither she nor Carice kept records.

An exploratory operation on Elgar in October 1933 – he had been suffering from sciatica and lumbago – revealed advanced cancer. Billy Reed promised Elgar that regarding the

Third Symphony, "no one would ever tamper with it in any way." One of Elgar's last jobs was to direct by land line from Marl Bank a recording of *Caractacus* in early January. He died on 23 February 1934 and was buried beside his beloved Alice.

Coda
"Did they have sex?"

> Today the questions that many would ask are 'Did they go to bed together?', 'Did they have sex?' (The latter such an unromantic description of making love!)
> [Michael Kennedy]

The most fascinating aspect of this question is that it is unanswerable. The large suitcase-full of letters Elgar sent Vera was burned after her death in 1963 by Don Cheeseman. On her deathbed, Vera had entrusted the fate of the letters to her partner's judgement, and Cheeseman decided to remove them for ever from the attentions of prurient biographers ...

However, the transition in Elgar's letters from "Dear Mrs Hockman" to "Sweetest and Dearest" may suggest a bedroom dimension. Purely co-lateral evidence is Elgar's known habit of pushing his luck in transient encounters. If he tried it on with Jelly d'Aranyi after so short a time, he is hardly likely not to have made advances in such an intense relationship as that with Vera.

***

Chapter 10

Gustav Mahler
"martyr to music" and "obsessional neurotic"
Born: Kalischt, Bohemia, 7 July 1860
Died age 50: Vienna, 18 May 1911

I keep on stumbling from one idiocy into another.
[Mahler on his early love life to his friend Fritz Löhr,
28 November 1885]

The touch of his hand deep inside me. – I shall never
forget it … I want to kneel down in front of him and
kiss his naked belly – kiss everything, everything!
Amen!
[Alma Mahler on her pre-marital lover, "Alex" Zemlinsky, the composer]

… in the early stages of our intimacy I found his body
odour offensive.
[Alma Mahler on her courtship with Mahler]

When will the hour arrive where you will be lying
completely naked against my body…? I know I live for
nothing but the time when I will belong to you entirely.
[Alma Mahler to Walter Gropius during their affair,
September 1910]

Everything [about Mahler] confirmed and strength-
ened the impression of demoniac obsession.
[Bruno Walter, Mahler's assistant at the Vienna
Hofoper]

*

Mahler's music, like that of Berlioz, is autobiographical to the
very core. Mahler himself told his young friend Ludwig Schieder-
mair in 1901 that his *First Symphony* had "not yet been grasped
by anyone who has not lived with me." And to his hopelessly
adoring, self-appointed chronicler Natalie Bauer-Lechner he said
(in the summer of 1893):

My [first] two symphonies contain the inner aspect of
my whole life; I have written into them everything
that I have experienced and endured – Truth and Poetry

in music. To understand these works properly would
be to see my life transparently revealed in them.

None of this is surprising in such a renowned egomaniac.
Mahler is surely the supreme egocentric and obsessional neurotic
of all the many men similarly cast in this volume. (Egocentricity
and high creativity seem to be inseparable.) Mahler took both
life and himself with deadly seriousness. So deadly, indeed, that
each of his symphonies (according to the psychoanalyst and
Freudian disciple Theodor Reik) was a new attempt "to answer
the same burning question about life and death, about the
meaning of life and the destiny of man."

Mahler realised all too correctly that his works would be
largely misunderstood before his death, though he had no doubts
at all about his assured future place in the pantheon of the great
composers. "Need one still be around when one becomes
immortal?" was how he put it to Natalie in the 1890s. The full
spate of Mahler mania would not overwhelm large parts of the
Western world for another sixty years and more.

*

Predictably, all Mahler's pre-marital romances and affairs
before his marriage to Alma Schindler in 1902 were agonised,
and they saturated his music. Two were unquestionably very
passionate, and Mahler was certainly not the virgin his wife
claimed him to be (in her memoirs) when they married. Once
married, however, he put music a long way before love and sex
in his scheme of things. Several writers on the composer agree
with Edward Seckerson's view that Mahler's sexual drive, "was
never very strong and that he sublimated almost exclusively
through his creative pursuits."

Immaculate conceptions

In Mahler's fraught, intense but short marriage of nine years,
there can be no question that in spite of her crucial part as muse
and mother figure in his life, Alma Mahler – extremely beautiful,
dark-haired, musically talented, and younger than her husband
by nineteen years – was increasingly and fatally neglected in
the bedroom. Long after her husband's death she complained to
Mahler's most renowned biographer Henry-Louis de La Grange
that her husband had been a "puritan" and that sex had played
only a very small part of his life. On one occasion she even told
La Grange that "her children were immaculately conceived."

To be fair, Mahler was not a complete puritan. We know from La Grange, for instance, that he approved of such lurid and voyeuristic dramas as *Frühlingserwachen* (Spring Awakening, 1891) by the then daring dramatist Frank Wedekind (1864-1919). The play includes a pregnant fourteen-year old girl, a young boy who commits suicide, and another who is seen masturbating in front of an engraving of Venus which he subsequently throws down the toilet!

*

"Mutterbindung", "Holy Mary complex"...
Early impressions never fade ... We carry our past within us; all our lives we still smell of our nurse's milk.
[Flaubert]

Mahler appears to have been mother-fixated, harbouring what Freud termed a "Holy Mary complex" after informally psycho-analysing the composer in August 1910 in Leiden. "Throughout his childhood," writes La Grange,

Mahler's love and affection for his mother never wavered, and if by chance he was momentarily unkind or brusque ... he always blamed himself afterward for adding yet another sorrow to all those that filled her life. ...

Perhaps it was his mother's lameness that caused him to develop in sympathy a lifelong peculiar gait – variously described as a "jerking foot," "arrhythmic limp," or "nervous tic" that caused him to change pace every three or four steps. A fellow musician described his step as "like a man walking with one foot in the gutter."

Natalie Bauer-Lechner tells another story of Mahler's devotion to mother:

Gustav told me that when his mother had a headache, as a small boy of three or four, he would hide behind her bed and pray that she would soon recover. Then he would go and ask whether she felt better now. And when she said she was, in order to please him, he would eagerly go straight back to playing.

Mahler's mother Marie clearly returned his love with interest. Here is a glimpse of the fondly-fussing mother before his arrival home from Vienna for Christmas in 1882 (he was then 22):

170

... you need not bring [home[]] any luggage, of course. If need be I will help you out with laundry, though if you have any torn socks or shirts you can bring them with you in the coach in your travelling bag ... Are you going to end up changing your lodgings every time you change your linen? And won't you finally find yourself without any linen or clothes? I know you: you will forget something in each place – and will go on moving until you have nothing left. Am I right?...

As to his father Bernhard Mahler, Gustav never spoke affectionately of him. Mahler senior owned a thriving tavern in Iglau (now renamed Jihlava) just inside Moravia, which is now part of the East Czech Republic. Bernhard Mahler was also a successful "manufacturer of liqueurs, rum, rosolio, punch, essences and vinegar." He had certainly pulled himself up by his bootstraps, since Gustav had been born in a miserable peasant hut (in Kalischt) in which "the windows did not even have glass."

In his domestic life, however, Bernard Mahler was distinctly less impressive. Not only did he rough his wife up from time to time. He also humiliated her by his lecherous pursuit of his servant girls.

Whether or not he was aware of his father's philandering, young Gustav certainly experienced a traumatic introduction to the facts of life at the age of eleven whilst lodging for a short time in miserable circumstances with a family (the Grünfelds) in Prague. One day Gustav entered a darkened room and stumbled across nineteen year old Alfred Grünfeld in the throes of passion with a servant girl. Mistakenly thinking the young woman needed help, Gustav was traumatised after discovering that, on the contrary, the couple were angry at being disturbed and swore the young lad to secrecy. The incident clearly lay embedded in Gustav's memory, since he related it to Alma many years later.

Gustav's childhood seems generally to have been a sad one, though relieved by many thrilling musical moments. As a wunderkind, he was able to play impressively by ear from age three on the concertina, and composed a polka and funeral march at age six. He also revelled in the music of the local village bands. Their Bohemian folk strains (what he called "the tootling of the Bohemian pipers") and oom-pah-pahs would repeatedly find their way decades later into his gigantic symphonies, along with gypsy,

Jewish and tavern songs. Likewise, much folk or folk-derived poetry – especially the treasure house *Des Knaben Wunderhorn* – would form the basis of his song settings.

Bernard Mahler was certainly not all bad as a father to Gustav, the second of the Mahlers' fourteen children, of whom only seven survived. Mahler senior seems to have nursed cultural aspirations and certainly did all he could – within the limits of the many other mouths he had to feed – to foster Gustav's musical and general education. In the family's street corner apartment above the tavern, Mahler was encouraged to make full use of the piano provided by his maternal grandfather, and also of the many books that clearly fuelled his vivid imagination.

At age six Gustav was sent to a good local music teacher Heinrich Fischer, (the musical director of the local St Jakob's Church) and later to the Vienna Conservatoire (1875). Bernhard had been persuaded that Gustav, his eldest surviving son, was destined for greater things than taking over the family business. Gustav was also given the opportunity of a sound general education, mainly at the Town Gymnasium in Iglau, though he was notably lax as a young scholar, barely managing to squeak through his Gymnasium exams in the summer of 1877.

Iglau was a market town with attractive buildings, and churches topped with those remarkable onion towers. It stood in "graceful surroundings" of "wooded slopes and particular magical places" up in the Moravian Heights. Here it was that Mahler learned to love so passionately the natural world that would so frequently inspire his music. One later close friend, Fritz Löhr, described Mahler's immersion in nature as "orgiastic" whilst Natalie would later note how, for example, the cuckoo's call played such a cheerful role in his *First Symphony*; and also how the cawing of ravens crept into the last movement of his *Second Symphony* (Resurrection).

At the Vienna Conservatoire Mahler survived on a small allowance from his father supplemented by an unreliable income from a few piano pupils. Given his bruised childhood, it is not surprising that as a student he became drawn towards friends in some cases more unstable and emotionally fragile than himself. The most notable included the composers Hans Rott (1858-84) and Hugo Wolf (1860-1903), who shared in whole or part Mahler's student enthusiasms for vegetarianism, socialism, Wagner and Bruckner. Poor Hans Rott, after writing a very promising symphony in *E minor*, was committed to an asylum, where he used his manuscripts as toilet paper, declaring "That's what human works are worth." He died of tuberculosis aged twenty-six. Wolf, composer of over 300 marvellous lieder, ended his life in syphilitic convulsions at the age of forty-two.

Instability also lurked within the Mahler family. One of his younger brothers Otto (twelfth of the Mahler brood) shot himself "in a friend's apartment after a discussion of Dostoevsky with her." Another brother Alois developed marked mythomanic tendencies and delusions of grandeur, telling falsehoods galore. He claimed, for instance, to have served as a volunteer in one of the most aristocratic Austrian cavalry regiments. Calling himself Hans Christian because it sounded less Jewish, Alois wore a top hat, flowered waistcoat and white spats, contracted many debts and even issued bouncing and forged cheques. After a spell as book-keeper and office manager in a Viennese confectionery, he ended up as a baker in Chicago and died between 1920 and 1930.

By contrast Mahler's favourite sister Justine (eight years his junior) seems to have been level-headed and became his closest and rather possessive confidante. From 1894 until his marriage in 1902 she lived with him (first in Hamburg, then in Vienna) and managed his household affairs.

*

"... a Jew who believed in Christ"

Mahler's Jewishness caused him a great deal of suffering. Bernhard Mahler was undoubtedly a practising (though clearly hypocritical) Jew who in 1878 was elected to the Iglau Jewish community's education board. At the correct time after his birth, Gustav was probably circumcised, and then at age thirteen put through the ritual bar-mitzvah ceremony.

Gustav gradually shed his Jewish orthodoxy. He probably dropped his attendance at synagogue when he went to study in Vienna in 1875. Then the death of his parents in 1889 left him free to cast off any last shreds of formal Jewish observance before his conversion to Catholicism, the Austrian state religion, on 23 February 1897. The conversion was a pre-condition for the post of Musical Director of the Imperial Opera House in Vienna (the Hofoper) that he took up that same year.

Although Alma Mahler referred to her husband as "a Jew who believed in Christ", he suffered repeatedly in his professional life from venomous anti-semitism. Of his Jewishness and generally dispossessed status he would later famously declare:

> It's like someone who comes into the world with one arm too short; the other arm must then learn to accomplish more, and ultimately perhaps it does things that two healthy arms would not have managed to do.

And also:

> I am thrice homeless, as a native of Bohemia in Austria, as an Austrian among Germans and as a Jew throughout the world.

*

A selection of romances and affairs

All Mahler's pre-marital adventures except the very first happened while he held conducting posts in a string of opera houses in Europe, before his appointment as Director of the Hofoper in Vienna. His route to this summit was via Bad Hall (1880), Laibach (now Ljubljana, 1881), Olmütz (Olomouc, 1883), Kassel (1883), Prague (1885-86), Leipzig (1886-88), Budapest (1888-91) and Hamburg (Chief Opera Conductor, 1891-97).

*

"... a racehorse in peak condition"

As a despotic, demon-driven maestro, with female singers' careers increasingly at his disposal, Mahler could, of course, more or less take his pick from the countless divas he directed on stage. Even had he been physically unattractive women would have endured his attentions. As it was, though certainly not conventionally handsome, he was supremely fit as a result of Spartan living and vigorous exercise that came to include fast walking, cycling, rowing and swimming. Even in his forties he retained "the perfect male torso", described as strong, slim, and beautifully made. The muscles on his sun-tanned back reminded his Viennese colleague Alfred Roller of "a racehorse in peak condition." La Grange refers to his sharp profile, sombre countenance, jet black hair, and features "evoking an ascetic monk." His eyes in particular had the power to transfix.

> Mahler was near-sighted [wrote Roller] and from his youth on wore glasses – sometimes spectacles, sometimes a pince-nez. ... His irises were speckled, mainly dark brown. His eye sockets stood out clearly

all round. The tear glands were small and flat. Since manhood his habit of opening wide his upper eyelids gave him an expression of lucid wakefulness. ... He had a clever, candid pair of eyes which could face things squarely.

*

The family of Josefa Poisl, one of Mahler's pupils in Iglau whom he met around 1879, turned him down flat as a suitor because of his poor prospects as a bread-winner. The painful Josefa experience induced not only three early songs and a quantity of poetry from Mahler but also, more importantly, a large part of *Das Klagende Lied* (The Lamenting Song) based on a grim German folk-tale, for soprano, contralto, tenor, bass, chorus and orchestra. Mahler completed the work on 1 November 1880, though later revised it at least four times.

Joanna Richter, a second rate though beautiful soprano whom Mahler met in Kassel in 1883, and who was "a source of endless suffering and anxiety" to him, fizzled out of his life when he left for Prague in 1885. Joanna's greatest claim to fame is as Mahler's main source of inspiration for his first outstanding work – the *Lieder eines Fahrenden Gesellen* (Songs of a Wayfarer), written in November and December 1884 for voice and orchestra (and later twice revised). Michael Kennedy considers these songs to be "one of the most moving and accomplished masterpieces in the history of the lied". The individual titles are:

> *When my love has her wedding day*
> *I went this morning over the field*
> *I have a glowing dagger*
> *The two blue eyes*

Another young singer with whom Mahler became involved was Betty Frank, whom he met in Prague. Betty had the distinction of giving the first public performance of any of his songs. With the composer accompanying her, they premiered his *Five Songs for Voice and Piano* on 20 April, 1886.

Marion Mathilda von Weber
Leipzig 1886

I have met a beautiful person here in Leipzig - and let me tell you at once, the sort that tempts one to do foolish things. Do I make myself clear, amice? But this time I mean to be careful, or else I shall be in trouble again.
[Mahler to Fritz Löhr on this latest conquest]

After becoming second conductor at the Leipzig Stadttheater, Mahler became violently involved for a while with a married woman four years his senior who was clearly overwhelmed by his talent and vitality. Marion Mathilda von Weber was the Jewish wife of the grandson of Karl Maria von Weber (1786-1826), composer of *Der Freischütz*, *Oberon*, and *Invitation to the Dance*.

While the Captain's away ...

The affair developed, perversely, through Mahler's contact with Marion's hapless husband. Baron Alexander Eduard Karl Maria von Weber, who was a Captain in the Leipzig regiment, invited Mahler to inspect the sketches for his grandfather's unfinished comic opera *Die Drei Pintos* (The Three Piebald Horses) and to complete them for performance. The task had already proved too much for the composers Meyerbeer and Franz Lachner. Mahler's successful completion of the project, however, brought him international fame and a handsome cheque which enabled him to send money to his ailing parents in Iglau.

While working on the commission, Mahler found an extra incentive to visit the Weber household in the shape of a very welcoming Frau Weber. He later described her to Natalie as a "luminous being entirely dedicated to Beauty and Good" who gave "a new meaning to his life."

Marion quickly took on the role of Mahler's muse. No sooner, for instance, had he finished the first movement of his *First Symphony* than he ran round to the Webers at midnight to play it. Marion was also an inspiring deity behind the first movement of his *Second Symphony*, entitled *Totenfeier* (Funeral Rites) in its original version. And no doubt it was mainly to please Marion that he also wrote a song for the family's children.

"This story is too good to check"
(Journalists' adage)

The lurid story of the affair is told by the redoubtable Ethel Smyth, lesbian, fiery suffragette and composer of such adventurous works as the opera, *The Wreckers*. In her memoirs *Impressions that Remained*, Smyth relates that Mahler's passion for Marion was reciprocated, "as well it might be, for in spite of his ugliness he had demoniacal charm". Captain Karl closed his eyes as long as possible, fearing a scandal that would force him to leave the army. But alas (writes Smyth), Mahler, although the finest conductor she had ever known, was

> a tyrannical lover [who] never hesitated to compromise his mistresses. Things were getting critical, when one day, travelling to Dresden in the company of strangers, Weber suddenly burst out laughing, drew a revolver and began taking William Tell-like shots at the headrests between the seats. He was overpowered, the train brought to a standstill, they took him to the police station raving mad – thence to the asylum. Always considered rather queer in the Army, the Mahler business had broken down his brain. I afterwards heard he had lucid intervals, that his wife in an agony of remorse refused to see her lover again ... and the rest is silence.

Smyth probably went over the top in declaring that Mahler's life was "full of incidents of this sort." Nevertheless she certainly had a point in saying that relating to Mahler was "like handling a bomb cased in razor edges."

Mahler himself admitted that he and Marion had planned an elopement. It all came to nothing, however, because she never turned up to catch the designated train that would have carried them away to certain future misery.

Incredibly, Captain von Weber seems to have born his adulterous rival no ill will, recommending Mahler's *First Symphony* to the President of the Leipzig Gewandhaus for performance that same summer (1888) after its completion in March.

Mahler later told his friend Max Marschalk that the *First Symphony* (originally entitled *Symphonic Poem*) had been inspired by a passionate love, though emphasised that "the real life experience was the reason for the work, not its content".

*

Love at the root of the *First Symphony*

Michael Kennedy sums up the musical fall-out in the *First Symphony* from three of Mahler's first four entanglements: the collective effects of Josefa Poisl, Joanna Richter and Marion von Weber:

> The use of themes from *Lieder eines fahrenden Gesellen* points to Joanna Richter as the inspiration of the work, although the song *Maitanz im Grünen* is the basis of the theme of the second movement and this was written

for Josephine Poisl. Yet the impetus to compose the symphony came from the passion for Marion von Weber ... so it would be accurate to say that 'a state of being in love' is at the root of the symphony.

*

1889: Annus Horribilis

There seems to have been no identified woman in Mahler's life while he was in Budapest (1888-91). Nevertheless the year 1889 is noteworthy because during it he endured a painful haemorrhoidectomy (a worse one was to come later), he lost both his parents and also his sister Leopoldine ("Poldi"). He also conducted the premiere of his *First Symphony* on 20 November. It was the first of many flops, with both audience and most critics.

In March 1890 Mahler was again on the move, this time to Hamburg – and to the most frenzied love affair of his life.

*

Anna von Mildenburg
Hamburg 1895

The intensity of his passion is conveyed in his letters to her and in the creative impetus he acquired to complete the third symphony.
[Lebrecht]

Anna von Mildenburg and Mahler are a book in themselves. She was his longest-lasting and most searing flame – and also proved far more difficult to snuff out than the others.

Mahler had been Chief Conductor at the Hamburg Opera for some four years when Anna crossed his path in 1895, having been given a job on the spot after her audition. "Over-sensitive, easily offended, hot-tempered, possessive, passionate, [and] demanding," Anna, Viennese-born and twelve years younger than Mahler, soon had him hopelessly hooked. He wrote some 180 letters to her altogether during their two years in Hamburg, though for copyright reasons these have regrettably not been released from the Austrian National Library and we must be content with snippets retrieved by La Grange.

Anna recalled her earliest encounters with the maestro, who was then thirty-five. A small sunburned man dressed in a summer suit, carrying a dark felt hat and a badly rolled umbrella, he looked at her coldly with clear grey-blue eyes. (Later, in more intimate encounters she would realise his eyes were in fact dark brown.) Terrified, she sang and was soon reduced to tears. But she survived the experience, and the following month she sang her first Brünnhilde (the rebellious leader of the Valkyries in three of Wagner's music dramas).

Mahler moulded Mildenberg in every way, valuing her – as he did all his favoured singers – as much for her gifts as an actress as for her exquisite singing. Little wonder, therefore, that for Anna, Mahler became "the incarnation of music ... the high priest, the initiator of a new cult that she wonderingly learned to worship." Nevertheless, she was apparently not very interested in her maestro's own compositions, no doubt finding them too long and complex.

When he was necessarily distant towards her in rehearsal she would retaliate by feigning indifference, and using other wiles to plunge him into abject misery. Tormented, and despairing he wrote:

> Anna! dear God! Forgive me for everything! The monster of repentance holds me in its claws. If it lets me go for a moment, another, more terrible still, will, come ... the monster of jealousy. ... If you have the slightest regard for me, write to me! If you need me, write to me! Oh Anna, forgive everything and forgive me!

Extracts from various other letters he wrote her during 1895 and 1896 reveal his total enslavement:

> Anna, never before have I felt such a pure and sacred love for anyone – and you do not love me! Oh God How can I ever get over it? ... You consent to grant me your esteem and confidence. Don't you realise these words pierce my heart like red-hot blades?

> Believe me, Anna, if you have asked me to die for you I would have done so, but oh, God, how could you only pretend to love me? ... Anna, I am in hell and without hope of redemption.

> I am in slippers because my shoes are soaking, but when I've finished this letter, I'll go out into the storm to post it so it will reach you in bed tomorrow morning and make you smile.

He tells her he loves it when she laughs, but begs her not
to do so in public,

> for how could I stop myself from taking you in my arms
> and covering you with kisses!
> ... My body burns, my blood is on fire, I have scarcely
> recovered from yesterday's heated battle; still full of
> daring, my eyes glint with the excitement of the
> struggle. ... I love you so much, Anna, just as you are!

Such sexual slavery could never last for Mahler. The balance
in the relationship changed during 1896 as her domineering
possessiveness cooled his passion. He had to insist on his right
to neglect her while he was composing his *Third Symphony*, telling
her he was on all such occasions "dead to the outside world." She
came to regard his work as her "rival" and inevitably there were
"countless small misunderstandings".

"What will come of all this?" he asked her gloomily in July
1896. Nevertheless they were still close enough for him to send
this frisky billet doux in the winter of 1896-97:

> You ask me if I miss you. How wicked of you! Can you
> doubt it? Do you think it is any different for me than
> for you? When one is accustomed to such a sweet
> 'tormentor'? when the time comes when one went to
> that horrible boarding-house in Magdalenstrasse, then
> enter a certain beloved room, take that usually, unruly
> little head in my hands and cover it with ... then of
> course one misses many things! Just wait: when you
> come back [from a Bayreuth audition] I shall show you
> what I mean!"

The most painful moments in their relationship came probably
just before Mahler left Hamburg for Vienna on 27 April 1897.
Anna was more demanding than ever as he was trying to ease
out. After performances (we read in La Grange), she would pursue
him through the dark lanes near the theatre, throw herself at
his feet, and burst into tears. She also disgusted him by parading
in front of him "completely naked." Her final trick was "to feign
illness and summon a Dominican priest [one Father Ottmar] to
marry them."

Au Revoir My Darling

> Au revoir my darling, my faithful little Anna ... May
> this forthcoming separation, which we must accept,
> be only physical!

180

Mahler's appointment to the Vienna Hofoper in May 1897 as a Kapellmeister (prior to his promotion to the Directorship) did not get Anna off his back. She was soon to take up an appointment in the same opera house! Although in early summer he continued to string her along with such assurances as "sooner or later everything will come right for us," in reality, he seems to have promised his sister Justi that he would never marry Anna.

Mahler warned Anna that if she accepted the offer from the Hofoper,

> It is essential that (I now perceive clearly) we restrict our personal relations to an absolute minimum. in order not to make life intolerable for one another again. ... the news of your engagement will burst like a bomb ... I feel we may be imposing an unbearable ordeal upon ourselves.

Anna accepted the conditions without really taking them on board. Rosa Papier (Anna's teacher and a former star diva) weighed in with Mahler, telling Anna that she had not been "compromised," even though her lover had often stayed "until late at night" in her Hamburg apartment.

> He did not dishonour you, thank God, [continued Papier] and for the two of you to marry would be calamitous, absurd, idiotic, sheer folly! ... if you were to see one another as often as you did in Hamburg and if you were to dominate him as you did then, you would both lose your jobs. Don't you realise that the poor man is suffering as a result of his foolishness? Don't you realise that, like all men, he is weak?

The news of Anna's appointment inevitably provoked a field day of press gossip on the lines that Mahler had imported his "girl friend" in to the Hofoper. Nevertheless many critics raved about Anna's singing — even the notoriously desiccated Hanslick, who praised "the ease of her runs, her trills, the chromatic scales that she unleashed with such amazing sureness and agility in the upper registers."

Anna's reported behaviour after Mahler's engagement to Alma Schindler must perhaps be taken with a pinch of salt, since most of the reports come from Alma talking about her husband's "ex". On one occasion Anna "made a scene, and even pretended to faint," urging him to address her as Du again (rather than the more formal Sie). There is a report of her prostrate on a sofa in a swoon, and another of a visit by Mahler and Alma to Anna in her "gloomy" hotel rooms. Anna soon found a pretext to get Mahler on his own where the conversation quickly degenerated into "a heated argument."

In spite of all this and much more, when Mahler quit his post at the Hofoper in 1907 he still clearly held Anna in deep regard:

> I can only send you these few heartfelt words and press
> your hand in spirit. I shall always watch your progress
> with affection and sympathy.

In 1909 at the age of 37 Anna married the writer Hermann Bahr "who had fallen in love with her stage persona." And, of course, she hadn't been lonely in the meanwhile: since her break-up with Mahler, her "admirers" had included the poet and philosopher Siegfried Lipiner and the music critic Ludwig Karpath, both friends of Mahler.

*

Interlude: Love Unrequited
Natalie Bauer-Lechner (1858-1921)
"Dear, merry old Natalie"(Mahler)

> I had two reasons for living – Gustav Mahler and the
> diary I kept of everything he said. Then I was
> abandoned. Simply cut adrift. I'm not sure I know what
> exactly happened after that, I didn't seem to notice what
> I was becoming – I think the word is 'destitute'.
> [Natalie to Lipiner in the Ronald Harwood's play,
> *Mahler's Conversion*]

Two years older than Mahler, Natalie Bauer-Lechner first met the composer as a student at the Vienna Conservatoire, and from the early 1890s became "his closest woman friend" and memoirist. The cultured daughter of a Viennese bookshop owner, Natalie was a professional viola player and member of the Söldat-Roger String Quartet. After the breakup of her ten-year marriage in 1885, Natalie (writes Lebrecht) "longed to marry Mahler and attempted on at least one occasion to seduce him, but he did not find her physically attractive and exercised his passions elsewhere."

The seduction attempt, after a supper party in Hamburg in 1896 – which had in turn followed booed performances of Mahler's *Todtenfeier* and the *Funeral March* movement of his

First Symphony is described in La Grange:
> Some minutes after they had said good night on the
> hotel landing, she knocked on his door, entered
> hurriedly, and without saying a word kissed his hand.
> Greatly embarrassed, he exclaimed, "Natalie, what are
> you doing?" but his passionate and faithful admirer
> had already fled, slamming the door behind her.

Poor Natalie was completely wiped out of Mahler's life when he met Alma, who obviously couldn't be expected to tolerate such a devoted acolyte hovering in the marital wings. For her part, Natalie could not have possibly endured a continuing friendship with the engaged man she had so passionately loved in vain.

Poor Natalie! She had seen all of her hero's works grow each summer in Steinbach am Attersee and elsewhere since 1893 – the *Second, Third,* and *Fourth Symphonies* and also many of the *Wunderhorn Songs.* In January 1902 after the public announcement of Mahler's engagement, she wrote:
> If I were to discuss this event, I would find myself in
> the position of a doctor obliged to treat his nearest and
> dearest in a life or death situation. Whether these pages
> are brought to a conclusion must rest with the Supreme
> and Eternal Master.

She bowed out broken-hearted but with great fortitude She had noted down in her private journal (published only after her death as *Recollections of Gustav Mahler*) countless details from Mahler's personal, professional and creative life that would otherwise have remained unrecorded – from his first attempts at composition (the polka at the age of six when he spilled ink over his paper) until the performance of his *Fourth Symphony* in Vienna on 12 January 1902.

The way she agonised so innocently and sincerely over his artistic traumas is infinitely touching:
> No one can have any idea of the agonies of creation
> (together with the ecstatic joys which come more in
> anticipation and as an aftermath than during the
> creative act) who has not experienced them with him,
> being sensitive to every tremor of his delicately strung
> soul.

She was the only woman who loved him unconditionally, body and soul, and received so little in return. Natalie died in obscure poverty on 8 June 1921.

**

Alma Mahler née Schindler
born Vienna, 31 August 1879
died New York, 11 December 1964

> [Alma Mahler's] books are often fearfully inaccurate, they may have offended individuals, but by their frankness and tactlessness as an unlikeable self-portrait they give an unrivalled, if distorted, picture not only of Mahler, but of a whole artistic circle.
> [Michael Kennedy]

"All the Muses seem to have gathered round her cradle," writes La Grange of Alma's cultured and exotic childhood and adolescence.

Her father was Emil Jakob Schindler who would become "the most celebrated landscape painter of the Austrian empire." He married Anna Bergen on February 1879, and by 1885, with the Kaiser himself as one of his customers, he could afford to rent from Prince Karl Liechtenstein a small Renaissance castle, Plankenberg, in Upper Austria. In this romantic home (writes La Grange)

> surrounded by woods and complete with legendary ghosts, he gave brilliant parties and sometimes musical evenings. It was here, in surroundings as idyllic and poetic as her father's landscapes, that Alma spent her childhood.

A childhood light years apart from that of Mahler in the family's hovel in Kalischt and the tavern at Iglau.

Alma always spoke admiringly of her father, extolling his handsomeness, his "inborn aristocratic nature," his friends in high places, his brilliant conversation, his passion for music, his fine tenor voice, his moving performances of Schumann's *Lieder* ... Experiencing little or nothing in the way of mother love, she predictably developed a father fixation that would later draw her continually towards older men in her romantic encounters.

Violent quarrels between Alma's parents merely reinforced her love for her father. The marital strife was hardly surprising in view of Frau Schindler's production of a lovechild, Grete, during her marriage, fathered by the painter Julius Berger.

Emil Schindler died in August 1892 and just over three years later his widow married his most distinguished pupil, Carl

Moll, with whom she had been having an affair even before her husband's death. But as far as Alma was concerned Moll was "a mere pendulum to her father's clock." At the age of thirteen she had lost what she called her "guiding star." She had lived to please him and his look of understanding had alone satisfied "all my vanity and ambition."

Men before Mahler

A born seductress who revelled in her powers, Alma Schindler caught elder men in her web as effortlessly as a spider traps flies. In some cases, she then twisted them on her pin like a boy with a beetle. One of her most besotted admirers was Max Burckhard, the adventurous director of the Burgtheater. Although unmoved by his advances, she looked up to him, accepted his presents of books, and was strongly influenced by his anti-Semitic and Nietzschean ideas.

Gustav Klimt (1862-1918)

> Klimt was the first great love in my life, but I had
> been an innocent child, drowned in music and remote
> from life. ... He was very close to me.

Klimt became the foremost exponent of the Viennese variation of Art Nouveau, best known for his erotic masterpieces in oil and gold leaf. He was also a member (with Alma's stepfather) of the Secession movement.

Seventeen years Alma's senior, Klimt, with his "peasant nature" and "monk's robes" certainly fell in love with her. But after just one "memorable and erotic kiss," Alma's mother put a stop to the romance! For his part, Klimt backed off, clearly valuing his friendship with Moll more than his passion for Alma. In 1899 he felt it necessary to put the record straight with Moll by assuring him that "the path of unrighteousness was not to be trodden."

"Alex"
Alexander von Zemlinsky (1871-1942)

Alma's sexual awakening crescendoed during her music lessons from the summer of 1900, when she and her teacher played through the score of Wagner's *Tristan und Isolde* together. Ideal music, certainly, for sexual arousal, since (according to the late critic Virgil Thomson) "in Act II the lovers ejaculate simultaneously seven times" at points that are "clearly marked in the music."

The fortunate teacher in question was Alexander von Zemlinsky, eight years older than Alma. Although a talented and respected musician and composer, Zemlinsky was certainly no oil painting, dismissed by Alma as "a frightful gnome ... small, chinless, toothless ... and unwashed." It seems she was hardly exaggerating.

For all that, the chemistry between teacher and pupil was clearly explosive. Alma records his "burning embraces," their "fiercest frenzies of passion" and more:

> And I long so madly for his embraces. The touch of his hand deep inside me. – I shall never forget it – such a glow - and such a blissful feeling swept through me ... one little [nuance] more and I would have been a god – And once again, everything is sacred to me. I want to kneel down in front of him and kiss his naked belly – kiss everything, everything! Amen!

Only her mother's daily sermons, she tells us, and her old-fashioned upbringing prevented the loss of her virginity. It was probably a close call since she wrote in 1901, "I want to be the mother of your children."

Most of this comes from her diaries, incidentally, rather than her memoirs, in which she conveys the idea of an altogether more innocent romance.

More than a hundred of Zemlinksy's letters to Alma have survived, about forty of them passionate and besotted on these lines:

> I want to kneel to you, kiss your dress, worship you like something sacred

Not surprisingly, it was Alma who made all the running, especially after she had met Mahler in November 1901. She drove Zemlinsky mad by blowing hot and cold with him. Interestingly, he found this very same inconstancy in her compositions:

> Look how your compositions start – warm, feminine, deeply felt – and then come the odds and ends, runs, passages without style.

For all that, some of Alma's songs have now been recorded, and acclaimed as "fascinating [and] imaginative in their word setting" and "bold and finely judged in their harmonies." Altogether she wrote around a hundred songs – of which a mere fourteen written at this time (1900-01) survive – and a number of instrumental works.

Zemlinksy was not Alma's only suitor after she met Mahler in late 1901. During one week in December she was besieged by two firm offers of marriage "like in a sixpenny novel!" One from a wealthy man named Felix Muhr, and another from François Hancke the Secretary of the Secession. She didn't remotely fancy either of them.

During her courtship with Mahler Alma would fall into "a terrible dilemma" about having suppressed her strong sexual attraction to Zemlinsky – "Alex" – to the awe in which she held Mahler. She would never ever feel the same raw passion for her fiancé and husband that she did for Alex. Indeed, it would not be until her abandoned extra-marital affair with Walter Gropius in 1910 that her sexual passion would again blaze furiously.

For all the agony Alma caused Zemlinsky, she seems to have been a lasting influence on his composing. Their affair was perhaps the conscious or unconscious inspiration behind his later opera *Der Traumgörge,* "the sad and romantic story of a young boy betrayed by his beloved." On Mahler's recommendation it was premiered by his successor at the Hofoper, Felix Weingartner.

*

Courtship with Mahler
"In November 1901 she at last meets Mahler face to face, mouth to mouth."

Alma and Mahler first met on 7 November 1901 and plighted their secret troths exactly a month later. The engagement was officially celebrated at Hohe Warte (the Molls' family home up in the Viennese suburb of Döbling) on 23 December, and officially announced in the *Neue Freie Presse* on 27 December. By the time they married on 9 March 1902 in the Karlskirche, Vienna, Alma was already pregnant with their first child Marie ("Putzi").

The story of their meeting has often been told. Alma had been persuaded to attend a dinner party given by her friends the Zuckerkandls on 7 November 1901 on the promise that her former admirers Klimt and Burckhard would be there. During that evening, Alma's perky forwardness captivated Mahler as it had so many others.

At one point she and Mahler had a furious row about the merits of Zemlinsky's opera *Das Goldene Herz* (The Golden Heart) which Mahler dismissed as "trash." Alma retorted that such an opinion was no excuse for the discourtesy of not replying within a whole year to Zemlinsky's proposal for a performance. When Mahler sarcastically asked her to explain the symbolism in *The Golden Heart*, she fired a return shot. Would he care to explain the absurd plot of Bayer's ballet, *The Korean Bride,* currently running under his Directorship at the Opera?

After the other guests dispersed, they became separated from everyone else – in True Stories vein, "by that void created around themselves by two people who have found one another."

Mahler was clearly already powerfully attracted, whilst Alma declared in her diary

> I must confess I liked him enormously. To be sure. he's
> very keyed up. He was like a bull in a China shop. He's
> pure oxygen. You get burnt if you get too close.

The next morning Alma, Berta Zuckerkandl, and Berta's sister Sophie Clemenceau attended a rehearsal at the Hofoper of Offenbach's *Hoffmanns Erzahlungen* (The Tales of Hoffmann.) At one point Mahler confessed to Alma that he hadn't "slept a wink all night."

Things moved very quickly. A rather pedantic love poem woven round the themes of love and music arrived at Alma's bedside the morning after the rehearsal. Then they met again on 11 November at the premiere of *Hoffmann*. Having flirted from the rostrum with Alma in her box, and entertained her to tea with her mother during the intermission, he agreed to visit Hohe Warte after returning from a trip to conduct his *Fourth Symphony* in Munich. They parted like a pair of lovers, "convinced," wrote Alma, "that something important and wonderful had entered our lives."

Both the ever-hopeful Burckhard and Alma's step-father Moll tried to warn Alma off marriage with Mahler. Moll stressed Mahler's unsuitability on grounds of his age, his debts, his poor health, and his "precarious' position at the Court Opera." The viciously anti-Semitic Burckhard minced no words about his own objections:

> But it would be a sin for so good-looking a girl of such
> good family as you to spoil it all by marrying that
> rachitic [rickets-ridden], degenerate Jew. Think of your
> children. It would be a sin! Besides which, fire and
> water can, at a pinch, get along together, but not fire
> and fire. You would be the one to suffer, not him, and
> you deserve better than that.

On 27 November after returning from Munich, Mahler conducted Hoffmann's *Erzahlungen* again but Alma was uppermost in his "heart and mind." He lost no time in calling at Hohe Warte where they argued about Nietszche before he accepted an invitation to dinner to eat Paprikahändl (chicken with cream and paprika, which he disliked).

They walked to the Post Office at Döbling — "their feet crunching on the fresh snow" — and on the way back he declared suddenly, after silence:

> It's not easy to marry a man like me! I must be entirely free. I can't allow myself to be hampered by any material responsibilities. I could lose my job at the Opera from one day to the next.

When they returned, they went up to her room and he kissed her for the first time. After that he regarded the marriage as decided. They went down to dinner where Gustav quoted Schiller at length.

"... without really wanting to"

Alma's wild vacillations over the relationship are clear from the beginning. She was utterly in awe of the demonic, charismatic man who for four years had held the Musical Directorship of the world's greatest opera house. Yet she confessed in her diary that she had allowed Gustav to give her that first kiss "without really wanting to." Years later she would even admit to Mahler that "in the early stages of our intimacy I found his body odour offensive." "That is the key to a lot of things!" was Mahler's perceptive reply. "You acted against your nature!"

A further problem for her was his music,

> which I find so utterly foreign to me ... To put it plainly, I don't believe in him as a composer! And I am supposed to bind my life to the man ...

Her consolation was that "whereas I was madly, passionately in love with Alex Z., I'm now filled with the most sacred feelings." And so she allowed Gustav, secretly, to fix the date for their marriage, on the grounds that

> these decisions are right and for the best and I can no longer live without him ... He's the only man who can give meaning to my life, for he stands head and shoulders above all the other men I've ever known.

Mahler's own misgivings about the marriage inevitably centred round their age gap. In a letter to Justi he wondered

> ... whether a man who will soon be old has the right to bind so much youth and freshness to his overripeness, to chain spring to autumn, missing out summer? ... what will happen when my fruitful autumn gives way to winter? Do you see what I mean?

In the ultra-chauvinistic fashion of those times, Mahler laid down the terms of their union – terms of near-slavery – in a diatribe of extraordinary length and tedium he sent her from the Hotel Bellevue, Dresden, on 19 December 1901. Future composing for her was utterly out of the question:

> Have you any idea how ridiculous and, in time, how degrading for both of us such a peculiarly competitive relationship would inevitably become? What will happen if, just when you're 'in the mood', you're obliged to attend to the house or to something I might happen to need ...

Her worry that she hadn't been working enough on her own theory and counterpoint was "incomprehensible" to him. So also was the thought that she could spend a whole afternoon with Justi "without talking lovingly of me and about me."

At least he was scrupulously honest with her! Not only about these demands on her, but also about his own fiercely uncompromising ideals for his music, whatever the consequential hardships. Would she be able to bear with him "all the adversity, the external trappings of shame, and joyfully take up such a cross?" For his part, he could bear all the "slaps of the Philistines and the scorn and hatred of the ignorant." He longed only "to inhale from your mouth and your life's breath the certainty and fullest awareness that my ship of life has come through the storms of the high seas and is now safe in its home port." ...

La Grange sums up the situation:

> It would be hard to imagine a woman less likely to bow to his demands than Alma. Flirtatious and selfish, capricious and vain, she was nevertheless momentarily swept away by the force of his personality and the intensity of his genius.

Alma's accession to all Mahler's demands on Saturday 21 December was "the greatest proof of love she could possibly have

given him." They played his *Symphony* together, and he said to
Frau Moll, "I still need your daughter's hand."

In her diary for 22 December Alma was carried away on a
tidal wave of love, both uxorious and protective:

> My longing for him is indescribable. ... Oh! – To have a
> child by him if only he's strong enough. He so
> desperately hopes for that. Nothing, nothing, nothing
> – other than to belong to him...
>
> I know everything – he's a sick man, my poor darling,
> he weighs 63 kilos (against my 117!) – far too little –
> I'll look after him as though he were a child. It's sweet
> that he can't pronounce his Rs and curious that he
> would like to call me Marie because he loves the strong
> R in the middle of the name ... I can just see him lying
> in a pool of blood.

If Mahler did in fact sometimes call Alma Marie (there
seems to be some doubt), then Freud was perhaps correct in
asserting that Mahler was seeking to replicate in his marriage
his relationship with his mother. (See below)

The Moment Men Dread

Alma's accounts of the consummation of their relationship need
no comment:

> [30 December]
>
> Rendezvous with Gustav ... We halfway united today ...
> he let me feel his strength, his life - and that with such
> a pure and sacred sensation that I would never have
> imagined possible ... He must be suffering terribly. I
> can guess his torment by my own .... No-one knows how
> unspeakably intense is my desire. And yet I can't
> imagine giving myself to him until the time is right. ...
> Why can't I just move in with him? - without the
> blessing ...

On New Year's Day 1902 the supreme moment seemed to
have arrived when

> suddenly he lost all his strength and lay limp on my
> breast, almost crying with shame. I comforted him, even
> though I was desperately miserable myself. ... I can't
> describe how frustrating I found the whole thing. First
> the turmoil deep inside me, then the goal so near – and
> no satisfaction ... My beloved!

The difficulty – possibly induced by Mahler's feelings of
guilt in marrying so much younger a woman – was fortunately

only temporary. Alma was able to record on 4 January, "Wonne über Wonne" (Bliss upon bliss).

A few days later Gustav's struggle had unfortunate consequences:

> My poor Gustav is undergoing medical treatment – an inflamed swelling – ice packs, hip-baths etc – Was it due to my prolonged resistance?

Alma's euphoria didn't last, of course, and already incompatibilities between the couple were surfacing. Alma, for instance, who had been nourished since her earliest days on a diet of philosophers like Nietzsche and Schopenhauer found herself "incapable of sharing Gustav's admiration for Dostoyevsky." On 16 January she was clearly unhappy:

> Now he's continually talking about protecting his art. I can't do that. With Zemlinsky it would even have been alright because I appreciate his art with him – he's a wonderfully gifted fellow ... I must be free, completely free!

*

The Marriage

> Gustav is so solitary, so distant! Everything is muted! I am alone! Everything in him is so deeply buried ... that it cannot surface! Even his love; everything is muted. I need warmth! I am alone! ... Oh, if only he were younger to enjoy life.
> [Alma writing on 16 December 1902]

For all Alma's complaints about her married life with Mahler, it was clearly sometimes an uplifting and inspirational experience for her – an ascent to what she called "a higher level" of existence where she was "drunk with joy." She did after all choose Mahler because he was "the purest and greatest genius" she had met and vowed to "sow the ground on which he walks with peace, contentment, equanimity." And there can be no question that at whatever personal cost, she did her best to fulfil this vow, even after she began her affair with Gropius. (Up to then she kept admirers at bay, though flattered by their attentions, especially those of Hans Pfitzner who dedicated a string quartet to her.)

For all its saddening later difficulties, the Mahlers' marriage was the lying-in room in which Alma was midwife to her husband's art. Michael Kennedy's tribute to her is undeniable:

The world can never repay her for her influence on his compositions. From 1880 to 1901 he had written four symphonies, a cantata and songs: no mean output for a busy conductor. Yet between 1902 and 1907 while in charge of the Vienna Opera and in increasing demand as conductor of his own and others' symphonic work, he wrote four enormous symphonies and the *Kindertotenlieder*. In the last three years of his life he wrote three symphonies ...

More specifically, Mahler would associate particular works and passages with Alma. The last of the five beautiful *Rückertlieder* (1901-1902) was intended as "a Privatissimum" for her and dedicated "To my dear Almscherl, my faithful and brave companion on all paths." The *Adagietto* of his *Fifth Symphony* was (according to Mahler's champion Willem Mengelberg) "a declaration of love" to Alma. Mahler himself told her that in the second main theme of the first movement of the *Sixth Symphony* he had "tried to personify you in a theme. I don't know if I've succeeded, but you will have to be content with it." Every note of the *Eighth Symphony* was, he said, addressed to her, and his anguished scrawlings over the incomplete score of the *Tenth Symphony* speak for themselves. (See below.)

*

Nevertheless, Alma was no Natalie Bauer-Lechner, who would have fulfilled herself in being the intelligent and intuitive slave Mahler needed to support his monumental labours. Young, highly sexed, volatile and vibrant, Alma was too severely deprived not only of sexual satisfaction, but of all those personal attentions, pleasures, presents and worldly comforts that many women need, but which her goal-driven, self-obsessed husband held in contempt. He had not even given her an engagement ring (which he regarded as being "totally absurd") nor a wedding present. In Alma's words, he wanted to "deprive her of all life but the life of the spirit." It is not surprising, therefore, to discover in La Grange that she sought some solace in drink, developing "a marked tendency towards alcoholism."

Given Mahler's colossal and draining workload at the Hofoper, day-to-day married life at number 2 Auenbruggergasse (in a neighbourhood that Mahler remembered for its strong winds and "endless smell of goulasch on the streets") left Alma with scant opportunities for family chit-chat with her husband. We read in La Grange that his daily routine in Vienna began early, with a working breakfast taken in his study. Travelling by tram, he arrived at the Opera at about 9.00 am and worked till 1.00 pm. He then phoned` home to make sure lunch would be ready. On arrival he rang the bell at the main entrance to the block of flats as an order for the soup to be served. He then raced up the four flights of stairs, slammed doors, washed his hands and ate. After a short nap he walked with Alma either in Belvedere Park (close by), or right round the Ring Road – something she found far too strenuous.

They took tea at 5.00 pm after which Mahler returned to the Opera. Even when not conducting he always stayed for at least part of nearly every show. Alma came to pick him up and sat in on the opera or ballet until he was ready to leave. After dinner he asked Alma to read to him! There was never time for a resumé of the day's domestic trivia.

Well might Alma write only a mere four months into her marriage:

> I don't know what to do. There's such a struggle going
> on in me! And a miserable longing for someone who
> thinks of ME, who helps me to find MYSELF! I've sunk
> to the level of a housekeeper!
> [July 1902]

Mahler's idea of a jolly evening at home was to have his young wife read aloud such works as Wolfram von Eschenbach's *Parsifal*, or Friedrich Albert Lange's *Geschichte Des Material-ismus* (History of Materialism), or poetry by Richard Demel ... Or then again, he might wish to discuss lectures on astronomy which he had bid her attend.

Well might one of Alma's friends tell her she had married "an abstraction for a husband, not a human being." And well also might Reik point out that it was typical of Mahler to wax lyrical to his wife on "the lofty, idealising concept of the Eternal Feminine" while "monstrously neglecting" the woman under his nose.

There are cameos galore of Mahler's "abstractedness" and other-worldliness. Of his dress Roller writes that

> His overcoat had only the top button fastened, his fists
> were crammed into the pockets; his tie had been wound

in three seconds into a crooked knot: the newest hat, jammed down over his ears with both fists, soon looked as shapeless as an old one.

Of Mahler's legendary absentmindedness here are just two stories. This one from Natalie's *Recollections*:

> He is extremely forgetful and absent-minded, because inwardly preoccupied and distracted. In fact, he used to be much more so. The strangest things would happen to him! The most extreme instance occurred in his youth, while drinking black coffee at a party. Without thinking, he stirred the cup with his cigarette instead of his spoon and then, imagining that he had smoke in his mouth, blew coffee across the table right into his hostess's face!

And Alma recalls how when Mahler had been gripped by an attack of toothache requiring immediate attention, he had to ask Alma "which tooth was it that hurt?"

*

Alma saw little more of her husband on their summer vacations in their idyllic country home (until 1907) at Maiernigg on the Wörthersee. We read (again in La Grange) that Mahler rose at 5.30 am, swam alone, hurried to his composing hut in the depths of the forest, ate a first breakfast, worked uninterrupted for seven hours and then swam again. Before lunch he might play music with Alma, and play with the children ("Putzi" and "Gucki"). Then after a brief nap, he took a daily long walk with Alma who again couldn't keep up with him. Neither, of course, did she share those passions for hiking, swimming, bicycling and rowing. The evenings were spent in intellectually demanding activity.

We can probably take Alma's word for her account of how Mahler tyrannised his household after some sort of panic attack – terrified that he was being "watched by the terrible smouldering eye of the god Pan" while he was writing his *Sixth Symphony* in the summer of 1904. For a while he would not return to his Häuschen (the log cabin he built to compose in) but worked instead at his desk on the top floor of the villa. Alma continues

> I had to run all over the three-storey-high house telling everyone to keep quiet. The cook was not allowed to make the slightest noise. The children were shut up in their rooms. I stopped playing the piano, didn't sing, didn't dare move around. And things stayed that way

> until he reached a 'break' in his work and surfaced
> radiant with joy, as always after he had finished
> working and wanted to re-establish contact with our
> life. Such were my experiences at that time. I no longer
> had any of my own. he didn't even notice that I had
> given up my own life.

*

Difficult to live with – and also difficult to work with! The
tales of Mahler's treatment of orchestral musicians and chorus
singers, who as a breed loathed him, are another story – or rather
a volume of stories. My favourite two are the time in Budapest
when he was challenged to a duel by some of the chorus members,
and the time in Hamburg when the police had to escort Mahler
home after a harassed flautist and his colleagues were waiting
outside the stage door to do him over.

*

Alma's nightmare

Alma's deepest anxieties about her life with Mahler surfaced in
her dreams. The most lurid seems to have been one she recorded
for 29 May 1903. At the climax of a succession of weird happen-
ings,

> a large green snake with long legs suddenly forces its
> way up inside me. I pull at its tail. it won't come out. I
> ring for the chamber maid. She pulls with all her
> strength. Suddenly she gets hold of it. It slides out
> with all my inner organs in its mouth. Now I am hollow
> and empty like a wrecked ship.

> To La Grange all this seems "clear enough." Alma
> continually rebelled against Mahler's physical and
> mental domination. All achievement, all personal
> fulfilment were prohibited by the permanent and
> obsessive presence of a husband whose real or phantom
> image pursued her everywhere, even into her most
> secret self.

More than this, the snake episode symbolises Alma's frust-
ration:

> ... the maternity resulting from sex with Mahler had
> mutilated her and deprived her of one of her basic
> needs: not only musical creation, but steady contacts
> with a group of close friends, and especially with men
> whom she usually bewitched with her wit and sed-
> uctive femininity.

*

196

Glimpses of a Family Man

Life in the Mahler menage was not, of course, total gloom, doom and work, though the happy times do not seem to have ever lasted long. At least from 1905, there were no more money worries, with Mahler earning a large salary of 36,000 kronen from the Hofoper (with a decent pension also), guest conducting fees for performances of his own works, and large sums for the publication of his later symphonies (10,000 guilders for his *Fifth* and 15,000 from for the *Sixth*). He could allow Alma 2,000 kronen for their Maiernigg holiday in 1904: plenty for a ménage that included two servants.

When he could spare the time Mahler was a good father, especially towards his favourite Marie ("Putzi"), born on 3 November 1902 and named in memory of Mahler's mother. Their second daughter Anna ("Gucki") was born on 15 June 1904.

In fact, fatherhood was initially much more to Mahler's taste than was motherhood (as then conceived) to Alma who felt more constrained than ever after Putzi's birth:

> Gustav, why did you bind to you this splendid bird so happy in flight, when a heavy, grey one would have suited you better? There are so many heavy ducks and geese who cannot fly at all!

Mahler loved to read his children grotesque fairy tales, and to Putzi in particular Brentano's *Gockel, Hinkel und Gackeleia*. Putzi would spend long hours with her father in the Häuschen at Maiernigg, often returning – to the distress of the family's English nanny Miss Turner – "splattered with jam from head to foot."

Mahler's happiness as a father was alas soon shattered. Two days short of his forty-seventh birthday, his beloved Putzi died age five from scarlet fever (complicated by diphtheria) at Maiernigg. Inconsolable with grief Mahler requested that when his own time came he be buried with her. Alma was also laid low by the bereavement – but when the doctor who attended her also examined Mahler's heart he had grim news to announce. The streptococcal infection that had caused Mahler so many sore throats and abscesses over the years (with attendant operations and convalescences) had by now attacked his heart. Mahler immediately knew the certain consequences and for some time was in creative paralysis.

The surviving Mahlers then fled Maiernigg – never to return there – for a holiday farm at Alt-Schluderbach in the Tyrol. Here Mahler began work on *Das Lied von der Erde* (The Song of the Earth), inspired by a collection of Chinese poems. Inevitably the songs were filled with all the grief and dread Mahler was then feeling. The message of the last song, *Abschied* (Farewell), lasting nearly half an hour, is that "our lives are short but that the beauties of the world go on":

> Everywhere and forever, the blue distance shines!
> Forever ... ever ... ever ... ever.

By the end of 1907 Mahler was a broken man – Putzi had died, Alma's heart and throat problems would require an operation, he had his own serious heart trouble, and he had resigned from the Hofoper. After ten arduous years of administration, planning and conducting, he had burned himself out. He had come to loathe "the most extreme laxity and deep-rooted weaknesses in the whole company" (as Natalie had written earlier), as well as the relentless repertoire system in which successions of different operas were recycled with only minimum rehearsal. After disagreements with the Imperial Chamberlain, Prince Montenuovo, his resignation came as a relief and his last performance at the Hofoper was a *Fidelio* on 15 October 1907.

Far from devoting his remaining life (three and a half years) solely to composition, Mahler accepted a lucrative contract to conduct at the Metropolitan Opera in New York, where he first appeared conducting *Tristan* on 1 January 1908.

*

Dr Walter Gropius (1883–1969)

> Almschi! If you had left me that time, I should simply
> have gone out like a torch deprived of air.

By the early summer of 1910 the Mahlers' marriage was at risk. Alma had been seriously destabilised since the death of Putzi in 1907, if not before. Unable to cope with Mahler's deteriorating physical and mental condition, she teetered on the precipice of a nervous breakdown. In May 1910, leaving her husband in the care of the servants at Toblach (in the Dolomites, where they spent their last three summers), she took Gucki with her to the sanatorium at Tobelbad (just south of Graz) where the doctor prescribed lettuce, buttermilk – and dancing.

She was soon engaged in more than dancing with the handsome Dr Walter Gropius (about four years her junior). Gropius released in her a flash-flood of pent-up passion, far stronger than any previous experience. "X's stormy ardour had opened my eyes" was how she described her sexual release in her memoir, though La Grange has unearthed far more explicit declarations, especially from a biography on Gropius.

Gropius was as high-powered in his own field as was Mahler in music. By the time of his liaison with Alma, he was already established as a pioneer in modern functional architecture, his glass-wall Fagus factory buildings at Alfeld in Germany (1910-11) being among the most advanced works in Europe. Later, in 1918, he would become director of the Weimar School of Art and reorganise it as the famous Bauhaus (1923).

After these burning encounters at the Sanatorium, by accident or (more probably) by unconscious design, Gropius sent one of his passionate letters to Alma in an envelope addressed to Herr Director, Mahler. Mahler's fury swiftly turned to intense remorse as Alma poured out as never before all her bitterness and frustrations of the past eight years, not least the suppression of her composing.

After a triangular meeting by happenstance in Toblach in early August, Mahler assembled the two lovers together at his family's holiday farm in Alt Schluderbach and told Alma to make up her mind over which man she wanted – while he retired to read the bible by candlelight in his room.

"I didn't have a choice," Alma wrote. "I could never have imagined life without him." He was "the hub of my existence." Mahler in turn knew he could not possibly manage without Alma. Finally realising the extent of the sacrifices she had made for him, he began to encourage her to compose, arranged for the publication of five of her songs (1910), and became "as devoted and submissive" as he had formerly been "tyrannical." In La Grange's view he now cut as pathetic a figure as "an amorous pigeon."

Mahler's desperate scribblings across the draft and incomplete score of his *Tenth Symphony* (realized much later from the sketches by Deryck Cooke and others) tell their own tale of his private hell during the crisis:

> Mercy! ... Oh God! Oh God! Why hast thou forsaken me? ...

> [Inscription above second scherzo]:
> You alone know what it means [the muffled drum at the end] ... Ah! Farewell my lyre!
> The Devil leads me in a dance.
> Madness seizes me, Accursed!
> Demolish me that I may forget my being!
> That I may cease to exist ...

> [Finale]:
> To live for thee! To die for thee! Almschili!

*

Dr Sigmund Freud

During his informal consultation with Freud in Leiden on 26 August in this year of crisis (1910), Mahler resurrected many childhood memories, including one in which he was confronted by a barrel organ after a scene between his parents. Freud told the composer that Alma was seeking her lost father in him. By the same token, Mahler had "unconsciously looked for a type like his own mother in every woman." Mahler's own mother had suffered and grieved and he had unconsciously wished his wife to be the same. Mahler therefore need have no guilt feelings about having married a woman half his age. Freud wrote to Theodor Reik after the analysis that conditions for the restoration of Mahler's "capability for love" were favourable.

On his way back on the train from Leiden, Mahler composed a poem for Alma (the first of a flood) in which he finally felt that "the shadows of the night" were "blown away by the power of one word" ... "I love you." Another poem refers to "my being flowing into yours in the bridal chamber".

There was, however, no sexual rejuvenation of their marriage. Alma wrote after the crisis of waking one night to find Mahler standing by her bed, and of one occasion when he had to be revived on the landing as if from a heart attack. On another occasion she found him lying on the floor of his studio weeping.

I knew that my marriage was no marriage and that my own life was utterly unfulfilled" [she wrote]. I concealed all this from him, and although he knew it as well as I did we played out the comedy to the end, to spare his feelings.

"Vertigo" on the Orient Express

Had he known the truth of the continuing love triangle, Mahler may very well have been felled by grief and shock. What is certain – and not too widely known – is that the affair between Alma and Gropius raged on behind Mahler's back at least until October of this same year, with a four-day tryst in Paris, and that Alma longed for it to continue indefinitely, corresponding with Gropius during the rest of her marriage.

La Grange traces the path of the affair after the summer crisis. As well as sending her lover several passionate letters, Alma spent some afternoons with him in September in the Hotel Regina-Palast in Munich, while her husband was slaving away in the city's Exhibition Hall with preparations for the premiere (10 September) of his *Eighth Symphony* – dedicated to Alma. Then in October, on her way to Paris from Vienna to meet her husband before they left for New York, Alma arranged for Gropius to join her on the Orient Express at Munich. She gave him precise instructions as to the date (14 October) and time of the train and her exact location on it – compartment number 13 in the second sleeping car. She also told him to use the pseudonym of "Walter Grote" just in case her husband caught sight of the list! After a night on the train of what Gropius described as "complete happiness" they then enjoyed four precious days together in Paris.

Alma's letters to Gropius over these several months explode with passion, using such unequivocal endearments as "your woman" (Dein Weib), "my dearly beloved" (Mein Geliebter) – and even "your fiancée" (Deine Braut). She longed to have Gropius "lying completely naked" against her body. She lived for the time when "I belong to you completely". She had "vertigo" when they met again on the Orient Express; and she more than once expressed an intense desire to bear his children. "Our two perfections must give birth to a demi god," was how she put it in a letter from New York dated 13 November 1910. About a fortnight before that she had urged him, provocatively, to "conserve your health for me. You know why!"

*

The couple's last winter in New York

Mahler's last season in New York shows him to be a pathetically deluded husband. As to Alma, the signs are that she found her trying role as reconciled spouse a huge strain.

One of the Mahlers' Viennese acquaintances who was in New York, Maurice Baumfeld, was obviously not privy to the true state of the marriage. He records that:

> In this last winter [1910-11], their harmony was of almost unbelievable intensity. For this woman above all, he composed, conducted, created, lived. If she once missed a concert because of illness, and he could not send up a glance at her box before he began, it was as if his right hand was gone. In his long illness, he would not let her leave his side for an instant. I seriously believe that he held on to her powerfully enough to fend off death itself.

Baumfeld helped Mahler buy Christmas presents:

> I walked for hours with him around New York stores and art shops. ... And when all the presents were assembled he, with the eagerness of a small boy who has just been allowed to spend his first dollar, asked me time and again: 'Do you think we have found the right thing? or should we perhaps buy something more?'

Finis

After the last concert of his career on 21 February 1911, Mahler again fell ill and handed over his baton in New York to Theodore Spiering. It was decided he must return to Europe where medical expertise in bacteriology was more advanced. He seemed to rally round briefly in Paris, but on reaching Vienna his physician Dr Franz Chvostek realised the bacterial encarditis he had contracted was beyond cure. Among his last words were "My Almschi" and "Mozart" before he died just after 11.00 pm on the night of 18 May during a thunderstorm. He was buried in the Grinzing cemetery beside Putzi.

In his last days he had often told Alma "I have lived wrongly" and had promised that if he recovered they would take long holidays in Egypt and the East.

*

After Mahler's death Alma did not immediately fall into the arms of Gropius, but first became the mistress of the Expressionist painter Oskar Kokoschka. She then married Gropius by whom she had a daughter, Manon, whose death in 1925 was commemorated by Berg in his *Violin Concerto*.

In 1929 Alma married Franz Werfel and settled with him in the USA. Her autobiographical documents colourfully chart (according to Grove) "the history of a Nietzsche-inspired New Woman of the 1890s who subsequently expressed sympathy with Mussolini and certain German fascists (not Hitler), whose anti-semitism she affected to share – to the distress of her Jewish friends and Werfel."

***

Chapter 11

Claude Achille Debussy
"Bewitching in music, Bastard in Love"
Born: Saint-Germain-en-Laye (near Paris), 22 August 1862
Died aged 55: Paris, 25 March 1918

There is a woman at each crossroad of Debussy's life.
Certainly women of all ages seemed fascinated by him,
and they attached themselves to him like ivy to a wall.
[Marcel Dietschy: *A Portrait of Claude Debussy*]

He was – it's all in his music – a very sensual man.
[Maggie Teyte, soloist in *Pelléas et Mélisande*, 1908]

Claude has still not recovered from the nibbles of your
dear little mouth.
[Debussy to Lilly Texier, 24 April 1899]

She knew what she wanted and had come prepared.
When, in reply to her knock, Claude opened the door,
he saw that she was nude under her fur coat.
[from Pierre La Mure's novel: *Clair de Lune*]

Let's not mince words. Where most of his many women were concerned Debussy was a bastard! After his death there was a roaring trade in grotesque wax effigies, demanded by screaming feminists, of this monster with the renowned bulging cranium and double-forehead. I made that up about the effigy, of course, though it's true that Debussy's double forehead was always his most distinguishing physical feature. Double forehead or not, Oliver Reed was certainly the right man to play Debussy in Ken Russell's BBC Omnibus Classic documentary of 1963, *The Debussy Film*, scripted by Melvyn Bragg. Russell selected Reed after seeing him on *Juke Box Jury* and being stunned by his physical resemblance to the composer. Debussy's heirs actually used their copyrights to ban the film because of the offence caused by one scene based on a play for which Debussy wrote incidental music, *The Martyrdom of St Sebastian* (see below). In Russell's film, a girl is shown in a t-shirt in the water, attached to a cross and being pelted with arrows.

No composer did more than Debussy to justify the feminists' adage that All Men Are Bastards. He drove two of his women, Gaby and Lilly, to desperate measures with revolvers. Although Gaby's hysterical pot shot at herself after finding a love letter in Debussy's pocket seems to have been aimed to miss, in Lilly's attempted suicide a bullet remained lodged in a vertebra under her left breast for the rest of her life.

And yet! Is not Debussy the finest composer in this volume? At any rate, he's easily my favourite. And not simply because like some readers, no doubt, I cherish happy memories of playing the *Golliwog's Cakewalk, The Girl with the Flaxen Hair, Clair de Lune, Jardins sous la pluie,* and *En Bateau* several decades ago. But where Debussy's treatment of women was concerned, the opening salvo cannot be mollified one iota.

He was incapable of selfless love for anyone except his beloved only daughter Chouchou, born in 1905 by the woman who became his umpteenth lover and second wife, Emma Bardac. Mary Garden, the Scottish-born lead soprano in the premiere of *Pelléas et Mélisande*, the opera that established Debussy's reputation as one of the world's greatest composers, had the full measure of Debussy the man:

> I honestly don't know if Debussy ever loved anybody really. He loved his music – and perhaps himself. I think he was wrapped up in his genius ... He was a very, very strange man.

Because of his brutal treatment of women Debussy lost many of his close friends over the years, including the man he had loved, homoerotically rather than homosexually, as much as any woman, Pierre Louÿs. Louÿs, whose half brother some claimed to be his father, was a poet, portrait photographer, and writer of novels that "oozed sex from every page": *The Crimson Man, New Sensual Delights, Aphrodite ...* Louÿs also provided Debussy with three poems that he set to music in his *Chansons de Bilitis*.

That Debussy treated women badly didn't of course mean they gave him a wide berth. On the contrary, as Marcel Dietschy has emphasised, "women of all ages ... attached themselves to him like ivy to a wall." However odious their behaviour, geniuses of either sex have never lacked strings of lovers if they wanted them. But Roger Nichols has suggested that one additional secret of Debussy's appeal for women was his playfulness. One of the many women who were enchanted by it was the celebrated French novelist Colette in 1910 (she of *Chéri, The Cat* and *Gigi* fame). Then in her late thirties, Colette chronicled Debussy's exuberant tomfoolery after being bowled over by his first hearing of Rimsky-Korsakov's *Scheherazade*:

> He sang scraps of this new music, accompanied himself with a glissando on the piano, imitated the timpani on a pane of glass, the glockenspiel on a crystal vase. He hummed like a swarm; he laughed with his whole astonishing visage – and we were delighted.

Little wonder that when Debussy was on such form "rumour had it that no pretty girl within 100 metres was safe from him." Nor did they wish to be! How could they resist a genius who compared beautiful music with beautiful women in such words as these?

> *The Ballade* [by Fauré] is almost as lovely as Mme Hasselmans, the pianist. With a charming gesture she readjusted a shoulder-strap which slipped down at every lively passage. Somehow an association of ideas was established in my mind between the charm of the aforementioned gesture and the music of Fauré. It is a fact, however, that the play of the graceful, fleeting lines described by Fauré's music may be compared to the gesture of a beautiful woman without either suffering from the comparison.'

"The kind of face women glance at twice"

Debussy's "Assyrian" looks were yet another of his magnetic attractions. With his "soft and silky" black beard and thick curly hair, his "vivacious black eyes under heavy, drooping lids," his "pale, matt complexion," plump cheeks, his wide-shouldered, "rather fleshy", body he exuded a languid, voluptuous aura, "partly feline, partly gypsy." "Byzantine priest," "an Indian Prince," "one of the magi" are other oriental labels included in Debussy cameos etched by various people at different times.

His outfits too were distinctly personal in his bohemian days: they included a huge sombrero-cum-cowboy hat, a beige overcoat with a wide black velvet collar, silk ties, button shoes, and a blue cane with delicate carvings on the knob.

*

As Edward Lockspeiser has clearly shown, the only constant aspect of Debussy's personality was his ambivalence, his constant wavering between violent extremes. Various pen portraits of the composer show that he was

> tender-hearted, infinitely sensitive, yet also brutal; he was shy and also outspoken; confident, even impetuous, yet devoured by doubts; independent but envious. Even his appearance belied his nature: he was noble, perhaps exotic, as it was thought, yet also a bohemian; he was wealthy and extravagant, as it seemed, but in reality almost a pauper. If there is a single key to the many conflicting aspects of Debussy's nature it is his ambivalence, the sudden and unaccountable veering from one extreme to another to which an artist of sensibility is perhaps inevitably condemned.

"The naked flesh of emotions"

Debussy was as unfettered in his music as in his personal life. His goal was to free music from all the shackles (form, tonality, rhythm) of the Classical school, which he saw as a form of Teutonic tyranny. (He once described Germans and their music as "so heavy, not clear" and Beethoven as "the old deaf man.")

"How much one must create and destroy whilst trying to touch the naked flesh of emotions," he wrote towards the end of his life. Here are two more of his bon mots that pinpoint his lifelong search for complete originality:

> Music in its essence is not a thing that can be poured into a rigorous and traditional mould. It is made of colours and rhythmical beats. All the rest is fraud, invented by cold-blooded imbeciles riding on the backs of the masters.
> [To his publisher Durand]

> There is no school of Debussy. I have no disciples. I am I.
> [To a Viennese journalist in 1910.]

His quest for such a kind of music took in all kinds of sources and inspirations: whole-tone scales, pentatonic scales (equivalent to the black notes only of the piano) and other scales deriving from Javanese gamelan music that bewitched him (as did the theatre of Annam) when he heard it at the Universal Exhibition in 1889. He also brought into his music twelve-tone chromatic scales, ancient church modes, medieval organum, and jazz progressions.

The painter in music
"I love pictures almost as much as music"
(Debussy to the composer Varèse in 1911)

Debussy's inspiration came far more from Impressionist painting and Symbolist poetry than from the music of other composers, save possibly that of Moussorgsky who was his ideal of the "instinctive" composer. If there is any label for Debussy, then Impressionist is the only one. Debussy himself, however, was ambivalent about the tag. In 1908 he said that it was "just about the least appropriate" but in 1916 he told his friend Emile Vuillermoz (a music critic) that

> You do me a great honour by calling me a pupil of
> Claude Monet.

Debussy's music gets as close as music can ever be to painting. It brings to mind the paintings not only of Monet, but even more so of his favourite painter Joseph Turner, England's most original landscape artist. The affinity between Debussy's *La mer* and Turner's abstract portrayals of light, space, and the elemental forces of nature – say in his *Rain, Steam and Speed* – is obvious.

Even many of Debussy's titles are in tune with the visual arts: Arabesques, Nocturnes, Images, Estampes (Engravings) ...

*

How to account for such a complex, secretive man? Debussy's teenage and adult love life was so packed with incident that we must skim over his childhood, which, according to Dietschy was fraught with "instability, lack of money, rebellion, hunger, fear, delusion, shame [and] defeat."

Debussy's volatile and domineering mother Victorine (née Manoury), was "passionately attached" to her eldest-born Claude, fussing, over-protective, and taking sole responsibility for his elementary education. (This wasn't a good idea in view of his lifelong shaky spelling and syntax.) Her death in 1915 would affect Claude "more painfully than I can say." His father Manuel Achille was largely ineffectual, Debussy once even referring to him, perhaps unfairly, as "a waster." Manuel Achille was by turns a china shop owner (at the time of Debussy's birth), a broker, a civil servant, a clerk in a printing works and twice a soldier – the second time getting off lightly with a year in prison and loss of civil rights for his role as a captain of the Communards in 1871. Manuel Achille's later disappointments in seeing his son reject the careers planned for him – first of sailor and then of concert virtuoso – would be finally compensated in 1903 when, purely to please both his parents Debussy received the Chevalier of the Légion d'Honneur. (He himself had no time for gongs.)

It was from both his parents that Debussy would acquire tastes that were both expensive and unaffordable. He would never be a man to allow arrears of rent to stop him somehow laying his hands on fine silks, yellowed prints, satsuma vases, walking sticks carved from pale wood, ivories, green or Vermeer-blue silk neckties, batiste ... He became a hedonist to the core, like the poet Verlaine, and like Wagner.

The key player in Debussy's musical beginnings was his fond paternal Aunt Clémentine, a true demimondaine whose life story is another ready-made novella. She found Claude his first piano teacher in Cannes, where he and other members of the family stayed with her over a few summers from 1870. Claude was happiest here when either losing himself in Aunt Clémentine's cardboard theatre – or doing absolutely nothing. According to his sister Adèle (the eldest of his four younger siblings), Claude was

> uncommunicative, and closed in upon himself, liking neither his lessons nor his games ... He would spend whole days sitting in a chair, thinking, no one knew of what.

Already he was a dreamer. And as Dietschy has said, "to dispute the primacy of the dream over reality is to fail to understand Debussy."

Nevertheless, for all his dreaming, his second piano teacher, a certain Mme de Mauté who claimed, dubiously, to have been a pupil of Chopin, spotted Debussy's wayward talent and managed to get him into the Paris Conservatoire in October 1872. Debussy was by then "a fat boy of ten or so, short, thickset, wearing a black coat enlivened by a loose spotted tie and short, velvet trousers."

*

"Mon plaisir"

Not surprisingly Debussy quickly became the despair of his professors Antoine Marmontel and Albert Lavignac who found him to be "a little backward in the rudiments". Ten years or so later he was hauled before the Conservatoire's irate registrar who asked him, "What rule do you follow?" "My pleasure," was the youth's supercilious reply, leaving the official dumbfounded. The one man who most encouraged Debussy's wayward genius was his easy-going composition teacher from 1880, Ernest Guiraud (who wrote the recitatives for Bizet's *Carmen*). By then Debussy had won no first prizes as a piano soloist, but had composed several songs set to the poems of Alfred de Musset.

*

Green-eyed Mme Blanche Vasnier
Debussy's "succubus"

everything he writes is for her and owes its existence to her.
[Paul Vidal, July 1884, in a letter to Henriette Fuchs]

To help make ends meet during his studies, Debussy was fortunate in acquiring two part-time jobs in the autumn of 1880: one as the accompanist to a choral society named La Concordia and another, at around sixty francs a month, as accompanist to a singing teacher by the name of Mme Victorine Moreau-Sainti. Predictably, Debussy often failed to turn up for the choral rehearsals when he had more interesting fish to fry. But neither hell nor high water would have kept him away from Mme Moreau-Sainti's studio with her potted palms and succession of pupils being put through their paces with technical exercises, Gounod's *Ave Maria* and *Carmen*'s Habañera.

Here it was that at the age of eighteen, Debussy fell madly in love with one pupil, thirty-two year old Mme Blanche Adélaïde Vasnier. Without ever deliberately intending to, it seems, she utterly enslaved Debussy for the next seven or eight years of his life.

True, he had "proposed" that summer to Sonia von Meck, flighty sixteen year old daughter of Tchaikovsky's idolater and patron Mme Nadezhda von Meck. (Debussy worked as one of Mme von Meck's house musicians for the three summers 1880-82, variously in Arcachon, Florence, Russia and Vienna.) But this had been a fit of adolescent fancy and he probably felt no lasting pain from Mme von Meck's curt refusal.

Mme Vasnier was the stuff of Debussy's dreams. Her eyes were his favourite colour, green. Her hair was red to brown, and she sang with a lovely light voice to professional standard. Daughter of a printer and man of letters, she was married to Eugène-Henry Vasnier, a reclusive, teetotal, workaholic legal expert (a "registrar of buildings"), eleven years her senior and extremely wealthy. She had thus always had every opportunity to pursue her expensive tastes and her passion for music to the full.

But it was with Debussy that she indulged, probably for the first time, her unsatisfied craving for passionate love. Hitherto she had merely titillated what Paul Vidal (one of Debussy's Conservatoire friends) called her "jealous vanity" by flirting with her many admirers.

It must have been while they were preparing for a concert they gave on 12 May 1882 in the Salle Flaxhand (Paris) that Love Walked In. Debussy was to accompany her in two of his own songs, *Les Roses* and *Fête Galante,* and the programme also included his *Nocturne* and *Scherzo* for violin and piano, in which he accompanied Maurice Thieberg.

Given Debussy's humble home in the rue Clapeyron, to have been so often made welcome by the Vasniers in their palatial apartment in the rue Constantinople, and also at their country home in Ville d'Avray (half an hour from Paris) must have been paradise. The Paris apartment (Dietschy tells us) sported

> Louis XV black-lacquered furniture, curtains of embossed red velvet, dazzling white cushions, pedestals adorned with dried flowers, paintings adroitly hung, heroic bronzes, and a selection of delicate bibelots.

The Vasniers' daughter Marguerite, who was thirteen in 1882, later recalled Debussy's almost daily visits to work in their Paris home:

> ... I can still see him in the little drawing room on the fifth floor. ... He used to come there nearly every evening, often in the afternoons too, leaving behind him the unfinished pages which were placed on a little table as soon as he arrived. He used to compose at the piano. ..or at times walking about the room. He would improvise for a long time, and then walk up and down humming, with the everlasting cigarette in his mouth,

211

or else rolling tobacco and paper in his fingers. When
he had found what he wanted, he began to write. He
made few corrections, but he spent a long time working
things out in his head and at the piano before he wrote.
He was rarely satisfied with his work ... He was very
quick to take offence and extremely sensitive. The
slightest thing put him in good humour or made him
sullen or angry. ...

Debussy was pouring out reams of lovely music – even if at
this stage often somewhat derivative of Massenet, for his idol.
She was the first woman ever to sing his songs. It only took a
brushing of fingers one day as he nervously handed over the
manuscripts; only a few seconds' lingering eye contact for Mme
Vasnier to lead her nervous adorer by the hand to her boudoir,
undo the buttons of his shirt and ask him to unlace the back of
her dress. ... And then the powder keg of passion exploded ... At
least that's how I imagined the first time. Pierre La Mure's
scenario is rather different. (La Mure wrote perceptive and well-
researched, if often wonderfully OTT novels based on the lives
of Mendelssohn and Debussy, and I have "borrowed" quite a few
vivid details from his *Clair de Lune*.)

Altogether Debussy wrote twenty-three beautiful songs over
nearly three years between 1881 and 1884. Here are two of the
dedications:

to Mme Vasnier, the only muse who has ever inspired
in me anything resembling a musical feeling (not to
mention anything else).

to Mme Vasnier, these songs which have come to life
through her alone, and which will lose their enchanting
gracefulness if they nevermore pass her melodious
fairy lips.

The eternally grateful author

Roger Nichols highlights one song in particular, a setting
of Verlaine's poem *En sourdine*, a portrait of two lovers in each
other's arms, completed on 16 September 1882. "From the very
first bar," writes Nichols, "the song is clearly describing a mystery,
almost a religious experience. ... the intention can hardly be
misinterpreted."

Grand Prix de Rome

In the grip of such a grand passion, it is hardly surprising
that Debussy abhorred the prize so many French musicians,

painters, sculptors, architects, and engravers craved for when he won it on the second attempt in 1884. Instituted by the French Académie des Beaux Arts in 1803, the Grand Prix de Rome required the winner to pursue three years of study in Rome at the Villa Medici. Debussy recalled much later that when he was informed that he had won the prize with his cantata *L'Enfant Prodigue,* "my heart sank ... I had a sudden vision of boredom ...I felt I was no longer free."

Especially no longer free, of course, to continue his affair with his "succubus". Thus did Paul Vidal damn Mme Vasnier in this letter to a friend in July 1884. (The literal definition of a succubus is "a female demon believed to have sexual intercourse with sleeping men!")

> So our friend Achille has won the prize despite himself! This sinister tale of adultery has been played out over a long period. Last year I had to persuade him to compete in the final round, against his wishes. Then during the winter he told me he wouldn't leave for Rome even if he won, that he was prevented from doing so. ...
>
> His succubus is battening on to all his little weaknesses. She's pretty and much pursued by admirers, ... everything he writes is for her and owes its existence to her. How can one expect him in the circumstances to exile himself for two years in Rome, which he already knows and abhors! ...
>
> His moral sense is undeveloped, he's nothing but a sensualist. ... But, with all that, he has such talent and such a personality!

Debussy found Rome initially unbearable. Within about two months of his arrival in February 1885 he was lamenting thus to his friend Claudius Popelin-Ducarre, father of one of his friendly and sympathetic fellow students, the painter Gustave Popelin:

> I must tell you that there has been no change in me during the last two months, if anything, my feelings have only been intensified during that time. ... I know this is not following the advice you gave me to try to reduce this passion, which I know is mad, to a lasting friendship, but it's because it is so mad that it prevents me from being reasonable. Thinking seriously about it not only makes it worse, but almost convinces me that I have not sacrificed enough to this love.

Debussy fled back to Paris twice, the first time as early as April 1885, the second in February or March 1886. He also spent part of the summer vacation (July 1885) with the Vasniers in Dieppe. By the time of his second flight, M. Vasnier, ever an assiduous and kindly mentor to Debussy over this entire period, must surely have rumbled the situation and wearied of his role as cuckold. He steered Debussy back in the direction of Rome, where he remained only until March 1887, flouting the Prize rules which specified a three-year stay.

Among Debussy's limited musical consolations during these two years in Rome were meeting Liszt – then a biretta-sporting half-priest in his mid-seventies – and steeping himself in the *Renaissance polyphony* of Palestrina and Lassus in one of Rome's churches, San Maria dell'Anima. Work wise, he abandoned two projects and wrote little of lasting interest. He did, however, steep himself in Shakespeare, Shelley, Verlaine, Baudelaire, and other writers.

Loulou: "Kissing in the villa ... nude under her fur coat"
There were also a few social diversions and consolations for Debussy in Rome, including a one-night stand or three. He was befriended by a certain Count Primoli ("a distant cousin of Napoleon III's daughter in law") who entertained him in luxury at his villa in Fiumicino in August 1885. And Primoli later revealed to the Principal's wife Mme Hébert (so she wrote in her diary for 9 February 1886) that Debussy and one, Loulou, had been seen "kissing in the Villa." Loulou turns out to have been another married lady, Mme Hochon. She and her husband were guests of the Héberts at the time. Being a "worldly woman" the presence of her husband didn't prevent Mme Hochon from offering the bereft Debussy "an evening of pleasure." The story goes (details unconfirmed) that the brazen hussy took a fancy to him at a reception at the Villa and, having given her husband the slip, appeared at the door of Debussy's room "wearing nothing but a wedding ring under a new fur coat!"

Given his good fortune, it may even possibly have been Mme Hochon rather than Mme Vasnier who inspired the song dated this very January 1886 that Debussy set to the poem *Green* (in the collection *Ariettes*) by Verlaine:

These final kisses ...
This heart that beats only for you

Back in Paris after his two-year ordeal in Rome, Debussy's contact with the Vasniers petered out – the last sighting of him in his role of lover being (according to Holmes) when the painter Jacques-Emile Blanche saw him climbing a rope ladder up to Madame's window in Dieppe in 1888. Debussy had maintained an entrée into the Vasnier household as Marguerite's piano teacher – an experience that the young lady found decidedly negative.

"A Rubens model"
Just one more glimpse of Mme Vasnier (from Dietschy) when she is 42. She appears in one photograph as

> buxom ... plump of face, her eyes dry, her arms crossed,
> the provocative thrust of her breasts balanced by the
> hips drawn back. ... Mme Vasnier had taken on the
> amplitude of a Rubens model.

The only large project Debussy was working on when he left Rome was his concluding obligation for the Prix: a setting of *The Blessed Damozel,* a poem D G Rossetti had written for his consumptive mistress Elizabeth Siddall. The work was finally premiered in April 1893.

*

1887 through 1892
"... almost abject poverty"
Debussy returned from Rome to his family in the rue de Berlin to find shortly afterwards that his father, now fifty-one, had lost his clerical job. Debussy was therefore forced to earn his living disagreeably, giving piano lessons and doing occasional hackwork for publishers. The trickle of money from the few compositions that were published in these next few years – including the *Ariettes* and *Deux Arabesques*, the *Petite Suite*, the *Cinq Poèmes de Baudelaire* and a cluster of piano pieces – was nowhere near enough to sustain his parents while he remained briefly with them. Nor often even himself after he moved into his seedy fifth floor apartment at 42 rue de Londre, hard by the Gare St Lazare.

The four or so years after his return from Rome were ones of "almost abject poverty" relieved by occasional spending sprees when he received a publisher's advance for a transcription, or other small commission. According to his plumber-poet friend and most intimate witness of these years, Vital Hocquet, Debussy lived through four Parisian winters without even an umbrella.

La Mure's imaginative scenario of a kindly concierge cooking him the occasional stew to supplement his diet of bread, potatoes and tea is all too believable.

However, having latched on for a while to a wealthy dilattante, one Etienne Dupin (who would later be murdered in Mexico), Debussy went in Dupin's company – and at Dupin's expense – to Bayreuth in the summers of 1888 and 1889. Over the two visits he saw two performances of *Parsifal,* two of *Die Meistersinger* and one of *Tristan und Isolde.* He returned from the first of these experiences "like a Muslim from Mecca," though fortunately for Western civilisation the infatuation wore off. Nothing would have been worse than Wagner à la française, as some of Debussy's contemporaries turned out to become.

Since his return from Rome he had begun mingling with the symbolist poets – Mallarmé, Baudelaire, Verlaine, Régnier and others – who met each Tuesday evening at Mallarmé's house in the rue de Rome, and whose work would so crucially inspire Debussy's own. Mallarmé himself believed that poetry should be "transcendental" and should strive for the abstraction of music. Not surprisingly many of his poems are exceedingly obscure.

Still on the symbolist front, in 1892 Debussy read a play by the symbolist dramatist Maurice Maeterlinck, *Pelléas et Mélisande*, set in the imaginary kingdom of Allemonde. Although a flop in Paris as a play, its other-worldly atmosphere was exactly what Debussy had been seeking for an opera:

> It had no action [writes La Mure], no suspense, no dramatic structure – nothing. The plot, if you could call it that, was the triangle, this hoariest, tritest of all plots. A young woman [Mélisande], lost, afraid, battered by life, married a kindly middle-aged man she did not love [Golaud]; later she met his younger brother [Pelléas] and fell desperately in love with him. It all ended badly, as such things usually did. The husband discovered the romance and in a fit of jealousy killed his brother, only to discover that his deed solved nothing. His wife did not love him any better than before, and she died, leaving him shattered with guilt and broken-hearted. As a play *Pelléas* was about everything a play should not be. In fact it was an unreal prose poem in which unreal people expressed real emotions. But music, not words, was the true language of emotions ... It was waiting for music to bring it to life.

Inspired by the play, Debussy immediately began working on music that would finally emerge before the world – a full ten years later – as his own opera of the same name. *Pelléas* sealed his reputation worldwide as the greatest French composer of the 19th Century.

In 1891 Debussy met a genius far more wayward than himself – a truly divine head case who was to become one of his most loyal friends in dire trouble, Erik Satie (he of *Gymnopédies* fame). The two men met in a Montmartre restaurant on the rue Trudaine, L'Auberge du Clou, where Satie was house pianist. (See Chapter 13 on Satie.)

*

"one navel looked astonishingly like another"

Now back to love! There is no reason to doubt La Mure's intuition that between Debussy's affairs with Mme Vasnier and Gaby Dupont he had any number of one night stands or short affairs with pickups as lonely as himself, only to discover that "one navel looked astonishingly like another" and that "kisses could be as tasteless as water." Nor that he had a brief and passionate liaison with another "Madame V.," a Belgian from Antwerp – "beautiful, rich, Jewish and married" – who was visiting relatives in Paris. The affair seems to have been more agonising on Mme V's side, since she also loved her husband "with all her heart" – though no longer, it seems, with her body which craved intensely for young Claude.

"A rickety table, three straw-bottomed chairs, something resembling a bed and, on loan, a splendid Pleyel piano."
Life with "Gaby-of-the-green-eyes", 1892-1898

a blonde with catlike eyes, a powerful chin and firm opinions.
[René Peter]

There were scandalous suggestions that Debussy and Gaby Dupont (1866-1945) first met "in some frivolous place" – a pickup joint, perhaps, rather than a brothel? Well, why not? All Parisian brasseries of the Toulouse-Lautrec type were pickup joints. Men and women must meet each other somewhere, and church socials were out of the question for a pagan like Debussy who declared that he "made mysterious Nature my religion."

Born in Lisieux in the Auge region of Normandy, twenty-four-year-old Gaby, the daughter of a dressmaker, had "an excellent figure, light brown hair which she dyed [blonde], a firm chin, blue-green eyes and a brilliant complexion," as well as full lips and a largish mouth. She arrived in Paris c.1887 to make her career as a courtesan in high society – and why not, when the only alternatives were dressmaking, millinery, or even soliciting and the like. You'll have to take it from me that on the testimony of one of her protectors (quoted by Dietschy), Gaby was unusually good at her job of pleasing men. A photo portrait of her, very Art Nouveau, by the aforementioned Louÿs shows her reclining languidly, eyes closed, on cushions and fabrics on a chaise longue. Head on hands, she is wrapped in a full-length loose-fitting gown. No wonder that after arriving in Paris she soon attached herself to "a black-sheep aristocrat," the middle-aged, corpulent Comte de Villeneuve.

Gaby must unquestionably have loved Debussy to reject a life of certain luxury as a protector's paramour to throw in her lot with him. Instead of being a kept woman languishing in bed all morning, she had to work her fingers to the bone as a milliner to help pay the rents; firstly for the couple's "dank attic" at 42 rue de Londres, with its borrowed Pleyel piano, bed, three chairs and a rickety table; and then, from autumn 1893, for their fifth floor apartment with three rooms, a kitchen and an inside loo at 10 rue Gustave Doré. After they parted Gaby admitted that their poverty was as much a cause of the split as Debussy's other women.

Even with an annuity of 6,000 francs settled on him in 1894 by George Hartmann (front-man for the publishing firm of Froment), as well as several well-paid engagements playing transcriptions of Wagner at society functions, Debussy was invariably penniless. And any hopes he and Gaby had nursed of money from *Rodrigue et Chimène*, the operatic project he had begun in 1890 and dedicated to her, were dashed after he abandoned it after the third act in 1892. (Debussy's life story is littered with such abandoned projects, over forty in all. He even scuttled the performance of one of his works, a *Fantasy for Piano and Orchestra*, on the day of its premiere.)

"... a relatively stable emotional life" (New Grove, 2001)
The world needs to be eternally grateful to Gaby for creating

some comfort in which Debussy could work on so many masterpieces during his developing career – the *String Quartet, the Proses Lyriques, Pelléas et Mélisande, Prélude à L'Après-midi d'un faune* (usually regarded as being the first and ground-breaking piece of "modern music"), the *Nocturnes* ... Gaby's background may have prevented her from being a full-blown muse. But even unworldly composers work better if all is done and dusted. If tiresome callers, plumbers, creditors, landlords and leaking roofs are all dealt with. And if light refreshments, meals (however so often frugal in this couple's case) and snifters are served at regular intervals. Especially as Debussy had by now established a habit of working through the night until dawn and sleeping in – perhaps because there was less racket from the train whistles and all the other puffing, hissing, clanking and clattering noises of the Gare St Lazare.

Debussy's young dramatist friend René Peter wrote vividly of the couple's lives in the mid nineties:

> [Claude] was living under the sway of Gaby. She was a blonde with catlike eyes, a powerful chin and firm opinions. She looked after the domestic side – there was not much Mélisande in her – and that was quite a big undertaking, first of all because they were poor and secondly because Claude, being a large, spoilt child who refused to allow himself to be manhandled by life, indulged all his whims and was impervious to reason. Was he suddenly struck with the desire for that brown Japanese engraving which he later gave me for my birthday? He emptied his purse without stopping to think where the next day's dinner would come from. And while he was lost in thought in company with his genius, Gaby would be out raising money on knickknacks at some sordid pawnshop.

In view of his indebtedness to Gaby, Debussy's dedications to her were rather scant:

À Mademoiselle Gabrielle Dupont

> [on the first page of the manuscript for the abandoned *Rodrigue et Chimène*]
> to my dear and very good little Gaby, with the sincere affection of her devoted Claude Debussy
> [Inscription on the short-hand score of the *Prélude à L'Après-midi d'un faune*]

> To Gaby, princess of the mysterious kingdom of
> Allemonde. Her old devoted friend Claude Debussy,
> June 1902.
> [inscription on a score of *Pelléas et Mélisande*, given to
> Gaby three years after they broke up]

Proposals, romances and affairs during the Gaby years

Given Debussy's affairs, and even two breathtaking proposals of marriage to other women while he was living with Gaby, it is a wonder that the liaison lasted six years. His infatuation with the sculptress Camille Claudel, an "ethereal, beautiful woman" who shared his love of Degas, was harmless enough. As later was an undeclared crush on Mallarmé's daughter Geneviève, who bowled over many other men besides Debussy as she served punch at her father's Tuesday evening gatherings of the Symbolists.

There were other such innocent infatuations with dream girls linked directly in Debussy's fantasies with his compositions: most notably, in February 1894, with a friend's daughter Yvonne Lerolle, aged 17 and of "of touching beauty." Debussy gave her a Japanese fan decorated with birds and flowers with the dedication

> To Mademoiselle Yvonne Lerolle, in memory of her little
> sister Mélisande.

Thérèse Roger (1866-1906)

Debussy's treatment of blonde, blue-eyed Thérèse Roger – "ravishing, young and all the rest" – in 1894 was of another order altogether, and brought him low in the eyes of many. The second child of a widowed singing teacher, Thérèse was already a renowned interpreter of Debussy's music. She had sung in the premiere of his *Blessed Damozel* in April 1893, and the last two of his *Proses Lyriques* in February 1894. She sang these works again the following month in a concert in Brussels that he rather grandiosely called The Debussy Festival.

In a state of dream-like euphoria, Debussy proposed to Thérèse after the February concert. Obviously being unaware that he was living with another woman, the hapless Thérèse, twenty-eight and maybe worried about being left on the shelf, accepted. From cloud-cuckoo land Debussy wrote thus to his composer friend Ernest Chausson, who as the brother-in-law of

Thérèse's father had paved the way for Debussy's proposal:

[8 March]

> Now that a sunny road is open before me I'm afraid at
> not having deserved such happiness, and at the same
> time I'm fiercely determined to defend it with all the
> power at my disposal! Your advice about marriage has
> touched me deeply, I assure you, and it seems to me
> (novice that l am in the business} absolutely right. ..I
> really feel I've offered my life once and for all and that
> from now on it will be lived for just one person.

When Gaby got wind of all this (there was even a notice in
the press) she went ballistic, as any woman would. Imagine the
scenes in the rue Gustave Doré! On 17 March the marriage was
called off. Poor Thérèse became a virtual recluse for another four
years. Eventually, at thirty-six, she entered into an unhappy
marriage with a divorced engraver and died four years later in
1906

Not surprisingly Debussy's treatment of Thérèse caused a
two-year rift with Chausson, as well as permanent ruptures with
other erstwhile admirers and supporters. The world is full of
such stories of course. A former good cellist colleague of mine
discovered purely by chance one day that her live-in partner – a
garage mechanic – was going to get married to another woman
in two days time. He wouldn't have told her even then if she
hadn't challenged him when he came home from work!

After the Thérèse debacle, Debussy and Gaby seem to have
rubbed along well enough between 1894 and 1897. There were
just the usual flaming rows and passionate reconciliations that
were par for the course between a volatile woman and an ab-
normally self-centred man who shared few interests in common
besides making love. A trip they made to the Hotel de Croisy,
Orbec (Calvados) at Whitsun 1894 resulted in the lovely *Jardins
sous la Pluie* (Gardens in the Rain). On 28 August 1894 Debussy
wrote to Lerolle:

> My life here is simple like a blade of grass, and I have
> no other joys than working.

The relatively happy couple would attend the literary
Fridays at the Chat Noir café in Montmartre, its walls covered
with Gauguins and paintings by the Impressionists. As well as
meeting painters, poets journalists and other composers, they

watched shadow plays in the top room. They also frequented the Reynolds Bar where they saw clowns performing, and the cakewalk from America. Other diversions included the circus, billiard matches, puppet shows, and the Alcazar Music Hall on the Champs Elysées.

When the odd cheque came through the box marked "letters," Debussy squandered it in on expensive meals. He had been a gourmet since childhood, his favourite dishes including timbales of macaroni, rose-flavoured pralines, curried oysters, tiny salmon trout, tarts, port ...

More affairs, a suicide attempt, and another proposal
These reasonably good times were bound to crumble. Debussy became involved with a Mrs Alice Peter, who was effectively separated from her husband and keen for a time to be seen as "the muse of the great man of the future." Debussy dedicated the second of his *Chansons de Bilitis* to her, *La Chevelure*.

He then cheated on Gaby in an affair with "a young and wealthy society woman" still unidentified – though La Mure gives her name as Hélène without, as he often does, quoting his source in a footnote. Debussy himself told the story of the ensuing crisis, including Gaby's suicide attempt, to Louÿs (who was then in Algeria acquiring an Arab lady named Zorah):

> [9 February 1897]
> Gaby with her steely eyes found a letter in my pocket which left no doubt as to the advanced stage of a love affair with all the romantic trappings to move the most hardened heart. Whereupon tears, drama, a real revolver and a report in the *Petit Journal*. Ah, my dear fellow, why weren't you here to help me out of this nasty mess? It was all barbarous, useless and will change absolutely nothing. A moth's kisses or a body's caresses can't be effaced with an India-rubber. Mind you, they might perhaps think of something like this and call it the Adulterer's India Rubber. On top of it all, poor little Gaby lost her father – an occurrence which for the time being has straightened things out.
> I was, all the same, very upset ...

This was far more histrionics rather than a serious suicide attempt. Although emotionally shattered, Gaby was unharmed and a few days later was able to attend her father's funeral in Lisieux. But Mme Chausson and Mme Ysaÿe (wife of the distinguished violinist who led the first performance of Debussy's string quartet) both publicly took Gaby's side, each giving her refuge for a time. Thereafter Debussy had only occasional contact with Chausson and Ysaÿe.

Around 1897 Debussy made his second proposal during the Gaby years, this time to Catherine Stevens, daughter of the Belgian painter Alfred Stevens. She declared that she would have married him, "despite everything that was being said about him at the time ... if I hadn't met Henry." Henry was Henry Vivier, a brilliant young doctor. Catherine did her best to spare Debussy's feelings with such words as "once *Pelléas* is performed, we will talk about it again!" However tempting he might have been for a fling, Debussy was definitely not husband material for the likes of a woman like Catherine, then in her early thirties and looking for a good match. Debussy was, she wrote, too "eccentric," a "man without a penny."

He was inconsolable for several days. Then once again it was back to Gaby and *Pelléas*. Desperately short of money he himself contemplated suicide in a rather whining letter to Louÿs (1 April 1898), part of which reads:

> I've got into this state of mind from continually fighting against silly and despicable impossibilities. You know me better than anyone and you alone can take it upon yourself to tell me that I am not altogether an old fool

Rags to riches

Soon after this it was crunch time for Gaby. According to La Mure, dire poverty had already driven her from Debussy for a few months from the early summer of 1897. At that point she took up with an unidentified protector whose money enabled her to rent a house and provide for her widowed mother in Orbec. But love drove Gaby back again to the draughty doors and squeaking shutters of the rue Gustave Doré.

Finally, however, fed up of being endlessly cheated on, and of living so often on bread and tea, she left Debussy for good, probably by September 1898, and collapsed into the welcoming arms of the aristocrat Comte Victor de Balbiani who lived on the Avenue Niel. There (writes La Mure) she was soon presiding over glittering receptions attended by diplomats, senators, cabinet ministers, even Aristide Briand, later to be ten times Premier of France. In due course Balbiani probably replaced her with someone younger.

Debussy later rebuffed Balbiani when approached by the count to write incidental music for his play *La Fille de Pasiphyé* (The Daughter of Pasiphaë). Aside of male rivalry, the play's lurid plotline, in which the heroine Pasiphaë (wife of King Minos) sleeps with a white bull and produces a son with "the head of a bull and the equipment of a man" (the Minotaur), was hardly one to tease out music from such a fastidious man as Debussy.

In September 1898 Debussy moved to another apartment, on the fourth floor of 58 rue Cardinet. He soon found some money to paper the walls in his favourite green, and decorated the room with Chinese silks and ornamental cats.

"She really loved him until she died."
[The pianist Alfred Cortot, who knew
Gaby well in her last years]

Gaby may have later been reported to be "a well-dressed tart," but neither she nor Debussy bore each other any ill will. On the contrary, he presented her with the earlier mentioned score of *Pelléas* in 1902, and some time much later she was seen attending a lecture on the composer's life and works.

Even when she was back in Rouen as an usherette, she held on to Debussy's scores as long as she was able. Later, she was reduced to satisfying her craving for tobacco by combing the pavements and gutters each night for cigarette ends "in an old coat and knitted woollen hat." She died on 12 May 1945 at Orbec.

*

Life with "Lilly-Lilo" (Lilly)
Rosalie Texier, Mme Claude Debussy (1873-1932)

She is unbelievable fair and pretty, like some character from an old legend ... Her favourite song is a roundelay about a grenadier with a red face who wears a hat on one side like an old campaigner – not very provoking aesthetically.
[Debussy to his friend Robert Godet, 5 January 1900]
"not much up top."
[Roger Nichols on Lilly, BBC 2: *Masterworks* 2,
19 January 2002]

Debussy was first introduced to Lilly Texier in the spring of 1898 during the terminal stages of his relationship with Gaby. Daughter of a widowed telegraph inspector, with a "slender figure, pale complexion, small dark mouth and dark chestnut hair," Gaby had come from the Yonne (in Burgundy) to Paris when she was twenty-five to work as a mannequin in a fashion house, the Soeurs Callot in the rue Taitbout. She first lived with "a nice fellow who dabbled in stocks" – the niceness however being infected with a streak of violence from which Lilly soon fled.

In a way that the French seem to manage better than anyone else, for a time Gaby befriended Lilly and even warned her of her suitor's less loveable qualities, especially his roving eye. Paul Holmes sketches this ménage à trois:

> For a while, all three could be seen in each other's company at their favourite haunts, especially in the Brasserie Pousset with its Pre-Raphaelite decor. Debussy and his two women, with their friends Mendès, Messager, various writers and journalists and the fantastic poet Paul-Jean Toulet, who wanted to co-operate on a libretto with Debussy, must have been a striking sight.

Lilly became very popular with many of Debussy's friends – not only for her "simplicity, her firmness, her lively and slightly earthy wit, her elegance, and her lithe body" but also because she laid on a very yummy "thé complet" – biscuits, brioches, canapés, macaroons, cream puffs .... Her least appealing asset was a harsh voice that Debussy was often prone to mock.

A year on, the relationship between Debussy and Lilly had clearly moved well beyond the platonic:

> [24 April 1899]
> My dear little Lilli, Claude has still not recovered from the nibbles of your dear little mouth. And he can hardly leave off thinking of that evening when you gave him so much unexpected pleasure in the nicest way, and with the most complete abandon in the world.

Although in mid May Debussy was telling Louÿs that "my old liaison with Music prevents me from becoming a bridegroom," by July he was describing Lilly as "marriageable." He had even been economical with the truth — or wildly optimistic — in telling her in the previous month that

> it is certain that *Pelléas et Mélisande* will be put on this winter and that my situation will improve very markedly.

All he had done at that stage was to play the score to Albert Carré, director of the Opéra-Comique. It would be another three years before it reached the stage.

"A time of spring"

With Gaby's warnings, and no doubt hearing other stories of Debussy's womanising, Lilly hesitated before plunging into marriage – even though in September Debussy threatened in eloquent style to kill himself. But she finally capitulated and they married on 19 October 1899. The witnesses were Satie and Louÿs. Every book on Debussy repeats the same story of the wedding day with minor variations. Debussy had to give a lesson for twenty francs (to a Mlle Worms de Romilly) so that he could pay for the ceremony and wedding breakfast. In the afternoon they went to the zoo at the Jardin des Plantes, and then dined at the popular Brasserie Pousset. Mme Claude Debussy then returned with her husband to his apartment at 58 rue Cardinet.

The couple enjoyed about three years of happiness. According to their matchmaker René Peter, "there followed perhaps the happiest period of his life – 'a time of spring', he used to call it – and a flowering of rare but marvellous works ..."

Debussy was able to work productively and undisturbed on *Pelléas,* as well as the *Estampes* (three piano preludes) and two of the *Nocturnes.* One caller at the rue Cardinet, Emille Vuillermoz, arrived and heard Debussy working on the opera but was firmly barred from entry:

> The door opened. A beautiful but stern-looking woman appeared, holding in her hands various menacing items of household apparatus. I can still see the long-handled broom on which she was leaning, like a Valkyrie on her spear! I asked politely to see Debussy. Brünnhilde listened to me with an outraged expression. My audacity seemed to take her breath away. ... 'My husband is not at home.'
> During all this, Debussy was playing and singing louder than ever, practically drowning our conversation. I ventured an unbelieving glance at the half-open door of the study from which this torrent of music was emanating. ... 'I tell you, my husband is not at home!' And satisfied with the solidity of this statement, the daughter of Wotan closed the door in my face. ...
> [Emile Vuillermoz: *Claude Debussy*]

Another caller Mme Gérard de Romilly, the now-married piano pupil he had taught just before his marriage ceremony, paints a cosy picture of wedded contentment:

There was an atmosphere of intimacy and calm in the two small rooms joined by a bay. One was Debussy's studio where, on the desk, manuscripts, inkwells and pencils were laid out in perfect order. There was also a divan, several Oriental carpets and, on the walls, pictures ... and drawings representing Lilo Debussy, then at the height of her beauty. ...

... The two cats, which Debussy cherished, occupied an important place in the family, and had all their whims respected. As silent as their master, they had the right to spend the day solemnly on the desk and, if they so wished, to sow disorder among the pencils.

This, of course, was all too good to last! One slowly increasing source of disappointment was their inability to have children. Between 14 and 23 August 1900, after a three week holiday in the Yonne, Lilly had an abortion in the Maison Dubois. On 25 August Debussy wrote to Louÿs:

Lilly...was operated on several days ago, but that's not all; it seems her body in general is in a poor state and (between ourselves) she has tubercular patches at the top of both lungs. We are having to take immediate steps to deal with these, namely sending her to the Pyrenees for three or four months! You can imagine what a torment it's all been, quite apart from my financial situation, desperate as usual! I don't know any more how to cope with so many contradictory events.

The convalescence in the Pyrenees probably never materialised – at any rate not for three or four months. By way of affordable recompense for Lilly, at the very end of the year Debussy dedicated the first two completed movements of his *Nocturnes* to her:

This manuscript belongs to my little Lilly-Lilo. All rights reserved. It is proof of the deep and passionate joy I have in being her husband. Claude Debussy. At the peep of January, 1901.

When these two *Nocturnes* were premiered the following December a discerning critic – there aren't many of those! – wrote that Debussy was "one of the most original and remarkable artistic personalities of the day" who was "intent on expressing the transient impressions of the dream he is in quest of, rather than the eternal passions of the world which he shuns."

Pelléas

Lilly's proudest months with Debussy were probably those surrounding the premiere of *Pelléas et Mélisande* on Monday 30 April 1902 at the Opéra-Comique on Place Boiëldieu – a full ten years after he first began reading Maeterlinck's play. Although unable to appreciate the real quality of her husband's genius, she felt that it was as much her piece as his. She had, after all, looked after him during its orchestration and completion – a process that went on even after the premiere since Debussy had to write some orchestral interludes to be played between the scene changes. Lilly will obviously have been thrilled that the opera played to fourteen good houses, and that in the last performance of the season on 28 June there were three or four curtain calls after each act.

Henri Büsser, who conducted the offstage chorus of sailors on the first night and later took over from André Messager as the main conductor, made some diary notes.

> 28 April: The great day finally arrives! Public dress rehearsal of *Pelléas*. ... Debussy takes refuge in Messager's office and nervously smokes one cigarette after another..
>
> 30 April [? 1 May]: The morning after the premiere I go to see Debussy ... [Lilly's] happy that *Pelléas* is being produced. 'It's my work too', she says, 'because I gave Claude encouragement when he was despairing of ever seeing his work reach the stage!'

This year of *Pelléas* was perhaps the climactic year in Debussy's rise to fame. He had written what many consider to be the most perfect music drama ever written. *Pelléas* would be performed over the next few years in Berlin, Munich, Milan (La Scala) London ... and even the New York "Met." (The Met's director Gatti-Casazza later forced an advance on Debussy for a second opera which, needless to say, was never written.) By the end of the year of Debussy's death *Pelléas* would be staged also in Brussels, Frankfurt, Cologne, Prague, Berlin, Rome, Boston, London, Chicago Buenos Aires, Geneva, Birmingham and Manchester.

Debussy's arrival to fame also sparked a cult which he came to loath of "Debussyism" in which acolytes proclaimed him their leader and wrote stuff "full of parallel fifths, unresolved sevenths and full-tone arpeggios."

Smelling Salts and Pistols at Dawn

Debussy's musical successes never came without enormous struggle – he was after all a man who would in his own words, "sometimes require weeks to decide upon one harmonious accord in preference to another." In the case of *Pelléas* there had also been an unholy fracas with the dramatist Maeterlinck. Suffice it to say that a huge row over Maeterlinck's choice of the lead soprano – his own mistress Mlle Georgette Leblanc, with Debussy's initial agreement – against the choice of the theatre, Mary Garden, (whom Debussy also came to prefer) climaxed into a Feydeau farce. Maeterlinck confronted Debussy with a cane, challenged him to a duel (even putting a bullet through his cat while practising for same), Debussy dropped into a chair, Lilly fetched smelling salts ...

It all, of course, came to nothing.

After all his public success, – including his acceptance of the Chevalier of the Légion d'Honneur – Debussy went to London for four days at the invitation of Messager. From the Hotel Cecil he sent this "soothing" letter to Lilly on 16 July (1902):

> My very dear little wife,
> Your letter did me immense good – if you knew how alone I feel in spite of everything; no longer hearing your imperious voice calling 'Mî — Mî leaves me as melancholy as a guitar. I loved your lack of courage very much. You see, it is very nice to be the strong little wife, but there are times when the strong little wife must have her weaknesses. That adds an extra charm to her graciousness. ... Would you believe that it is impossible to get a cup of good tea? That makes me think of my rue Cardinet and the dear little wife, who, among other gifts, possesses that of making tea! Ah! in England there are no such wives as that; here they are wives for horseguards with their complexions of raw ham and their movements like those of a young animal. ...

He came back to find Lilly, rarely in robust health, "in the grip of kidney stones". "Will she never get well?" Debussy asked in a letter to a friend. But they spent that summer in the peace of the Burgundy countryside at Lilly's father's home in Bichain. Here he worked on, amongst other things, an opera based on

Edgar Allan Poe's *The Devil in the Belfry* – another obsessive project that would come to nothing after years of agonising.

"His love for Lilly was oozing out of him like water from a cracked jug." (La Mure)

By 1903 life with Lilly was beginning to pall. He secretly admitted that her voice and shrill laughter grated on his nerves. At the age of 30 she was also ageing prematurely, developing jowls and her eyes becoming ever more "doe-like." She was unable to identify with his ever intensifying need to withdraw from the world in his search to express himself.

Their holiday photos at Bichain in 1903 (where he began working on his first set of *Images* and *La mer)* "have a glum aspect," writes Dietschy. Debussy is bored with her. And they were still childless, and still sometimes short of money. In his correspondence with others Lilly became "my poor wife," "my little wife" ...

Enter Emma Bardac
a woman of "commanding presence"

Things would no doubt have drifted on, in the way that men, more than women, always let them, had Debussy not met someone else. She had money and she made a beeline for him, as she had done for other distinguished artistic men.

In October 1903 a young pupil of Debussy, Raoul Bardac, introduced his teacher to his mother, forty-one-year-old Emma Bardac, the Jewish wife, since she was seventeen, of a wealthy banker Sigismond Bardac. Their marriage had been "open" for some time, he consorting with an actress and she with various artists including most notably, a decade earlier, Fauré, who had dedicated his song cycle *La Bonne Chanson* to her. Others who had fallen for her auburn hair and topaz-coloured eyes included Debussy's composer friends Charles Koechlin and Albert Samain.

Debussy had long admired Emma's voice, and after dining with the Bardacs, readily accepted further invitations for music

"The conflagration of 1903-1904"

"Elle l'a eu par la gueule." ("She's hooked him.")
[Lilly's comment on Emma]

Things moved quickly over the next few months, with Debussy and Bardac, according to one unconfirmed report, taking a romantic drive in her carriage along the Bois de Boulogne and

Debussy, in French novella style, successfully proposing an affair.

In Dietschy's opinion, Debussy's *Deux Danses* of April 1904 for harp and strings (*Danse sacrée et danse profane*) convey his "unease and anticipation" of this time. This letter of 6 June from Debussy to Emma thanking her for some flowers is surely the language of lovers:

> How kind of you and how good they smell! But above all, I am made profoundly happy by your thought. That entered my heart and remains there, and it is for such things as these that you are unforgettable and charming. ... Forgive me if I have kissed all these flowers as though they formed a human mouth. Perhaps it is crazy ...

In this same month Debussy also completed his second set of *Fêtes galantes* to poems by Verlaine, dedicating them to Emma – "To my little darling [À la petite mienne] to thank the month of June," Of this music Nichols writes:

> The third and last song, *Colloque sentimental*, Debussy's farewell to the poet, sounds like a farewell to Lilly as the two ghostly lovers converse:
> 'How blue was the sky, and great our hope!' 'Hope, crushed, has fled toward the black sky'

On 15 July 1904 Debussy packed Lilly off to her father's at Bichain and moved to Emma's house. On the 16th he wrote to Lilly that:

> for some time I've been worried that I'm going round the same circles of ideas. Now that I seem to have found a new direction, that's why I dare not let go of it, whatever it costs me

Over the next weeks he hinted several times at how things were going to turn out.

"The works born of his passions"
Masques, L'Île Joyeuse ...

Later in July Debussy went with Emma to Jersey where he completed his *Masques*. They then moved on to Dieppe for most of August and part of September, where he completed the work that on every hearing sounds incandescent with his new passion: *L'Île Joyeuse*. Both this and the *Masques* were sparked off by the eighteenth-century painter Watteau's *The Embarkation for*

Cythera, depicting masked lovers leaving for Aphrodite's island of love. There are obvious parallels with Debussy's own flight to Jersey with his beloved. In Dietschy's words, *L'Île Joyeuse* with its profusion of oriental arabesques

> is in every regard the isle of Jersey, an isolated place
> and a place of uninhibited joy – the composition proves
> it overwhelmingly.

Both these works, Dietschy feels, embody Debussy's "uncontrollable feeling" for Emma Bardac.

*

Mayhem

For all this passionate elation, Debussy had to come down to earth. He had to ditch his wife. There was a "painful meeting" on 13 September when he told Lilly that he was moving out of the rue Cardinet and moving in with Emma, first to 19 Avenue Alphand. Lilly would threaten suicide at least four times.

Debussy wrote to Messager on 19 September 1904 :

> My life during the last few months has been strange
> and bizarre, much more so than I could have wished.
> It is not easy to give you particulars, it would be rather
> embarrassing. ... I have had many a fall, and have
> hurt myself so much that I have felt utterly exhausted
> for hours afterwards ... I have been mourning the
> Claude Debussy who worked so joyfully on *Pelléas* ...

The crisis came on 14 October 1904, perhaps because Lilly couldn't face their imminent fifth wedding anniversary. In the very public space of the Place de la Concorde, she pointed a revolver at herself and fired. Mary Garden describes her visit to Lilly in a clinic on the rue Blomet:

> ... When Lilly had finished telling me the story, the
> surgeon came in to dress her wound ... and opened
> her night dress, and in my life I have never seen
> anything so beautiful as Lilly Debussy from the waist
> up. It was just like a glorious marble statue, too divine
> for words! ...
> And lying underneath Lilly's left breast was a round
> dark hole where the bullet had gone in, without
> touching anything vital ... That little token of her love
> for Claude Debussy stayed with her till she died, and
> that was in 1932.

Curiously, in June of this very same year Debussy had told Mary Garden that he was "obsessed with love" of *her*! Clearly

Mary was another Mélisande in his imaginary love life. Mary, however, although deeply respecting Debussy, didn't remotely fancy him.

Now that Debussy was a public figure, Lilly's suicide attempt received coverage in every newspaper including *Le Figaro* (4 November). Later even a play based on it appeared, *La Femme nue* by Henry Bataille.

It is not surprising to learn that Debussy never visited Lilly at the clinic, nor did he pay her bills. Ravel and Pierre Louÿs collected money amongst their circle to help her. Louÿs openly quarrelled with Debussy, while Fauré also refused to speak to him – no doubt also piqued by Debussy inheriting his mistress! Other erstwhile friends who had been fond of Lilly and who temporarily or permanently broke with Debussy included René Peter, Paul Dukas, André Messager, Pierre Lalo ... Inevitably some accused Debussy of pursuing Bardac for her money. Only Satie, Louis Laloy, his new publisher Jacques Durand, Ricardo Viñes (who premiered many of Debussy's piano works), Koechlin, and a few others stood by him.

In the run-up to his divorce, Debussy turned to the offensive in one of his *Note Books* (quoted here from Nichols) that also contained sketches for *La mer*:

> Anger – even in front of her family -violence with the servants; quarrels about money ...; lies of every kind. ...; constant dissimulation – my friends, for example, never liked – was only after a slightly better situation — she made a mistake there and avenged herself by exercising a daily tyranny over my thoughts and dealings ...; ... If Mme D had been an honest person, it is probable that my friends would not have been so attentive to her – !! [exclamation marks added in blue]

Debussy never saw Lilly again, though even as late as March 1905 during divorce proceedings she was still resisting a break-up. The divorce – rightly punitive for Debussy – was finalised on 2 August. (Emma's divorce, more favourable than Debussy's, had come through on 4 May.)

Even allowing for the futility of laying blame in love, it is easy to see why so many of Debussy's friends deserted him. He had once loved Lilly and, (as Holmes reminds us) had even put her into a play on which he collaborated with René Peter, *Les Frères en Art*. There he said of her:

'You don't pretend to be a muse who frightens the
sparrows away. You don't do your hair like the women
in the frescoes. You have a lovely perfume and you are
as sweet as a peach. ..'

Lilly's story closes by mentioning that in 1910 Debussy
stopped paying her alimony, and that on 15 July 1916 he had to
make a down payment of 30,000 francs to fund her alimony of
400 francs a month. In doing so he moaned to his lawyer that
"an artist is much less interesting than a mannequin".

Lilly died in 1932.

*

By the Spring of 1905, life had become so unbearable for Debussy
and Emma in Paris that they left for England via Jersey. Before
leaving Debussy wrote to his new young friend the scholar and
critic Louis Laloy:

[14 April 1905]
You should know how many people have deserted me.
It is enough to make one sick of everyone called man.
I shan't tell you everything I have gone through. It's
ugly and tragic and ironically reminds me of a novel a
concierge might read. Morally, I have suffered terribly.
Have I some forgotten debt to pay to life? I don't know,
but I've often had to smile so that no one should see
that I was going to cry .

In Jersey, Debussy took up *La mer* once more and wrote
thence to Durand:

The sea has been very good to me, she has shown me
all her moods.

Debussy was glad of Durand, who in August 1905 signed with
the composer an exclusive contract paying him a monthly income
based on anticipated future royalties.

That same August the couple moved on to London where,
he told Laloy, he spent several days

without much joy, except for the music of the grenadiers
who used to pass every morning with their joyful
bagpipes and the wild little fifes playing marches in
which the Scotch song seemed to melt into the
cakewalk.

Debussy noted one march down and was to use it four years
later in his *Children's Corner Suite* for piano. Children were now
very much on his mind, since to his joy Emma was now some
seven months pregnant.

From London they moved on to Eastbourne where once more Debussy wrote to Laloy:

> I've been here a month. It's a little English seaside place, silly as these places sometimes are. I shall have to go because there are too many draughts and too much music - but I don't know where ... I have written a certain amount of music as I have not done for quite a time.

In spite of the distraction of seafront bands in Eastbourne playing military marches and arrangements of Sullivan and Edward German, he finished the orchestration of *La mer* ("three symphonic sketches") while overlooking the sea from the windows of the Grand Hotel. *La mer* would be premiered later that year on 15 October in a fiasco of catcalls and hisses followed by a "cool" press response. (One problem was that the conductor Camille Chevillard was not up to the job.) However, the tide soon turned when Debussy himself conducted the work successfully in 1908, and it is now perhaps his best-loved orchestral work. Here is one eloquent tribute in a memoir by Nicholson Baker:

> I was amazed by how true to liquid life it all was. ...
> How did [Debussy] turn an orchestra, a prickly ball of horsehair and old machinery, into something that splashed and surged, lost its balance and regained it?
> ...

[from *Granta* magazine, issue 76]

*

Family Man: whisky and strong tea

With the birth on 30 October 1905 of Claude Emma Debussy – ever to be known as Chouchou – Debussy, although not yet married to Emma Bardac, was indeed a de facto family man living also with Emma's twenty-three year old son Raoul, her daughter Dolly (for whom Fauré would later write his *Dolly Suite*), two servants and Kim the dog. Debussy also ensured that his ageing parents were living in decent accommodation.

With Emma's funds, they had all moved shortly before Chouchou's birth from the Avenue Alphand to 80 Avenue du Bois de Boulogne (now Avenue Foch): a pleasant detached house whose rear garden backed on to the familiar ceinture railway line that circled the city.

According to Dolly Bardac these were days of happiness, with Debussy sending from his study to her mother elsewhere in the house billets doux "full of love and tenderness." For nearly two years there were no money problems, with Emma's alimony keeping her in the style to which she was accustomed and Debussy in a position to indulge in all those luxuries that he had always in any case regarded as essentials. Dolly later numbered among her step-father's treasured acquisitions a big wooden toad, a Chinese ornament called Arkel, various Chinese antiques, beautiful silver ... And from across the Channel books of English literature, original paintings by Turner, Whistler and D G Rossetti, drawings by Arthur Rackham, William Morris furniture ... not to mention supplies of whisky and strong tea.

From now on Debussy also became more conventional and meticulous in his dress, abandoning his broad-brimmed hat "nearly as big as a parasol" for a thoroughly bourgeois derby.

Debussy was besotted with his Chouchou, and made up for her a whole series of stories about a Monsieur Gros, a fat butterfly hunter who got into scrapes with lions, tigers and crocodiles. Later, from Vienna, he would send her post card instalments of *Les Mémoires d'outre-Croche* signed "Le Papadechouchou." In 1908 he dedicated his *Children's Corner Suite* to her "with her father's apologies for what is to follow." Some of the pieces were inspired by toy animals in her nursery and some of the titles were suggested by Chouchou's English governess, Miss Gibbs. Later, in 1913, Chouchou and her collections would also inspire *La Boîte a Joujoux* (The Toy Box) – "a little work to amuse children, nothing more."

The singer Maggie Teyte ("the graceful Miss Teyte" as Debussy referred to her) left a telling picture of Debussy in 1906-07 in the Debussy-Bardac household in the Bois du Boulogne. (She sang *Mélisande* at the Opéra-Comique in 1908, taking over from Mary Garden.)

> So it was, that at the age of eighteen, very small and light, I found myself on Debussy's doorstep, with the score of *Pelléas* under my arm.
>
> ... he sat at the piano without even moving. There seemed to be hours of silence. At last he turned round: 'Vous êtes Mlle Teyte?' 'Oui Monsieur .' Silence. 'Vous êtes Mlle Maggie Teyte?' 'Oui Monsieur.' Silence. ...
>
> ... Strange to relate he never shook hands with me. He said to me, 'I will have Mélisande as I want her.' I was only too ready to agree.

As a teacher he was pedantic ... He sat one day at the piano. He never played without getting into the mood. This took two or three minutes. I sat and waited. He raised his arms and was just ready to play when he saw a little bit of white cotton on the floor. He stopped and picked it up. He rolled it up and looked everywhere for a place to put it. Dead silence for another five minutes ...

... He was such a many-sided character. ... He was volcanic: a volcano that smouldered. I once saw him so white with anger, then red with the sheer effort of control. There was a core of anger and bitterness in him ... No one seemed to like him. Jean Perrier, who played Pelléas to my Mélisande, went white with anger if you mentioned the name of Debussy ...

1907
When poverty comes through the door
love flies out of the window.
[Lancastrian adage]

Once again the good times for Debussy didn't last. Sigismund Bardac soon began to renege on his alimony payments and had to be pursued through the courts. Worse still, in 1907 the couple's hopes of a bonanza from the will of Emma's Uncle, Osiris, were dashed when they discovered that owing to his displeasure with her conduct, he had left her a mere 5,000 francs a year.

A letter from Debussy to Laloy of 15 October 1907 is one of all-too-familiar moroseness:

> An ordinary rain is falling on Paris, but I do not see its purpose very well ... peace does not dwell in my soul. Is it the fault of the landscape of this corner of Paris? Or is it that I am clearly not made to put up with domestic life? So many questions, which I cannot find the strength to answer.

Tough! With Chouchou now a dearly beloved child of two, absconding was not even an option. Instead he sealed his relationship with Emma by marrying her on 20 January 1908. Debussy realised that from now on, much to his loathing, he would have to hit the road regularly as a conductor of his own works in order to bring in some money.

Loathsome long train journeys, hotel rooms, rehearsals,

concerts, receptions ... Merde! Between now and his death Debussy would visit London, Vienna, Amsterdam, Budapest, Moscow, St Petersburg, Turin, Rome, The Hague, and Brussels. His very last trip would be to London in 1914 to earn a sou performing for Sir Edgar and Lady Speyer.

On the composing front, he would have to labour on commissions – including the bizarre five-act "mystery" by Gabriel d'Annunzio, *Le Martyr de Saint Sebastien* (inspired by the love bites of d'Annunzio's mistress who was the star of the show!), and also the ballet *Jeux* for Diaghilev and the Ballets Russes. Inevitably these and other projects reduced the time he could spend writing for himself. But praise be that he could somehow continue to produce such masterpieces as the *Rondes de Printemps, Ibéria,* the two sets of *Images* (for orchestra), his ineffably beautiful two sets of *Préludes, Le Promenoir des deux amants, the Trois Ballades de François Villon, the Trois Poèmes de Mallarmé* ... And then would come his explosion of creativity in the summer of 1915 (see below), followed by the last creative spurts before his death.

Debussy's increasingly morbid state must have made him hard to live with. In 1908 he began to identify himself with the character of Roderick, in Poe's *The Fall of the House of Usher*, who feels the walls of the house suffering ... A year later, still immersed in Poe's gloomy mansion he wrote to Durand

> I spend my existence in the *House of Usher* ... and leave with my nerves as taut as the strings of a violin.

His recurring gloominess wasn't improved in 1909 by the appearance of the first symptoms, in the form of daily haemorrhages, of the cancer that would kill him in 1918.

It Had To Happen

Of course it did! Debussy had his last known affair with an unknown woman in March 1910. Approaching the male menopause he wrote to André Caplet on 23 March,

> I am – and this happens to me often – at a dangerous turning point in my life.

"There was a final attachment," writes Dietschy, "secret and very tender, but it led to no rupture." Did Emma know? Did she by now care? Probably, just about.

The reluctant "travelling salesman"

Debussy's first letters to Emma from abroad date from Vienna late November and early December 1910. Coming from a man compelled to abandon the comfort and tranquillity of his study and present his wares all too often to "idiots," they are not those of a happy man:

> You realise that I have undertaken this journey for us, because of our persistent poverty without which I shouldn't be so far away from you, so deprived of your caresses.
>
> It was with much difficulty that I kept myself from weeping ... Everything annoys me. My nerves are on edge and I find that a composer of music is required to excel these days in those qualities of toughness possessed by a travelling salesman.
>
> If only you could see my expression – something like the mask of Beethoven or that of Dante on his return from Hell.

Certainly the marriage was going through a rocky patch, perhaps not the first. Emma wrote to a lawyer about a possible separation, complaining among other things about her husband's mania for table-tapping. (Debussy's interest in Occultism is another chapter.)

Nevertheless she stuck with him and supported him crucially through the ordeal of the above-mentioned project with d'Annunzio in 1910 and 1911. When it was all over, Debussy recorded his gratitude to Emma in June:

> For my own little one, in memory of three months of Martyrdom which she alone knew how to alleviate with the happy phrase: "What does a work like this matter to you!"

*

By now Debussy was heavily in debt, his obligations to Durand alone in 1911 amounting to 27,000 francs. (By 1914 the figure would rise to over 56,000 francs.) To make matters worse, Emma refused to let him to sail to Boston in the final months of 1911 to see a production of *Pelléas* conducted by Caplet. He also felt he had dried up musically; he was no longer reaching "the naked flesh of emotions."

The Debussys were unable to afford holidays in either 1912 or 1913. Of the latter year Nichols writes:

It is implicit in one or two remarks in his letters that Emma refused to countenance any diminution of the luxurious lifestyle she was accustomed to. At the same time she regularly refused to let him travel without her and no less regularly suffered illnesses of one sort and another: in this summer of 1913 a temperature and accompanying insomnia, which prevented Debussy travelling to London and earning a fairly easy 5,000 francs for accompanying Maggie Teyte in the *Ballades de François Villon*.

Debussy's trip to Russia in December 1913 did have some pleasant moments – including hearing *Sorochinsky Fair* by his favourite composer Moussorgsky – but basically the trip was a "a grim ordeal." He suffered continuously from insomnia, one of the symptoms of his cancer condition. The letter he wrote to Emma on his first night in Moscow is like many others:

I went to sleep broken-hearted. ...After an hour, not being able to sleep, I got up and walked about like a demented one, from one room to another. ...I drop into an armchair, fall off to sleep and am awakened by the cold. ...I lie down again and try to get to sleep by doing the silliest things such as counting to a thousand forwards and backwards. Then some-one comes in to ask what I want for breakfast.

Even more alarming is this letter of 6 December:

What's going to become of us? Your letters are more and more miserable! Like you, I feel nothing will calm you and that makes me very uneasy. ..Once again, I beg you, grant us both a little patience and goodwill.

Two days later the real rub, perhaps, in their marital problems surfaces: a rub that causes so many creative artists to change partners frequently or to end up living alone. Emma is jealous of his composing. He gives her insufficient attention:

Do you realise that you wrote: 'I don't know how I'll manage not to be jealous of your music'? Don't you think that's enough to upset one's equilibrium somewhat? ...

Concert-wise, this Russian trip to Moscow and St Petersburg was a huge success with both audience and critics. Even more to Debussy's liking will have been a homage signed by twenty Russian musicians assuring him that their expectations of his music had not been disappointed and that

we have lived with you days that will never fade from
our memory.

Debussy's melancholia continued in 1915 when between
leaving Paris on 18 February for Rome (where audiences went
"delirious" over his music) and returning home on the 24th, he
sent Emma twelve letters and telegrams of despair: at having
received no letters from her, at her having to face their creditors
alone, at his being in a hotel room in which he felt that 'everything
is crumbling round me' ... One letter reads:

> In the course of a sleepless night I was convinced I
> was going to die and decided to give up conducting
> concerts throughout Europe. I hardly dare write this
> down but I confess my terrible fear of losing your love.

After Rome came a four-day trip to Amsterdam and The
Hague for a fee of 1,500 francs. Again successful concerts were
no consolation for personal distress:

> The fog is murky; that's the only word for it. I'm again
> in a dismal state, but with my nerves on edge, and I'm
> off to rehearse.

The death on 23 March of his mother after his return only
plunged him further into despair. "Does one know what happens
at such moments?" he asked.

*

"Probably the three most productive months of his life for quality and quantity"

> Ouff! the most intricate Japanese woodcut is child's
> play compared to some of those pages, but I am content.
> It is a good work.
> [Debussy to Durand of the *Piano Etudes*]

Having helped Emma in her war efforts by organising a concert,
Debussy and his family went in July 1915 to Mon Coin, Pourville,
near Dieppe. Exactly what now sparked off such an explosion of
creativity – probably the three most productive months of his
entire life – is a mystery. First came a two-piano suite *En Blanc
et Noire*, followed by six *Etudes, A sonata for piano and cello,* six
more *Etudes*, then the *Sonata for flute viola and harp* ... All these
works testified to Debussy's newfound enthusiasm for the French
tradition in music — hence his signing himself Musicien Français
in the scores. (This was, of course, wartime.)

In October he had to return to Paris. On hearing of the
destruction of French villages, at the beginning of December he

wrote his little heartfelt *Le noël des enfants qui n'ont plus de maison* (Carol for Homeless Children) – one of the last spurts of his flickering genius. Only the *Violin Sonata* was still to be written. Before his debilitating colostomy for rectal cancer on 7 December he bade Emma to "continue to love me in our little Chouchou".

From 1916 life became a long calvary. "He is so thin and pale" wrote Emma to Pasteur Valléry-Radot. The composer Widor was "profoundly moved by his thinness and weakness." "If I must soon die, I hope at least that I have tried to do my duty," Debussy wrote to Durand on 3 July 1916. His morale was not improved by taking up and abandoning once again his project on the *House of Usher*, of which he completed only a sketch for one scene.

In March 1917 he finished his *Violin Sonata*, begun the previous year, and took part in its premiere on 5 May. His last-ever concert engagement was to accompany Gaston Poulet in the *Violin Sonata* in September at St Jean de Luz (at the Atlantic end of the Pyrenees). Back in Paris he soon took to his bed for the rest of his life.

A cryptic note to Emma at New Year 1918 was his last ever to her. He had not put pen to paper for two months.

> But if it is agreed that love is ... How will it not be ...

Pasteur Valléry-Radot saw him on 8 February:

> I acted as though I knew nothing and she did likewise ... As if this war did not kill enough people, this illness had to strike a man like him. What injustice, what blindness of fate!

His last days were relieved by visits from Viñes, who played him the *Etudes,* then from Durand who embraced him and handed him ... a cigarette. One of the hundreds and thousands that he had rolled and savoured with such pleasure throughout his adult life and that surely helped to kill him.

He died on Monday 25 March 1918 at 10.00 pm during blasts of the German's infamous monster long-range canon "Big Bertha". Emma, André Caplet and Valléry-Radot were beside him. The funeral ceremony took place on 28 March amidst another shelling. Of the fifty or so mourners present, only a handful arrived at the Père Lachaise cemetery where he was buried. Shortly afterwards, his body was re-interred at the Passy cemetery.

***

Chapter 12

Johan Julian Christian (Jean) Sibelius
"The worst skirt-chaser of us all"
Born: Hämeenlinna, Finland, 8 December, 1865
Died age 91: Järvenpää, 20 September, 1957

There is much in my make up that is weak ... When I am standing in front of a grand orchestra and have drunk a half-bottle of champagne, then I conduct like a young god. Otherwise I am nervous and tremble, feel unsure of myself, and everything is lost. The same is true of my visits to the bank manager. ... You can see from this that my drinking has genuine roots that are both dangerous and go deep. I promise you to try and cope with it with all my strength.
[Sibelius to his brother Christian, 1903]

Never write any unnecessary notes, because every note should have a life of its own.
[Sibelius's advice to aspiring composers, radio interview, 1948]

How capricious are the gods! Only they can explain why Sibelius's lungs and liver kept going well into his ninety-second year whilst so many other nicotine and alcohol addicts are felled in their fifties or sixties. Obviously, an iron constitution helped Sibelius to reach such a ripe old age in decent health.

Powerful composer that he was – the best of his music matching anything composed over the past hundred years – Sibelius cannot detain us too long here. As a student about five feet nine inches tall – "slender and handsome, with a mop of unruly hair and a luxuriant moustache" – he was dubbed "the worst skirt chaser of us all" by his comrades in Vienna in 1890. Yet in his married life, apart from a period of seven years on the wagon, he was surely too much of a soak to be a serious womaniser. Though who knows? Perhaps during his mammoth benders he came across a moll or two who relieved him of more than the contents of his wallet.

All this may come as a surprise to the millions of fans of Sibelius's perennial pops: the ever-rousing *Finlandia* (the zenith of nationalism in Finnish music and banned by the Russian government!); the hauntingly evocative *Valse Triste*; the patriotically inspired *Karelia Suite*; and the *Violin Concerto* (one of the most difficult in the repertoire). It just goes to show, for the umpteenth time in these stories, how beautiful music can flow from boorish men.

*

Since it is impossible to write anything about Sibelius without mentioning Finnish nationalism, let me remind you (thanks to Microsoft Bookshelf 94) that Finland had been a Russian Grand Duchy since 1809. Nationalist feelings became ever more fervent during the nineteenth century and Sibelius reflected them powerfully in his music. An elected Finnish parliament was finally established in 1906. After Finnish independence was proclaimed in 1917, a civil war followed between the nationalist White Guard (supported by the Germans – and Sibelius) and the defeated leftist Red Guard (supported by the Russians). A republic was finally established in 1919.

*

Love requited or unrequited in his personal life does not seem to have drawn any music from Sibelius – apart, that is, from a little piano waltz he wrote for the woman who did not become his fiancée, Betsy Lerché, the daughter of a Finnish senator. His finest music is far more immersed in the wind, light, space and solitude of his native country – with its vast forested interior plateau dotted with some 60,000 lakes, and its barren region north of the Arctic Circle. From his study at Ainola (his country home from 1904) Sibelius could look out across the tree tops to the lake beyond, Tuusulanjärvi. It was an undying source of inspiration, as were the birds, especially the cranes, geese and curlews. In Julian Barnes's short story *The Silence*, Sibelius's music and his natural surroundings are one and the same:

> I heard the cranes today but did not see them. The clouds were too low. But as I stood on that hill, I heard, coming towards me from above, the full-throated cry they give as they head south for the summer. Invisible, they were even more beautiful, more mysterious. They teach me about sonority all over again. Their music, my music, music. This is what it is. You stand on a hill and from beyond the clouds hear sounds that pierce

the heart. Music – even my music – is always heading south, invisibly.

*

Feminine environment

Sibelius's only dim but abiding memory of his father, the town's heavy-drinking physician who died bankrupt before the toddler Johan was yet three, was of the heavy odour of tobacco smoke. It "permeated every fibre of his father's clothes and every nook and cranny of the house" in Tavastehus, the Swedish name for Hämeenlinna. (Swedish was always the language spoken in the households of Sibelius father and son.)

More important in Johan's childhood development was his attractive mother, Maria Charlotta (née Borg). He was never close to her for, as a preacher's daughter straight out of Ibsen, she was strict, formal, and not at all touchy-feely with baby Johan, the second of her three children. All this left Johan (rather like Debussy) inverted, dreamy and remote. And maybe it explains why as an adult he would often crave to be caressed, his wife Aino duly obliging.

Called Janne by his boyhood friends, Sibelius changed Janne to Jean in his teens after inheriting some calling cards belonging to a late uncle, inscribed "Jean Sibelius." He and his younger brother Christian grew up in an almost wholly feminine environment. Besides his sister Linda, there was the ever-looming presence of his maternal grandmother and her two unmarried daughters. And on the other side of the family, there was his paternal grandmother and her daughter, Johan's dearly loved Aunt Evelina, with whom the Sibelius children spent the summers. The only man sometimes around was Sibelius's much loved paternal uncle Pehr.

Such a female-dominated environment has certainly fostered creativity in other composers (Saint-Saëns and Puccini come immediately to mind), and it may also have been a factor in that of Sibelius – along, of course with his precocious talent. Although he was no high flyer in his school lessons, at the age of nine Sibelius could repeat at the piano, from memory, extracts from Handel's *Harp Concerto* he had heard at a concert.

*

"The prettiest girl in Finland."
(Martin Wegelius, Director of the Helsinki Institute
of Music, on Aino Järnefelt.)

The overpowering impression gleaned from Sibelius's life-story is the sacrifices made on his behalf by his wife Aino née Järnefelt. She was the sister of his best friend and fellow student Armas Järnefelt, an important conductor in his day but now best known for his *Praeludium* and *Berceuse* for small orchestra. Never losing faith in his genius, Aino would tolerate to repeated breaking points the scourge of her husband's alcoholism and also what Guy Rickards so very aptly calls "the blind egocentricity of the artist."

It was love at first sight when Sibelius and Aino met at the Järnefelt family's Helsinki flat in 1889. Aino was so transfixed that she could not go through with a pantomime part assigned to her. Her family however, considerably more well-to-do than that of Sibelius, were not initially keen on the match and Sibelius rather callously courted for a time the above mentioned Betsy Lerché.

After completing his studies in 1889 at the Music Institute in Helsinki (where one of his closest friends was the great pianist and composer Busoni, a member of staff there) Sibelius spent a year in Berlin. Here he steeped himself in music he had never before heard (*Don Giovanni, Tannhäuser, Die Meistersinger,* Richard Strauss's *Don Juan...*) and studied counterpoint with "an old-line drill sergeant" named Albert Becker. But when not working, Sibelius was also boozing to excess and frittering his money away in the circle of Christian (Rustle of Spring) Sinding. "The circle was completed," writes Sibelius's eight-volume biographer Erik Tawaststjerna, "by some young ladies who studied musicians more closely than music."

After Sibelius's engagement to Aino in October 1890 (her iciness over his relationship with Betsy Lerché having melted) he spent a further year of study in Vienna. Here his skirt-chasing became legendary. So assiduous, indeed, was his devotion to Venus that he caught the disease named after her, concealing the truth from his fiancée by informing her he had had an operation for the removal of a kidney stone. However, he was more honest with his friend Robert Kajanus (see below) and his long-suffering brother Christian, who had to cough up funds for the treatment before the hospital would release its patient.

Eventually leaving the hospital in June 1891, Sibelius passed through Berlin where he indulged in another bout of benders that left him penniless. Selling most of his clothes to fund the fare home, he arrived back in Helsinki in evening dress! Matters were not then improved with his fiancée when a novel was published by Sibelius's friend Adolf Paul – *Em bok om en människa* (A Book about a Man) – purportedly depicting the composer as a boy-genius, Sillén, addicted to womanising.

Sibelius did, however, redeem himself somewhat by composing and conducting his first major work, the *Kullervo Symphony*, actually more a cantata based on the national epic *Kalevala* which relates the exploits of three semi-divine brothers in mythical Kaleva, land of the heroes. On the strength of its roaring success at the premiere on 28 April 1892, and with a pending appointment to a teaching post at the Helsinki Conservatoire, Sibelius married his Aino in early June and they set up house in a rented flat in the capital. Sibelius's brother Christian, a medical student, joined them as a lodger. Aino would bear her husband five daughters, one of whom, Kirsti, died of typhus at fifteen months in 1900.

At least Aino knew where she stood before she married. Sibelius had warned her briefly and to the point that

> The last thing [a composer] must become is the kindly, drowsy, pipe-smoking head of the house. He must be free to continue his imaginative life undisturbed ... that is absolutely essential! The sort of marriage centring solely on rearing children is anathema to me – there are other things to think about if you are an artist.

Mahler would make similar points to his fiancée Alma Schindler in December 1901, though of course he took a thousand times as many words to say it. (The same went for the two men's music. Sibelius's symphonies are marvels of compression, the structures winnowed down to the bare bones. But Mahler, at least for some of us, never knows when or how to stop.)

"The Symposium" and "The Problem"

It didn't, alas, take long for cracks to appear in the marriage. Soon after the birth of the Sibeliuses' first daughter Eva in March

1893 (the year in which he completed the *Karelia Suite* and the *Swan of Tuonela),* Sibelius felt a need to escape the nappies, burping, puking and all the rest. His bolt hole was The Symposium, an "intellectual drinking circle" convened by the distinguished painter Axel Gallén-Kallela, where Sibelius spent all the housekeeping money on drink and cigars. A painting of *The Symposium* by Gallén ("The Problem") shows himself, Sibelius and two other friends far gone around a table. One of them is out for the count while a bleary-eyed Sibelius is fixated senselessly on the great beyond. Music and discussion did take place however, often at inordinate length.

Later, in April 1898 when Sibelius was on his own in Berlin contemplating his *First Symphony*, Gallén revived *The Symposium*, one session of which ended with Sibelius injuring his head in a drunken brawl with some Polish workers. Nevertheless, he completed the symphony (soon to be revised) and conducted its premiere on 26 April 1899. The Finnish authorities were so impressed with it that they awarded him a state grant of 2,500 marks – on top of his state annuity for life awarded in 1897. Yet, despite these and other sources of income including commissioned compositions, Sibelius was for many years close to insolvency.

Flight from Reality

Sibelius had been unable to cope with the loss of his baby daughter Kirsti from typhus in 1900, but had sublimated his grief somewhat in an interesting but little-known piece for cello and piano, *Malincholia*. However when his second daughter, six-year-old Ruth caught typhus while the family were staying at Rapallo in Italy in March 1901, Sibelius simply fled to Rome for a fortnight. The combined burdens of a serious shortage of money, composer's block (he had abandoned work on a series of tone poems) and Ruth's illness were more than he could face. While her husband was visiting Roman art galleries and listening to Palestrina masses in church, Aino was left trying to manage on a few hundred lire. Only "the blind egocentricity of the artist" can explain such a letter as this sent by Sibelius to Aino:

> I realise what hell both Rapallo and Berlin were for me [sic]. I am working very hard here and – I hope – writing well. And there are so many artistic diversions when my imagination runs dry. I seem to need this

248

stimulus and it also seems that I need total solitude
when I am working ... I have now fallen fatally in love
with my orchestral fantasy [actually the work that
would become the *Third Symphony*]. I can't tear myself
away from it.

Well – at least he had warned her of the life to expect with him!
He did not, however, blame only himself, writing to Aino,

You must also love me, otherwise our relationship will
perish.

That Aino stayed with him shows that either she loved her
husband regardless, or else felt that for the sake of Music and
Finland she ought to endure the problems. Posterity is as deeply
indebted to Aino as it is to so many other composers' wives in
these sagas. For without the all-coping, all-forgiving (or at least
endlessly-tolerating) mother figure Sibelius had in the shape of
Aino, he may well have cracked up altogether and never have
written the *Violin Concerto,* the music to *Pelléas et Mélisande,*
the last five of his seven symphonies ...

The culmination of Sibelius's work while escaping in Rome
was the tight and sinewy *Second Symphony*, in which, according
to Rickards, "a brief, mournful episode" in the Finale was a
reaction to the suicide of Aino's sister Elli. Another programmatic
feature in the work was "an urgent call to arms" against the
Russians who still ruled the country and "a concluding defiance
and triumph." Premiered with huge success on 8 March 1902
and repeated a further three times that same month, the *Second
Symphony* with its "combative tone and blazingly affirmative
conclusion" was seen very much as a reflection of the spirit of
the times.

After The Symposium, The Euterpists

After returning from a triumphant trip to Germany in the fall of
1902, Sibelius joined another bibulous cultural circle centred
round the art periodical *Euterpe* (she being the Muse of lyric
poetry and music) run by the critic and composer Karl Flodin.
Endless bouts of heavy drinking added to the strains Aino was
already enduring in the final stages of her fourth pregnancy.
Sibelius would not only disappear for days at a time, but also
refuse to see his wife if she managed to track him down. Around
the time "Nipsu" (Katarina Elisabet) was born on 12 January

1903 Sibelius was usually to be found in one of Helsinki's bars rather than working on his *Violin Concerto* or, heaven forbid, offering his wife a little TLC. Jean's brother Christian, who as a student had been dissecting the brains of alcoholics, urged Sibelius to sign the pledge, but to no avail:

> There is much in my make up that is weak [wrote Janne to Christian] ... When I am standing in front of a grand orchestra and have drunk a half-bottle of champagne, then I conduct like a young god. Otherwise I am nervous and tremble, feel unsure of myself, and everything is lost. The same is true of my visits to the bank manager. ... You can see from this that my drinking has genuine roots that are both dangerous and go deep. I promise you to try and cope with it with all my strength.

"Ainola"
"In Helsinki every song within me dies." (Sibelius)

Aino and Christian decided that the only long-term hope (a rather fond one, alas) of solving Sibelius's drinking problem was to get him out of Helsinki. The result was a new family home, "Ainola," a two-storey wooden house with a steep roof and a porch of round logs in the village of Järvenpää, some twenty miles north of Helsinki. Designed for free in the Art Nouveau style by a leading architect, it was completed in 1904. Sibelius and Aino would live there for the rest of their lives. Inside (we discover in *Virtual Finland*) Ainola herself designed the staircase to the upper floor as well as the kitchen cupboards and cabinets. She also landscaped the garden with flowers, herbs, and fruit bushes.

Meanwhile, pending the completion of Ainola, the drinking continued and the Finale of the *Violin Concerto* was often neglected unless Sibelius was dragged out of a bar to finish it by Aino and Robert Kajanus. (Kajanus was the first and most loyal of Sibelius's champions, and as a prominent conductor would pioneer the recordings of his work in the 1930s).

Although now a standard of the Violin repertoire, the *Concerto* was not an initial success at its premiere in Helsinki on 8 February 1904, nor even after Sibelius made extensive revisions to it. The turn in its fortunes was due to its passionate promotion by Jascha Heifetz in the 1930s.

Alcohol-wise, domestic matters came to something of a head when on his thirty-ninth birthday in 1904, Sibelius, on his way to conduct a concert in Uleaborg, received a "furious letter" from Aino about his drinking. His letters home certainly justified her anger, showing as they did signs of "the shakes" in the handwriting as a result of delirium tremens.

Alas, Aino's outburst was to no lasting avail. True, he managed the first of his five visits to England in November 1905 with commendable aplomb, enjoying the generous hospitality organised by Granville Bantock and noting with characteristic pleasure that he never even "made the acquaintance of English coinage." But he returned to the bottle with a vengeance in 1907, unable to cope with the pressure of a deadline for the completion of the *Third Symphony* for a London premiere in the spring. (In the event it was premiered in Helsinki on 25 September.) Sibelius confessed to Gallén that "something [had] to be done" about both his drinking and his financial management:

> Aino is quite at the end of her tether [he continued]. I really must have it out with her. Its not just the boozer Sibb who is at stake but the composer in whose music I believe, and which can develop into something much bigger ... All this is not easy for me to admit to myself, as I am spoilt, superior and weak-willed.

Thirteenth time lucky; seven years on the wagon

Persistent and worsening sore throats Sibelius suffered during and after a trip to St Petersburg in November 1907 resulted in two operations, the second performed in Berlin by a Dr Fränkel in July 1908 for the removal of a tumour. Dr Fränkel prescribed a total ban on alcohol and cigars.

Dreading the consequences of disobeying Dr Fränkel — who had succeeded in removing the tumour only on the thirteenth attempt – Sibelius somehow managed without booze and tobacco for seven years. The colossal strain this deprivation caused him, particularly on social occasions, is only too clear in the diaries he started keeping from 1909. However, this same crisis, which inevitably also focused his mind on his own mortality, would have a productive outcome in the *Fourth Symphony,* his finest, bleakest and most concentrated. It seems, in Rickards's words, to embody "an at times desolate landscape, half real, half of the mind, in the icy grip of winter."

Intimations of mortality were being compounded by heavy debts. The construction of Ainola and the retinue of staff employed there were essentially beyond Sibelius's means. At the end of May 1909 he arrived home from a foreign tour to realise, to Aino's acute distress, that he had mounted up a total debt of 100,000 marks and that his annual expenses exceeded his annual income by 6,000 marks. Fortunately, his long-time fan and valued mentor Baron Axel Carpelan secured a substantial donation from a wealthy family that kept the bailiffs at bay. Sibelius reciprocated by promising to write the *Fourth Symphony*. Carpelan may therefore be credited with having created the conditions in which Sibelius could complete his masterpiece premiered in Helsinki on 3 April 1911.

Although not yet off the wagon, in the spring of 1914 Sibelius enjoyed the lavish hospitality offered to him at the Norfolk Festival in Connecticut, USA. He travelled there to conduct the premiere of his tone-poem *The Oceanides*. The visit was one of the high points of his career, in which he even enjoyed the luxury of a private barber to shave him daily. However, it did nothing to improve his marriage. As with the London trip, there was insufficient money for Aino to join him. Left behind again to cope with the creditors, she could be forgiven if she saw her marriage at this point as twenty-one years of "disappointments, frustrations and tragedies" with a man so inordinately self-obsessed.

Sibelius's hopes of clearing all his debts with a return visit to the USA in 1914 were wiped out by the beginning of World War I.

*

Back to the Bottle

Not surprisingly, Aino regarded her husband's seven years of abstinence as the happiest (least unhappy?) of her chequered married life. However, in 1915 the boozing (wines rather than spirits at this stage) and cigar smoking gradually resumed. By the summer, when Aino was away, Sibelius was drinking to excess with one of his sons-in-law Arvi Paloheimo. It was very much a hand-to-mouth existence as progress on the first version of the *Fifth Symphony* proceeded in fits and starts towards its premiere in December 1916. Early the following year Aino left her husband for a whole month to visit her daughter Eva and her husband in Petrograd (now St Petersburg). On her return there were "heated rows," writes Rickards

> Centring with some ferocity on the subject of alcohol
> ...weeks might go by without 'a smile or a laugh' and
> 'always tears and tears. Her whole life thrown away'.

Sibelius voiced thoughts of a separation, though only to himself in his diary.

"Sodden with champagne"

In 1919, the year of the definitive version of the *Fifth*, the marriage continued to nosedive. While attending a Nordic Music Festival in Copenhagen in June, Sibelius flew into a rage: when asked to pay for his champagne, he threw his money on the floor. Somehow Aino managed to bring him to his senses.

In 1920 he was tempted by an offer of appointment as head of the Eastman School of Music at Rochester, New York, but ultimately turned it down. In this same year, having avoided spirits so far since resuming drinking, he turned to the whisky bottle:

> Poor Aino [he wrote]. What a dreadful fate. Alone, alone
> with her sick children. I cannot bear to think about it.
> ... We are both down and she avoids my gaze and then
> there's that implied criticism of me in all her
> movements. But cheer up .... death is round the corner.

In 1922 Sibelius was foolish enough to tell Aino that his *Valse Chevaleresque,* one of several salon pot-boilers he wrote that year, would be a money-spinner. She dismissed the piece savagely as "the product of someone whose senses were sodden with champagne." The atmosphere at Ainola "could be cut with a meat cleaver."

The following year Sibelius totally disgraced himself in Göthenburg. Well after the hour when he should have been on the podium for the start of a concert he was conducting, he was found eating oysters and drinking champagne in a restaurant! After he finally made it to the hall, the first piece broke down and had to be restarted. After the concert, in a fit of self-disgust, he flung a miniature bottle of cognac on to the steps of the hall. Then to round off a great day, he had to be woken to hear a speech given in his honour by the Swedish composer Ture Rangström.

Aino took yet another stand in the following year, 1924. She would not accompany him to Stockholm in March for the premiere of his *Sixth Symphony* (originally entitled *Fantasia Sinfonica*) since he had so disgraced himself in Göthenburg. The tension at Ainola would now often be unbearable. Sibelius would stay up all night drinking and (sometimes) composing. When Aino came down in the morning she invariably found him comatose, and took the bottle away. Not a word would pass between them all day.

We could go on and on, but it would be only more of the same. Though perhaps, like many life-long hard drinkers, Sibelius moderated his intake as an octogenarian. Let's end this doleful marital saga with one more dose of self-recrimination in 1927 –

> Isolation and loneliness is driving me to despair. Not even my wife is talking to me ... In order to survive I have to have alcohol. ... Perhaps it is all my fault.

– and one more embarrassing incident. In 1928 when he was picnicking with a Masonic colleague, Wäino Sola, he tried to grasp a cup made of folded paper containing wine. He had the shakes so badly that he crushed it, showering the wine everywhere.

*

Sibelius officially entered into his twenty-eight years of retirement in 1929, the year of his last published work with an opus number *Three Pieces for Violin and Piano* Op 116. His last work of real importance had been his cataclysmic tone poem, *Tapiola*, of 1925 – a supreme creation in music of "Nature's terrifying infinities of time and space." Thereafter he mainly stayed at home, received visitors, read books from his extensive library, and welcomed the many honours conferred upon him. He also listened to his own music and that of younger distinguished composers on the wireless, on 78 rpm shellacs and (in his last few years, presumably) on long-playing vinyls. He gave just one radio interview in 1948 in which he gave aspiring composers the precious advice "never to write any unnecessary notes, because every note should have a life of its own." Whatever else he composed, including, perhaps, a promised *Eighth Symphony,* seems to have been thrown onto the fire.

In 1949, Canadian photographer Yousef Karsh, whose magnificent portrait of the composer in his eighties is widely known, found "a happy man, full of infectious laughter... His hands shook but his mind was wonderfully alert, and he followed the news of the world in careful detail."

The poetic but accredited story of Sibelius's death and its harbinger in the form of one of his beloved cranes comes from Tawaststjerna:

> On October the 18th, 1957, Sibelius was returning from his customary walk. Exhilarated, he told his wife Aino that he had seen a flock of cranes approaching. "There they come, the birds of my youth," he exclaimed. Suddenly, one of the birds broke away from the formation and circled once above Ainola. It then rejoined the flock to continue its journey. Two days afterwards Sibelius died of a brain haemorrhage.

He was given a state funeral ten days later, and buried in the grounds of Ainola, where he had lived for more than fifty years. Aino died on 8 June 1969, two months before her 98th birthday, and was also buried there.

***

Chapter 13

Erik Alfred Leslie Satie
"The Velvet Gentleman"
Born: Honfleur, France 17 May, 1866
Died age 59: Paris 1 July, 1925

... she has a tender little belch which is often inspiring. [Satie on his lover the model and painter Suzanne Valadon]

He was a wily old card. He was full of guile and intelligently mischievous. I liked him from the start. [Igor Stravinsky]

His strange sparse scores, often written without bar lines in red ink are peppered with whimsical instructions: "Light as an egg", "Here comes the lantern", "Open your head", "Muffle the sound", "With astonishment", "Work it out yourself".
[Michael Furstner: Website: Jazclass: *Erik Satie*]

"Those who aren't satisfied are advised to **** off."
[On-stage poster in Satie's ballet *Relâche*, roughly translatable as *No Performance*]

Not for nothing did Debussy dub Satie "Le Précurseur" (The Forerunner). By far the most way-out, eccentric character in this volume, Satie nevertheless commands total respect on two counts. Firstly for his whimsical, iconoclastic and highly original music, which anticipated most modern developments in "minimalism" and "serial techniques" (the latter meaning very roughly music based on a twelve-tone row of semitones rather than on familiar Western scales). Satie also commands esteem for the integrity of each of his wildly varying lifestyles. He played every role from bohemian to "deferential bourgeois functionary", Communist fanatic, and Dada freak.

It is hardly surprising that no woman elected to live out her life with Satie. Even the one who most loved him, the painter Suzanne Valadon, decided after six months with him to abandon their drafty, freezing floorboards and zero comforts for the feather mattress and coal fires provided by her other lover, a wealthy lawyer by the name of Paul Mousis.

Satie's childhood was hardly conducive to stability. He lost his mother when he was six. Then after being sent from Paris back to his home town of Honfleur (on the Seine estuary) to be brought up as a Catholic by his grandparents, he lost his grand-mother when he was twelve, after she drowned in "mysterious circumstances." On returning to Paris he was educated informally by his father and continued his musical studies with the woman who soon became his loathed stepmother, a piano teacher and second-rate composer by the name of Eugénie Barnetsche. When he was forced into the Conservatoire things went from bad to worse. He regarded it as "a sort of local penitentiary," while for their part one teacher condemned him as "the laziest student in the Conservatoire" and another as "worthless." Satie's only reason for slogging out seven years there, on and off, was to reduce his compulsory military service to one year from five. Even that one year was reduced further when he deliberately contracted bronchitis in April 1887 to escape call-up to the 33ʳᵈ Infantry Regiment.

Later in this same year, he was thrown out of the house after reportedly being caught in delicto flagrante with his step-mother's housemaid. Heading for Montmartre he acquired a room at 50 rue Condorcet, close to the famed Chat Noir restaurant and cabaret. Soon becoming part of the furniture there, he styled himself "Erik Satie – gymnopédiste", a label that connected directly with his piano miniatures of a year later, *Gymnopédies* (1888) – still hugely popular, of course, with those haunting plainsong overtones. By 1890 he was conducting the band that played for the shadow spectacles at the Chat. A year later he fell out with the management and moved on as second pianist to the Auberge du Clou, where he began his twenty-five-year friendship with Debussy.

At this stage Satie's image as a man about town was ostentatiously anti-bohemian, with his top hat, pince-nez, high collar, and frock coat. It was a style he could ill afford and in 1890 he moved higher up the hill to the slummier Butte Mont-martre "to escape his creditors," taking tiny rooms at 2 rue Cortot. It was "furnished only with bed, chair, bookshelf and chest." Here it was that he conceived his *Rose+Croix* pieces, following his appointment as composer to the – wait for it! – Order of the Catholic Rose – Cross of the Temple and of the Grail. This was a mystic sect run by another brilliant head-case Joséphin Péladin, who styled himself as "Sâr Merodack" and was author of the best selling novel *The Supreme Vice*, replete with Sodom, Gomorrah, diabolism, "salacious mysticism", and "hermaphrodite frolics". Péladin's sect attempted to reconcile Catholicism with Rosicrucianism. (The Rosicrucians or members of the Ancient Mystic Order Rosae Crucis dedicated their lives to the study of esoteric, mystical, philosophical, and religious beliefs.) Music Satie wrote for this sect includes a *Prelude for the heroic entrance-gate to the heavens* (incidental music to an *Esoteric Drama* by Jules Bois), and also a *Mass for the Poor*.

It was at the meetings of Péladin's sect that Satie gained his first public hearings, also developing his interest in "static sound décor," meaning, undoubtedly, musical wallpaper. For Satie, music was not an expression of emotions but rather a representation of "stasis and chastity". Well – after one violent love affair, Satie knew all there was to know about chastity.

Ever totally his own man, Satie publicly broke off from Péladin in August 1892 and formed his own sect – of which he was the sole member – The Metropolitan Art Church of Jesus Conductor. From the headquarters of his "Abbey Church" (those two tiny rooms in the rue Cortot) he published paranoiac attacks on his artistic enemies. At the same time, although he hadn't a chance in hell of ever gaining acceptance, he made his first of three attempts to get elected to the Académie des Beaux-Arts.

In November 1892 Satie and his poet friend J.P. Contamine de Latour concocted a "Christian ballet", *Uspud*, intended to scandalise the establishment. Indeed, in an attempt to secure a staging of it, Satie challenged the manager of the Opéra to a duel! – All to no avail of course. The ballet, which had only one dancer, was based on Flaubert's *Temptation of Saint Anthony* and was dedicated to the Holy Trinity. Debussy was the only musician who could understand the serious intent behind the project.

*

Suzanne Valadon ("Biqui")

Satie conducted his only known love affair, wild and traumatic, with Suzanne Valadon in the first six months of 1893. He probably met her for the first time on 13 January in the Nouvelle Athènes in the Place Pigalle – another favoured haunt of the poets, painters and musicians who cocked a snoot at official art. (Some say they first met at L'Auberge du Clou.) The illegitimate daughter of a seamstress-charwoman who had settled in Montmartre, Valadon first worked in a dressmaker's sweatshop, then moved on to selling vegetables from a barrow, mucking out stables, and dancing on horseback. She first made her mark in the world as an artists' model for sixty-year-old Puvis de Chavannes, known for his chaste murals with allegorical figures – though needless to say his relationship with young Suzanne was far from chaste! Valadon then sat for, and snuggled up to both Renoir and Dégas, and also met Toulouse-Lautrec, at the same time gradually becoming known as a painter in her own right. Nowadays, of course, she is overshadowed by the son she had at age eighteen, Maurice Utrillo, known especially for his Parisian street scenes and landmarks.

Satie himself recalled his marriage proposal to Valadon on their first encounter:

> It was my last chance. It was then three o'clock in the morning – an impossible time to get to the mairie. After that it was always too late. She had too many things on her mind to get married; so we never brought up the subject again.
> [John Storm: *The Valadon Drama*]

Although she was already the mistress of Paul Mousis, Valadon soon took up with Satie, moving into a studio next door to him in the rue Cortot. (There was no room in either pad for them to live together.) The affair was to be "volcanic and transitory and not without an element of the bizarre". Gillmor continues:

> The sensuous young woman and the impecunious cabaret pianist spent idyllic days together sailing toy boats in the ponds of the Luxembourg Gardens; often he would buy her necklaces of sausages and send bouquets of flowers to her ten-year-old son, and once

on her birthday he brought her a paper sack "with all
the wonderful smells of the world in it".

Although not remotely musical, Biqui inspired Satie to compose. "She will never get a rapt expression on her face like a spaniel or a critic," he remarked approvingly, "and she has a tender little belch which is often inspiring." If her belch inspired him, did her early morning little farts do the same? Scholars may reasonably assume so.

They certainly roughed it together, sleeping wrapped in blankets on the bare floor of Suzanne's studio. Here it was that she painted her first picture in oils: a portrait of Satie in bohemian garb, bearded, moustached, red-cheeked, intensely blue-eyed, and projecting "a personality conscious of and unafraid of its own originality."

Satie reciprocated with a snippet of song, *Bonjour, Biqui, Bonjour*, dated Easter Sunday 1893, and adorned with an "authentic portrait" of his beloved in pen and ink.

An intimate letter Satie sent to Suzanne on 11 March 1893 offers an extremely rare glimpse into his deepest feelings.

Dear little Biqui,
Impossible to stop thinking of your whole being; I am
completely full of you; wherever I go I see nothing but
your lovely eyes, your gentle hands and your tiny feet.

Alas, the triangular arrangement obviously became increasingly painful for Satie, and there were scenes of rage and violence. As Biqui presumably spent more time opting for Mousis's silk sheets and maid service, Satie sunk into dejection:

For me there is nothing but icy loneliness which makes
my head go empty and fills my heart with sadness. ..."

The end came on 20 June, and soon after Suzanne went back to Mousis, apparently settling with him close by. It must have been searingly painful for Satie to meet Suzanne in the boulangerie, or spot the couple arm-in-arm on the way home from their favourite bistro.

By way of revenge Satie posted a series of placards excoriating Valadon on the outside of his front door. Recalling the break with her in later years to one of his acolytes, Satie said:

The Master [i.e. Satie, Master of my sect] was the most
melancholy of humans. He bawled and he threw
himself to the floor to weep bitter tears. Suzanne was

the only one in the world from whom he could draw the spirit his soul required. She was the anchor to his sanity. If she left him, all would be lost. He sobbed and fainted.

*

That concludes Satie's known love life, but a few titbits from the rest of his life may be of interest.

1895-1911

• In 1895, with a small inheritance, Satie purchased "seven identical dun-coloured suits" or (sources vary) "twelve identical grey corduroy suits", or even "twelve identical grey velvet suits". This change of image signified the end of his *Rose+Croix* period, and his search for a new artistic direction.

• In 1898 he moved to even more spartan accommodation over a café in the working class suburb of Arceuil on the south side of Paris, and "closed his door to the world for the rest of his life." He reportedly nicknamed his apartment 'Notre Dame de Basses'. (Our lady of the Double Bass, or Bass Singers, perhaps, though goodness knows why.)

• From this point he changed his image for the third and last time. He walked the ten kilometres into Paris every day dressed as a "deferential bourgeois functionary" with bowler hat, wing collar and an umbrella. He stopped at numerous cafés en route to compose, a snifter always to hand (there were too many of those), and returned home either on foot or by the last train in the small hours of the next day. Actually preferring wet weather, he did not open his umbrella when it rained but hid it beneath his coat, concealing also a hammer in case of assault. "The unsolved question," Grove ponders,

> is how he emerged from his filthy room each day in pristine condition, 'like an actor stepping out from the wings'.

• His most revelatory experience in these drifting years, in which he earned his living in various kinds of "degrading" cabaret work, was hearing the premiere of Debussy's *Pelléas et Mélisande* in 1902. He described it as "absolutely astounding". His café songs and music hall pieces include (from 1900) *Je te veux,* an elegant French waltz, and *Le Piccadilly*, a ragtime number in Scott Joplin vein.

- His only significant work in these same years was *Three Pieces in the Form of a Pear* for piano duet (1903), mainly based on earlier pieces. He wrote them in response to Debussy's criticism that he ignored form in his compositions.

- In 1905 he finally decided to make up for his wasted youth and get down to serious study at the Schola Cantorum, which specialised in medieval music. (Debussy once called Satie "a gentle medieval musician lost in this century".) His diploma in counterpoint in 1908 was quite an achievement, since by now he was seriously hitting the bottle.

1911-1925

- The real turning point in Satie's career came in January 1911, when some of his earliest pieces were performed by Ravel at a concert of the Independent Musical Society. Thereafter his works were performed increasingly, especially by the virtuoso pianist Ricardo Viñes, and also by Debussy. Best of all, in 1912 one publisher issued Satie's humorous piano pieces, *Truly Limp Preludes*, and requested more of the same.

- His next lucky break came when Jean Cocteau (1889–1963) heard Viñes playing those bite-sized Pear pieces in 1916. Cocteau was mind-blowingly versatile: a poet, novelist, dramatist, film director (*Les Enfants Terribles, The Blood of a Poet, Beauty and the Beast*), choreographer, drawer, librettist ... all invariably in surrealistic vein.

- Cocteau's interest in Satie led to the composer's collaboration with Diaghilev (co-founder of the Ballets Russes in 1909). In 1917, the first Cubist ballet and a riotous succès de scandale, *Parade* pushed Satie firmly into the limelight. The inclusion in the orchestral score of typewriters and pistols, the choreographer Leonid Massine, and Picasso for a ballet, along with Picasso's cubist costumes and the absurd plot created an uproar. In James Harding's words,

> Cocteau reported vividly that there were insulting cries of "Boches!" and demands that the perpetrators be sent to the Front. He pictured women charging with hatpins at him and his collaborators. He spoke of fights in the auditorium after the curtain fell, of a female who tried to put out his eyes with a hatpin, and of the man who said to his wife: "If I'd known it was going to be so silly I'd have brought the children." A bayonet charge in

Flanders, he declared, was as nothing compared with
that unruly scene. Though Cocteau over-dramatised
the incident, there is no doubt that the audience was
shocked and confused.

•   Satie only narrowly escaped a prison sentence in the
wake of *Parade* when a failed composer-turned-critic, Jean
Pouiegh, successfully sued him for libel. Satie had dubbed him,
on an open postcard, "not only an asshole [un cul], but also an
unmusical asshole." Satie had been especially enraged by
Pouiegh's turnabout since the show, the creep then having been
effusive with congratulations.

•   From now on Satie worked mostly to commissions,
owing most of them to Cocteau, whom he nonetheless disliked
because of his egotism and interference. Cocteau also encouraged the emergence of the group of composers headed by Satie
known as Les Six – the others being Honegger, Milhaud, Poulenc,
Georges Auric, Louis Durey, and Germaine Tailleferre. They were
united by their reaction against the Impressionism of Debussy
and Ravel.

•   Possibly Satie's "greatest" work was his "studiedly un-
emotional" symphonic drama *Socrate* of 1918, based on Plato
and commissioned by that magnificent patron of the arts,
Princesse de Polignac, heiress to the Singer sewing machine
empire.

•   The year 1920 saw two festivals of Satie's music and
the first performance of his *Furniture Music,* designed to be part
of the background. When the piece started, he ran about among
the audience urging them to talk.

•   In 1921 he joined the Communist Party and became
increasingly involved with the Dada movement in Paris. (The
Dadaists flouted convention by producing works marked by
"nonsense, travesty, and incongruity.")

•   In 1924 two ballets for which Satie wrote the music,
The Adventures of Mercury (in "three plastic poses") and *Relâche*
(translatable roughly as No Performance) provoked more first-
night furores. The latter featured on-stage obscenities including
a poster inscribed "Those who aren't satisfied are advised to ****
off" and a surrealist film by René Clair. At the end Satie and the
stage designer Picabia took their bows from a miniature Citroën
car which Satie drove onstage.

- In 1925 Satie paid the price for his years of alcohol abuse with terminal attacks of cirrhosis and pleurisy. When he could no longer drag himself about, he was first installed in a hotel room, and then later hospitalised.
- When his brother Conrad, Darius Milhaud, and three other friends entered his squalid room at Arcueil after his death, they had to clear out two cartloads of rubbish before they could begin to sort out his papers and manuscripts.

According to the American critic Virgil Thomson, all Satie's music, in its "gentleness, sincerity and directness of statement" was based on the composer's conviction that "the only healthy thing music can do in our century is to stop trying to be impressive." Amen to that!

***

Chapter 14

George Percy [Aldridge] Grainger
"Pianist Extraordinaire, Pervert, Peroxide Blonde"
Born: Brighton, Melbourne, Australia 8 July 1882
Died age 78, White Plains, New York, 20 February 1961

... the only truly passionate relationship of my life.
[Grainger referring to his mother in a letter to Alfhild
Sandby, 26 November 1929]

It just boils down to this: that I hardly think of anything
but sex & that all my sex thoughts are full of evil &
cruelty.
[Letter to Cyril Scott, 23 July 1956]

The idea of incest was obsessive with Grainger for most
of his life.
[John Bird: *Percy Grainger*]

We will now hear Percy Grainger tear the guts out of
the grand piano.
[Poulteney Bigelow introducing Grainger to his guests]
Note:
It will be clear to readers that in writing this chapter
I am deeply indebted to the work of John Bird. Mr
Bird generously scrutinised my draft script and
suggested a few changes. I adopted most of them and
am deeply grateful to him.
                                        *
Music biography springs a thousand staggering surprises. Few,
however, can be more startling than the case of Grainger, who
wrote so many gorgeous arrangements and tunes and yet was
such an extreme sexual deviant. He is surely classical music's
most severe case of murky mother-fixation, flagellism, and so
many other-isms of perversion. Not least among these were a
passion for pornography (indulged to the full in Amsterdam in
1900), and his fantasies of paedophilia and incest. Of these he
wrote to his Danish girl-friend Karen Holten on 6 November
1908:

You know that I long to flog children. It must be
wonderful to hurt this soft unspoiled skin ... & when
my girls begin to awaken sexually I would gradually

like to have carnal knowledge of them. ... Why should a
man not be sensual with his own children?

The man who arranged or composed such glorious numbers
as *Irish Tune from County Derry* (the Londonderry Air), *Molly
on the Shore, Mock Morris, I'm Seventeen Come Sunday, Country
Gardens* (his top money-spinner), *Handel in the Strand, Brigg
Fair* (perhaps the best folk-song setting ever written), *Shallow
Brown, Shepherd's Hey, Willow Willow, Lincolnshire Posy*, and
To a Nordic Princess, was always totally open about the darkest
corners of his life. "I hardly think of anything but sex & ... all my
sex thoughts are full of evil & cruelty," he wrote in a letter to his
friend Cyril Scott in 1956. And in that same year he deposited a
small parcel in a Melbourne bank containing an essay and
photographs giving details of his sex life with a view to their
future use by an institute of psychology.

Grainger's compulsive perversions seem to have set in early.
Even by the age of sixteen he was indulging in experiments in
sado-masochism. As a child he would sometimes be cruel to cats,
and revel in the gory depictions of pain (javelins, battleaxes and
all the rest) in Homer, the Icelandic sagas and even the cruelties
described in Dickens.

In his adulthood all the women with whom he was
intimately associated – with the possible exception of Mimi Kwast
(see below) – co-operated with his deviant practices. He would
even record these on camera: "not only the exact time of day,
location of session and number of lashes with what kind of whip,"
writes John Bird, "but also the type of film used in the camera
and the exposure and aperture." And he nearly always laundered
his own shirts to hide the tell-tale stains from his bloodletting
sessions.

"Whip in My Valise"

On his arduous concert tours in Australia, Scandinavia
and elsewhere he used to pack a selection of whips
along with his white tie and tails. (Remember Adam
Ant's punk classic *Whip in My Valise*, 1977?) Were the
floggings a way of psyching up for a concert, one
wonders, or of winding down afterwards? Presumably
he also carried his gear with him on his ground-
breaking tours collecting folk songs in rural England
and in Scandinavia. Some of the old countrymen from

whom he coaxed songs handed down through the centuries in Lincolnshire villages would have been stunned had they known how the renowned Mr Grainger rounded off his evenings.

*

Grainger also developed a virulent racist streak, symptoms of which included a hatred of Germans and Austro-German music (Beethoven, Mozart and Haydn included). A twist in his racist kink was his crackpot obsession that blond, blue-eyed Nordics were the only worthwhile composers. But then Grainger was an archetypal Nordic himself, with his "exquisitely proportioned", delicate, rather feminine features, his intense blue eyes, ivory skin, and a Paderewskian mop of golden hair to which his mother, Rose Grainger, used to apply hydrogen peroxide.

Very pretty and young-looking, his mother Rose was complicit in all her son's deviant sexual activities. Although she sometimes worried about them she connived at his coded references to them ("blue roses" being one such) in their correspondence. We know for certain from one of Grainger's doctors, Dr K K Nygaard (in a letter to Bird dated 2 December 1975), that she even went so far as to give "advice on sex matters to the deviant offspring".

Rose Grainger would tolerate anything in her adult son – except the loss of him to anyone else. Until her suicide in 1922, each of the hapless women who entered Percy's life would walk like a bridesmaid in the train of his life while Rose remained at his side like a permanent bride-to-be.

*

Grainger and his Mother
I only wanted to see if you still love me.
[Rose Grainger to her son after feigning death]

... with Grainger one of the pinnacles of his sex-fantasy was to unite the parental or filial with the lover's emotion.
[Both quotes taken from Bird]

Turning back to Grainger's childhood, it is hardly surprising that he wandered into deviant ways. His mother horsewhipped him regularly and severely as punishment until he was fourteen or fifteen for bad behaviour or for skipping his piano practice. For good measure Rose (née Aldridge) also whipped her ineffectual, alcoholic and womanising husband John Grainger when he was drunk. In 1890 she threw him out for good, and no wonder: he had infected her with syphilis that led to her first breakdown in that same year.

Percy saw his father only occasionally thereafter, though he always valued his paternal love and solicitude. But from the age of eight Percy was effectively brought up by his mother alone. And though she rarely touched him as a baby, she would regularly sing him to sleep with the lovely tunes of Stephen Foster – memories of which (especially *Camptown Races*) Percy would cling to all his life.

The result of all this was that young Percy loved his mother to bits. She was "omniscient, omnipotent and omnipresent". All the classic conditions for a homosexual orientation were in place, and although Percy never developed any known overtly physical relationships with men, there was undoubtedly an erotic dimension to some of his male friendships. Especially in the case of the fine Danish cellist he would refer to as "my closest male friend", Hermann Sandby. Indeed, he would write to Sandby's fiancée Alfhild on 11 November 1905:

> There can be in his tone a quietly-ruthless slowly
> pushful & sending force that if I were a woman would
> lay me out wholly submissive, I wish I had the chance
> – I should be splendacious to him of possibilities.

Sandby returned the compliment, though indirectly, by telling Alfhild that "you are the Percy I love in the shape of a woman". Maybe she wasn't too thrilled to be told that!

All her life Rose Grainger was obsessively protective of her adored son: not only of his career as a solo pianist (she was his concert manager), but also of his time, his relationships, his social life – everything. Mother and son lived together throughout his student years (1895-1901) in Frankfurt – where he was a member of the so-called Frankfurt Group – and then also in London from 1901 to 1914 during his ascent towards international stardom. Rose still clung to her son's side after they moved to New York in 1914. They eventually settled in the leafy suburb of White Plains until her tragic death on Sunday 30 April 1922. Demented by rumours of an incestuous relationship with her son, Rose Grainger jumped out of a window in the Aeolian building and landed in the adjacent Central Building fourteen storeys below.

It will be no surprise to learn that Grainger described his bond with his mother as "the only truly passionate relationship of my life". Because Rose retained her pretty and youthful looks, she and Percy were often mistaken for wife and husband or sister and brother. But whatever the ambiguous physical attractions between mother and son, they were never, according to Bird, "given any explicitly incestuous outlet".

The ties between mother and son were intensified after Percy took on the role of breadwinner when Rose had a second syphilitic breakdown (1900). Thereafter he was forced to sweat on what he called "the rack of the concert platform" for his lucrative living, leaving only very limited time for composition. Nevertheless these performing years were well spent, not least because he introduced the keyboard works of such composers as Debussy, Ravel, Albeniz and Granados to English audiences.

Rose gripped her son in an emotional vice. After his first separation from her for more than a very few days, his admission to her that he had enjoyed himself while staying with friends in Bath caused her to throw a hysterical fit. She never baulked at emotional blackmail, even when Grainger was in his early forties. She would, for instance, "stretch herself out corpse-like on the floor shamming death". When convinced of his distress she would say "I only wanted to see if you still love me."

Such tyranny eventually drove even Percy's closest friends away. They became fed up with having their social calls timed literally to the minute between Percy's piano lessons. What really baffled them was the passive way he accepted such control.

No wonder there were rumours of incest! "Longing to hold you in my arms once more," was how Percy would round off his letters and telegrams to her. The extant missives between mother and son run into thousands and offer, writes Bird, a "fascinating, if frightening picture which is almost impossible to grasp in its enormity and complexity".

After what Grainger called the "torture" of his mother's death – which caused him to age swiftly in appearance – he spared no labour or expense to enshrine her memory. He paid £800 for the publication of several thousand copies of a memoir introduced thus:

> Photos of Rose Grainger and of three short accounts
> of her life by herself, in her own hand-writing
> reproduced for her kin and friends by her adoring son,
> Percy Grainger – also table of dates, & summary of
> her cultural tastes.

Over thirty-three years after Rose's death, and only four
before his own, the wounds were still causing pain. On 3 July
1957 he wrote

> Beloved mother would have been 95 today. I have felt
> the tragic influence of her death more in this year 1957
> than in any other year.

*

Dotty titles and mad music machines

No matter how wayward Grainger's love life was – and who has
a "normal" one anyway? – some would say that ten minutes of
his ravishing lollipops are worth infinitely more than ten times
ten hours of the symphonies of Mahler. It must, however, be
admitted that Grainger's bids to be accepted as a heavyweight
composer came to little – though that doesn't mean that history
has not thereby done him an injustice. Like Sir Arthur Sullivan,
he tended to look down on his best-loved gems as mere money-
spinners and was ever mortified that his more avant-garde
creations were invariably viewed as barmy. Grainger perhaps
sometimes lost the plot in his inventions, though to me he was
overall more of a marvellous madman than a mere crackpot.
The world needs its quota of Graingers even if they come with
whiplashes.

The titles and "machines" (rather than instruments)
Grainger used for his largely unknown music offer some cor-
roboration of a wayward personality. How about such titles as
Arrival Platform Humlet (including a version for massed violas),
A Lot of Rot (cello and piano, later renamed), *Pritteling Prattling
Pretty Poll Parrot* (two pianos), *Let's Dance Gay in Green Meadow*
...?

His "free music" machines were intended so that notes could
glide into each other, or move in microtones (i.e. intervals less
than a semitone) rather than in the semitones of the piano. "Free
music", he believed, should "tally the movements of clouds, water,
trees, birds, fishes, & so on." We learn from Bird that one of his

microtone instruments made use of pencil sharpeners, milk bottles, bamboo, roller-skate wheels, the bowels of a harmonium, linoleum, ping-pong balls, children's toy records, egg whisks, cotton reels, bits of sewing machines, carpet rolls, a vacuum cleaner, a hair dryer, and miles of strong brown paper and string.

Others were constructed under such names as the *Estey Reed Tone Tool*, *The Crumb-catcher and Drain Protector Disc*, and – take a deep breath – *The Cross Grainger Double-Decker Kangaroo-pouch Flying Disc Graph Model for Synchronizing and Playing 8 Oscillators*. Apparently the roots of Grainger's "free music" ran deep down to his childhood when he so often heard "the sounds of the wind as it howled through the telegraph wires of the Australian country roads".

And what about his short work for huge forces *The Warriors*? – described as "an orgy of war-like dances, processions, and merry-making, broken or accompanied". One Grainger admirer, Charles L. Buchanan, writing in *Musical America* in August 1917 found in it evidence of a "fundamental instability" and an undisciplined imagination. In one Chicago performance of *The Warriors*, Grainger had thirty pianists playing nineteen pianos. At his summer schools in Chicago, fifteen to twenty pianos and a vast array of tuned percussion were common.

"The Siegfried of the piano"

Some comments on Grainger at work on the ivories seem to corroborate his sadistic proclivities. Although his playing was universally admired for its freshness and originality of interpretation, he had a predilection (like Beethoven) for murdering the piano. One friend and host of Grainger, a man named Poulteney Bigelow, would at his house parties often cue in Grainger with the line, "We will now hear Percy Grainger tear the guts out of the grand piano." Grainger was not remotely offended. Indeed, after a music critic in the 1940s accused him of having a touch "as hard as nails" Grainger expressed his wholehearted agreement, attributing the fault to having been forced as a child to overplay in Melbourne's vast Exhibition Building. This same brutal streak is very much in evidence in the recording Grainger made for Columbia in 1925 of Chopin's momentous *B Minor sonata* – played, according to Bird, with "a ferocity and wild abandon that is at times frightening".

For all that, Grainger became Edvard Grieg's preferred exponent of his famous *Piano Concerto*. Grieg admired not only Grainger's clarity of rhythm but also his "robustness, tenderness and broad tonal palette".

*

Pips, pith and skin

For all his musical eccentricities, however, Grainger remained a populist, as his deep admiration for Duke Ellington and his superb arrangements of Gershwin numbers – *Love Walked In* being a ravishing masterpiece – and of the *Warsaw Concerto* show. Grainger also held very sincere beliefs in social welfare and international peace – though after the Great War broke out he did his bit by signing on as a US artillery bandsman in 1917, before becoming an American citizen in 1918. His ideal, he said, was

> to wrench the listeners' hearts with my chords. ... Perhaps these assaults on the tenderness of men's hearts (as we find in tragic poetry & music based on the same) will play their part in weaning men from massed murder of mankind in war, & massed murder of animals for food.

An ardent vegetarian, Grainger's preferred diet was reportedly nuts, plain boiled rice, wheatcakes (especially Berlin pancakes), bread and jam, cream cakes, ice cream, and oranges, which he ate with pips, pith, and skin. His most favoured meal was reportedly stale bread and hard cheese. He never, ever, consumed alcohol.

Although Grainger performed most often at the social functions of high society, being a royalty darling both in England and in Norway, he did his bit to bring culture to the masses. He was the first pianist of international repute to appear at the silent movies that were then in their infancy. Between showings of *Famous Ride on a Runaway Train* and *Officer Cupid* (at the Capitol Theatre, New York, April 1921) he played to 5,500 people with the aid of a "Duo-Art" Player Piano. Grainger noted that his audiences were far more attentive than those at the Carnegie Hall, the Aeolian Hall and the Met. He was, incidentally, a movie fanatic, his favourite stars being Marlene Dietrich, Ginger Rogers and Ingrid Bergman.

*

Before we end with a brief survey of Grainger's admiring though long-suffering women, we must add a few more dabs of paint to his portrait.

One of the first signs of his eccentricity was when on 14 May 1895 (at age 13) he took a rusty dustbin lid on stage with him "as a soldier would hold a shield." After his last bow "he picked up his precious dustbin lid and marched off again, grinning with pride."

Grainger was never a jacket-and-tie man. After meeting the Maoris in New Zealand and hearing Maori and Raratongan folk music he had his mother make him shorts and shirts in brightly coloured towelling that was warm in winter and cool in summer. He taught and jogged in them. Cyril Scott, a friend of Grainger since their Frankfurt days, recalls in *My Years of Indiscretion* that having managed to fix one of those "lightning appointments" with Rose to see Percy,

> I ... found my friend dressed in a most astonishing costume consisting of a blue and red shirt, very much open about the chest, and a pair of shorts made out of coarse, dark-coloured Turkish towels. Round his calves were twisted, very far apart, puttees of white linen, under which he wore neither socks nor stockings.
> " Good Lord! " I ejaculated as I entered, " is it football, Buffalo Bill, or a penance ? "
> "Percy wanted something cool he could wear," Mrs Grainger explained, "so he got me to make him that."

For underwear, boots and socks Grainger favoured army surplus. He also sported a jacket to which short lengths of string were attached securing his manuscripts, pens, pencils and other paraphernalia.

Grainger was a fitness fanatic. During the Australian leg of a tour in 1903-04, he would run up to sixty miles and more overnight from one gig to the next. Then during the ocean voyage from Australia to Cape Town (1904) he was feeling so under-exercised that he obtained permission from the captain to shovel coal, stripped down to the waist, each day in the boiler room — until, that is, he developed painful whitlows and had to stop. When in South Africa he was spotted on one occasion approaching the concert hall behind a "group of ferocious looking Zulu warriors" whom he had wanted to invite to the concert!

More than thirty years later, during the building of his Museum in Melbourne, which still looks rather like a public loo, Grainger himself worked on the site from 5.00 am till well after midnight.

Spell-checker crasher

On a different tack, Grainger developed the most bizarre prose style in a bid to avoid all words other than those with Anglo-Saxon roots. Here is a brief example of his "blue-eyed" or Nordic prose – enough to crash any computer's spell-checker:

> I have always believed in the "wish-for-ableness" of building up a mainly Anglo-Saxon-Scandinavian kind of English in which all but the most un-do-withoutable of the French-begotten, Latin begotten & Greek begotten words should be side-stepped & in which the bulk of the put-together words should wilfully & owned-up-to-ly hot house-grown out of Nordic word seeds ....."

*

Pre-marital "affairs"

It cannot be stressed too strongly that Grainger's mother decided "the beginning, termination, extent and nature of all [his] outside friendships" – all of them, of course, subservient to mother and son. One reason why Grainger rather emphasised to his mother his lust for little girls in preference to women of his own age was to spare her the agony of a potential rival.

Women, most often his piano pupils, were forever in hot pursuit of him – for his looks, his stardom and his undoubted charisma. Bird reports that after his first highly successful season in America (1915-16) he received "more than 200 invitations from the mothers of attractive and marriageable daughters to spend the summer months at their homes." He turned them all down!

In true Freudian mode, Grainger sought in all his women a replication of his mother. They were, writes Bird, all "strong-willed, forceful and musical."

Mimi Kwast, 1897

"Won't you take Mimi's arm?" was how Rose set her son's first romance in motion two years after they arrived in Frankfurt. Grainger, now fifteen, became besotted. Mimi, however, who was a pupil in one of Rose's English classes, and the daughter of James Kwast (Grainger's Dutch-born piano professor at the Conserv- atoire) soon realised that Rose was the only person Percy would ever truly love. But in any case, her real passion was for the composer Hans Pfitzner. Described as anxiety-ridden, romantic and dreamy, Pfitzner (whose later opera *Palestrina* would become enshrined in the German repertoire) threatened Mimi with suicide if she didn't return to him. Defying fierce parental opposition, Mimi eloped with Pfitzner to Canterbury in 1899.

First orgasm: Mrs Frank Lowrey, 1902

Half-Irish, half-Polish, and possibly a fleeting mistress of Edward VII who made "visits" to her, Mrs Lowrey was a tall and handsome woman in her forties when Grainger first met her at her Chelsea home in 1902. A mover and shaker in artistic circles, she made a point of encouraging talented young musicians in their careers by providing them with openings that included performances for "The Queen's House Manuscript Music Society" that she had formed. Grainger's entrée into this circle was very much at a price. Mrs Lowrey made it clear that the price of her patronage was his sexual favours. Thus it came about that Grainger (then age 20) experienced his first orgasm. Although throughout intercourse Grainger "thought he was going to die," he did, however, have the consolation that his "sexual equipment" was in working order.

Alfhild de Luce, 1905

> ... mother must have looked something like you when
> she was young.
> [Grainger's highest compliment to Alfhild]

Before Alfhild de Luce married Hermann Sandby (already-mentioned as Grainger's "closest male friend"), this engaged Danish couple for a while entered a bizarre threesome with Grainger – who was unable to stop himself from declaring his love for Alfhild on bended knee. For his part, Hermann seems not to have taken amiss his closest friend's "veiled attentions" to his fiancée, which included showers of kisses. Although Alfhild managed gently to deflect Grainger's attentions by reminding him that she had a fiancé and that he had his mother to look after, she annoyed him by telling him that his mother "looked like a devil" on a photograph.

Karen Holten, 1905

> I was rather in love with Karen ... and at the time (as
> now and as always) only felt two needs – art and sex.
> [Grainger, 31 December 1940]

A friend of Hermann Sandby, Karen first met Grainger during his tour of Denmark in 1905 and she accompanied Grainger back to England. This beautiful young Danish girl arrived in London (writes Bird) in a "blue velvet suit with a matching cape edged with fur," and a "tiny embroidered cap" above her "dark curly hair" and "sparkling blue eyes". After eight years of a courtship that was conducted mainly by correspondence Karen finally ended the relationship because of Rose's jealous rages and tantrums.

Margot Harrison, 1911
"charming and impulsive"

This was yet another of those scores of relationships in music that developed at the piano stool between teacher and taught. One of Grainger's private pupils, and the daughter of the art connoisseur Peter Harrison, Margot became engaged to Percy just over a year after she began lessons with him in 1911.

Rose felt that the couple were rushing things and suggested a trial marriage in which Margot would accompany Percy and herself on his tour of Norway in 1913 "to get some idea of what life would be like as the wife of a travelling virtuoso".

Margot's father put a stop to that idea, of course, and the relationship soon cooled off.

"E –"

The identity of a mysterious "E –", who along with other admirers of Grainger spread rumours of incest in 1922, has now been revealed. She was Else Permin, an Englishwoman who had fallen in love with Grainger years earlier at her first piano lesson with him in London. Later the Graingers had invited her to stay with them at their new home in White Plains in 1921.

Ostensibly coming more round to the idea that Percy should get married, Rose had even offered to move out of White Plains to give Else Permin "a clear run"! Inevitably, Rose became unhinged when she learned of the incest rumours in April 1922 – denying them to all and sundry, demanding apologies, and begging Percy by telegraph (he was on tour in Los Angeles) to stop sending her passionate letters, and to destroy hers to him.

The rest of the story has been partly told. Her fall from the Aeolian building resulted in a fractured skull and multiple internal injuries. Rushing back to New York after receiving a telegram announcing only her death and requesting his immediate return, he read the full story of Rose's death in the *New York Times* during the train journey.

Rose left less than $3,000 in her will.

Grainger's Nordic Princess
Marriage to Ella Viola Ström, 1928
half boyish yet wholly womanly ... To meet her is to have all one's boyhood fairy dreams and hero dreams come true.
[Grainger in his programme note: *To A Nordic Princess*]

... hell to be with him and hell to be without him.
[Ella on Grainger]

For Grainger it was love at first sight after he met Ella in a passport queue in Auckland, New Zealand in 1926. She was then thirty-seven, "radiantly beautiful" and of course, Danish, fair-skinned and blue-eyed. She had already been pursued by Prince Iyemasa Tokugawa of Japan. A talented painter and ceramicist, she had studied at the Slade School of Art and worked with the Swedish diplomatic service.

Ella owned a seaside retreat home at Pevensey Bay where she and Grainger spent "two blissful months" in the summer of 1927. On 2 October, while at sea returning from a final folk-song-collecting expedition in Jutland, Grainger sent her a letter proposing marriage and was accepted.

That a marriage might work for Ella was clear from her tolerance of the letters from his dead mother that Percy wore round his neck. And although at first horrified by them, Ella was also prepared to tolerate his sexual preferences, declaring that it was "hell to be with him and hell to be without him".

The story of their wedding day shows Grainger at his most wildly exuberant and extravagant – but it was an indulgence he could readily afford from his now colossal earnings.

On 9 August 1928, having expected a quiet wedding, Ella found herself as his bride (wearing a rose pink tulle gown and

sporting three camellias in her hair) on the stage of the Hollywood
Bowl, suitably decked out with huge flags of the Stars and Stripes
and the Union Jack. The ceremony took place before an audience
of "between 15,000 and 23,000" after Grainger had conducted
126 musicians in a concert that ended with his scrumptious
composition *To a Nordic Princess*, specially written, of course,
for Ella.

Grainger's marriage to Ella survived – even though he was
at one point sued to the tune of several thousand pounds for
"inciting to disaffection" the wife of an irate husband. Let John
Bird have the last word on the sex life of this extraordinary man:

> There were even periods when, because of his demands,
> she left him for a short time. She discovered that her
> burden involved shouldering much more than Rose's
> mantle. Only she knew the full measure of his joys and
> frustrations, his saintliness and cruelty and his genius
> and aberrations. In the early 1930s he composed a letter
> which had instructions on the envelope that it was to
> be opened only in the event of his or Ella's or their both
> being found dead covered in whip-lashes. It explained
> that no blame should be placed on either since
> flagellation was for him the greatest pleasure and the
> highest expression of his love.

*

Like many great artists in their declining years Grainger's star
waned: he might have been wiser to retreat sooner from the
concert platform. The star who had wowed them all in the Royal
Albert Hall, the Carnegie Hall and in so many other places ended
his days playing to Women's Afternoon Clubs.

His last words to Ella at his bedside were "You're the only
one I like" before he died of abdominal cancer on February 20,
1961. Although a life-long atheist, he received two Christian
burials (entirely against his wishes) before his body was taken
back to Australia.

***

Index

Acknowledgements and Bibliography

The author wishes to thank the following publishers and authors for their kind permissions to quote from copyright sources, details of which are given below: Cambridge University Press, Oxford University Press, Faber and Faber, Phaidon Press Ltd, Kevin Allen, The Random House Group Limited, John Bird, and Peter Kemp. In some cases, because of the scale and frequency of company mergers, efforts where appropriate to trace publishers for permissions have failed.

The author and publisher welcome any information on any inadvertent errors or omissions so that corrections can be made in future printings.

Allen, James: *Dictionary of Opera* (Bloomsbury 1989, © James Allen 1989)

Allen, Kevin: *Elgar in Love: Vera Hockman and the Third Symphony*. (Kevin Allen 2000, © Kevin Allen)

Barnes, Julian: *The Silence* (short story published in Granta 76: Music)

Bauer-Lechner, Natalie: *Recollections of Gustav Mahler* (Edited and annotated by Peter Franklin, translated by Dika Newlin, Faber Music, 1980. English translation and annotations © 1980 by Faber Music Ltd)

Bird, John: *Percy Grainger* (Faber and Faber 1982, © John Bird 1982)

Budden, Julian: *Verdi* (Master Musicians Series, J.M. Dent, 1985, © Julian Budden 1985)

Burley, Rosa: *Edward Elgar: The Record of a Friendship* (Barrie & Jenkins, 1972 ©)

Curtiss, Mina: *Bizet and His World* (Secker & Warburg, © Mina Curtiss 1958. Extracts used by kind permission of Random House)

Dean, Winton: *Georges Bizet: His Life and Work* (J. M Dent, 1965, © Winton Dean 1965)

Dietschy, M: *A Portrait of Claude Debussy* (Clarendon, 1994, © OUP)

Franklin, Peter: *The Life of Mahler* (CUP, 1997©)

Gillmor, Alan M: *Erik Satie* (MacMillan Press Music, © G. K. Hall & Co, 1988)

Greene, David Mason: *Greene's Biographical Encyclopedia of Composers* (Collins 1985, © David Mason Greene 1985)

Grove's Dictionary of Music and Musicians (© Macmillan 1980)

Harding, James: *Erik Satie* (Secker & Warburg, 1975 © James Harding 1975)

Harding, James: *Gounod* (© George Allen & Unwin, 1973)

Harding, James: *Saint-Saëns and His Circle* (Chapman and Hall 1965, © James Harding)

Harwood, Ronald: *Mahler's Conversion* (Faber and Faber, 2001, © Sea Point Productions Inc, 2001)

Hogwood, Christopher: *Handel* (Thames and Hudson 1988, © Christopher Hogwood 1984)

Holmes, Paul. *Debussy* (Illustrated Lives, Omnibus Press, 1989 © Paul Holmes 1989)

Janácek, Leoš: *Intimate Letters to Kamila Stösslová*, edited and translated by John Tyrrell (Faber and Faber, 1994 © John Tyrrell)

Janácková, Zdenka: *My Life with Janácek*, edited and translated by John Tyrrell. (Faber and Faber, 1998 © John Tyrrell)

Kemp, Peter: *The Strauss Family* (Omnibus Press 1989, © Peter Kemp 1985 and 1989). The chapter on the Strausses relies heavily and with thanks on Peter Kemp's book. His is the only readily available detailed source in English on the family.

Kennedy, Michael: *Mahler* (The Master Musicians, JM Dent & Sons Ltd, 1990 © Michael Kennedy 1974, 1990)

Kennedy, Michael: *Portrait of Elgar* (Clarendon Paperbacks 1993, © Michael Kennedy 1987)

La Grange, Henri Louis de [4 volumes] : *Mahler: A Biography* (to 1902), Victor Gollancz Ltd. © 1973 La Grange. *Gustav Mahler: Vienna, The Years of Challenge* (1897-1904), OUP, 1995 © La Grange 1995. *Gustav Mahler: Vienna, Triumph and Disillusion,* OUP, 1999 © La Grange 1999. *Gustav Mahler: Le génie foudroyé* (Fayard, © Librairie Arthème Fayard 1984)

La Mure, P: *Clair de Lune* (Random House, 1962)

Layton, Robert: *Sibelius* (J. M Dent, 1992, © Robert Layton 1992)

Lebrecht, Norman: *Mahler Remembered* (Faber and Faber, 1998 © Norman Lebrecht 1987, 1998)

Lockspeiser,E: *Debussy* (Master Musicians, J.M Dent, 1980 ©)

Lockspeiser, E: *Debussy: His Life and Mind* (2 vol, CUP 1978)

Mahler, Alma: *Gustav Mahler, Memories and Letters* (2nd enlarged edition trans. Basil Creighton, © John Murray, 1968)

Mason Greene, David: *Biographical Encyclopedia of Composers* (Collins 1985 © David Mason Greene 1985)

Microsoft Bookshelf 94 (© 1994 Microsoft Corporation)

Moore, Jerrold Northrop: *Edward Elgar: A Creative Life* (OUP ,1984, © Jerrold Northrop Moore 1984)

New Grove Dictionary of Music and Musicians (© Macmillan 2000)

Nichols, R: *Debussy Remembered* (Faber and Faber, 1992©)

Nichols, R: *The Life of Debussy* (CUP, 2000 © Roger Nichols 1998)

Niemi, Irmeli (Chairman of the Board the Ainola Foundation): article written for the website, *Virtual Finland.*

Orrey, Leslie: *Bellini* (The Master Musicians series, J.M Dent and Sons Ltd, 1969 © Text, Leslie Orrey, 1969

Phillips-Matz, Jane: *Verdi: A Biography* (OUP, 1993 © Jane Phillips-Matz 1993)

Rickards, Guy: *Jean Sibelius* (Phaidon, 1997 © Phaidon Press Limited 1997)

Rosselli, John: *The Life of Bellini* (CUP, 1996, ©)

Rosselli, John: *The Life of Verdi* (C.U.P. 2000 ©)

Southwell-Sanders, Peter: *Verdi* (Illustrated Lives, Omnibus Press, 1978 © Peter Southwell-Sanders 1978)

Studd, Stephen: *Saint-Saëns: a Critical Biography* (Cygnus Arts,1999 © Stephen Studd 1999)

Thomas, Gary C: *Was George Frideric Handel Gay?* in *Queering the Pitch* (chapter), *The New Gay and Lesbian Musicology* (Routledge 1994, ©)

Walker, Frank: *The Man Verdi* (University of Chicago Press, © The University of Chicago 1982)

www.charles-gounod.com

Cover painting (detailed) by John Singer Sargent, 1899.
Acknowledgements to Houston's Museum of Fine Arts.

About the Author

Writing is Basil Howitt's third career, following successful long stints in education and professional cello playing. The writing took off in the early nineties with a series of articles in *Classical Music* magazine on the lifestyle of the freelance musician. These were compiled into his first book, *Life in a Penguin Suit*. Then followed *Love Lives of the Great Composers* (Sound And Vision, 1995) and *Grand Passions and Broken Hearts* (Robson Books, 1998)

Basil Howitt has written for *The Guardian, The Sunday Times, The Mail on Sunday,* the *News of the World, Private Eye* and the BBC Radio 4 series on tormented geniuses.

Nowadays he does much of his work in the French Pyrenees where he and his wife Clare spend as much time as possible in their remote village home. He is a very enthusiastic cook and enjoys fine wine, walking and reading.

More Love Lives of the Great Composers
© Basil Howitt 2002

First published in Canada by
Sound And Vision
359 Riverdale Avenue
Toronto, Canada, M4J 1A4
www.soundandvision.com

First printing, September 2002
1 3 5 7 9 - printings - 10 8 6 4 2

National Library of Canada Cataloguing in Publication
Howitt, Basil
More love lives of the great composers
by Basil Howitt.
Includes index.
ISBN 0-920151-36-1

1. Composers—Biography. 2. Composers
—Sexual behavior. I. Title.
ML390.H825 2002   780'.92'2   C2002-904217-8

Typset in ITC New Century Schoolbook
Printed and bound in Canada

Other books of interest

Other books by David W. Barber,
with cartoons by Dave Donald:

A Musician's Dictionary
preface by Yehudi Menuhin
isbn 0-920151-21-3

Bach, Beethoven and the Boys
Music History as It Ought to Be Taught
preface by Anthony Burgess
isbn 0-920151-10-8

When the Fat Lady Sings
Opera History as It Ought to Be Taught
preface by Maureen Forrester
foreword by Anna Russell
isbn 0-920151-34-5

If It Ain't Baroque
More Music History as It Ought to Be Taught
isbn 0-920151-15-9

Getting a Handel on Messiah
preface by Trevor Pinnock
isbn 0-920151-17-5

Tenors, Tantrums and Trills
An Opera Dictionary from Aida to Zzzz
isbn 0-920151-19-1

Tutus, Tights and Tiptoes
Ballet History as It Ought to Be Taught
preface by Karen Kain
isbn 0-920151-30-2

Compiled & Edited by
David W. Barber
Better Than It Sounds
A Dictionary of Humorous Musical Quotations
isbn 0-920151-22-1

Love Lives of the Great Composers
From Gesualdo to Wagner
by Basil Howitt
isbn 0-920151-18-3

The Composers
A Hystery of Music
by Kevin Reeves
preface by Daniel Taylor
isbn 0-920151-29-9

1812 And All That
A Concise History of Music from 30.000 BC
to the Millennium
by Lawrence Leonard,
cartoons by Emma Bebbington
isbn 0-920151-33-7

Opera Antics & Annecdotes
by Stephen Tanner
Illustrations by Umberto Táccola
preface by David W. Barber
isbn 0-920151-32-9

How to Stay Awake
During Anybody's Second Movement
by David E. Walden, cartoons by Mike Duncan
preface by Charlie Farquharson
isbn 0-920151-20-5

How To Listen To Modern Music
Without Earplugs
by David E. Walden, cartoons by Mike Duncan
foreword by Bramwell Tovey
isbn 0-920151-31-0

The Thing I've Played With the Most
Professor Anthon E. Darling Discusses
His Favourite Instrument
by David E. Walden, cartoons by Mike Duncan
foreword by Mabel May Squinnge, B.O.
isbn 0-920151-35-3

A Working Musician's Joke Book
by Daniel G. Theaker, cartoons by Mike Freen
preface by David W. Barber
isbn 0-920151-23-X

I Wanna Be Sedated
Pop Music in the Seventies
by Phil Dellio & Scott Woods
Caricatures by Dave Prothero
preface by Chuck Eddy
isbn 0-920151-16-7

Quotable Pop
Fifty Decades of Blah Blah Blah
Compiled & Edited by Phil Dellio & Scott Woods
Caricatures by Mike Rooth
isbn 0-920151-50-7

Quotable Jazz
Compiled & Edited by Marshall Bowden
Caricatures by Mike Rooth
isbn 0-920151-55-8

Quotable Opera
Compiled & Edited by Steve & Nancy Tanner
Caricatures by Umberto Tàccola
isbn 0-920151-54-X

Quotable Alice
Compiled & Edited by David W. Barber
Illustrations by Sir John Tenniel
isbn 0-920151-52-3

Quotable Sherlock
Compiled & Edited by David W. Barber
Illustrations by Sidney Paget
isbn 0-920151-53-1

Quotable Twain
Compiled & Edited by David W. Barber
isbn 0-920151-56-6

Note from the Publisher

I would like thank David Barber, Luca Di Nicola, Bruce Surtees & Mike Walsh for the help in preparing this manuscript for publication.

Sound And Vision books may be purchased for educational or promotional use or for special sales. If you have any comments on this book or any other books we publish, or if you would like a catalogue, please write to us at Sound And Vision 359 Riverdale Avenue, Toronto, Canada M4J 1A4.

We are always looking for original books to publish. If you have an idea or manuscript that is in the genre of musical humour including educational themes, please contact us. Thank you for purchasing or borrowing this book.

Please visit our web site at http://www.soundandvision.com.

Geoff Savage
Publisher